Turned Around by Love

The Montgomery Family Trilogy
- Book Three -

by Vikki Vaught

First Edition

Copyright © 2012 by Vikki Vaught

All rights reserved. No part of this book may be reproduced in any form or by any electronic or mechanical means including information storage and retrieval systems, without permission in writing from the author. The only exception is by a reviewer, who may quote short excerpts in a review.

This book is a work of fiction. Names, characters, places, and incidents either are products of the author's imagination or are used fictitiously. Any resemblance to actual persons, living or dead, events, or locales is entirely coincidental.

ISBN:1477634878
ISBN-13:9781477634875

Chapter 1
- Late June 1823 -

While Jonathan St. John, the Marquess of Sutherland, lay in bed looking around the room of his latest mistress Alana, he realized that even though she was beautiful with her long, rich, sable-brown hair, startling golden eyes, and a figure as voluptuous as any man could ask for, he was already tired of her.

Jonathan was thirty years old and had had a dozen of mistresses over the last eight years. While all of them were beautiful, none of them could hold his interest for very long. Oh, they were all sexually alluring and well trained in all the sensual arts, but after a while he lost interest in every one of them. He found himself growing bored faster than usual with his most recent mistresses. It was as if he'd even lost interest in sex. Physically, his body still responded, but mentally, he was somewhere else.

At two and twenty, Jonathan had returned from Waterloo a broken man. He'd joined the army when Bonaparte escaped from Elba. Because his father didn't want him to enlist as a foot soldier, he'd bought him a commission, and since his brother Roderick refused to stay behind, he came along also.

The injuries Jonathan sustained during the battle still pained him today. Because of his bad knee, he'd lost his fiancée, Susannah, when he came back from the war. She had refused to marry a cripple. He suffered from terrible nightmares and…he was a drunk. In essence, he was going through the motions of life and letting it pass him by.

Alana stretched, purring like a cat. He knew he'd pleasured her well because he was an expert lover, but he was completely unmoved by their sexual encounter. It was definitely time for their liaison to end. Jonathan rolled out of bed and stood up, leaned over, and pulled on his black satin knee breeches over his muscular buttocks and thighs.

Alana sat up and gave him a sultry look. "Darling, why are you getting out of bed? I thought you were going to spend the night. Please come back. I'm sure I can revive you, if you'll give me a chance." She pulled him to her and began stroking his cock through his breeches, but he remained unmoved by her touch.

"Alana, I'm not in the mood, and I just want to go home. It doesn't have anything to do with you. I just need to leave. Besides, I never stay all night. You know that."

He reached for his startling-white, fine lawn shirt, pulled it over his head and broad shoulders, then tucked it into his breeches. He put on his deep blue embroidered waistcoat and pulled his dress coat on over it. Once he finished dressing, he ran his fingers through his thick, jet black hair and smoothed it down, giving it some semblance of order. He took a deep breath, clenched his straight white teeth, and turned around.

Softening the expression in his brilliant blue eyes, Jonathan gave her one of his sardonic smiles. "My dear, I've enjoyed the time we've spent together. However, I've decided that it's time to end our liaison."

"What do you mean it's time to end our liaison? We had an agreement that I would be your mistress for twelve months, and we've only been together for three. I turned down several very good protectors for you!" She stood up, her eyes on fire with indignation as she walked over to him. "I've given you no reason to want to end our liaison. Sexually, we're extremely compatible. Give me a chance to prove it to you." She lifted up on her tiptoes and gave him a searing kiss as she stroked his cock.

He felt a stirring of desire and returned her kiss but then pushed her away. "I know what our contract states. I'll fulfill those terms until you can find another protector. I'm sure one of those men you turned down will be happy to take my place. You're more than welcome to stay in this house while you find a new protector. My secretary, Stebbins, will pay all your expenses, within reason of course, and you'll receive a new diamond necklace for your trouble. I'm leaving London at the end of the week, so I will bid you adieu."

Jonathan turned around, picked up his silver-headed walking stick and left the room. As he closed the door, he heard a crash and breaking glass, and Alana shouting profanities. Obviously she wasn't taking their parting well at all. He made his way down the stairs, picked up his top hat and kidskin gloves, then laboriously made his way out of the house.

When he stepped down onto the sidewalk, he motioned to his driver to bring him his carriage. When the carriage pulled to a stop, he gingerly pulled himself inside. His knee was killing him, and it was beginning to swell.

As Jonathan fell back against the tufted dark red velvet cushions, he rubbed his knee, trying to alleviate some of his pain. His leg was acting up, so he knew the weather was getting ready to turn. He tapped the roof and told his driver to take him to his club. Pulling his flask from the inside pocket of his dress coat, he took a large swig of brandy. Jonathan needed the brandy to steady his nerves. He knew he was drinking too much, but couldn't seem to help it. It was the only thing that seemed to deaden the pain.

When he arrived at White's, he carefully got out of his carriage, climbed the stairs, and went into his club. While he stood at the entrance to the card room, he scanned the room, looking for his friend Baron Kenneth Jenkins. He spied him sitting at a table involved in a card game with Bentley, Masters, and Wilkins. Jonathan slowly made his way across the room. "Good evening. Can I join you gentlemen?"

Jenkins glanced over at Jonathan and grinned. "What are you doing here? I thought you were spending the evening with the delectable Alana. Of course you can join us. Masters just folded so you can take his place."

Jonathan sat down, and they began a round of whist. He enjoyed the occasional game of cards, but he was very careful that he didn't lose too much money. If the cards were against him, he would fold and discontinue playing. Luck was with him tonight, and soon he had a pile of coins in front of him. Bentley and Wilkins folded and left the table.

While he sat there smoking a cigar and enjoying a brandy, he looked over at Jenkins. "I ended my liaison with Alana tonight. I've become bored with her and no longer want her as my mistress."

Jenkins took a sip of his brandy and then laughed. "Sutherland, you go through mistresses faster that anyone I know, but even for you this is fast. You've only had her for what, three months? Have you already found someone new?"

Jonathan leaned back in his chair while adjusting his intricately tied cravat. "No, I haven't. I've decided I'll take a break and not have a mistress for a while. If I feel the need for sex, I'll go to a house of pleasure instead. That will be less trouble. Mistresses are too demanding, and I can't be bothered trying to please them. Oh, by the way, I'm leaving London at the end of the week. I haven't been to my estate since March, and I'm bored with the season."

With a look of astonishment on his face, Jenkins asked, "When did you decide to leave London? You didn't say anything about leaving this morning when we went to Tattersall's. Aren't you supposed to buy that matched pair of dappled grays you were looking at? We both agreed they're real goers and would be perfect for your new phaeton."

"Oh yes, I'm definitely buying the pair, but that won't keep me from leaving. I've been thinking of leaving London for a while now, but I just didn't say anything about it. The amusements of London have lost much of their appeal. I made the decision to go back to Bath this evening when I realized how utterly bored I am. Why don't you come with me? I have a lake on my estate and we can do some fishing. You can't tell me you're not getting tired of the season. Besides, it's almost over anyway, and I'd enjoy your company."

"I haven't been fishing in years. I find the idea very entertaining. I'll be happy to come for a visit, but I can't leave town until next week. Would it be all right if I came then?"

"Come whenever it's convenient for you. I'll look forward to you joining me next week. Well, I'm going to head home. I have quite a bit to accomplish if I'm leaving town by the end of the week. I'll see you soon." Jonathan stood up and almost lost his balance. He realized that the brandy was beginning to affect him.

Jenkins stood up, grabbing Jonathan's arm to help steady him. "Do you need help getting to your carriage? I can tell your knee's bothering you."

"No, I'm fine. See you next week," he said, as he staggered out of the room.

Jonathan went outside, hailed his coach, and went to his townhouse in Bloomsbury. It was no longer one of the best parts of town, but his townhouse had been in the family for several generations. When he arrived, he climbed out, went up the steps, and unlocked his door. He picked up a candelabrum that was waiting for him and slowly made his way up the stairs.

His valet, Hatton, was waiting for him, but Jonathan wasn't in the mood to have Hatton fuss over him, so he sent him off to bed. He made it as far as the chair by the fireplace and collapsed. His knee was causing him a great deal of pain tonight.

When he was injured, the surgeons had wanted to remove his leg, but thankfully, he was lucid enough to refuse the procedure. His brother Roderick had been there to make sure they didn't proceed. Roderick could be very intimidating since he was such a large man, and he had convinced the surgeons to leave Jonathan's leg alone.

While it pained him a great deal much of the time, he would still rather have it than the alternative. It bothered him most late at night, especially if it rained.

Once Jonathan sat there relaxing for about thirty minutes, he was finally able to get up and remove his clothes. He went to the basin and washed off the smell of sex before donning his dark blue silk banyan. He went over to the table, poured a large glass of brandy, and proceeded to drink until he knew he would finally be able to sleep.

Jonathan hated the fact that he needed so much brandy, but it had been that way ever since Waterloo. Lately it seemed to take more and more brandy before he felt any relief. He felt himself begin to doze off, so he made his way to his bed and fell into an exhausted sleep.

Around three in the morning, he began tossing and turning in his sleep. *Oh God, no. Everywhere he looked he saw dead and dying men. He was fighting off three Frenchmen when one of them shot his horse out from under him. He felt himself falling. He was able to roll clear of his horse, but just as he gained his footing, something slammed into him. As he hit the ground, he knew he was done for, and he felt himself begin to lose consciousness. The next thing he knew, he heard the surgeons talking about his leg, saying that it needed to come off. He started yelling, "No, you will not...cut off...my leg! Dammit...leave...me...alone!"* Jonathan let out a scream as he woke up from his nightmare.

Covered in sweat and his heart pounding, it took a few moments for Jonathan to realize it had only been a dream. He hated the nightmares. That was one of the reasons he drank so much before he went to bed. It helped to keep the nightmares away and helped him deal with the pain. He must have failed to drink enough last night.

Why couldn't he get some peace from this torment?

Jonathan lay there fighting the need to go back to sleep, fearing more nightmares. Pulling himself out of bed, he made it to the table where he kept his decanter of brandy and poured a glass. He gulped it down, refilled it, and drank that too. He limped over to his chair, collapsed into it, and continued to drink. Slowly he lost his battle to stay awake and slipped back to sleep.

The next morning Jonathan woke up exhausted. When he looked at himself in the mirror while shaving, he wasn't surprised that he looked so haggard. There were dark circles under his eyes, and the lines on his forehead looked deeper than usual. He looked like hell and felt years older than thirty. In many ways, he felt as if he were a hundred.

Jonathan tried to shake off the melancholy and slowly finished his ablutions. He had a blinding headache and felt nauseous. He knew it was from all the brandy he drank the night before. Hatton was there with his restorative, which he mixed for him each morning. He dressed in the clothes Hatton had laid out for him and tried to concentrate on the things that he needed to take care of that day.

Once Jonathan was dressed, he went down to the breakfast room and attempted to eat his morning meal, but he just couldn't stomach the thought of food and gave up. Even though it was only noon, he craved the oblivion that the brandy gave him, but he resisted the temptation. There were quite a few things he needed to do today if he was going to be able to leave town in three days.

Jonathan left for his solicitor's office, since he had an appointment with him at one o'clock. They were going to go over some recent investments he'd made. Although he was a wealthy landowner with holdings scattered all over England, he religiously looked for new investments to enrich the marquessate for future generations. He had always enjoyed a challenge and dabbling with investments was definitely that. It was just about the only thing in his life he could still get excited about.

The next two days were brutal. Each day, Jonathan needed more brandy to sleep, and the pain in his knee was worse than it had been in a long time. Hatton kept trying to convince him to take laudanum, since he believed it would work better on his pain than liquor, but Jonathan refused.

Finally it was Sunday, and Jonathan was ready to leave town. The trip to his estate took three days, and he stayed drunk the entire time to make the trip tolerable. Sitting in a cramped carriage was hell on his knee, and bouncing around on the rainy rutted roads wasn't helping.

As he drew near his home, he watched as the landscape changed to grassy limestone hills, woodlands, and cool, green ravines. Breathing in the clean countryside air, he felt himself begin to relax.

His family seat was in Weston, which was south of the Cotswold Hills, and about five miles from the center of Bath. The closer he came to his estate, the better he felt. St. John's Wood had been in the family ever since Queen Elizabeth gave it to the first marquess shortly after she ascended to the throne in 1558.

Looking out of the window as the coach turned into the drive to his home, Jonathan noticed how neatly trimmed the boxwood hedges were, which ran along each side of the drive, and he anxiously awaited his first sight of his ancestral home, St. John's Wood Manor.

When it came into view, his heart swelled with love for his home. It was a Jacobean mellow-red brick manor with white stone window casings. There were wings on each side of the main house that had been added at the end of the last century. The overall effect was very pleasing to the eye — his home was as lovely as he remembered. Jonathan often wondered why he stayed away for so long whenever he came home and saw the beauty of his principle estate.

When his carriage pulled up under the portico, his butler was already there to greet him. "My lord, it's so good to see you. I received your message. Everything is ready, as you requested."

"Thank you, Goodman. Where's my sister? I would have expected her to be here to greet me." Just as Jonathan spoke these words, out of the corner of his eye, he saw a whirlwind coming his way. He turned and his little sister ran into his arms. She must have run quite a distance because her pretty pink cheeks were flushed from her exertion, and her long, golden hair was hanging down her back, having lost all its hairpins.

Grabbing Elaine around the waist, he hugged her close as she laughed up at him. "Jonathan, I'm so thrilled you've finally arrived! How long are you planning on staying? Please say you plan to stay for a good long time, because it's dreadfully dull when you're away!"

"Hello, Princess. It's good to know you missed me. I'm not sure how long I'm staying, but I know it will be at least through harvest time. After that, we'll just have to wait and see. I've become terribly bored with town and just want the peace and quiet of home for a while. I received a letter from Roderick. He wants us to come for a visit, but I'm going to try to convince him to bring his family here instead."

"Oh, that would be wonderful! I just love playing with my niece and nephew. Frankford and Jane are such sweet children. I haven't seen them since last Christmas. If they can't come, can we please go visit them?"

"Yes, if they can't come here, we'll just have to make the trip to see them. Well, let me go in and get settled. We can talk more over dinner. Since we have no guests, you can dine with me tonight."

Jonathan and Elaine went into the house, and Jonathan went upstairs to his suite so he could wash away his travel dirt. Hatton came rushing into the room, began unpacking his belongings, and started putting them away. He was a very good valet, but Jonathan wished he wouldn't hover over him quite so much.

All the inactivity of traveling for three days had taken a toll on his knee and it was aching fiercely. Jonathan stripped down to his smalls, sat down in his deeply cushioned chair and put his leg up on the matching ottoman to take some strain off his knee.

Hatton could always sense when Jonathan's knee was bothering him, so he hastily applied a soothing balm, prepared the cold compresses, and wrapped them around Jonathan's knee. Jonathan didn't know what was in the special liniment that he used, but it always seemed to help. Hatton handed him a glass of brandy, and he drank it quickly, hoping that it would deaden the pain.

"Thank you, Hatton. That feels much better. Why don't you go up to your room and get all your things put away? I won't need you again until it's time to get ready for dinner. I just want to relax for a while."

"Here's your brandy decanter. I'll just leave it on the table beside you, my lord. I'll return in plenty of time to help you get ready for dinner."

Hatton left the room and Jonathan breathed a sigh of relief. Finally, he was alone. He poured himself another large glass of brandy and settled back into his chair. It was so good to be at home at last. He knew he had made the right decision to come back here.

As Jonathan looked around his room, he felt a huge sense of peace roll over him. His room was so comfortable with his large oak bed and his oversized chair by the fireplace. He found the deep moss-green colors that decorated his room restful. It made him wonder why he ever left St. John's Wood to begin with. He thought back over the last few months and had no regrets over leaving town, or breaking it off with Alana.

Turning his thoughts to other things, Jonathan certainly hoped he could get his brother to come here because he didn't want to have to go to him. He picked up his travel writing desk, pulled paper and quill out of it, and wrote a letter to his brother asking him to come home and bring his family. He would get Goodman to post it tomorrow morning. Jonathan leaned his head back against the cushions of his chair and fell fast asleep.

Later that afternoon, Hatton woke him in plenty of time for dinner, and Jonathan enjoyed spending the evening with Elaine. Dinner was pleasant, and after they finished eating Elaine entertained him by playing the pianoforte and singing. She had a lovely contralto voice that he always found soothing.

Yes, he was very glad to be home again.

Over the next few days, Jonathan rode around his estate visiting with his tenant farmers and catching up with his steward, Whetherby. The tenant farms were all doing well, and the harvest promised to be bountiful again this year. So far, rain had been steady throughout the summer, which helped the crops, even though it aggravated his knee.

Jonathan enjoyed his morning rides with Whetherby. Thank God, he had no problems riding a horse. He had to use his thigh muscles to compensate for the weakness in his knee and lower leg, but his horse, Demon, had adapted well, and Jonathan could get him to respond to the lightest of pressure followed by a verbal command.

He'd had Demon since he returned from Waterloo. He found him at Tattersall's, and one of the fastest racing horses of the century had sired him. Since he was a gelding, he was less temperamental than a stallion would have been. While Jonathan was still an excellent rider, he doubted he could control a temperamental horse.

A few days later, as Jonathan sat in his study drinking brandy and going over some reports that Whetherby had left for him to peruse, Goodman brought him the post. There was a letter from his brother telling him to expect him to arrive on Saturday, the twenty-eighth. He was definitely looking forward to seeing his brother again.

Jonathan enjoyed spending time with Elaine. They went riding every afternoon. He was pleased to see that Elaine had turned into an excellent equestrian. He remembered how scared she was the first time he had put her on a horse when she was six years old. Elaine had certainly come a long way.

She had also turned into a real beauty, and he knew he would have his hands full in a few years when she made her bow to society. Elaine appeared much older than most fifteen-year-olds did. With her long golden blonde hair and gorgeous green eyes, he was sure young men would flock around her once she had her come out and presentation at court. He just hoped she wouldn't give him any problems anytime soon.

Elaine was fairly well behaved, but she did tend to get into mischief when he was away. Again, he was so grateful that his brother had married. His brother's wife, Allison, would be there when it was time for Elaine to have her come out. She would help make sure Elaine didn't get into trouble. Pouring himself another glass of brandy, he continued going over his reports.

Chapter 2

The next day, when Jonathan returned from his ride with Elaine, his friend Jenkins had arrived. Jonathan dismounted, grabbed his walking stick, and made his way over to him. "Jenkins, glad you could make it. I figured you'd be here any day now. You remember my sister, Lady Elaine, don't you?"

Jenkins glanced over at Elaine and smiled. "Surely this can't be little Lady Elaine! I remember you as a little girl in braids, and now you're a lovely young lady. It's a pleasure to see you again."

Elaine coyly looked over at him. "Hello, my lord. I'm almost sixteen years old now, so I'm no longer a child. I'm pleased to see you again." As Elaine laughed up at Jenkins, she added, "It's been far too long since you came for a visit. I hope you'll be staying for a while."

Jonathan didn't like the way Elaine was acting at all. He couldn't believe his eyes. His little sister was actually trying to flirt with Jenkins. "Elaine, why don't you go into the house and let Mrs. Rollins know we have a guest and make sure she readies a room for him?" Elaine looked back at him with an exasperated look, but went into the house as directed.

Turning to Jenkins, Jonathan said, "Sorry about that. Elaine's trying out her feminine wiles on you. She thinks she's grown, now that she'll be sixteen in five months. I hope she didn't offend you. I'm glad you've arrived."

Jenkins looked over at Jonathan and shrugged his shoulder. "I have a sister the same age, so no, I wasn't offended. Actually, it's a boost to the old ego to have her trying to flirt with me, since I'm almost old enough to be her father. You're probably going to have to watch her when she has her come out. She's turned into a real beauty. I'm glad it's you and not me who will have to contend with all her beaus."

"I'm certainly not looking forward to it. Thank God, I'll have Allison to guide her when she makes her come out in a few years. Now, are you ready to do some fishing?"

"I'm more than ready to do some fishing. Have you done any since you arrived here?"

Jonathan pulled his flask from his pocket and took a drink. "No, I haven't, but I'm certainly looking forward to it now that you're here."

"Is your knee giving you more problems? You seem to be drinking quite a bit lately. Does it help with the pain?"

Jonathan ran his fingers through his hair in frustration. The last thing he needed was a friend commenting on his drinking. He turned a stoic look towards Jenkins. "My knee has been giving me more problems lately, and I do find the brandy helps to deaden the pain a bit. Hatton wants me to take laudanum, but I don't want it. How was the trip over here? Did it take you long to get here?"

"The trip was pleasant. I stopped by my estate and spent a couple days there. Since I was only coming from Wiltshire, I left at dawn this morning. Oh, by the way, Alana already has a new protector. She's with Haversham now. I've heard that he's set her up in a townhouse in Mayfair, and she's loving every minute of it."

"That relieves my mind and my pocket. Your room should be ready, so let's go in and get you settled. We keep country hours here, so dinner's at seven." They went into the house where Mrs. Rollins was waiting to show Jenkins to his room.

Jonathan went to his study, poured himself a glass of brandy, and sat down. His knee was bothering him more than usual today, so he knew they would probably have rain tonight. He was relieved to hear that Alana had already found another protector. Now he didn't need to feel guilty about ending their liaison early.

Thinking about Jenkins's comment about his drinking, Jonathan realized that he would need to be more careful about drinking in front of people. He didn't want anyone thinking that he had a drinking problem. He knew he was probably drinking too much, but it helped with the pain and the nightmares.

That evening, as they dined on pheasant and roasted potatoes, Jonathan said, "Will ten o'clock work for you in the morning? The fish should be biting at that time."

"That sounds good to me."

"Why don't we adjourn to my study so we can finish our conversation?"

When they went to his study, they sat in front of the fireplace and started talking about the good old days. Laughing, Jonathan asked, "Do you recall the time we were caught sneaking those barmaids into our rooms while we were at school?"

"I'd forgotten all about that! We were a couple of rogues back then. I thought we were going to get expelled for sure, but you came up with that brilliant tale about them being there to clean our rooms. I still can't believe Professor Higgins bought it. I miss those days."

Jonathan grinned. "Me too. I don't know how we ever made it to graduation."

"You and I would never have made it through without Roderick. Having a prefect as a friend kept us out of trouble most of the time."

Jonathan sipped his brandy as he resisted the temptation to swill it down in one giant gulp. He was determined to limit himself to one glass since Jenkins had commented on his drinking earlier that day.

"We've been friends for a long time now. The only time we've been apart was when you went to war. I still regret not going to fight, but as you know, I'd already inherited my title by then. I couldn't risk anything happening to me. My title would have become extinct, and that would have left my sister without a guardian. Do you ever regret going? I know you experience a lot of pain because of your knee."

"I hate that I'm a cripple, but no, I've never regretted going to fight. Bonaparte had to be stopped, and I wanted to do my part. My only regret was how it affected my father when I came back. My injury devastated him. God, I miss him so much."

"I miss your father too. He was a good man. He helped me immeasurably when I lost mine. I was so young. I didn't have a clue about running my estate."

"Yes, my father was a great man. A day doesn't go by that I don't miss him. Oh, by the way, while you're here, I'll take you into Bath so we can visit Madame Angela's House of Pleasure. It's the most exclusive brothel in Bath. She has quite a few lovely ladies to choose from. I know you'll enjoy yourself."

"Oh, I'd love to go with you. Can we go tomorrow night?"

"Yes, tomorrow would be perfect." Jonathan stretched and stifled a yawn as he looked at Jenkins. "Since we're going fishing in the morning, I think I'll retire early. It's been great talking about old times. We can continue our conversation tomorrow. I'll see you to your room."

By the time Jonathan entered his room he was shaking. He poured a large glass of brandy and drank it down in three gulps. He hated needing the damned brandy, but he just couldn't seem to go very long without it. Maybe it was time to try something stronger. He looked through his liquor cabinet and found a bottle of scotch whiskey. He drank a large glass of it and felt the immediate warmth as it made its way into his body.

Ah, yes, that was much better.

Jonathan could feel his pain ease up just a little. Since he had told Hatton to not wait up for him, he undressed, put on his banyan, and sank down into his chair as he continued to drink the whiskey. Eventually he passed out in the chair.

Hatton woke him up the next morning and immediately handed him his restorative beverage. He didn't say anything to him, but Jonathan knew Hatton was disappointed when he bent over, picked up the empty whiskey bottle, and sighed deeply.

Jonathan and Jenkins went fishing that morning as planned. They didn't catch many fish, but they enjoyed each other's company tremendously. They laughed and joked, and it felt as if they were young again, before war had gotten in the way.

That night they went into town and visited Madame Angela's House of Pleasure. Jonathan picked out a luscious, tall, slender, blonde-haired woman and spent half the night having great sex. He decided that coming to Madame Angela's was much better than having a mistress. Mistresses always wanted to talk, and they were just too damned expensive. Here it was all just mindless sex, which was all he wanted anyway.

For the next three days, Jonathan and Jenkins went fishing during the day and to Madame Angela's at night. It was the most enjoyable time he'd had in years. Jenkins left on Friday, and Jonathan was sorry to see him go, but Jenkins needed to get back to his estate, and Roderick was due to arrive the next day.

Roderick and his family arrived the following day in time for tea. There was an entire entourage because they also brought the children's governess, Allison's maid, and Roderick's valet. Once they had the children settled, everyone went down to tea. Since it was only family, Elaine was allowed to participate. Jonathan looked at his brother and said, "I'm so pleased that you were able to come for a visit. How have you been lately?"

Roderick sat down and took a plate of sandwiches from Allison. "I was glad you wanted us to come. We've been spending quite a bit of our time out on our new yacht. The weather has been superb this summer, and I dread it when it gets too cool to take her out anymore. Allison loves it as much as I do, and we've even taken the children out a few times. I wish you would come over so I can take you out. I know you'd enjoy it."

Jonathan sat back in his chair and took a sip of his tea. "I know you love being out on the sea, but I've always had problems with seasickness, so I think I'll pass. How long can you stay? I would like to spend some time with Frankford. After all, he is my heir."

Roderick looked over at Jonathan and sighed. "You're welcome to spend time with him, but I wish you would reconsider your decision about marriage. Marriage has been the best decision of my life." Roderick turned to Allison and said, "Isn't that right, my dear?"

"I hope you feel that way!" Allison replied, with delight dancing in her light-blue eyes. Then she looked over at Jonathan and asked, "Do you think we could go into Bath on Monday? We would like to visit the city while we're here. The shopping is so much better than in Bristol. I would also like to visit the Pump Room, just to see who's in town, of course. I can't stand the mineral water, even though I know everyone drinks it. Oh, and I would like to go to the assembly rooms on Wednesday night, if that would be convenient?"

"Whatever you'd like to do is fine with me. We can definitely go on Monday. I might like to take the waters myself. They could help my knee. I'm free to go to the assembly rooms on Wednesday as well. I remember how much you like to dance."

After tea, Jonathan took Roderick to his study so they could talk. Jonathan poured both of them a glass of brandy.

Once they had taken their seats, Roderick said, "I know that you're set in your mind to never marry, but I hate that you've allowed Susannah to have so much power over you. She was a shallow, conceded bitch. Please don't let what she did to you ruin your chance at happiness."

Jonathan glared at Roderick. "God, you're worse than our elderly aunt was! And I'm *not* giving power to that bitch!"

"I'm sorry, I don't want to make you angry, but you've been through so much, and you deserve to have some contentment in your life. I've watched you through the years, ever since Waterloo. If you keep drinking, carousing around with your reprobate friends, and debauching women, you'll end up a bitter old man or die before your time. How many mistresses have you had over the last eight years anyway?"

"To be honest with you, I can't even tell you. I lost count a long time ago. I just got rid of my last one, and I've decided to do without one in the future. Now if I want sex, I'll just go to a house of pleasure instead. I drink…because it helps the pain. I carouse with my friends…to keep the boredom away. You know that."

"I know you believe that, but Jonathan, marriage would be good for you. You deserve to have someone in your life that could give you comfort."

"I know your views on marriage, but I don't have anything to give to a woman. Look at me! I have to walk with a cane, and I can't dance. What woman's going to want me?" Jonathan felt his blood begin to boil the more they talked about the subject. He pulled at the neck of his cravat, which suddenly felt too tight. "Besides, I'm too set in my ways. I could never marry some silly young debutante. I wish you would just accept my decision and drop it."

"Sorry, I don't want us to fight over this. I'll drop the subject. Frankford, by the way, is thrilled that you want to spend time with him. That was all he talked about the whole way here. I hope you know what you're getting into with him. He's a very rambunctious lad and can be hard to handle at times. Maybe I should go with you tomorrow when you take him fishing after church."

"We'll be fine. I just think it's important that Frankford gets to know me. In a few years, I'll be teaching him about managing the marquessate. He'll be more receptive if he knows me. Since I'll never have a son of my own, he'll have quite a bit of responsibility when he grows up. I want to help him be ready for it. Father used to spend quite a bit of time with me, and I want to do the same for Frankford. You're welcome to come along with us tomorrow if you think that would be better. After all, I am a cripple, and I wouldn't want anything to happen and then not be able to get to him fast enough."

Roderick looked directly into Jonathan's eyes. "I'm sure you'd manage just fine. I'm more concerned that Frankford will irritate you with all his nonsense. He's only six years old and all boy. You can remember what we were like at that age."

"All right, we'll all go tomorrow. Well, I think I'll go up to my rooms. It's time for Hatton to treat my knee. It's going to rain tonight. I can always tell when it's going to rain when my knee starts bothering me more than usual. See you at dinner." Roderick and Jonathan stood up and left the study. Jonathan went to his room, and Roderick went to find Allison.

Everyone was in a jovial mood at dinner that night. After the meal ended, Allison entertained Roderick and Elaine by singing as Jonathan played the pianoforte. It had been years since he'd played and he quite enjoyed it. Allison had a beautiful soprano voice, and it was such a pleasure to hear her again.

Once Jonathan entered his rooms, he sent Hatton off to bed. Just as soon as he left, he pulled out the bottle of scotch whiskey, poured himself a large glass, and drank it down. As soon as he felt the warmth of the whiskey hit his body, he let out a sigh of relief, and his hands stopped shaking. He sat down in his chair with the bottle and continued to drink long into the night until he eventually passed out.

The next morning, Hatton found Jonathan asleep in the chair and the empty bottle of whiskey lying on the floor beside him. When Jonathan woke up, his head was splitting, and he felt great waves of nausea roll over him. Hatton didn't say a word, he just shook his head as he handed him a morning glass of the obnoxious concoction he always mixed for him. Jonathan was glad Hatton kept his opinion to himself. Once his stomach settled down, he allowed Hatton to dress and shave him.

After Hatton left, he looked in the mirror and knew that he looked awful. He was bleary-eyed, and the bags under his eyes looked terrible. He took a deep steadying breath, but it didn't help. His hands were trembling and his palms were sweaty. He wanted a drink, but he resisted the temptation and left his room.

After church, even though it was muddy from last night's rain, Jonathan still took Roderick and Frankford to the lake so they could go fishing. Frankford was full of energy, but overall he was a good boy. He asked a million questions and never seemed to stop talking. They didn't catch any fish, but they still had a good time. Jonathan was content because he knew Frankford would make a good marquess someday.

Chapter 3

Jonathan and his party left for Bath at nine o'clock the next morning. It took them about an hour to get to the Pump Room, which was over the ancient Roman Baths. When the Romans occupied the area, they built a temple dedicated to the Goddess Minerva over the hot mineral spring located there. The hot mineral spring had become such a phenomena, that the city of Bath had been a premier spa resort in England since the last century. The older members of the ton flocked to visit each year, just to drink the healing waters.

As they made their way around the room, Allison spied her aunt, Lady Milsom, and they went over to her. Allison hugged her aunt. "Hello, Aunt Harriet. It's so good to see you here. I'm visiting my brother-in-law, so I'll be in the area for a few days. Are you here to take the waters?"

Allison's aunt returned her hug and kissed her cheek. "My dear, it's a pleasure to see you, as always. You'll have to come for tea so we can catch up. My doctor told me that he thought the mineral water would help my aching joints. Please, let me introduce you to my friend." Lady Milsom turned to the woman on her right. "Your Grace, this is my niece Lady Roderick and her husband, Lord St. John, and this is the Marquess of Sutherland and his sister, Lady Elaine."

Allison and Elaine curtsied to the duchess as Allison said, "I'm pleased to meet you, Your Grace. My aunt has mentioned to me several times that you're now living in Bath and that you're one of her dear friends."

The duchess barely acknowledged Allison, but turned all her attention toward Jonathan. "It's a pleasure to meet you, my lord. Let me introduce you to my daughter. Here she comes now."

Jonathan looked up and saw a young lady approaching. This woman had the most incredibly thick red hair he'd ever seen. With the sunlight radiating through the window, it was as if a halo of fire floated around her head. As he met her gaze, he noticed that her eyes were such a deep blue that they were almost more violet than blue.

As she approached, she brushed something from the bodice of her deep lavender muslin day dress, which molded her tall, slender figure to perfection. She was truly lovely, but since she was obviously a lady, he'd never be able to have her, even though one look at her had aroused his desire in a way that took him entirely by surprise.

The duchess motioned for her to come over to them. "My lord, this is my daughter, Lady Kathryn Montgomery."

Kathryn met his gaze and curtsied. "It's a pleasure to meet you, my lord."

Jonathan took her delicate white hand, raised it to his lips, and kissed her long, slender fingers as he continued to gaze into her eyes. "I'm pleased to meet you, Lady Kathryn. Let me introduce you to my sister, brother, and his wife." He turned to them. "Lady Kathryn, this is my brother, Lord Roderick St. John, and his wife, Lady Roderick. And this is my sister, Lady Elaine."

Nodding in acknowledgement of the introduction, Katherine said, "It's a pleasure to meet all of you."

Allison gave her a welcoming smile. "I'm pleased to make your acquaintance. We live in Bristol, and we've come to town for a visit."

The dowager duchess spoke up as she looked over at Jonathan. "My daughter is visiting me for the rest of the summer. She just graduated from the Art Institute in London, and she's painting my portrait. She's actually quite a gifted artist. She's done quite a few portraits of my son and his wife, the Duke and Duchess of Sanderford, and their children."

Jonathan looked over at Lady Kathryn. "I'm sure you're very talented if you attended the Art Institute. I've never known them to accept female students before. It sounds as if you enjoy painting portraits. Do you also paint landscapes?"

Kathryn smiled enthusiastically. "I do enjoy painting some landscapes, but I prefer painting portraits. I find it more challenging to paint people. I'm going to be doing the Marquess and Marchioness of Ralston's family portrait, once I've finished visiting my mother this fall. It will be my first commission since I graduated, and I'm looking forward to it."

"So are you planning to take on other commissions?" Jonathan asked. "If you would be interested, I haven't had my formal portrait done since I inherited my title, and I would be interested in seeing some of your work. If you're that good, I would like you to do mine."

"I'd love to paint your portrait. I have several miniatures I've done of my nieces and nephews at my mother's house, and I'd be happy to show you my mother's portrait. It's almost finished." She turned to her mother and asked, "Mother, could we have them come for tea this afternoon so I can show Lord Sutherland my work?"

"Certainly, we would be delighted to have Lord Sutherland. Of course, the rest of his family can come as well." Turning to Jonathan, the duchess asked, "Would four o'clock be convenient for you?"

Jonathan looked at his brother, sister, and sister-in-law, and they nodded in agreement. "We would be pleased to come for tea, and four o'clock would be convenient, Your Grace. Where do you live?"

"We live at number three Royal Crescent. We look forward to your arrival." The duchess turned to Lady Milsom and asked, "Lady Milsom, would you like to come for tea also?"

"I would enjoy that very much. It will give me a chance to spend some time with my niece, Lady Roderick. Oh, gracious, look at the time. I'll see all of you later. I have an appointment with Madame Bovary, so I need to leave right away." As Lady Milsom hurried away, the others took their leave, agreeing to meet again for tea that afternoon.

Jonathan and his party continued to stroll around the room to where the waters were. Jonathan drank a glass, hoping it would relieve some of his pain. Of course, the water tasted so vile he wasn't sure that it would be worth it. He'd have to feel considerably better after his first taste to even consider drinking it again. Since it was approaching luncheon, they went across the street to the White Hart Inn.

Once everyone sat down to eat, Roderick turned to Jonathan. "Since when did you decide to have your portrait done? I've never heard you mention a thing about it. It wouldn't have anything to do with the fact that Lady Kathryn is young and attractive, would it?"

"I haven't had my formal portrait done, as you well know. I'm at the age when most of our ancestors had theirs done. Since she's so conveniently located, it just made sense to me to have her do it, *if* she's any good, which she probably is since she graduated from the Art Institute. I'm astonished they accepted her. She has to be very gifted. She's a very attractive young woman, but that's irrelevant. She's off limits to me anyway. I'm not interested in marriage, as we've already discussed numerous times." Jonathan took a sip of his ale as he looked over at Roderick in disgust.

Elaine spoke up. "Well, I think she's quite nice, and pretty. I don't understand why you're so opposed to marriage. I wish you would tell me so I can understand. None of you ever want to tell me anything, and it's just not fair!"

Jonathan, with a supercilious expression on his face, replied, "I agree she did seem very nice. I'll explain to you why I'm opposed to marriage when you get a little older. I know you hate to hear that, but for now, you'll just have to accept that I have some very good reasons. Now, here's our food. May we please relax and enjoy our luncheon?"

The White Hart Inn was well known for their excellent food, and they weren't disappointed. Once everyone had dined sufficiently, they left to go shopping. After all, that was one of the reasons Allison wanted to come to town. Since both Allison and Elaine needed to freshen up their wardrobes, they went to Madame Bovary's, as she always had the latest styles, and she did such exquisite work. Roderick and Jonathan told them they were leaving, but would return in two hours.

When Jonathan and Roderick returned to pick up the ladies, Allison and Elaine were raving about all the new clothes Elaine had ordered. Elaine, in her enthusiasm, almost fell when she tripped on the sidewalk in front of the carriage. "Oh, dear. I need to be more careful. Jonathan, thank you so much for allowing me to order some new gowns." Then turning to Allison, she said, "I really appreciate your help. That fashion plate you found of the gown with the rosettes embroidered on the bodice and at the hem is going to look wonderful in that yellow silk we picked out."

"Elaine, I enjoyed helping you. I also think that new emerald green riding habit will look excellent on you." Looking over at Jonathan, Allison asked, "Would it be all right, since it's only three o'clock, if we strolled along the delightful streets of Bath until it's time to go to the duchess's house?"

"Certainly, my dear. I'll just follow along in the carriage. You'll enjoy seeing the Abbey Church courtyard and the Roman Baths. I'll pick you up at Queen Square."

Once they passed the park, they joined Jonathan in the carriage and went on to Royal Crescent.

By the time Jonathan and his party arrived at the duchess's house it was almost four o'clock. Jonathan knocked on the door, and a tall, distinguished-looking man opened the door and showed them into the drawing room where the duchess and Lady Kathryn were sitting. Shortly after they arrived, Lady Milsom entered the drawing room, and the duchess served tea.

Once everyone finished their tea, Lady Kathryn asked, "Would you like to go up to my studio so you can view some of my work? If you're ready, please follow me."

Everyone enthusiastically agreed, and they followed Lady Kathryn upstairs. They entered a large, well-lit room with mullioned windows along the wall. In the center of the room was an easel with the duchess's portrait displayed on it. Jonathan made his way over to the easel and could immediately see an astonishing likeness to the duchess. Lady Kathryn had captured her arrogant expression perfectly. The duchess's startling blue eyes glowed with life. It was as if she were standing right in front of them.

"Lady Kathryn, this is a marvelous portrait of your mother. I can see that you're a talented artist, and I would like you to paint my formal portrait. When would you be able to start?"

"But don't you want to see these miniatures first, before you decide? Here's one that I did of my nieces and my nephews, and here is another one of my brother."

After Jonathan perused the miniatures, he said, "These are all exquisite. Now when can you start my portrait?"

Kathryn's lovely violet eyes were glowing with enthusiasm. "I get the best light in my studio in the morning, so that's the best time for me. Would nine o'clock work for you? I'll be finished with my mother's portrait by the end of the week, so I could start yours this coming Saturday, if that is convenient for you."

"Saturday will work well for me. My brother and his family are leaving very early that morning, so I would easily be able to be here by nine."

Once Kathryn and Jonathan agreed upon everything, they went back downstairs to the drawing room and joined the duchess. Shortly after that, Jonathan said, "Your Grace, thank you for having us for tea. We'll be attending the assembly rooms on Wednesday, so hopefully we'll see you then. It grows late, so we'll take our leave now."

The duchess smiled graciously over at him. "It's been a pleasure, Lord Sutherland, and we will definitely be attending the assembly rooms on Wednesday evening. We will see you then."

When everyone was back in the carriage, Allison said, "Lady Kathryn is probably the most gifted artist I've ever seen. Did you notice how she caught the duchess's arrogance perfectly? It was as if she were standing right in front of us. Roderick, I'd love for her to do our children's portrait. Once she's through with Jonathan's, we should commission her to do them, don't you agree?"

"She truly is an extraordinary artist, and I agree wholeheartedly that she should do a portrait of our children. I think we should get her to do one of our entire family." Roderick turned to Jonathan. "I'm sure she'll do a superb job on your portrait. Just imagine spending hours with such a lovely young woman. I would think you'll get to know each other quite well while she does your portrait."

Jonathan glanced over at his brother, frustrated with his brother's attempts at matchmaking. Roderick just wouldn't leave him alone on this issue. "I look forward to her painting my portrait, and I'm sure that we'll get to know each other, just not in the way you mean, Brother."

Since it was close to dinner when they arrived back at St. John's Wood, they all went up to their rooms to get ready. Jonathan could tell that Elaine was thrilled that she would be able to dine with the rest of the family, instead of her governess, Miss Tilton. Part of him wanted to keep her a child, but he knew Elaine was indeed growing up. He would have to let her have some additional freedoms, now that she was going to be sixteen soon.

When Jonathan entered his rooms, Hatton was there to apply the liniment and cold compresses to Jonathan's knee. After being on it for so long, Jonathan was in quite a bit of pain. Hatton tried to get him to take some laudanum, but he again refused. Besides, he knew several men who had become addicted to it. He didn't want to have that happen to him. Jonathan had Hatton pour him a glass of brandy instead. He decided he would try to stay away from the whiskey, even if he did like the way it made him feel.

While relaxing in his comfortable chair, Jonathan thought about Lady Kathryn and knew he was very attracted to her. He certainly hoped there would by a chaperone in the room with them while she was painting him. Jonathan had never felt such an instant attraction to such an innocent young woman. Most of the time he never even noticed them at all. She had such glorious red hair and the most gorgeous violet eyes he'd ever seen. Her figure was actually quite spectacular too. Her curves were in all the right places, and her legs had to be incredibly long. He could just imagine them wrapped around his hips.

Oh, this wasn't a good sign at all.

He couldn't allow himself to feel this level of attraction for her if they were going to be spending so much time together.

Well, there was no use thinking about it right now.

He needed to finish getting ready for dinner.

Vikki Vaught

On Wednesday evening, Jonathan, Roderick, and Allison went back to Bath to the assembly rooms. Jonathan didn't usually attend functions like this, but since Allison wanted to go, he felt it would be rude if he didn't come along. When they arrived, he was surprised at how crowded the rooms were. Since the season wasn't over in London yet, he hadn't thought there would be this many people. He hated functions like this because everyone was dancing, and, of course, he no longer danced. He used to enjoy dancing quite a bit, and that was just one more thing he could no longer do because of the battle.

As Jonathan stood over by a potted plant, he scanned the room, looking for anyone he might know. His eyes caught sight of Kathryn, and he was stunned once more by her incredible beauty. Her fabulous red hair was in a top knot on the crown of her head with curls cascading down around her shoulders. He could just imagine pulling out her hairpins and all those fiery curls tumbling down her back. Her gown was a soft shade of silvery blue, and it draped her figure to perfection. It had a low décolletage, which showed her breasts off magnificently. For such a slender woman, she filled out the top of her gown enticingly well.

Jonathan was by no means a short man, but he knew she would probably come up to his nose. He had always been attracted to tall women with deliciously long legs that could wrap around his hips as he sank deeply inside her tight sheath.

God, he had to quit thinking about her like this.

Jonathan felt his trousers tighten against his loins as he became aroused.

This was getting ridiculous!

It was a good thing he was standing partially behind this potted plant. He had to think of something else or people would notice his condition. Immediately, he imagined himself taking a cold bath, and then he was back to normal.

Slowly, Jonathan made his way around the room to where his brother and Allison were standing. They were talking to Lady Milsom when he approached. Allison looked over at Jonathan. "There you are, Jonathan. We were wondering where you were. Have you seen anyone here that you know? We're surprised that there are so many people here, since the season isn't over yet. Thank you for bringing us tonight. I know this can't be much fun for you, and I'm sure it's difficult to watch all the dancing. I remember how much you enjoyed it before your injury."

"I'm as surprised as you are. I never dreamed it would be this crowded tonight." He looked over at Lady Milsom. "The only people I've seen tonight that I know are you, of course, Lady Milsom, and I saw Lady Kathryn a few minutes ago." He turned toward Allison and added, "I was happy to bring you tonight. I do miss dancing. You're right, I did enjoy it quite a bit. Are you having a good time this evening?"

Roderick spoke up. "She's having a marvelous time, and it's getting ready to get even better." He grabbed his wife's hand. "Come with me, my sweet. I want to dance. It's a waltz, and I particularly enjoy waltzing with you."

With envy in his eyes, Jonathan watched as Roderick and Allison went to the dance floor. Watching them dance was like watching beauty in motion. He was so glad they had such a wonderful marriage. Roderick and Allison made such an attractive couple, what with Roderick being so tall with dark brown hair and bright blue eyes, and Allison, so petite with light brown hair and lovely light blue eyes.

As they danced, it was easy to see the love shining on their faces. If Susannah hadn't broken up with him, they would have been married eight years, and probably would have had several children by now, but he doubted they would have been as happy. She would have ended up being unfaithful to him just as she had been to the man she had married.

For Christ's sake, why was he thinking about her tonight?
He never thought about her!
He needed to get a grip on himself!

He turned to Lady Milsom. I'm going to the drink table. Would you like me to bring you a glass of lemonade?"

"Oh, yes, that would be lovely. It's quite warm in here tonight, and a glass of lemonade sounds delightful," Lady Milsom replied, as she waved her fan in front of her face.

Jonathan made his way over to the drink table, picked up a flute of champagne, and took a sip. As he picked up the glass of lemonade, he realized that he wouldn't be able to manage two drinks and still be able to use his cane, so he finished his glass and sat it down. It was such a nuisance, having to use his cane all the time. As he approached Lady Milsom, he noticed she was now standing with the dowager duchess and Lady Kathryn.

"Here's your lemonade, Lady Milsom." Jonathan looked over at Lady Kathryn and the duchess and smiled. "Your Grace, Lady Kathryn, it's a pleasure to see you tonight. I hope you're enjoying the evening. Can I get either of you ladies a glass of lemonade?"

The duchess said, "That would be simply splendid. It is quite warm this evening, and that sounds divine. Why don't the two of you go over to the drink table and get us some champagne? I would rather have that instead of lemonade."

Kathryn glanced at Jonathan. "I'll be happy to go with you. It will give us a chance to talk about your upcoming sitting." Jonathan held out his arm for her, she placed her hand in the crook of his arm, and they headed toward the drink table. "My lord, I'm sorry about my mother. She's always trying to play matchmaker whenever a handsome man is around. I keep telling her that I'm not interested, but she won't listen to me."

With surprise in his voice, Jonathan asked, "Aren't you interested in marriage? I thought that was what all young women wanted."

"I feel that having a husband would interfere with my art. I doubt very seriously that any man would want their wife painting portraits," Kathryn said, with determination on her lovely face. "I've known since I was a small child that I wanted to be an artist, and I won't let anything get in the way of that."

"Well then, we can become fast friends because I have no desire to get married either." This was an interesting turn of events. Now he could at least relax around Kathryn since he now knew she didn't want to get married. Of course, that didn't help the attraction he felt for her. If anything, it made it worse. This attraction puzzled him because he had never felt such strong feelings so quickly. It wasn't just sexual either — he found everything about Lady Kathryn fascinating.

As they approached the drink table, Kathryn answered, "I'd like that very much. Being at the Art Institute, I had several male friends who understood that I was just as serious about my art as they were and had no more desire to marry than they did. I'd be happy to be your friend."

Jonathan smiled at her, picked up a flute of champagne, and handed it to her. Then he picked up another one for the duchess, and they turned around and walked back to her mother. Jonathan appreciated how she understood he couldn't offer her his arm on the way back and felt even more relaxed in her presence.

Once Jonathan handed the duchess her champagne, he said, "It's been a pleasure seeing you this evening. I hope you have an enjoyable time tonight. I think I'll go to the card room. Excuse me, ladies." Then he bowed and left the room.

Chapter 4

When Jonathan entered the card room, he saw one of his old school friends and made his way over to him. "Hello, Shelton. It's been a long time since I've seen you. What have you been doing with yourself? It's been, what, five years since we last saw each other?"

Shelton pointed toward the chair and said, "Here, take a seat Sutherland. We were just getting ready to find a fourth, if you'd like to join us in a game of whist. It's been close to five years indeed. Since I've gotten married, my wife and I have been too busy to make it to London for the season, what with having a child almost every year since our marriage. I suppose you're still a confirmed bachelor, aren't you?"

"Of course. I haven't changed my views on marriage, and I never will! Since Roderick is happily married, I won't have to worry about becoming leg-shackled. He's already taken care of the succession by having a son."

Deciding to join them, Jonathan sat down, and soon he was relaxing with a glass of brandy by his side and a great hand of cards. He partnered with Shelton, and they were winning the set easily. He was on a winning streak and was feeling quite mellow from all of the brandy he'd been drinking. He knew he was getting drunk, but he couldn't seem to stop himself. They continued to play, and he continued to down glass after glass of brandy, smoking one cigar after another.

More than a few glasses of brandy later, Jonathan saw his brother approaching and sat up straighter. Roderick stopped in front of him. "Jonathan, my wife and I are ready to leave. I've taken the liberty of ordering the carriage."

"Hello, Brother," Jonathan drunkenly replied. "I'm not ready to leave yet. I'm on a winning streak, and I'm playing with my good friend Shelton here. Why don't you sit down and join us? Have a glass of brandy."

"I think you've had enough tonight. It's time for you to leave." Roderick turned to Shelton. "It's good to see you, Shelton. It's been a long time. Can you help me with my brother?"

"No problem. He's just had a bit too much to drink tonight." Shelton stood up. "Come on, old friend. It's time for you to go home. I'll help you up, all right?"

Jonathan looked at them with bloodshot eyes. "I don't need anybody's help. I can leave on my own!" He pulled himself up out of his chair but then fell over onto the floor, laughing as he tried to get up. Shelton and Roderick managed to get Jonathan up on his feet, encouraged him to lean on them, and finally got him out to the carriage. The footman helped get him inside, and his head fell back against the cushions as he passed out.

"Shelton, thank you for helping me with him. I'm not sure why he drank so much tonight. I would appreciate your discretion on this, all right?"

Shelton clapped him on the shoulder. "We've all had our moments. Don't worry about it. Here are his winnings from tonight. It was good to see both of you. I hope it won't be another five years before we see each other again. If you need anything else, just let me know."

Roderick went back into the ballroom and found his wife talking with her aunt. "Hello, my dear. I found Jonathan. He's already in the carriage, so we can leave now." Roderick bowed to Lady Milsom and smiled as he added, "It was a pleasure seeing you again. I look forward to seeing you tomorrow at four o'clock."

When they entered the carriage, Roderick helped Allison take her seat, took the seat next to her, and told the driver to take them home. Allison looked over at Jonathan with concern in her eyes and asked, "Roderick, what happened to Jonathan? Why is he sleeping? Is he all right?"

With a disgruntled tone to his voice, Roderick said, "He's not asleep. He's passed out. I found him in the card room drunk. Shelton had to help me get him out to the carriage."

"Oh, dear. I've never known him to do this kind of thing before," Allison replied. "Do you think this happens often?"

"I had noticed that Jonathan was drinking quite a bit," Roderick answered, "but I didn't realize to what extent. It's getting out of hand. I'll talk to him tomorrow. If he doesn't change his ways, he's going to die before his time. I'm really worried about his health. He looks years older than what he really is. Well, we've got quite a drive, so why don't you lay your pretty little head on my shoulder and rest a bit, my darling."

Allison smiled up at him with love shining in her pretty blue eyes, kissed his cheek, and snuggled close as they made their way back to St. John's Wood. When they arrived at the house, two footmen helped carry Jonathan up to his room. Hatton didn't look surprised when he saw the condition that Jonathan was in—he just shook his head. "I'll put him to bed, my lord."

Roderick looked Hatton in the eye and asked, "Does this happen often? He's quite drunk tonight, and I'm worried about him. Thank God, he's got you to look out for him. I appreciate your help with him tonight."

"My lord, his lordship's been drinking to excess every day for quite some time, and lately, he doesn't seem to be able to hold it as well. I've been quite worried about him."

"I'll talk to him in the morning. Well, it's late. I'm off to bed."

When Jonathan woke up the next morning, he had the worst headache he could remember having in years. Nausea rolled over him. He couldn't even remember coming to bed last night. The last thing he remembered was sitting down to play cards with Shelton. That was very troubling. He'd never been so drunk that he forgot how he made it to bed. When he tried to sit up, he barely had time to reach for the chamber pot before he cast up his accounts. Hatton came into the room, assisted him, and gave him some water to rinse out his mouth.

Jonathan rubbed his hand over his face. "Hatton, what happened to me last night? I can't remember coming home nor coming to bed. Did I do something stupid last night?"

"My lord, evidently you drank too much and passed out. When Roderick got you home, two of the footmen carried you to your bed. You'll have to talk to your brother to find out what happened. We've been together for a long time now, and I know it's not my place to say anything, but I'm worried about you. You've been drinking a lot more lately, and not just brandy. I know that you drink because of the pain. If you'd just take some laudanum, it may help you could cut back on the drink."

"Maybe you're right about the laudanum. I guess it wouldn't hurt to try it, instead of drinking. Hatton, please know that I do value your opinion. You've been with me a long time, and I know you have my best interests foremost in mind. Help me get dressed so I can go talk to my brother."

Once Jonathan was dressed, he went downstairs and found Roderick in his study. Jonathan could tell by the expression on his brother's face that he wasn't going to like what he had to tell him.

As Jonathan took his seat, he asked, "What did I do last night? The last thing I remember was sitting down to play cards with Shelton. Tell me what happened."

Roderick sat down across from Jonathan. "I found you in the card room, and you were extremely drunk. You made quite a scene and fell out of your chair. You were in such an inebriated state that Shelton and I had to help you out to the carriage, and once we got you in, you passed out cold. Jonathan, I've noticed that you've been drinking quite a bit lately. I think that you need to cut back. I realize you drink to deaden the pain, but surely, there's a better way to deal with it. What can I do to help?"

"Hatton has suggested that I try taking laudanum for the pain, and I've agreed. I'm sorry I was such an ass last night. I normally can hold my liquor better than that. Please apologize to Allison for me." Jonathan hung his head in shame. He certainly hoped he didn't run into Shelton any time soon.

"No apology is necessary. Allison knows how much pain you're in. We both helped nurse you when you came back from Waterloo, remember? Just try to lay off the liquor for a while, all right? I'm worried about you. Now, are you up for our morning ride?"

"Thank you for being so understanding. I promise I'll at least cut back on my drinking. I know it's getting out of hand. I'm afraid I'll have to pass on this morning's ride, but I'll be fine by tomorrow. I'm just going to sit here and go over some reports that Whetherby left for me. I'll see you later this afternoon for tea, since I've missed luncheon." Jonathan slumped down in his chair and reached for his reports.

Roderick stood up and turned to leave the room. "Why don't you have Goodman bring you a tray? You really need to eat something. You've lost quite a bit of weight lately."

"You're right, I have lost a bit. I promise I'll try to eat something."

"Well, I'll leave you now. I'll see you this afternoon."

Jonathan ordered a tray, and when it arrived he tried to eat something, but his stomach was still so nauseated that he was unable to eat much at all. He sat there all afternoon, fighting the desire to drink. His hands were shaking badly, but he was determined to stay away from liquor, at least for a few days.

Thank God, Roderick was so understanding.

He still felt he owed Allison an apology, and he would deliver it at tea later.

Kathryn woke up the morning after seeing the Marquess of Sutherland at the assembly rooms, thinking about him. She was glad they had talked, and since she now knew he had no more interest in marriage than she did, she could relax and not worry about doing his portrait. Not that she thought every man she met wanted to marry her. For some reason the marquess made her very nervous. She wasn't sure why, but he did. Kathryn got an odd feeling in the pit of her stomach every time she met his gaze. His eyes were such a penetrating blue, and he had such a beautiful, sensual mouth.

She couldn't remember ever noticing a man's eyes, let alone his mouth before.

Goodness!

What was this all about?

Lord Sutherland seemed to be a somber man, and she doubted that he smiled often. Kathryn wondered why he seemed so sad. He'd obviously sustained an injury at some point in the past, because he relied heavily on his cane. She would guess his age to be a few years older than Henry, who was three and thirty. His face was interesting with his strong jaw, high cheekbones, aquiline nose, and high forehead. While he certainly wasn't what she would call handsome, he was, nonetheless, quite attractive. She would enjoy the challenge of capturing his face on canvas.

Yes, she was very pleased about painting his portrait.

Well, this wasn't going to get her day started.

It was very unusual for her to woolgather like this. It must be because she was anxious to get started on his portrait. Kathryn rang for her maid, Sarah, and soon she was ready to meet her day.

When she arrived at the breakfast room, she was surprised to see her mother already there. Normally her mother didn't come down for breakfast, preferring to break her fast in her rooms. Kathryn's eyes narrowed. She knew her mother must be up to something.

While her mother buttered her toast, she said, "Good morning, Kathryn. I hope you had a restful night. I thought we could have a nice little chat this morning. Go ahead and get your breakfast and then sit here beside me. Did you enjoy the assembly rooms last night?"

Kathryn looked at her mother in astonishment, but did as her mother asked. Now she knew something must be up because her mother was never this pleasant. Kathryn went to the sideboard, filled her plate with her usual breakfast of coddled eggs, bacon, and toast with fresh creamery butter, then sat down across from her mother. "I had a very pleasant evening last night. You look refreshed this morning. You must have had a pleasant night's sleep. It's unusual for you to join me for breakfast. Is there something that you would like to chat about?"

The duchess slyly glanced at her. "I want to talk to you about painting the Marquess of Sutherland's portrait. I'm not pleased that you're accepting payment for doing it. That's so... bourgeois. He's quite an attractive gentleman, don't you think?" Taking a sip of her tea, she continued. "He would be a very good match for you. I'm sure that spending time with him will help you catch his eye. It would be wonderful if you could bring him up to scratch. He would be an even better match for you than your sister Helen made by marrying Lord Collingswood."

Kathryn interrupted. "Mother, I've told you repeatedly that I'm not interested in marriage. I have not changed my mind. I will *not* allow anything or anyone to interfere with my art. Besides, I already know that Lord Sutherland is a confirmed bachelor."

"How do you know he's not interested in marriage? He will need an heir, after all."

"He told me he already has an heir. Since his brother Roderick already has a son, there's no need for him to marry. I told him I wasn't looking for a husband, and we've agreed to become friends. So please, don't start trying to play the matchmaker! Remember, you promised me that you wouldn't do that if I agreed to come visit you here, and I expect you to honor your promise."

"Oh, all right, I'll leave you alone as I promised, but I can still hope that you'll change your mind. Surely, you don't want to be dependent on your brother your entire life?"

Kathryn took a deep, cleansing breath, trying to get her temper under control. "Henry and I have discussed my independence, and he has agreed to allow me to set up my own household in three years, once I've turned five and twenty. I'll hire a female companion so I won't be living alone. Henry understands how I feel about my art, and he supports my plans. I'm eventually going to have a studio in London, where my patrons can come to me."

Her mother started to interrupt, but Kathryn held up her hand to stop her saying anything. "I know you're not happy about my decision to be a portraitist, but you'll need to accept it, because I'm determined to succeed. I'm thrilled that I've already gotten two commissions, and I'm sure that as word gets out, I'll receive more. Now, I'm going upstairs to work on your portrait. I want to have it completed by Saturday so I'll be free to concentrate on Lord Sutherland's portrait. I'll see you at luncheon."

Kathryn went upstairs, put on her smock, and mixed the paint colors she needed to finish her mother's painting. Soon she was lost in her creativity. As she added the finishing touches to her mother's portrait, she thought about her upcoming meeting with Lord Sutherland. She was looking forward to Saturday. This would be her first commission, and she wanted to make sure she was mentally prepared for the sitting. Kathryn estimated that it would take about three weeks to do his portrait. Kathryn hoped he would be willing to sit for her at least twice a week.

She stood back and looked at her mother's portrait. She wasn't satisfied with her hair, so she went to work on getting it right. Her mother's hair was red-gold just like her brother and her sister, however her mother now had some strands of white mixed in, and that was what she needed to get right.

Finally, Kathryn was satisfied with her result, and since it was time for luncheon, she cleaned her brushes with oil of turpentine and laid them out to dry. She removed her smock, hung it up, and went to her room to freshen up.

That afternoon Kathryn received a letter from her sister. Helen was four years older, but they were very close. Helen had married the Earl of Collingswood three years ago, and their estate was on the coast of Devonshire. She would be staying there in November when she went to do the Marquess and Marchioness of Ralston's family portrait.

Helen wrote that she was trying to have another child. Helen and Matthew already had two-year-old twin boys, Winston and Nelson, plus Christina and Catherine, Matthew's twin daughters from his first marriage. They were all delightful children, and Kathryn loved them very much.

After she wrote a return letter to Helen, she took it downstairs to Abernathy so it would go out in tomorrow's post. Since it was such a lovely day, she called for Sarah so she could take a walk to Queen Square. The gardens were so lovely that she pulled out her sketchpad so she could capture the beauty of the summer blooms. While her first love was portraits, she also enjoyed painting landscapes. As she sat there lost in her art, she didn't realize someone had approached.

A noise disturbed her concentration, and she looked up to see Lord and Lady Roderick standing in front of her. Lady Roderick said, "Excuse me, Lady Kathryn, I couldn't help noticing you. I hope I'm not interrupting you, but I wanted to tell you how much I enjoyed seeing you last night."

Smiling, Kathryn replied, "It was a pleasure seeing you also."

Lady Roderick returned her smile as she said, "We want to talk to you about painting our children. I know that you're committed to do my brother-in-law's portrait, but once you have completed his, we would love to have you do our children. We greatly admired the paintings you showed us of your brother's and sister's children. We'd love to have you come to our home. Would you consider doing this for us?"

"I'd love to do their portrait. It should take me about three weeks to do Lord Sutherland's, which will mean that I could come out to do your children around the first part of August. Would that be convenient for you?"

Lady Roderick sat down on the bench beside Kathryn. "That would be wonderful. We may even decide that we want you to do our entire family. Would that be a problem?"

Kathryn closed her sketchbook. "Whatever you decide will be fine with me. I just want you to be happy with your decision. You live in Bristol, don't you? I've never been there, so I would enjoy visiting the area."

"We have a yacht, and we'd be happy to take you out in it, if that is something you would be interested in?"

"Oh, that sounds marvelous. I've never been out on the sea before, but my sister has. She loves it, so I'm sure I will too. Once I'm through painting Lord Sutherland's portrait, I'll write you and give you a firm date of when to expect me."

"Thank you so much. Well, we'll let you get back to your drawing now. We look forward to you coming in August." Lady Roderick and her husband turned around and walked away.

Kathryn watched them as they continued on their walk. She was so pleased that they wanted her to do their portrait. This would mean she now had three commissions already lined up. This was wonderful. At this rate, she was on her way to having a steady flow of patrons. Noticing the time, she called to Sarah, and they started home.

Chapter 5
- July 1823 -

Jonathan enjoyed the next couple of days with his brother, Roderick. Every morning they went for a ride around the estate. Roderick was able to see several of the tenant farmers that remembered him as a child. They were able to talk about old times and just enjoy being together again. They had always been the best of friends, not just brothers.

Jonathan held true to his promise and didn't drink anything accept wine with his dinner. He was feeling better, so he knew he would be better off leaving the liquor alone. The temptation to take a drink was strong all day long, but he was determined to resist the lure of the oblivion that liquor brought him, at least until Roderick and Allison left on Saturday.

On Friday, while they were out riding the estate, Roderick mentioned, "I have something wonderful to tell you. You know that Allison and I have wanted more children for several years now. Well, Allison is finally with child, and the baby should be born around the middle of January."

Jonathan grinned. "That *is* wonderful news. I hope this child is a boy. Frankford needs a brother. I'm sure Allison is thrilled."

Roderick threw back his head and laughed. "You're just looking out for your own interests. You want a spare. We're both extremely pleased. I still wish you would change your mind about marriage." Jonathan started to interrupt and Roderick quickly said, "I know...I know. I won't say any more about it."

After they finished their ride, they took the children to the lake and let them go swimming. Jonathan had never spent much time with children before, but found that he enjoyed himself. Frankford swam like a fish. He would jump off the limb of the tree and let out a big yell as he plummeted to the water's surface. Even little Jane was an excellent swimmer. It did his heart good to see how happy his brother was. They were both such good parents, and Jonathan knew they would mold Frankford to accept his future responsibilities as the next marquess.

After getting back to the house that afternoon, Jonathan went to his room, and Hatton wrapped cold compresses around his knee. Instead of brandy, he took a dose of laudanum. The laudanum did seem to help. His hands weren't shaking as badly since he'd been leaving the liquor alone, and his appetite had improved dramatically. He fought the temptation every day, but he knew he needed to stop drinking.

Jonathan hated to see his brother and his family go back home tomorrow. Elaine had really enjoyed spending time with Frankford and Jane, and so had he. The children were delightful, and Frankford was such a bright child. Maybe he should send Elaine with them when they left tomorrow, and then he could go get her next month. She could do with a break from her studies. He would talk to Roderick and Allison about it at tea that afternoon.

When Jonathan entered the drawing room that afternoon, he joined Allison on the sofa. "I've been thinking about how much fun Elaine's been having with the children. I wondered how you would feel about having her come stay with you this next month. She gets so bored here with just me for company. I thought she would enjoy a little holiday from her studies. What do you think?"

With a pleased expression on her pretty face, Allison replied, "I'd love to have Elaine come. She's so helpful with the children, and they love her so much. I'm sure Roderick would be fine with it." Then looking up, she saw Roderick enter the room. "In fact, here he is now. You can ask him what he thinks."

While accepting a cup of tea from Allison, Jonathan brought up the subject. "Roderick, I just asked Allison if it would be all right if Elaine came for a visit. She could go back with you tomorrow, and I'll come and get her next month. Would that be all right with you?"

"I think it would be delightful to have her. We can take her out on our yacht. I'm sure she would love that. I just wish you'd come with her. I'm determined to get you out on it." Roderick sat down in the chair beside the sofa, and Allison handed him his tea.

"I've already committed to having my portrait done, and I have quite a bit of work around here I need to take care of. I've been spending so much time in London the past few years that I've been neglecting my responsibilities to the marquessate. I promise that when I come to get Elaine, I'll go out on your yacht, all right?"

Allison passed Roderick a plate piled high with sandwiches, and then Roderick admitted, "I forgot about you sitting for Lady Kathryn. I wouldn't want to take you away from that. I know how much you're looking forward to having your portrait done. Of course, I understand. If I were a single bachelor, I'd want her to paint my portrait too."

Jonathan stiffened. He was getting quite tired of all Roderick's comments regarding Lady Kathryn. "I'm not interested in her that way. I thought you promised to quit trying to marry me off. You're worse than those marriage-mad mamas who are always trying to get me to talk to their daughters. Lady Kathryn has assured me that she's not interested in marriage either, and we've agreed to become friends. Now, will you leave it alone?"

"Oh, all right. I got the impression that you're attracted to each other, but I'll leave you alone. Let's have Goodman ask Elaine to come down so we can tell her she's coming for a visit." They sat and finished their tea while Goodman went to ask Lady Elaine to come downstairs.

When Elaine joined them, Jonathan asked, "Hello, Princess. How would you like to go back with Roderick and Allison for a visit?"

Elaine immediately jumped up from her seat, ran over to him and hugged him. "You're the best brother in the world. I'd love to go for a visit. How long can I stay?"

"I thought you could stay for three or four weeks. I'll come get you the first part of August. How does that sound? Oh, and you can take a holiday from your studies also."

"Oh, thank you! I'm going to have so much fun! You're the best brother ever." She turned to Roderick and asked, "Can I go out on your yacht? I've been dying to do that. I love the sea!"

Roderick hugged her, laughing. "Yes, I've already thought of that. I remembered how much you have always loved the sea. I promise to take you out."

The rest of the day and evening passed, and everyone had a pleasant time. Jonathan knew he was going to miss all of them so much, but he knew it was the right decision, allowing Elaine to go for a visit.

After dinner, they went to the drawing room, and Allison entertained them by playing the pianoforte, and Elaine sang. He found music very soothing and used to play the pianoforte often, but now he rarely did. Since they would be leaving early the next morning, everyone retired to their rooms at nine o'clock.

That night, Jonathan had another nightmare. He woke up fighting his bed sheets and yelling. He was shaking all over and had to have a drink. He tried to fight the temptation, but he had to have something to calm his nerves. He decided he would drink one glass of whiskey, just enough to take the edge off.

As soon as Jonathan drank the whiskey, he could feel his heart rate slowing to normal, and his entire body relaxed as the warmth spread throughout his body. It was the most wonderful feeling in the world. The whiskey took all his aches and pains away and dimmed the memory of the nightmare.

Jonathan knew that he had to get up early in the morning to see Roderick, Allison, and the children off, so he would only allow himself one more glass and no more. After each glass, he told himself no more, but he continued to drink until he passed out and dropped the empty whiskey bottle on the floor.

The next morning, Jonathan woke up with a start when he felt someone shaking him. He looked up into Hatton's face with Roderick staring at him over Hatton's shoulder. Jonathan looked at them through bloodshot eyes, and then he dropped his head in his hands. His head felt as if it was splitting in two. "I had a bad dream last night, and I was only going to drink one glass. I know you're disappointed in me, but no more than I am in myself. Let me get dressed, and I'll meet you downstairs in thirty minutes." As Roderick left the room, he looked back at Jonathan with pity in his eyes. It made him feel so ashamed.

Oh, hell!

Why couldn't he leave the drink alone?

It was the whiskey...he knew it. If he just left it alone...he'd be all right. From now on, he was only going to drink wine and maybe a little brandy. Hatton handed him his restorative and he drank it down, then got up and dressed. Hatton shaved him, and then he went downstairs to see them off.

As the carriage pulled away and Roderick, Allison, and Elaine waved goodbye to him, he felt so miserable and alone. Even though he would miss Elaine, he knew she deserved this break from her studies. He had to get a handle on this drinking. He went back into the house, went into his study and sat down. Then he remembered he was due at Lady Kathryn's house at nine o'clock, and it was already after eight o'clock. He rushed out to the stables as quickly as he could — damn his bad knee! He had Demon saddled, since he would have to ride into town if he was going to get there in time.

As Jonathan headed towards Bath, he remembered how disappointed his brother was in him. When he saw the pity in his eyes, it had cut him deep. The last thing he wanted from anyone was pity. From this point on, he wouldn't drink any more whiskey. When he got back to the house, he'd have all of it removed from the house and thrown away.

The closer Jonathan got to Bath, the better he began to feel. He was really looking forward to seeing Kathryn again. She was certainly a beautiful woman. Too bad she was a lady, because he'd love to have her in his bed. Unfortunately, that wasn't going to happen.

He needed to find a woman. That was half the problem. He wasn't used to going this long without sex. It had been over a week since he had last visited Madame Angela's. Once he was through with his sitting, he would go see the Madame. He'd pick out a woman and relieve the sexual tension he was feeling.

Ah…yes, now that was a great plan!

Jonathan arrived at Kathryn's house by nine o'clock, and the butler showed him upstairs to Kathryn's studio. When he saw her, he was again struck by how beautiful she was with all that glorious red hair casually caught up at the top of her head, tendrils curling around her face. He wanted to run his fingers through all that gorgeous hair.

Hell's bells, he needed a woman badly!

He approached her, took her hand, and brought it to his lips as he gazed into her lovely eyes. "Hello, Lady Kathryn. I hope you're feeling well today. I've been looking forward to seeing you again."

"Good morning, my lord. I'm pleased you could come. I feel excellent today. Why don't you sit down so we can talk, and I'll tell you what we're going to be doing?" She took her seat, and Jonathan sat down, looking expectantly at her. "Today, I'll be doing some preliminary sketches of you. Have you thought about how you would like to be portrayed?"

Jonathan thought a moment. "I know I don't want to be dressed in formal attire. I'd prefer to be dressed much as I am today. Would that be a problem? I'm not a formal person, and I want to appear relaxed in my portrait."

"That would be no problem at all. When I did my brother's portrait, he wore riding clothes. Is that what you had in mind?"

"Yes, that's exactly what I had in mind. Should I wear the same clothes to each sitting?"

Kathryn shook her head. "Not until I'm ready to actually do the painting. During these first few sittings, I'll be sketching you in different positions to find out what will work best for you. I'd like you to come at least two times a week, but more would be preferable. How often could you come for a sitting?"

"Since you want me to come in the morning, three times a week would be the best I could do. I normally ride my estate each morning with my steward, so Saturday, Tuesday, and Thursday would work best for me. Would that fit your schedule?"

"That would be fine. Since I'm basically on holiday and don't have an estate to run, I can be as flexible as you need. Now that we have that settled, why don't you take a seat over there by the window, and we'll get started." There was a straight-back chair by the window, and Jonathan went over and sat down. "Just relax and try to look natural. Think about something pleasant, that way I'll get some good sketches. Tell me a little bit about yourself. What kind of things do you like to do? For example, do you like to read?"

Jonathan shifted in his seat, trying to get comfortable before answering her. "To be honest with you, what I like best is riding my horse, Demon. As I'm sure you've noticed, I have a bad limp, and when I'm on a horse, I'm more comfortable. I do like to read, and I also enjoy music. I play the pianoforte, but I don't sing. I used to love to dance, but since my injury, I'm no longer able to."

As Kathryn continued to sketch, she asked, "Tell me about Demon. Have you had him for long?"

Jonathan smiled with pleasure. "I bought Demon just as soon as I was healed enough to think about trying to ride again, and that was eight years ago. At first, I wasn't sure if I'd even be able to do that. The surgeons told me that I would never walk again, let alone ride a horse. Demon is a gelding, and he's very in tune to me. I have to use my upper leg since I can't use my knee, but he responds to the slightest pressure and my voice command. I was very fortunate when I found him."

As he talked, he observed Kathryn as she worked. Her hands were in constant motion. It was fascinating to watch. She held her head a little to the side, and as she concentrated, she bit her bottom lip. He was getting aroused imagining what it would be like to kiss her. His breeches grew taut across his loins.

Obviously, he needed to find a woman, and fast, if he was going to be coming here three times a week. And of course…there was no chaperone as he'd hoped there would be.

"My sister, Helen, Lady Collingswood, loves to ride. She and her husband live along the coast of Devonshire, and they ride on the beach every day. I enjoy riding, but not as much as my sister does. You said you were injured eight years ago. If I may ask, how did you get hurt?"

Jonathan normally hated to talk about his injury, but for some reason he wanted to tell Kathryn about it. "When Bonaparte escaped in 1815, I joined the army. I met your brother, by the way, when we were waiting around for something to happen. During the battle, my horse was shot out from under me. A Frenchman took advantage and shot me. My brother found me, and when the surgeons wanted to amputate my leg, he wouldn't let them. I'm so grateful that he was there. While I hate that I have to limp, I prefer that to the alternative. I don't like to complain since I'm lucky I survived when so many others didn't."

Kathryn stopped drawing and glanced over at him. "That still doesn't negate all your suffering. You've had to live with discomfort for eight years. My brother was injured at Waterloo, but he doesn't like to talk about that time."

"I can understand that," Jonathan remarked. "I vaguely remember hearing about you losing your father several years back. That's when your brother inherited his title, wasn't it?"

"Yes. I lost my brother, Nelson, and my father—both within three weeks. Thank goodness we still had Henry to inherit, or I don't know what would have happened since there were no other male heirs on my father's side of the family."

"I'm sure that must have been a dreadful time for your whole family," Jonathan stretched out his leg in front of him, trying to get more comfortable. "I lost my father five years ago, and I think of him every day. We were very close while I was growing up. He was so relieved when my brother and I both made it back. The only time that I can remember arguing with my father was when both my brother and I decided to go fight Bonaparte. He was so worried the entire time we were gone, and was devastated when I came back so severely wounded."

"I can understand why he worried. When Henry had to go fight, we were all terribly worried, especially his wife. I'm sure it was hard on you, being so severely wounded."

"I was very melancholy for a long time after my injury," Jonathan admitted. "I regret my behavior before my father died. I spent most of my time in London, when I should have been home helping him run the marquessate. When he died of a heart attack, I felt so guilty because I wasn't with him when it happened. Neither my brother nor I were able to get to him before he died."

Kathryn resumed sketching. "I'm sure your father knew that you loved him, even if you weren't there. My father had a heart attack also. He only lived for a few days after his attack. Henry had gone to London when it happened, but he did make it back before he died."

Jonathan gazed over at Kathryn, once more becoming transfixed as he watched her nibbling on her bottom lip, and wishing that he could taste her. She probably tasted as sweet as cherries.

Oh God, he had to quit thinking this way.

He moved in his seat trying to find a way to ease the front of his breeches. At least his riding coat should cover his arousal.

Kathryn looked over at him and smiled. "Well, that's enough for today. When you come on Tuesday, I'll need to make some sketches of you standing up. Will that be a problem for you? I'll let you sit down and rest between sketches. Will that be all right?"

"That will be fine. I don't have a problem standing. It's walking that causes me problems. I'm amazed that I've been here for two hours. May I see your sketches?"

"I hope you'll understand, but I don't normally let my subjects see my work until it's complete. You wouldn't be able to understand what I'm trying to do. I'll do this: once I've got a complete sketch, I'll let you see that."

Jonathan shrugged his shoulder. "That's all right. Whatever works for you is fine with me. Well, I'll leave you until Tuesday."

"Let me show you out. I want to thank you again for allowing me to do your portrait. I think you'll be pleased with the final result." Kathryn walked with him until they were back downstairs. Then she turned him over to their butler and he showed him to the door.

Once Jonathan was outside, he led his horse to a mounting block and managed to get on. He left and headed over to Madame Angela's House of Pleasure. A part of him felt guilty about what he was getting ready to do, but he was so aroused from the time spent with Kathryn, he needed relief badly. Besides, he had no reason to feel guilty. After all, he'd just met her six days ago, and he was definitely not interested in having any kind of relationship with her.

When Jonathan arrived, Madame Angela curtsied. "Good afternoon, Lord Sutherland. It's a pleasure to see you again. Where's your friend Baron Jenkins?"

Jonathan smiled sardonically. "Jenkins has gone back to his estate, so it's just me today."

Madame Angela smiled suggestively. "I'm sure you'll find what you're looking for here. Please look around and pick out any of my ladies."

Jonathan looked around the room, spied a tall gorgeous redhead, pointed toward her. "I would like to spend time with her. What's her name?"

"My lord, you have very good taste. That's Suzette, and she's just come here from Paris. I think you'll be pleased with her." Madame Angela motioned Suzette over. "Suzette, Lord Sutherland would like to spend some time with you this afternoon. Take him upstairs so that you can entertain him in the privacy of your room."

Jonathan followed Suzette upstairs. She was quite tall and slender, and her hips gently swayed as she walked up the stairs. His desire spiraled upward as he thought with anticipation of what was to come. When they entered her room, she led him to the bed and he sat down. Suzette gazed seductively at him, reached down, and stroked his cock through his breeches, and he grew even harder than he had been before. As she rubbed up against him, she slowly unbuttoned his breeches, reached inside his smalls, and took out his rigid member.

As Suzette began to stroke him, he saw Kathryn's beautiful face. Jonathan closed his eyes and imagined it was Kathryn touching him as his desire spiked to fever pitch. Suzette leaned over and took him into her mouth and started sucking and running her tongue up and down his shaft. Again, he imagined Kathryn was doing this to him. He pulled Suzette up, leaned her over the bed, and entered her from behind. He stroked in and out, harder and faster, all the time picturing Kathryn's beautiful face. In mere seconds, he exploded in an incredibly powerful climax.

Jonathan had never reached satisfaction so quickly, at least not since he was just a green boy with his first whore. As he came back down to earth, he felt embarrassed and a little ashamed by his visualization of Kathryn. In a way, he felt as if he had betrayed her, which made no sense since they weren't involved. After all, he'd only met her last Monday. Even though he obviously desired her, he knew that since she was an innocent, nothing could ever come of it.

Standing up, Jonathan buttoned his breeches. "Thank you, Suzette, for an enjoyable time. I'll be sure to tell Madame that you pleased me tremendously."

Suzette rolled over and sat up. "Don't you want to do anything else? I'm sure I could revive you, if you would let me." She reached for him, but he backed away.

"No, that's all right. I'm fine. You've more than satisfied me. Here's a little extra for the enjoyable time you've given me. I'm going to take my leave now."

After Jonathan left Madame Angela's, he realized that he shouldn't have gone there. While it was extremely erotic, he shouldn't have thought of Kathryn while he was in a brothel. He knew that he must never do that again. If he couldn't stop thinking about her, he would just have to try to do without sex until he was over this obsession he was having with Kathryn.

Chapter 6
- July 1823 -

Kathryn watched as Jonathan departed her mother's house. She realized that she was now thinking of him as "Jonathan" ever since his sister-in-law had used his given name. In her sketches of him, she was able to capture the sad expression in his brilliant blue eyes. Kathryn longed to see him smiling and happy. She just knew he would have a dazzling smile with those white teeth and sensual mouth. Every time she was around him, she experienced odd sensations coursing through her body, and it was very disturbing. These sensations were new to Kathryn, and she wasn't sure what was causing them, but she wished they would stop.

Oh goodness, she had to stop thinking about him like this!
She never thought about other men this way.

It was such a shame that Jonathan's knee had been so severely injured at Waterloo. So many fine young men either lost their lives or were permanently injured in that terrible battle. It all seemed so senseless to her. She realized that Waterloo had been necessary, but it still didn't make any sense to her. War was so brutal, and she wished it didn't exist. Of course, wars had been around since the beginning of time, and she was sure there would be other wars in the future. She just hoped there wasn't another one in her lifetime.

Her heart went out to Jonathan. Kathryn could sense that he felt a keen sense of guilt over not being there when his father died. It must be horrible to live with that kind of guilt. If he could just let go of it, she knew he would be a happier man. She looked forward to getting to know him better. She definitely found him fascinating.

Why did she keep thinking so much about him?

This was so strange for her. She had never thought about a man like she was thinking about Jonathan.

Kathryn went back upstairs and put away her drawing supplies. She pinned the drawings that she'd made of Jonathan to the canvas on her easel and stood back, looking the drawings over. His eyes had quite a few lines at the corners, and he looked bone-weary tired. She wondered if he had trouble sleeping. Henry had suffered from nightmares for years after his injuries at Waterloo. That could be what was wrong with Jonathan, and why he probably slept so poorly.

Kathryn understood about nightmares. She'd suffered from them since she was a small child, along with sleepwalking. Her nightmares were brought on by the abuse she'd suffered at the hands of her uncle, Viscount Manningly. He was her mother's brother, and in her mother's eyes, her uncle could do no wrong. He came to visit frequently while she was growing up.

Uncle Theodore started abusing her when she was about six years old, and it continued until she was sixteen. That Christmas, he'd tried to rape her, but Henry and Melody stopped him before he could finish the rape. Of course, they didn't know it, but her uncle had raped her many times.

Kathryn was twelve years old the first time he raped her, but before that, he made her do disgusting things. Even when she was six years, he would get her alone and touch her. As the years went by, his depravity grew worse. Kathryn had a hard time understanding why he had picked her. He told her that it was because she was bad, and that he needed to show her the error of her ways, but she always thought that it must be something about her that caused him to choose her.

Still to this day, every time Kathryn would remember what he did to her, it made her quite ill, especially when she remembered how he made her take him into her mouth. The rapes themselves had been excruciatingly painful, but the other thing was worse. It was because of her horrible experience with her uncle that she had decided that she would never marry. As much as she would like to have children, she knew she could never stand to be intimate with a man.

Kathryn would shower all her maternal love on her dear nieces and nephews. Henry and Melody had four children. Mary Elizabeth was their eldest, and she was now seven years old and grew to look more like Kathryn's sister, Helen, as each day passed. Mary Elizabeth was small for her age, so she took that after Melody, who was very petite. Brandon had just turned six years old, but Henry wasn't his real father. Then in 1818, they had Magnus who was three years old, and then the baby William, who was nine months old, and a delightful baby.

Helen had four children also, and Kathryn looked forward to seeing them in November when she went to paint the

Marquess and Marchioness of Ralston. She would be staying with Helen and Matthew while she did the portrait.

Yes, she was truly blessed with all her nieces and nephews.

Kathryn was so grateful to have them in her life. She looked over at the clock on the wall and noticed that it was almost time for luncheon. She hurried to her room to freshen up before she went down to join her mother.

Kathryn entered the dining room, sat down across from her mother, and the footman served her. As they were eating her mother asked, "How did the sitting with Lord Sutherland go this morning? Did you have a chance to talk while you were sketching? I'm sure that he's a very interesting gentleman."

"The sitting went extremely well, and I was able to do quite a few sketches that will help when I actually start painting his portrait. I found him to be very interesting. He actually met Henry in Brussels shortly before that terrible battle. Lord Sutherland was a captain in the army, just as Henry was, so they met right before the battle. In fact, that was how he was injured. From what he said, he's very fortunate that he didn't lose his leg. What do you have planned for this evening? Are we going anywhere?"

"Oh my, yes," her mother said. "I thought that we would attend the opera tonight. I know how you've always enjoyed that. I want you to enjoy your visit with me. Do you realize that this is the first time that we've ever spent time together without the rest of the family around? I'm so pleased that you agreed to come."

Kathryn realized that she was enjoying this time with her mother. They had never been close, so maybe this was the ideal opportunity to forge a closer bound. "I'm enjoying my time here. Bath is such a lovely city, and your townhouse is beautiful. I'm sure you love living here, but I'm sure you miss Sanderford Park. What opera is playing tonight?"

"It's one of Mozart's operas, *Le nozze di Figaro*. Have you ever seen it before?"

"Yes, and it's actually one of my favorites, so I look forward to attending tonight. I love the comic operas, and that one is delightful,"

"I'm glad you're enjoying your stay with me. I do love Bath. Since so many of my friends live here, there are constant parties and soirees to keep me entertained. Of course, Sanderford Park is wonderful, but I've always enjoyed city living much more than living in the country. If you are going to establish a studio in London, you'll need to adjust to city life."

"While I was attending the Art Institute, I enjoyed London tremendously. Even though I'm not thrilled with balls and such, I do love the other amusements that are available in London. Melody's aunt, Lady Helton, has offered to allow me to continue to stay with her whenever I'm in London, so I'll be returning there in the spring." They continued talking as they finished their meal. It was one of the most pleasant conversations she'd ever had with her mother.

Once they were finished with their meal, Kathryn stood up. "I'm going to take a walk this afternoon. I'll see you later at tea." She left the dining room and went to find her maid so she could go for her walk.

Kathryn enjoyed walking tremendously, and she could walk for miles without growing tired. Fortunately, Sarah enjoyed walking as well, since she had to come with her. She felt constrained by the rules that governed unmarried females while in the city. When she was at Sanderford Park, she could walk for miles by herself and never leave the park. Here, if she wanted to stick her nose out of the door, she had to take her maid with her. She was quite fond of Sarah, but it would be so nice to be able to take a walk by herself.

While Kathryn was on her walk, she stopped by the bookseller and found an excellent book on art, and a new novel, so she purchased them both. Then she went to the confectionery and picked out some delicious looking chocolate sweetmeats. Kathryn loved anything chocolate. On the way back to her mother's, she ran into Lady Milsom and they chatted a bit. Over all, Kathryn had a very pleasant afternoon.

When Jonathan returned home, he went to his rooms and had Hatton wrap his knee with cold compresses and put liniment on it. Since he was in quite a bit of pain, he took a dose of laudanum and fell asleep. When Jonathan woke up several hours later, he felt much better, since his head was no longer pounding from his excessive drinking the night before. Jonathan had promised Roderick that he would stay away from liquor, but he had broken down and gotten drunk when he woke up from his nightmare. It pained him when he remembered that he'd let his brother down this morning.

Jonathan felt that the problem was the whiskey, so he had ordered Goodman to remove all of it from the house. He loved the way the whiskey made him feel while he was drinking it, but he didn't enjoy the aftermath. His head always felt much worse the morning after. It was not so much the drinking, but what...he'd been drinking. From now on, he was going to stick to wine and a little brandy before he went to bed. That should be all right.

That night, after Jonathan retired to bed and sent Hatton away, he sat in his chair to read. While he read, he sipped his glass of brandy, no more drinking it quickly. He would savor it and nurse it along, that way he wouldn't drink as much. It worked for a while, but then as he started to feel mellow, he told himself that he could drink a little bit faster. By midnight, he'd passed out in his chair and never made it to his bed.

When Jonathan woke up the next morning, he had another pounding headache, and his stomach was extremely queasy. Since Hatton hadn't come up yet, he hurriedly hid the evidence of his drinking and got in bed.

When Hatton got his bath ready, he didn't tell him that he needed his morning brew. He made himself do without it. Once Hatton had shaved him and helped him dress, he went down to his study. As soon as he was alone, he poured a glass of brandy and drank it down in three gulps. As soon as the liquor hit his stomach, his hands quit shaking. He spent the entire day in his study drinking. By bedtime, he was too drunk to go upstairs.

The next morning, Goodman found Jonathan passed out in his study. He sent for Hatton, and together they helped him upstairs to his bed. He felt so horrible that he slept away most of the day. When he woke up at eight o'clock that night, he rang for Hatton, and then sent him to the kitchen for food. He realized that he hadn't had anything to eat in two days.

This had to stop.

He had to be up early tomorrow as he was due at Lady Kathryn's at nine o'clock. That night he was determined not to drink, since he didn't want to have a headache when he went for his sitting. After he ate, he got back in bed and eventually fell asleep from sheer exhaustion.

Hatton woke Jonathan up the next morning at seven, and he felt much improved. He was even able to eat some breakfast. Obviously, he had to stop drinking brandy too. From now on, he was only going to drink wine, and only with his meals. Surely, he would be all right if he left the brandy alone.

Jonathan had a pleasant drive into town. Instead of riding Demon, he went in the carriage this time. When he arrived at Kathryn's house, since he was a bit early, the butler showed him to the drawing room and told him that Lady Kathryn would be down shortly.

About ten minutes later Kathryn arrived. "Good morning. I appreciate your promptness. I hope you had a restful night."

While Jonathan and Kathryn walked upstairs to her studio, he replied, "I did have a pleasant night's sleep. Thank you for asking. I hope you slept well. I must say you look very pretty today. That blue looks lovely with your eyes."

Kathryn entered her studio ahead of him, looked back and said, "Thank you. Remember how I told you that I wanted to do some sketches of you standing up? If you will go over to the window and put your hand on the ledge, I'll get started."

Jonathan went over to the window and did as she had requested. "Is this how you want me?"

Kathryn looked over at him. "Yes, that's perfect. I hope that it doesn't bother you when I direct you, but I'll need to do that so I can get the right poses. It's all right to move a little bit, but try to stay as still as possible." Kathryn walked over to her easel and started drawing. "Why don't you tell me more about yourself? I enjoyed meeting your brother and his wife, and of course, your sister, Lady Elaine. She's quite a bit younger than you, isn't she? By the way, I've found that talking will help to pass the time for you."

"Roderick and I are extremely close. Since we are only a year apart in age, we did everything together. My father waited to send me to school so Roderick and I could go together. We went to Eton and we both liked school. It's hard to separate my story from Roderick's because we've always been together, especially when we were young."

"That's all right. It's the same for me and my sister, Helen. We were quite inseparable as we were growing up. Tell me more."

"Roderick and I joined the army together. We ended up apart during the fighting, and that was when I received my injury. I think I told you he was the one to find me after the battle. He wouldn't allow them to amputate my leg, and I'll always be eternally grateful to him for that."

"I can understand why you're thankful he was there with you."

"When we got back to England, he married Allison right away, just as soon as we arrived at St. John's Wood. They nursed me back to health, or at least as healthy as I could be. It took me four months before I could even attempt to get out of bed and walk. Roderick and my valet, Hatton, wouldn't give up on me, and eventually I was able to walk using my cane."

"It sounds as if you're quite close to your valet. You've mentioned him before. Was he in the army with you?"

Jonathan shifted his weight to his good leg, and then continued talking. "Yes, Hatton was my batman. I'm very fortunate to have him. Once I was up and walking, Roderick and Allison left for Westland Acres. After they left, my mental attitude was terrible. My father tried to cheer me up, but I was just too miserable to care. Eventually, I went to London. I started drinking, carousing around with my friends, and living my life quite recklessly. I think that a part of me wished I'd died over there."

Jonathan realized he had completely failed to answer her question about Elaine. "I'm sorry, you asked about Elaine, didn't you?"

Kathryn glanced over at him and smiled. "That's all right. I enjoyed hearing you talk about your brother. Now tell me about Elaine."

"Elaine is fifteen. She has a different mother than Roderick and I had. Our mother passed away when I was twelve. My father was remarried a couple of years later to a woman quite a bit younger than he was. My stepmother got with child right away, but unfortunately, she passed away when she gave birth to my sister," Jonathan said, as he flexed his hand, and then put it back on the windowsill.

"Do you need to take a break? I'll be through shortly, if you can just bear it for a few more minutes. So Elaine never knew her mother, did she?"

"No, Elaine didn't have the benefit of knowing a mother's love. I'm fifteen years older than she is, but even though there's a big age difference, we're very close. When my father died five years ago, I left her alone with her governess. I'm not proud of that. I should have tried to be more of a father to her, but I didn't. She's actually turning into a wonderful young lady, thanks to her governess. She went with Roderick and Allison when they left to go back to their home. I thought it would give her a holiday. I'm sorry. I didn't mean to rattle on like this."

Kathryn stopped drawing. "You did exactly what I wanted you to do. As you talked, I was able to get different facial expressions that will help when I start to paint your portrait. I think that's enough for today. On Thursday, I'll get you to pose in a different position. I should be able to start painting on Saturday. I'm sorry this session ran over a bit."

"Please, don't worry about it. I was fine until the end. In fact, I lost track of the time completely as I was talking. Were you able to get what you needed today?"

"Definitely, and what I need you to do now is figure out what you want to wear for your portrait. I'll need you to wear whatever you decide on at all your sittings starting Saturday. Let me show you out, and then I'll see you on Thursday." Kathryn stepped away from her easel and together they left her studio.

"You know this isn't very fair. I'm telling you all kinds of things about me, but you haven't told me anything about yourself. Next time, it will be your turn to talk, and I'll listen." When they arrived back downstairs, Jonathan bowed, kissed her hand, and left.

The next two days, Jonathan didn't drink any brandy, and only drank wine at his meals. He was starting to feel much better. He now realized that he could never drink brandy again. His knee was bothering him quite a bit, but he ignored it as much as possible and took laudanum before bed, which also helped him sleep. His first thought when he woke up Thursday morning was about seeing Kathryn again. He was so attracted to her, and he definitely wanted to know more about her. Today, he planned on getting her to talk, instead of him doing all the talking.

Jonathan arrived on time, and the butler took him up to her studio. As he entered, Kathryn said, "Good morning. You certainly look cheerful today. Are you ready for your sitting?"

Jonathan smiled, walked over to her and raised her hand to his lips, then kissed it. "Good morning to you. I do feel cheerful. May I say how lovely you look today? What position do you need me in?"

Kathryn smiled shyly, looking somewhat embarrassed. "I'm going to have to touch you to pose you today. I hope you don't think I'm too forward, but it's the only way."

Smiling, Jonathan walked over to the window. "No problem. Do whatever you need to do. I think that I can handle you touching me."

Kathryn walked over to where Jonathan was standing. "I need you to stand facing my easel. Please put your hand on your hip and stand with your right foot slightly forward, putting more of your weight on your left leg." He did as she asked, and then she said, "No, that's not quite right. Let me place your hand. Please let me know if it will bother you to stand in this position."

Kathryn touched his hand, and he immediately felt a jolt of energy shoot through his body. As she picked up his hand and placed it where she wanted it, he became aroused. He kept trying to think of something else, but it wasn't working.

"Ah, that's better. Are you all right? You appear a little flushed. Is it too warm in here for you?"

Jonathan continued to try to get himself back under control. "Yes, it is a little warm, but I'll be all right. Am I standing correctly for you?"

"I'll just open the window a little bit, but don't move. You're just perfect, and I don't want you to lose your pose."

She reached behind him brushing against his arm as she raised the window. He immediately felt a cool breeze, and a further tightening in his loins. "That's much better. I promise I'll try to draw quickly."

The breeze did help, but he was glad his riding coat covered his breeches. "I'll be fine. Thank you for opening up the window. There's a cool breeze blowing now, and I feel much cooler. Now remember, you promised you would do the talking today. Tell me a little about yourself."

Kathryn walked over to her easel, picked up her pencil, and started sketching. "You already know about my family. As a child, I spent most of my time painting. I started painting when I was about six years old. I painted my dog, my cat, my sister, and both of my brothers. They were incredibly patient with me, and they always told me that my paintings were wonderful."

Laughing, Jonathan asked, "Did you keep your early work? When did you start painting with oils, or did you start that as a young child?"

"At first, I only used watercolors, but when I started with oils, I knew it was the medium for me," she replied, "My parents didn't take my art seriously for a long time. In fact, if it wasn't for Henry, I wouldn't have gone to art school. He paid for my first art instructor since my parents wouldn't. That was when I was fourteen."

"Well, it's good that your brother took your talent seriously."

Kathryn glanced up from her work and gave him a determined look. "Henry made them accept me into the Art Institute. I know he gave them a huge donation so they would let me attend, but I didn't care, as long as I was able to go. I knew I was good enough, and my instructors realized it too, once the Institute let me in. I graduated top in my class. I found all the instruction invaluable, and I plan to open my own studio in London in three years."

"Why do have to wait three years? Once more people see your work, they'll all want you to paint them."

Kathryn stepped back from her easel. "Henry has promised that I can set up my own household when I turn five and twenty. His only requirement is that I hire a companion to live with me."

"All this is very interesting, but surely you have some other interests besides art. What other things do you like to do?"

"Well, let me think." She continued to sketch, as she thought about his question she got an adorable quizzical expression on her face. "I like to walk. I would go exploring when I was a child, and I'd walk for miles. Sanderford Park is huge, and so I could walk anywhere I wanted. There's a lake at Sanderford Park, and I used to go there quite a bit. In fact, my brother Nelson taught me how to swim. We spent most of our afternoons during the summer swimming in the lake, so I definitely like to swim."

"I have a lake on my estate, and Roderick and I spent many wonderful days there fishing when we were children. In fact, one of my friends came to visit me a few weeks ago, and we went fishing there. Now, what else do you like to do?"

"I do enjoy reading. I owe my love of reading to Melody. She got me started on novels, and I've loved them ever since. She's an avid reader," Kathryn explained. "I also enjoy the opera tremendously. I recently went to see *Le nozze di Figaro*, and it was marvelous. I've always loved to sing, and singing lessons were something I enjoyed as a child. I know you told me you play the pianoforte, but do you like opera?"

It pleased Jonathan that they had music in common. That just gave him one more thing to like about her. "I do enjoy going to the opera. I like all types of music, and I find it very soothing to play the pianoforte. I've barely touched my pianoforte since I came home. I'll have to correct that immediately. Where did you live while you were going to the Art Institute?"

Kathryn looked over at him. "Oh, Melody has a wonderful aunt, Lady Helton, and she invited me to stay with her. I'll be returning to her home when I go to London in the spring. She has turned one of her bedrooms into a studio for me. I could stay at Sanderford House when Henry and Melody are in town, but they really prefer to be at Sanderford Park, so they're rarely there. They only go to London when Henry attends Parliament. Do you attend Parliament?"

Jonathan thought of the importance that his father placed on being active in Parliament. His father had believed it was his main responsibility as a peer of the realm. He knew his father would be disappointed in him because of his lack of interest.

Feeling somewhat discomforted because he knew he wasn't living up to his responsibility, Jonathan replied, "I did take my seat, but I hate to say this, I'm not very active. I know that your brother is very active. I find it difficult to sit for long periods of time, and to be honest with you I grow bored quite easily. Of course, that's no excuse for me to shirk my responsibilities."

Kathryn stopped drawing and looked up. "My brother wasn't sure he would like Parliament in the beginning, but now he enjoys it quite a bit. He thinks he can help his people by attending. Well, I'm finished for the day. I'll be ready to start painting on Saturday. Have you picked out what you'll be wearing? Remember that you'll need to wear whatever you pick out to all our future sittings. I hope that isn't too much of an inconvenience?"

"Not at all. As I told you in the beginning, I'll be dressing casually. I'll make sure that I wear the same clothing each time from here on out. How long will it take you to complete my portrait? I promised my brother that I would be in Bristol to pick up Elaine by the first part of August. Will you be finished by then?"

"Your sittings should be done by then. I won't need you when I add the finishing touches. You know, your brother and his wife have asked me to come to Bristol and do their family portrait. I told them that I'd be able to come just as soon as I finish yours."

"If we added another session each week, could you be ready to go to Bristol by the first of the month? If so, you could travel with me when I go to pick up Elaine, if that would be convenient for you?"

Kathryn looked a bit taken aback at this, but then she smiled. "That would be excellent. I'm so pleased that they want me to do their portrait. I'm sure that as long as I take my maid, my mother should have no objections to me going with you. After all, it will only take one day to get to Bristol from here. I'll just make sure she's all right with it, and I'll let you know on Saturday. Now what day will you add to your sittings?"

"I could add Wednesday. Will that work for you?"

"Yes that would be fine. Since we're through for the day, I'll walk you out."

Jonathan was pleased that she would be able to come with him. He knew Roderick and Allison would be ecstatic that he was bringing Kathryn to them. He just hoped he would get over this obsession he had with her. Maybe spending time with her every day would help that. Once they were downstairs, he turned to her and kissed her hand, and then left.

Chapter 7

On Friday morning, Kathryn worked on getting the canvas ready for Jonathan's portrait. She chose tightly woven linen for the canvas and stretched it over the frame until it was taut. Then she securely fastened the canvas to the frame. Once the canvas was ready, she mixed the primer, which would seal the canvas so it would be ready for tomorrow's sitting. Once she had the first layer of primer on the canvas, she set it on her easel to dry. She should be able to apply the second coat of primer that afternoon when she returned from her daily walk.

Kathryn had some excellent sketches of Jonathan. She liked the way she'd posed him on Thursday. While he appeared almost regal, he still looked quite natural. She noticed that his color was much better yesterday than it had been in the previous sittings, and there was much less tension in his face, especially around his eyes. Kathryn hoped he would be as relaxed tomorrow as he'd been yesterday. While he talked about his brother, she could see the love for him shining in his brilliant blue eyes, and she hoped she could capture that look in his portrait.

Tomorrow, she would be working on the background to get it set before she started on him. She was going to use a library scene as the backdrop, so she had two of the footmen carry up a bookcase, as well as the books to fill it, and place it by the window. She would have Jonathan standing in front of the bookcase with the sun shining through the window. Jonathan would be holding a book as if he had just selected it and was anticipating the enjoyment of reading it. Since he'd shared that he enjoyed reading, she felt that this would be a good background for his portrait.

That afternoon, while Kathryn was taking her walk, she picked up some additional art supplies. That was the beauty of living in the city, she could easily get the supplies she needed right away. When she was at Sanderford Park, she had to order her supplies from London and that could take a couple of days sometimes.

Amazingly enough, Kathryn was actually enjoying her stay with her mother. Ever since Henry had her mother turn the running of the house over to Melody, she seemed to have mellowed, especially since she had moved to Bath. Kathryn had never been close to her mother growing up, so it was nice that they were getting closer now. She had finally accepted Kathryn's desire not to marry and hadn't brought the subject up again. Moving to Bath had been a good decision for her mother. She seemed much happier.

When Kathryn returned to the house, she went to her studio and put away the supplies that she had purchased. She touched her canvas and it was dry, so she applied the second coat of primer. Since she was doing such a large painting, she had a footman find her a stool. This was definitely going to be the most challenging project she had committed to do so far. She just hoped Jonathan would be pleased with his portrait.

After her talk with Jonathan yesterday, she realized she was a bit obsessed with her art, but it was all that had kept her sane when her uncle had been abusing her. Henry told her she would never have to worry about seeing her uncle again because he'd passed away this past winter. It was a great sense of relief to know that her uncle was no longer able to hurt her, or anyone else, ever again. As she gazed around the room, making sure that everything was ready for tomorrow, she noticed the time. If she was going to be ready for Lady Milsom's soiree, she'd better hurry.

When Kathryn entered her room, Sarah had her bath drawn, and soon she was luxuriating in the tub as the bath water lapped against her soft skin. Bathing was such a sensual feeling, one of the few she allowed herself to experience. While she'd been out today, she'd purchased some lavender-scented milled soap and bathing salts, which were her favorite.

Ducking under the water, Kathryn came back up and lathered her hair as the scent of lavender filled the air. When she stood up, Sarah poured fresh water over her to wash the soap away. She stepped out of the tub and wrapped a big fluffy towel around her body, allowing it to caress her flushed skin, still heated from the warm bath. Once she was dry and dressed, she adjusted the skirt of her shimmering blue silk gown that she had purchased from Madame Bovary's Boutique.

While she gazed at her reflection, she liked the way Sarah had arranged her hair with braids woven around her head resembling a coronet. She wished Jonathan would attend the soiree tonight, so he could see her in her new dress.

Goodness, where did that thought come from?
What did it matter what he thought of her gown?

Kathryn was a bit alarmed that she was thinking this way. She never had thoughts about any other man the way she thought about Jonathan. Thank goodness, he wasn't going to be at the soiree. With thoughts like these, she could end up falling in love with him, and that could never be. Even if she were to fall in love, nothing could come of it, because she could never be intimate with any man. Since it was time to leave for the soiree, Kathryn went to the door and left her room to go downstairs.

When Kathryn and her mother arrived at Lady Milsom's soiree, Lady Milsom immediately greeted them with a polite smile. "Welcome, Your Grace. I'm so pleased you're able to attend my party this evening." Then she turned to Katherine, "Lady Kathryn, you look marvelous this evening. I'm sure that all the gentlemen will want the opportunity to dance with you."

"Thank you, Lady Milsom. I didn't realize that there would be dancing this evening. I look forward to it,"

Lady Milsom turned to greet some new arrivals, and Kathryn glanced around the room. She knew Jonathan wouldn't be there, but she could always hope.

Oh, goodness! She had to stop thinking like this!

The majordomo announced dinner, and everyone went into the dining room. Of course, her mother sat to the right of Lady Milsom's husband since she was the highest-ranking person in the room. Kathryn was seated several places away between Lord Shelton and Lord Ellington.

As dinner progressed, Lord Shelton commented, "Her Grace told me you were coming for a visit. I hope you're enjoying your stay in Bath. Have you met any interesting people?"

Kathryn glanced over at him and straightened her napkin before speaking. "I've met several lovely people, and I do like Bath. It's one of the loveliest cities I've ever visited, and the architecture is incredible. Recently, I met the Marquess of Sutherland, and when Lord Sutherland found out that I was an artist, he asked me to paint his portrait, which I'm currently working on now."

"I know Lord Sutherland quite well. We went to Oxford together, and I recently saw him at the assembly rooms the other week. That was the first time that I had seen him in about five years. Once I got married, I quit going out with the fellows, so we grew apart. Do you do portraits for other people?" Lord Shelton asked.

"Yes, I plan to open a studio in London in a few years, but for now I take commissions when people ask. After I finish Lord Sutherland's portrait, I'll be going to Bristol to do a portrait of his brother's family, and in November I'll be traveling to Devonshire where I'll be doing a portrait of the Marquess and Marchioness of Ralston. I hope that when more people see my work, I'll have more commissions."

Lord Shelton looked appraisingly at her. "I'd be interested in seeing some of your work. My wife and I haven't had our portrait painted yet. Do you have any work that we could see?"

Kathryn sat her wine goblet down as she enthusiastically answered him. "I just finished my mother's portrait, and I have several miniatures of other members of my family that I would be happy to show you. Would you like to come for tea on Sunday, and I could show you my work then?"

"I feel sure my wife will want to see your work. I'll introduce you to her when dinner is over, and you can ask her if Sunday is convenient."

They talked a bit more, and then she turned to Lord Ellington, making sure she didn't ignore her other dinner partner. Soon Lady Milsom led all the ladies to the drawing room and left the gentlemen to their port and cigars.

When the men entered the drawing room, Kathryn watched Lord Shelton approach with a lovely young woman, whom she assumed was his wife. He stopped in front of her. "Hello, Lady Kathryn. Please let me introduce you to my wife, the Countess of Shelton." He turned to his wife and added, "My dear, this is Lady Kathryn, the daughter of the Dowager Duchess of Sanderford."

Kathryn acknowledged the introduction with a smile. "Good evening, Lady Shelton. It's a pleasure to meet you. Your husband mentioned that you might be interested in having me paint your portrait. Would you be able to come for tea on Sunday so you can see some of my work?"

Lady Shelton smiled pleasantly. "I'm pleased to meet you as well, Lady Kathryn. My husband mentioned that you have some of your work we could see. We would love to come for tea on Sunday. I've told him that we need to have our portrait done for several years now, so I'm sure that we'll want you to do our portrait."

"I appreciate your interest in my work, and I look forward to showing you several portraits that I've done. As I told Lord Shelton, I've just finished my mother's portrait, and I have several miniatures that you can see. I look forward to seeing you on Sunday."

Lord and Lady Shelton left Kathryn to join some friends of theirs across the room. When the duchess returned from the retiring room, Kathryn said, "Mother, I invited the Earl of Shelton and his countess to tea on Sunday. They want to see some of my work. They may want me to do their portrait. Isn't that wonderful?"

The duchess sighed in resignation. "I am happy for you. I know how much you love to paint, but I'm concerned about you being paid for these portraits. You don't need the money. What will people say when word gets around that you're accepting money? You'll never find a husband." As Kathryn got ready to interrupt, the duchess hurriedly said, "I know...I know...you don't want to get married, but you could change your mind, and then it will be too late. Just try to be discreet."

Shortly after talking with Lord and Lady Shelton, the dancing started, and Kathryn had a pleasant evening dancing with Lord Ellington, Lord Shelton, and several other gentlemen. Finally, her mother was ready to leave, which suited Kathryn just fine since her feet were tired from all the dancing.

As Kathryn was getting ready for bed, she thought of Jonathan. She would tell him about meeting Lord Shelton, and that he might want her to do his portrait. It bothered her that she wanted to share her good news with him. She was spending too much time thinking about Jonathan. They had agreed to become friends, but she had never thought of any of her other friends as she did him. As she drifted off to sleep, she wondered what it would feel like if Jonathan kissed her.

Friday was a productive day for Jonathan. He spent the entire morning riding his estate with Whetherby. As long as the weather continued to be fair, the crops should be excellent again this year, as they were last year. He had an invitation for a soiree at Lady Milsom's. Even though he never attended parties, he was tempted since he knew that Kathryn would be there. Jonathan had to quit thinking about her so much. Kathryn aroused his desire whenever he was around her, and it was starting to alarm him since he knew nothing could come of it. Jonathan needed a woman very badly, but he couldn't go to the brothel if he was going to think of Kathryn while being entertained by one of the Madame's delicacies.

Maybe if I go and pick out a woman that doesn't resemble her in the slightest, then surely I'll be fine.

Yes, that is what he would do.

Thank God, because he really needed a woman badly.

He wasn't used to going so long without sex.

While Lady Milsom's soiree was going on, he went to town for a different reason. When he entered Madame Angela's, she immediately greeted him, "Good evening, my lord. It's a pleasure to have you here again. What is your pleasure tonight? Would you like Suzette again?"

"Ah...Good evening. I would like a brunette tonight. Someone petite, but plump in all the right places." Jonathan scanned the room and saw a chubby brunette across the room and said, "Who's that over there?" pointing to the petite brunette.

"That's Diane. She's new, just in from the country. I'm sure that she'll be happy to entertain you tonight." Madame Angela motioned for her to come over. "Diane, this is Lord Sutherland, and he'd like to have the honor of your company tonight. Please take him upstairs to your room and show him a good time."

Diane smiled beguilingly at Jonathan. "I'd be honored to spend the evening with you, my lord. Why don't we go upstairs to my room?"

Jonathan bowed. "Lead the way."

Ah, this was going to work.

Diane didn't look anything at all like Kathryn.

Once they entered her room, Diane gave him a sultry look. "What is your pleasure, my lord? Just say it, and I'll be happy to comply."

She approached, took her hand, and rubbed it over his chest and purred. Jonathan pulled her close and gave her a hard, hungry kiss. He ran his hands over her luscious curves and felt his desire rise. Diane took his hand and led him over to her bed. Picking Diane up, he dropped her in the middle as she pulled her chemise off over her head. Diane truly had a lovely body. Her breasts were large and plump. Leaning over, he suckled her nipple as he rolled her other one between his forefinger and thumb.

Diane pulled him down on top of her, ran her hands over his cock, and seductively unbuttoned his breeches. His shaft sprang upward when Diane squeezed it as she pushed his breeches down. He kicked them off the bed, pushed her thighs wide apart, and surged home. It felt so sublime to be inside a woman again.

Jonathan started stroking in and out, harder and faster. Over and over again, he pumped into her passage. He knew he was close to his release, and because he always made sure his partner found her release, he stroked her love bud. Once he felt her muscles tighten around his cock, he let himself lose control. He felt his sac contract, and just as he found his release, he called out, "Oh, my God...yes...Kathryn!" In shock, he quickly pulled out and rolled off Diane onto his back.

He put his arm up to his face, covering his eyes. "Who's Kathryn?" Diana asked. "Is she your wife or a lost love? I could hear pain in your voice when you called out her name."

Jonathan sighed. "No, she's not my wife. She's a woman that I've recently met, and I can't stop thinking about her. She's an innocent young lady, and since I have no intention of ever marrying her, or anyone for that matter, I have to stop thinking about her. She's an artist, and I've hired her to do my portrait, so I'm with her several times a week. It's killing me to be with her and know that I can never have her."

"Why are you so determined to never marry? If you care for the young lady, you should pursue her and make her your own. Clearly, you have deep feelings for her. Would it be so terrible if you did marry?"

"I'm not good enough for Kathryn. She's an angel, and I'm a drunken rake. She deserves someone far better than me. Besides, she says she doesn't want to get married, since she feels that it would inhibit her ability as an artist. No, marriage is out of the question. Thank you for listening to me though. You're very kind and quite lovely. I appreciate you sharing your time with me this evening. I'll leave you now, and I'll tell Madame that you were delightful. Here's a bonus for you. Good evening." Jonathan hurriedly put his clothes on and left.

Jonathan felt so ashamed about what had happened. This had to end. He couldn't keep doing this. He had to find some way to get over his fascination for Kathryn. He now realized he couldn't be with another woman until he got over this obsession. No sexual gratification was worth it, if he had these strong feelings of guilt afterwards. Until he could move beyond this, he would just have to live a celibate life.

That night, Jonathan had another nightmare. This pattern was becoming all too familiar. Shaking and upset, he went to his study to pour himself just one small drink. When Hatton woke him up the next morning, Jonathan knew he had again crossed the line. He looked over at the clock and realized that he was going to be late for his sitting with Kathryn. Then he remembered what he'd done the night before at Madame Angela's, and waves of guilt washed over him. This was getting ridiculous. He wasn't even involved with her.

Jonathan allowed Hatton to shave him, and he finished his morning ablutions. After retrieving Demon, he headed for town. On his way there, he began to feel a little better, but the guilt was still with him. He told himself again that he had to stop relying on liquor to deaden the pain and keep the nightmares away. Roderick was right about him either turning into a bitter old man or dying at too young of an age. He was only thirty, yet he looked closer to forty and felt even older. He would just have to be stronger and leave the liquor alone, at least for a while.

Jonathan was fifteen minutes late when he arrived at Kathryn's house, and the butler immediately took him up to her studio. As he entered, he said, "I'm sorry, I'm late. I overslept this morning. I hope this doesn't inconvenience you?"

Kathryn gazed at him with concern in her eyes. "If you feel badly, we can skip this sitting. I can tell you don't feel well. Did you sleep poorly last night?"

Jonathan felt sick when he looked at Kathryn. She was so innocent and pure. How could he have thought of her while he was with a whore? He felt as if he'd defiled her, which didn't make any sense. It wasn't as if they were engaged, or married, or anything.

He had a hard time meeting her sympathetic gaze as he replied, "No, I'll be fine. I did sleep poorly, but I don't want us to get behind. Where do you want me this morning?"

"All right, if you're sure you're well enough. Please go over by the bookcase and the window. Can you remember how I had you stand last time? I'm going to start on the actual painting today." Jonathan went over and stood in the correct pose. Kathryn walked over to him and handed him a book of poetry, and opened it up. "Please, hold this book as if you have just selected it and opened it up to your favorite part. Think about what pleasure you will receive when you read it."

Jonathan tried to do as directed, but instead he thought about how lovely her violet eyes were. He wanted to bury his hands in her glorious red hair. At that moment, he realized...he wasn't just infatuated with Kathryn—he was in love with her. He felt a sharp pain in his chest.

No wonder he felt so awful about last night.
God, he was such a wretch.
He wasn't even good enough to wipe her slippers.

Even if he did ask her to marry him, she would refuse. She was determined to never marry. He pulled himself together and smiled as pleasantly as possible so she would think that he was doing as she asked.

"Ah, that's perfect." She went over to her easel and put on her smock, picked up her palette, and as she softly hummed to herself, she began to paint. She took his breath away — she was so beautiful. Jonathan knew that he would remember this moment for the rest of his life. He wondered what she would do if he went over there and kissed her. The very thought caused his desire to rise to fever pitch. He knew that he had to stop thinking about her, or she would notice the effect that she was having on him. He felt his breeches strain with his hard shaft.

Thank God, she was so absorbed by her art that she didn't seem to notice.

As Kathryn painted, she asked, "How did your brother meet his wife? They seem quite fond of each other."

Jonathan sighed in relief, hoping that talking would take his mind of his attraction to her. "We all grew up together. Allison's father was the vicar of our Parish. Roderick and Allison realized that they loved each other while they were quite young. They were planning the wedding when Bonaparte escaped from Elba. When I decided to join the army, Roderick immediately said he was going with me, so they delayed their marriage until he returned. Allison knew he couldn't let me go without him, and even though she was scared that something would happen to him, she still supported him."

"That had to have been difficult for Lady Roderick, knowing he was going off to war. Thank goodness he returned safely."

Jonathan looked over at Kathryn. "Yes, it was. I think I told you they got married just as soon as possible after we returned back from Brussels. You know the rest of their story. They're deeply in love, and I'm happy for them."

"I could tell they loved each other when I met them. I'm looking forward to going to Bristol. I'm sure we'll become good friends while I'm painting the portrait. I know you told me you don't want to marry. Why do you feel that way?"

"I was supposed to get married when I returned from the continent, but when my fiancée realized I had returned a cripple, she decided that she couldn't marry me after all. That's why I decided to never get married. Knowing what I know now, I realize she did me a favor when she broke off our engagement, but at the time, I didn't handle her rejection very well. Just as soon as I could walk, I left for London and never looked back. I don't know why I just told you that. I've never talked about this with anyone before."

Kathryn brushed a stray lock of her glorious red hair out of her eyes. "I'm pleased that you feel comfortable enough with me to share that. I had a very unpleasant experience when I was eighteen years old, and that is part of the reason I decided I didn't want to get married."

"I'm sorry. You know if you ever need to talk, I'll be happy to listen."

"Thank you. I hope that we'll continue to be good friends even after I finish your portrait. I've always been so wrapped up with my art that I haven't taken the time to get to know many people. I'm glad that we have gotten to know each other."

Jonathan gazed at her beautiful face and felt his heart seize. God, she was so lovely. So sweet. "I'll always be your friend, and if you ever need anything at all, all you have to do is ask, and I'll do my best to be there for you. I respect and admire you greatly, and I'm honored you want to continue being friends."

"Thank you, Lord Sutherland. I appreciate that. I think that we've done enough today, so you can relax and move around." Kathryn lowered her brush, then walked over to her worktable and started cleaning her brushes. As she opened a jar of oil of turpentine, the aroma filled the air.

Jonathan realized he would always associate the smell of turpentine and lavender with Kathryn. He watched her as she cleaned her brushes. "Don't you think that we know each other well enough to use our given names? Please…call me Jonathan."

"Only if you'll call me Kathryn. Oh, by the way, I met your friend Lord Shelton. He and his wife are coming for tea tomorrow, and they may want me to do their portrait. Isn't that wonderful? Theirs would be my fourth commission."

Kathryn's whole face lit up as she talked, and he felt his heart flip over as he remembered how unworthy he was of her. "That's wonderful, Kathryn. I'm happy for you. I'm sure that after they see your work, they'll want you to do their portrait. Again, I'm sorry that I was late today. I promise I'll be on time on Tuesday. Well, since you're through with me today, I'll take my leave. Don't bother to show me out. I'm sure that you need to finish getting your brushes cleaned up. I hope the rest of your day goes well, Kathryn."

Jonathan left in a state of shock. He was in love with Kathryn. He never meant it to happen, and he knew he could never act on his feelings. But as he promised her, he would always be there to care for and protect her. She just wouldn't know…that he loved her.

―――∞◦▷◁◦∞―――

The next morning, Kathryn was so excited about Lord and Lady Shelton coming to tea that she couldn't even concentrate on the vicar's sermon. She certainly hoped they would decide to have her do their portrait. The fact that Kathryn was also overjoyed that Jonathan wanted them to continue their friendship didn't help her focus either. He was such an interesting man, and he was truly a wonderful person. She realized she thought of him as one of her best friends. The more she found out about Jonathan, the more she admired him.

When Lord Shelton and his wife came for tea, they loved her work and decided they wanted her to do their portrait. Since she was going to Bristol in August, she told them she would do their portrait in October, which they said would work out well for them. They had three children, so it would be a family portrait.

The next two weeks flew by. Today, Jonathan would be coming for his final sitting, and Kathryn would finish his portrait. She was expecting him to arrive any moment. She was pleased with his portrait, and she hoped that he would like it.

There was a knock on the door and Jonathan entered the room. "Good morning, Kathryn. I hope that you slept well. You certainly look lovely today. Are you sure that you'll be finished with my portrait today? Do I finally get to see it?"

Kathryn gave him a big smile. "Hello, Jonathan. You look refreshed. Yes, I'll definitely finish today. Please go take your pose, and I'll get started."

As Jonathan took his place, he said, "I'd like to leave for Bristol on Friday. I thought we could leave around eight o'clock in the morning, if that's convenient for you. I received a letter from Roderick and Allison, and they're eager for you to come. They told me to tell you that they want to take you out on their yacht, so bring some casual clothing that you won't mind getting wet. I know they want me to go out too, but I really don't enjoy the sea. Even though I get a little seasick, I've promised I'll go out with them when you go."

"I'll be ready. I'm looking forward to it, and I certainly hope I don't get seasick, because I really want to go out on their yacht. I told you that my sister Helen loves it, and she has assured me that I'll enjoy it also." Kathryn noticed that Jonathan looked well rested. He must be sleeping better lately. The lines around his eyes weren't as pronounced, and he seemed more relaxed. She looked at his portrait, added the finishing touches, stood back, and said, "Well, it's finished. Do you want to come take a look?"

Jonathan walked over and stood by Kathryn. When he saw the portrait, his eyes lit up with appreciation. "This is incredible. It will look marvelous in my family gallery. Thank you, Kathryn. You flattered me so greatly that my future ancestors will think I was much better looking than I really am. When will it be dry enough for me to take home?"

"I'm glad you like it. I'm pleased and honored that you want to hang it in your family gallery. It will be dry by this time tomorrow, so you can come pick it up any time after that. I want to let you know that I'm glad that we've become friends, and I'm pleased we're going to remain friends even though your portrait is finished."

"I value our friendship tremendously and definitely plan to continue seeing you. I'll come by tomorrow afternoon to pick up my portrait. I hope you take a break from all your work and rest between now and Friday. Well, since you're through, I'll take my leave. Take care, my dear, and I'll see you tomorrow." As Jonathan left the room, he turned back to

Kathryn and smiled. Kathryn returned his smile and gave him a little wave of her hand as he left the room.

Kathryn realized that she was looking forward to spending more time with Jonathan. He was truly a fascinating person. It was so strange, but for the first time in her life, she realized that she trusted a man other than her brother and that had never happened before.

Chapter 8
- Early August 1823 -

As Jonathan headed home after leaving Kathryn's house, he felt a little sad because now that the portrait was finished he would no longer be spending so much time with her. At least he would still see her every day while she was painting Roderick's portrait. He hadn't had anything to drink, other than wine at his meals, for two weeks. Each day that he went without any brandy, he felt better. He had finally accepted that he couldn't touch anything stronger than wine.

The nightmares still bothered him, but when he had one now, he would just read for a while or go and play the pianoforte. He had not visited the brothel again, either. He couldn't even think of being with any other woman now that he had acknowledged his love for Kathryn. Once he came back from Bristol and the harvest was in, he would go back to London and try to forget her, but for the next month, he would just savor the time he spent with her.

Jonathan had gone and picked up his portrait, and it now hung in the family gallery. He would go there at night and just stare at it, thinking about Kathryn and how much he loved her. He just wished that he weren't such a broken man. If he were different, then he would try to win her love, but he knew he was just not good enough for her.

At eight o'clock on Friday, he picked up Kathryn and her maid for the trip to Bristol. The weather was fair, so they were able to make the trip in record time. Roderick and Allison actually lived about five miles west of Bristol. Their estate was along the waterway that led out to the Bristol Channel. It was a small estate, but it had a lovely old manor house of red brick with mullioned windows. As they arrived, the door opened, and out came Roderick and Allison to greet them.

Roderick bowed to Kathryn. "I hope you had a pleasant journey. We're so pleased that you could come and do our portrait. I have a bedroom upstairs that has very good morning light, so I thought you could use it for your studio while you're here."

Allison spoke up. "Please, feel free to ask for anything that you need. We want your stay to be an enjoyable one. While we're anxious for you to do our portrait, we hope you can relax and look at this as a little holiday. We want to take you out on our yacht, which we hope you'll enjoy. Let me show you to your room so you can get settled in."

Kathryn went with Allison, and Jonathan followed Roderick into his study. "Did you have a pleasant trip? At least the weather cooperated. We've enjoyed having Elaine with us this past month. The children just adore her. How did your portrait turn out?"

Jonathan sat down across from Roderick. "We had a very pleasant trip. Kathryn is an amusing travel companion, and we became good friends while she was painting my portrait.

It's incredible, by the way. Much better than I anticipated. I look very distinguished, yet casual at the same time. I've already placed it in the family gallery. I'm glad Elaine has had a good time. How are your crops doing this year? Mine are looking very good, and I expect a bountiful harvest."

"We're having such nice weather this year that I'm also expecting an excellent harvest. I noticed you watching Kathryn as she went upstairs with Allison. You're attracted to her, aren't you? I could tell by the gleam in your eyes. Has she changed your mind about marriage?"

Jonathan laughed, much more relaxed over Roderick's matchmaking than before. "Yes, I find her attractive. If I did want to get married, Kathryn would make me a wonderful wife, but I'm not nearly good enough for her. You know how I've lived my life for the past eight years. Besides, she's not interested in marriage. She told me from the very beginning of our friendship she never plans to marry."

"You'd make a fine husband, and any woman would be proud to be married to you. I wish you wouldn't rule marriage out. As far as her saying that she's not interested in marriage, women do change their minds."

Jonathan felt a twinge in his heart, because he knew Kathryn wouldn't change her mind even if he had changed his. "Enough said about that subject. How is Allison feeling? Is everything going well with her pregnancy?"

"All right. I shan't bring it up again. Allison is feeling wonderful. Just a little morning sickness, but other than that she's fine. How have you been feeling lately? I must say, you look much better than the last time I saw you."

Jonathan thought about telling Roderick that he was in love with Kathryn, but he knew Roderick would tell him he should pursue her. Kathryn was too sweet and innocent for a rake like him, so he refrained from saying anything.

"I'm feeling much better. I haven't had a drink, other than wine at my meals, in over two weeks. I have accepted that I can't drink any hard liquor. It really didn't help the pain that much anyway. The laudanum does a much better job. Now when I have a nightmare, I either read or play the pianoforte."

"I'm relieved that you've stopped drinking. It was ruining your health and making you look years older than you really are. Now, if you could just stop the carousing, you'd be in good shape. I'm sure you'd like to go to your room, so let me show you where you'll be staying," Roderick clapped him on the back, and they headed upstairs to his room.

When Jonathan entered, Hatton had already put everything away and was ready to give him his daily treatment. After he applied the ointment and wrapped the cold compresses around his knee, he gave him his daily afternoon dose of laudanum, and Jonathan fell asleep.

After Jonathan woke up from his nap, he felt refreshed, and once he was dressed, he went downstairs and joined everyone in the drawing room. Kathryn was already there, and she looked incredibly beautiful. Her dinner gown was lavender, and it made her lovely eyes a deep violet. Her abundant fiery red hair was arranged at the crown of her head with ringlets of curls cascading down to her creamy white shoulders. He had to fight his desire and was doing a very poor job of it, because his trousers pulled tight against his loins. He wanted to go over to her, grab her, and carry her up to his room where he would make mad, passionate love to her all night.

Dammit, he had to stop thinking about her like this.

Elaine rushed over to him and gave him a big hug. "I've been having so much fun. Thank you for allowing me to come. I love going out on their yacht, and we've gone swimming almost every day. I've been having a wonderful time with Frankford and Jane."

Jonathan smiled indulgently. "Hello, Princess. I'm glad that you've been having a delightful time. I'm sure you've enjoyed their yacht. I don't care for it myself because I get seasick. I did promised Roderick that I would go out one time anyway. I would rather it be sooner than later and get it over with. Lady Kathryn is very excited about going out."

Roderick looked over at Jonathan and said, "Since the weather is so nice, we'll try it tomorrow and put you out of your misery. You never know, it may not make you sick this time." He turned to Lady Katherine and added, "I hope that you'll enjoy it as much as the rest of us do."

"I'm looking forward to it. My sister lives along the coast of Devonshire, and she goes out on their yacht all the time and loves it. I'm sure that I won't get seasick."

Jonathan spoke up. "We'll find out tomorrow. I hope that for your sake you don't." He turned to Allison and asked, "Are you still all right going out in your delicate condition?"

Allison rolled her eyes at him. "I have no problems at all. We've been taking the yacht out a couple times a week, and I love it as much as ever."

The butler came in and announced dinner, so they all went to the dining room. The first course was oyster stew, which was delicious. Conversation flowed freely around the table, and soon it was time to go to the drawing room. Roderick and Jonathan chose to forgo their port and cigars, and when they got to the drawing room, Allison asked Jonathan if he would play the pianoforte for them. He started playing a Mozart concerto and became lost in the music. Since they had planned to go out on the yacht early the next morning, they retired to their rooms at ten o'clock.

That night, after Sarah finished brushing Kathryn's hair, she sent her away. Kathryn gazed around the room, noticing the pretty lace curtains at the window and felt the cool breeze coming in off the water. She breathed in deeply and inhaled the tangy scent of salt water and sand. It was so refreshing and exhilarating. Now she could understand why Helen loved the ocean so much. She was looking forward to going out on the yacht tomorrow morning. It was too bad that Jonathan hated it. She hoped he wouldn't get too ill tomorrow.

Jonathan looked so much better lately. His color was clearer, and his eyes were no longer filled with as much pain. She wondered what had changed for him. Of course, she was pleased that he was doing better, and he was much more attractive now than he'd been before. In fact, she thought he was quite handsome with his incredible jet-black hair and startling blue eyes. It almost made her change her mind about men. He was such a gentle and kind man that she couldn't help wondering what it would feel like if he kissed her.

Oh my, where did that thought come from?

Kathryn had never even thought about what a kiss would feel like before, and then there was that strange feeling in the pit of her belly every time she met Jonathan's gaze. All this was slightly troubling for Kathryn.

Oh well, it was getting quite late, and she had a full day ahead of her tomorrow.

With that thought, she climbed into bed, yawned, and soon she was fast asleep.

When Kathryn awoke the next morning, the sunlight was streaming in through her bedroom window, and she could hear the sea gulls flying around outside. She hurried to the window and looked out to see an amazingly beautiful summer day, perfect for going out on a yacht. Kathryn hurried through her morning ablutions and went downstairs for breakfast.

After everyone had their breakfast, they went down to the shore. Taking a small boat out to the yacht, soon they were all on board and headed out to sea. Once they entered the Bristol Channel, the yacht picked up speed, and they were sailing across the ocean at a pace that surprised Kathryn. She enjoyed the beauty of the sea but was beginning to feel a bit sick at her stomach.

Oh dear, she'd so been looking forward to this experience.

The longer she stood there, the sicker she felt.

As Kathryn glanced over at Jonathan, she noticed he was turning green, so she knew he was probably feeling worse than she was. She went over to where he was standing. "I'm beginning to feel slightly ill. You look as if you are feeling ill too. I hope this feeling passes soon."

Jonathan groaned. "I hope you get to feeling better, but it doesn't work that way for me. I'll continue to feel ill until we are back on the beach."

Allison came over to them, and when she looked into their faces, she sighed. "Oh dear, both of you are feeling ill, aren't you? I had hoped that it wouldn't affect you this way. I'll go tell Roderick, and we'll turn around and go back."

Allison went to the helm to speak with Roderick. "We're going to have turn around and go back to shore. Both Jonathan and Lady Kathryn are turning green, they're so ill. I hate that they're feeling so poorly."

Roderick shrugged his shoulders. "Oh well, at least they tried. God, it's a glorious day to be sailing, but I guess we have to go back. Tell them that I'll get them back as quickly as possible. At least Elaine doesn't get seasick. She'll be disappointed that we have to go back."

Allison went over to Jonathan and Kathryn and assured them. "I spoke with Roderick and he's turning around now. We should have you back on dry land shortly."

Roderick steered the yacht back into the waterway, and soon they were back on dry land. Since it was still early, Roderick, Allison, and Elaine decided to go back out when Kathryn and Jonathan assured them they would be fine now that they were back on land.

Kathryn had a pensive look on her face as she watched the yacht head back down the channel. "They were so disappointed when we became ill. I'm disappointed as well. I really thought I'd like it. At first, I was enjoying it when we were still in the waterway, but once we got out on the open sea, it was horrible. I feel fine now that we're back on land. Isn't it odd the way that works?"

"I knew what it was going to be like, because I've tried to go out several times, but I always react the same way. It's a good thing that I joined the army instead of the navy, or I would have been in trouble. I guess we had better go back to the house. What do you want to do for the rest of the day?"

As the wind blew Kathryn's hair, she tucked a lock behind her ear. "I guess I'll go up to the room they have given me to use as my studio and get everything ready to start the portrait tomorrow. What are you going to do?"

Jonathan smiled as he watched her play with her hair.

God, she was so gorgeous.

Jonathan wished he could relive these last eight years in a way that would make him worthy of her. "I think that I'll go play the pianoforte for a while. I find it very relaxing. I've been playing almost every day for the last few weeks. I'm not sure why I ever stopped." Jonathan knew it was because of his conversations with Kathryn that he was playing again. She had enriched his life so much.

God, all he wanted to do was pull her in his arms and hold her close to his heart.

If he could do that, he would be content.

As Kathryn and Jonathan walked back to the house, Kathryn said, "You play beautifully. I tried to learn, but while I could play with my right hand and also my left, when I tried to put them together it was a disaster. My sister-in-law, Mary, is an incredibly accomplished pianist. I could sit and listen to her play for hours."

"I didn't realize you had another sister-in-law. You've never mentioned her before. She was your other brother's wife, I suppose? I didn't realize that he was married. Did they not have any children?"

"They had a daughter, Angela, and she's almost six years old and adorable. Mary also has a son, Roderick, from a previous marriage. Poor Mary didn't have very good luck with her husbands. Her first husband was killed in Portugal, and then Nelson died of a wasting disease."

"I imagine that she must have had a difficult time when your brother Nelson died. How many nieces and nephews do you have?"

Jonathan watched her as she talked about her nieces and nephews. Her face glowed. "I have ten that I claim. I adore children, and I think that's why I enjoy painting them so much. I look forward to painting your niece and nephew. They're both beautiful children. Frankford looks quite a bit like you, did you realize that?"

By this time, Kathryn and Jonathan were back at the house, and he opened the door for her. "I never really thought about it, but you're right, he does look like me. I'm so grateful that Roderick married Allison, and that they have two beautiful children with another one on the way. It makes my decision not to marry easier to abide by."

"With what happened with your ex-fiancée, I do understand why you don't want to marry."

"I still don't understand why you're so opposed to marriage. I know you feel that a husband wouldn't want you to paint," he hesitated, then quickly continued, "but if I were to marry you...for instance, I'd never stand in your way." Looking at Kathryn, he tried to gauge her reaction, but couldn't see anything in her expression that would let him know what she was feeling.

"Jonathan, you're quite different than most men. Of course, this is all hypothetical since we both know you're not interested in marrying."

"I still say you have an incredible gift, and I don't believe any man who cared about you...would keep you from your art. I would think that you'd want to marry so you can have children of your own since you love them so much."

"My art is important to me, and I do feel that most men would stand in my way, but the bigger reason," she paused, then continued, "is because of what happened to me when I was sixteen. I won't bore you with the details, but I could never think about marrying because of what happened."

Seeing how distressed this conversation was making Kathryn, Jonathan quickly said, "I'm sorry. I didn't mean to pry or make you uncomfortable. Please forgive me."

Looking away, Kathryn answered, "I'm all right, but I think I'll go on up to my studio now. I'll see you at luncheon."

Jonathan watched Kathryn as she went up the stairs. He didn't know for sure, but he suspected that a man had assaulted her when she was sixteen. He couldn't think of any other incident that would turn her so strongly against marriage. If he ever got his hands on whoever it was, he would kill him for hurting her.

What was he going to do when he didn't see her anymore?

How was he ever going to forget her?

Jonathan's heart filled with love for her. While he desired her desperately, it was more than just sexually. He wanted to protect her from harm and help her achieve her goals as an artist. He realized that he would want her even if he could never be with her intimately. He would rather have her friendship than nothing at all. As hard as it would be, he wouldn't go to London and try to forget her. He realized he could never forget her, even if he lived to be a hundred.

He knew…he would love Kathryn…for the rest of his life.

Roderick, Allison, and Elaine were back in time for tea. Kathryn was quiet during tea, and wondered if their earlier conversation had upset her. Jonathan went over to her and asked, "Kathryn, are you feeling all right? You seem to be a little quiet this afternoon. I didn't say anything that upset you earlier when we were talking?"

"No, it isn't anything you said. I just started thinking about being childless my entire life, and it had made me a little sad. I do love children. When I'm in London, I volunteer at St. Mark's Orphanage. Melody has volunteered there for years and got me involved."

Jonathan reached for her hand and stroked it. "I admire you tremendously. If you ever need to talk, or anything, please let me know. I want to be there for you. You're an incredibly beautiful person, and you deserve to be happy. If you would just tell me who hurt you, I would take care of him for you. I don't need the details to know that a man hurt you in some way. Please just tell me who it was."

Kathryn's gorgeous violet eyes filled with tears. "Thank you. You are such a dear friend. The man who hurt me died this past winter, so he can never hurt me, or anyone else, ever again."

Without thinking, Jonathan brushed a tear from her cheek. "Well, good. Now, let's talk about happier things. Did you get everything ready to start the portrait tomorrow?" Jonathan asked.

Kathryn wiped the rest of her tears away, and answered him with a smile. "Yes, everything is ready. Did you enjoy playing your music this afternoon? I listened at the top of the stairs. You do play beautifully. I could listen to you play for hours. How old were you when you started playing?"

Jonathan continued to hold her hand, just enjoying the feel of it nestled in his firm clasp. "My mother taught me to play. She played magnificently, and I started playing when I was about five years old. I wanted to be as good as she was. I got away from it when I came back from Waterloo. I'm glad I've started to play again, since I find it so soothing."

"I'm glad you've started playing again too. You have an incredible gift," Kathryn said. "You play as well as Mary."

Hesitantly, Jonathan said, "The main reason playing is so important to me is…Kathryn…I have a drinking problem. Since I met you, I've tried to stop drinking. It's been over two weeks since I drank anything stronger than wine. Having to go into Bath for my sittings helped me realize that I needed to stop. While you were painting my portrait, I had a lot of time to think, and I realized that I've been abusing myself for eight years, and it's time that I stopped. I hope you don't think less of me because I told you this."

Kathryn squeezed his hand. "I could never think less of you. I'm honored that you feel you can confide in me. I understand how easy it is to need something as a crutch. After what happened to me when I was sixteen, I was in so much emotional pain that I began taking laudanum. I came close to losing my life because of it. If it weren't for Melody and Helen, I would probably be dead. It takes a very strong individual to overcome an affliction, so I'm proud of you for realizing that you have a problem, and that you're trying to do something about it."

Jonathan gazed directly into her eyes. "You're the bravest, most wonderful person I've ever known. I count myself fortunate that you've decided to be my friend. Again, if you ever need anything, all you have to do is ask."

"Thank you, Jonathan. I value your friendship more than I can ever say. The same goes for me, if you ever need anything or you just need to talk, I'll be there for you. It looks like everyone has left the drawing room. I think that I'll go up to my room and lie down before dinner." As she walked out of the room, Jonathan was again overwhelmed by the love he felt for her. Just knowing Kathryn had drastically changed his life.

Chapter 9

- Late August 1823 -

Kathryn started on the portrait the next day. She did sketches of the children individually and together. She did the same for Roderick and Allison. By the end of the second week, she was ready to start painting. She had to keep the sessions short because of the children, but they sat for her every day. When she wasn't working on the painting, she was spending time with Jonathan.

They took long walks along the shore together, and she felt a great sense of peace and serenity when she was with Jonathan. Kathryn wished she weren't so afraid of men, because if she ever could get over her fear, she realized she could marry someone like Jonathan.

Roderick, Allison, and Elaine went sailing almost every afternoon as long as the weather cooperated. She envied the relationship that Roderick and Allison had with each other. It was obvious they were in love. Allison just glowed every time she gazed at Roderick. If her uncle had left her alone, she could have had what they had. She tried not to be bitter, but sometimes it was very hard.

The end of the third week of her stay, Kathryn was more than halfway finished with the portrait. The children were being very cooperative, and it was making the project go much quicker than she had expected. She estimated that she would be finished by the end of next week. That afternoon, Roderick and Allison went sailing by themselves. Since Elaine had a cold, she was too miserable to go with them. About an hour after they left, the sky started to cloud up, and Kathryn heard thunder rumbling in the distance.

Kathryn went to look for Jonathan and found him in the music room playing. "Jonathan, did you hear that thunder? It sounds as if a storm is coming. Do you think Roderick and Allison will be all right?"

Jonathan smiled reassuringly. "I'm sure Roderick and Allison will be fine. Roderick is a very good sea captain, and I'm sure he has already turned back. I expect they'll be coming home before it gets too bad. How's the portrait coming along? Do you have any idea when you'll be finished?"

"I'm more than halfway finished, so I expect I'll have it finished by the end of next week. The children have been so well behaved that it's made it easier to paint than I expected. When I painted Melody's children, it took much longer because they weren't as well behaved. I'm going to my room to rest before dinner, so I'll see you then." Kathryn turned, but then she turned back around, gave him a beatific smile, and left the room.

When Kathryn woke up from her nap, she noticed there was a terrible storm raging outside. The wind was blowing so hard that the windows were rattling. She certainly hoped

Roderick and Allison had made it back before the storm hit. She splashed some water on her face, then rushed out of her room to make sure they had come home.

She found Jonathan in the drawing room, pacing back and forth. "Jonathan, did Roderick and Allison make it back before this storm hit? It sounds awful out there. The windows in my room were rattling terribly."

Jonathan stopped pacing for a moment to look up at her, but then started back up again. "No, they haven't come home yet. I'm hoping that they pulled in somewhere else, and they're riding out the storm. I'm very worried, but I keep telling myself that Roderick is very skilled. I just hope this storm stops soon, and then I'm going out to look for them."

The storm raged on for several hours—long after dark. Finally, it stopped at about ten o'clock, but it was too dark and muddy out for Jonathan to go look for them. Kathryn sat up with him, but she eventually fell asleep on the couch. At daybreak, Jonathan gently woke her. "Kathryn, wake up, my dear. We both fell asleep. Since it's getting light outside, I'm going out to look for Roderick and Allison. Why don't you go upstairs and sleep for a few hours?"

Kathryn could see the worry in his face. "Jonathan, I'm sure you'll find them safe. I'll keep Elaine and the children entertained while you go look for them. Be careful. It's probably terribly muddy and wet outside. I'll be praying that you find them safe."

Jonathan nodded his head and then rushed from the room.

Kathryn went to her room, but she didn't go to bed. She rang for Sarah and had her prepare her bath. Since she had slept in her clothes, she thought that a bath would help relieve some of the tension she was feeling. She knew that it was dangerous for Roderick and Allison to be out on a yacht in a storm. She hoped that Jonathan was right, and they had taken shelter somewhere else along the coast.

Once Kathryn was dressed, she went downstairs to breakfast but was too nervous to eat. At nine o'clock, she went and checked on Elaine, but she was still asleep. Then she went to the nursery and checked on the children. They had just finished their breakfast, and their governess was starting their lessons, so she didn't disturb them. She went back downstairs and waited in the drawing room. By this point, she was praying that Roderick and Allison were all right.

Elaine came down for luncheon, but she still looked miserable. "Where is everyone? I haven't seen either of my brothers today, and I went looking for Allison but couldn't find her anywhere."

Kathryn didn't know what to say, but she knew she had to tell Elaine something, "Jonathan is out looking for Roderick and Allison. They didn't come home last night. They must have taken shelter from the storm along the coast. Jonathan left early this morning to go look for them. I'm sure they're fine. Jonathan will send word when he finds them." Elaine started crying and Kathryn went over, pulled her into her arms and said, "I know that it's frightening, but I'm sure that Roderick and Allison are fine. The best thing we can do for them is pray. Would you like to pray together?"

Elaine nodded her head, and they knelt down and clasped hands. Kathryn bowed her head and began to pray. "Dear Lord, please let Jonathan find Roderick and Allison, and let them be safe. Keep them in your loving arms until Jonathan can find them. Amen."

Kathryn led Elaine to the couch and sat her down, then sat down beside her and pulled her into her arms. They sat like that for a long time. Exhausted from crying, Elaine fell asleep around three o'clock. Kathryn continued to pray for their safe return, but as each hour went by, it seemed less likely that Jonathan would find them unhurt.

Elaine, still miserable from her nasty cold and exhausted from worry, went to bed at nine o'clock, but she made Kathryn promise to wake her when everyone returned. When Jonathan showed up at ten o'clock, his clothes were disheveled, he looked completely undone, and was so tired he could barely stand.

"Have you heard anything? You look exhausted. I sent Elaine to bed about an hour ago. Poor thing has cried all afternoon, ever since I told her Roderick and Allison were missing." Kathryn sat on the sofa twisting her hands in fear, but she knew she needed to be brave for Jonathan's sake.

Jonathan looked at Kathryn with anguished eyes. "I've been out all day riding from one coastal village to another, and no one has seen them. I rounded up some of the fishermen in the area, and we've been searching everywhere. I've left word at all the villages with my directions, so if they hear anything, they'll know where to contact me."

"Why don't you sit down?"

Jonathan sank down on the sofa next to Kathryn, and she reached out for his hand as he said, "We called off the search once it grew too dark to look. Kathryn, I'm so scared that something has happened to them, and I don't know where else to look. We're going to start searching again in the morning, just as soon as it gets light enough."

"Jonathan, have you had anything to eat? Let's go to the kitchen and find you something, and then you need to get some sleep. Your knee is bothering you terribly, isn't it? What can I do to help?"

Jonathan's face had lines of fear etched on it, and he had deep circles under his eyes. Kathryn wished there was something she could say to help him, but until Roderick and Allison were found, he would continue to worry. She couldn't blame him. She knew the longer they were missing, the more likely it was that they had come to harm.

Leaning back against the cushions of the sofa, Jonathan wearily replied, "I haven't eaten, but I'm not hungry. I'm too worried to eat anyway. I'm going upstairs, and I'll get Hatton to rub some ointment on my knee and wrap it in cold compresses. Then I'll try to get some sleep. You look exhausted too. I'm sure you didn't get much rest on that couch last night. Thank you for taking care of Elaine for me. I'm sure that she's worried sick."

"Elaine is still battling her cold, so I'm sure she'll sleep through the night. Please don't worry about her on top of everything else. She asked me to wake her when you returned, but since you don't have any news, it's probably better to let her sleep."

"How are the children? Have Frankford and Jane asked for their parents?"

"The children are fine. I spoke with Miss Mills and she has been keeping them busy. I told the children that Roderick and Allison were away visiting some friends, since they wanted to know why Allison didn't visit them the night before."

"I know I shouldn't ask this, but can I just hold you for a minute?" Kathryn opened her arms to him, and Jonathan hugged her close. Overcome, he began to weep.

Kathryn held him close and rubbed his back in a soothing manner. After a few minutes, he stopped crying. "I'm sorry. I know it's unmanly to cry, and I never do, but I'm just so scared. He's not just my brother, he's my best friend. If something has happened to them, I don't know what I'll do."

She continued to rub his back, trying to comfort him. "Let me help you to your room. Here, lean on me, and we'll get you upstairs."

They finally made it to Jonathan's room, and Hatton was there to help him. Kathryn kissed him on the cheek and told him if he needed her for anything to come and get her. Then she left him alone.

When Kathryn got to her room, the floodgates opened, and she cried until she had no more tears to cry. She knew in her heart that something terrible had happened to Roderick and Allison. She had sent Sarah to bed hours ago, so she twisted and turned, but finally she got herself out of her clothes. Thank goodness, she hadn't worn a corset that day, or she would never have gotten it off. Once she was in her nightclothes, she went back to Jonathan's room. She just couldn't leave him all alone when she knew how much he was hurting.

Kathryn knocked on his door and heard him say, "Come in." When she walked into the room, Jonathan was standing there naked except for a pair of loose sleeping trousers slung low on his hips. Taken aback, she couldn't help noticing his amazing chest. Some of the very handsome models she had seen while she was at the Institute were nothing compared to

Jonathan. He grabbed his dressing gown and quickly put it on as he asked, "Did you need me?"

Walking over to him, Kathryn looked into his eyes. "I wanted to make sure you're all right. I know how worried you are about Roderick and Allison. I thought you might want some company until you can go to sleep."

"Thank you, Kathryn, but I know that you have to be tired. Please go back to bed. I'll be fine. I'm worried, but I'm so exhausted, I'm sure that I'll be able to sleep." Jonathan gently touched her arm and she turned to him. He pulled her into his arms and just held her.

Kathryn laid her head on his chest. "I want to be here with you. I know that if it were my brother or sister who had gone missing, I wouldn't want to be alone. Let me just stay with you until you go to sleep."

"All right, Kathryn, but I've got to lie down, because my knee is killing me. I just took some laudanum, so I should fall asleep quickly." Jonathan crawled into bed, pulled the covers up, laid his head on his pillow, and then closed his eyes. Kathryn sat down in the chair by his bed, and soon she heard his breathing become slow and deep and knew he was asleep, but for some reason she didn't want to leave him. She leaned her head back against the chair, closed her eyes, and fell fast asleep.

The first thing Jonathan saw when he opened his eyes was Kathryn's beautiful face, all aglow in the soft lamp light. She had fallen asleep in the chair. Her head was back, her mouth was slightly open, and she was softly snoring. He wanted to gather her up in his arms and never let her go. He looked over at the clock and noticed it was five in the morning. It would be light soon, so he got up, went over to Kathryn, and gently shook her shoulder. She looked so peaceful, but she had to go back to her room before Hatton came to his room.

She slowly opened her eyes and smiled up at him. "Is it morning yet?"

Jonathan gently stroked her cheek as he murmured, "Almost, sweetheart. You need to go back to your room. Hatton will be here any minute, and you don't want him to find you here. Let me escort you to your room."

Kathryn suddenly looked embarrassed as she stood up. "I'm sorry. I didn't mean to fall asleep. You don't need to escort me. I'll leave you now. Will you be leaving soon to continue your search?"

"I'm going to leave just as soon as you go to bed. Promise me that you'll get some sleep. I may need you later, if anything...happens." He hung his head and shuddered when he thought about what could have happened to Roderick and Allison.

"All right, Jonathan." Kathryn rose up on her tiptoes and kissed his cheek before turning around and leaving his room. Jonathan watched as she went through the door and took a deep breath. What an incredible woman she was.

God, he loved her so much!

How he wished she could return his love.

At that moment, he knew he would give anything to win her love.

Hatton arrived just seconds after she left. He didn't say anything, so Jonathan felt sure he didn't see her. He went to the washstand and hurriedly washed as Hatton laid out his clothes. He didn't bother to take time to shave. He knew that he probably looked horrible, but he had things that were more important on his mind.

Just as he opened the door, Ellsworth, the butler, was getting ready to knock on his door. "My lord, there are some men downstairs asking for you. They look like some of the local fishermen. Do you want to see them?"

"Where are they?"

"They are at the servants' entrance, my lord."

"I'll go to them right away." Jonathan's heart was pounding, and his palms were sweating. He knew that these fishermen had news for him. When he saw them, he asked, "Have you found them?"

"Milord, we came straightaway. Two bodies have washed ashore. Do ye want t' come and take a look?" one of the fishermen asked.

Jonathan felt ringing in his ears. His heart was beating so fast that it felt as if it would jump out of his chest. "Take me to them right away!"

They lead him down to the shore, and he saw two bodies lying on the sand. As he approached, he saw Roderick and Allison's white faces and knew...they were dead.

"Oh God, no...not Roderick...not Allison...why...why," he cried to the heavens. He threw himself down beside them and screamed. The pain was so intense that it tore through his chest. He felt someone touch him, and it was Hatton.

Hatton offered Jonathan his hand. "My lord, there's nothing you can do for them. Let these men carry them up to the house. Come, let me help you up."

Jonathan sat up, trembling from his outburst. He had to get a grip on his emotions. Elaine and the children would need him to be strong. There would be time later to give into his grief. He nodded his head, and then he let Hatton pull him up. He stood there as two men carefully picked Roderick up. Roderick was such a big man that they had a hard time carrying him. Hatton picked Allison up with great gentleness and care, and they slowly made their way up to the house.

Ellsworth opened the front door and showed the men where to lay Roderick in the dining room, and Hatton gently laid Allison down beside her husband. All the men removed their hats and lowered their heads as one of them said a prayer for their souls. Jonathan wanted to say something, but he had such a lump in his throat, he just could not. Ellsworth showed the men out. Everyone left Jonathan alone with his brother and Allison.

Jonathan stood there in a state of shock. Icy chills ran down his arms. He kept saying, "No...No...they can't be dead...Oh God, please let this be a bad dream!" His voice filling the room with his anguish, he felt someone touch his arm, and he looked over. It was Kathryn, tears streaming down her face. She held her arms open and he fell into them. She held him in her arms for a long time as he cried out his grief. She didn't try to console him, she just held him.

Pulling himself together, Jonathan stood straight and tall, then said, "I need to go get the doctor and the vicar. Will you stay with them until I return? I don't want them...to be alone."

"I'll be right here with them. I won't leave their sides. Go, do what you need to do." With quiet dignity, Jonathan left the room.

Kathryn told Ellsworth to get Roderick's valet and Allison's maid and bring them to her. She quietly stood there waiting until they arrived. When they appeared, Allison's maid was crying, and Roderick's valet's lip was trembling.

"I need both of you to go get fresh clothes to bury them in. Please hurry. I want them dressed before Lord Sutherland returns with the doctor and the vicar." They left quickly, and Kathryn silently stood there watching over them until the maid and valet returned.

They soon returned with clothes and steaming water. The valet quickly washed and dressed Roderick as Kathryn stoically stood vigil. When he was through, he left the room. Kathryn watched as Allison's maid cleansed her mistress for the last time. The maid cried when she saw the bruises on Allison's body, but she went about her business, and soon Allison was dressed. Kathryn tenderly placed their hands on top of each other as if they were holding hands. The maid slowly left the room. Kathryn continued to stand vigil. The door opened and Jonathan was standing there with the doctor and the vicar.

Jonathan walked over to Kathryn, hugged her and said, "Thank you. I'll take over from here. Elaine should be awake. Can you try to keep her upstairs until I can come...tell her? I know...it's a lot to ask."

"Whatever you need me to do. I'll keep her upstairs until...you can come tell her." After stroking his shoulder, she turned and left the room.

Jonathan looked at the vicar and asked, "How do I go about getting caskets for them? I'm not from around here so I don't know where to get them." Jonathan turned to the doctor. "Doctor, can you tell how they died?"

The doctor went over to Roderick and Allison and started examining them, while the vicar said, "My lord, I will take care of it for you. When do you want to have the service? I know many of their neighbors will want to attend. They were well loved by everyone."

"I want the best caskets money can buy. Spare no expense. There is no family outside of my sister and myself—oh, and Lady Roderick's aunt, Lady Milsom. I'll be taking them back with me to St. John's Wood, and they'll be entombed in our family mausoleum. We can have the funeral service here just as soon as we can get the caskets. Thank you for your help. Please let me know when you have the caskets." After the vicar left, he turned to the doctor and asked, "Could you tell what...killed them?"

The doctor shook his head. "They both have severe blows to the head. They could have died from the blows alone. The only way to know is if I check their lungs for water, but even then, it will be hard to tell for sure. It's up to you, my lord."

"I don't want them disturbed. It doesn't really matter how they died anyway. The fact is...they're lost to me. Thank you for coming, Doctor. I'll get Ellsworth to show you out." Jonathan knew he had to go to his sister. He needed to be the one to tell her.

Oh God, how would he explain this to the children?

He went to the door, and Ellsworth was waiting there. "I need you to stay with my brother and Lady Roderick until Lady Kathryn comes back downstairs. I'll send her right down. I'm going upstairs to tell...my sister."

When he got to Elaine's door, he knocked and Kathryn answered. He quietly asked, keeping his voice low so Elaine wouldn't hear, "Will you go back downstairs and stay with Roderick and Allison until I can return?" She nodded her agreement, and then left the room. He looked over at Elaine.

"I need to speak with you. Come here, Princess, and take a seat. I found Roderick and Allison. They're downstairs in the dining room. Princess…they're…they didn't make it. I'm sorry."

Elaine looked at him with shocked terror on her face. "No…No…it can't be true. They…can't be dead. Not Roderick…Not Allison. She was going to have a baby. Please tell me it's not true!"

"Elaine, I know that it's hard to accept, but it is true."

Tears streamed down her sweet face. "Oh no, who will take care of Frankford and Jane? Do they know yet?"

"I've got to tell them just as soon as I know that you're all right."

Elaine turned her brave face to him, and with tears rolling down, she said, "I want to be with you when you tell them. They know me better than they know you. Let me just…catch my breath, and then we'll go…tell them together. Who is with Roderick and Allison? I don't want them to be alone."

"Princess, Roderick and Allison are in the dining room, and Kathryn is with them. She won't leave their side. I promise they won't be alone."

Elaine stood up, walked to her dressing table, and picked up her handkerchief. She wiped her eyes, then turned back to Jonathan, and with a tremulous voice, she said, "I'm ready."

Jonathan and Elaine went up to the nursery. The children were eating breakfast as they entered their room. They got up and ran to Elaine, and then Frankford asked, "Where is Mama? She didn't come see us again last night. She always tells us a story every night. Does she have a cold, like you do?"

Jonathan looked at their sweet faces, and his heart was ripped from his chest, yet again. This was the hardest thing he'd ever had to do. He took a deep breath, to gain some composure, then said, "Frankford, Jane, you know that we love you. I...have something that I need to tell you. Children...your parents were out on the sea the day before yesterday during the bad storm. Their yacht went down in the storm. Frankford, Jane...your parents...died. I'm so sorry."

Frankford and Jane looked at him and started crying. "My mama and papa are not dead," Frankford shouted. "You're lying!"

Jane just stood there and asked, "What does dead mean? Why is Frankford so mad? I want my mama," Jane wailed.

Jonathan picked her up, hugged her close. "Your mama and papa went to heaven to be with God. They're angels now. Do you know what angels are?"

"But that's so far away. I want to go see them. Will you take me, Uncle Jonathan, please?" Jane asked.

"Darling, you're right...heaven is far away, and we can't go there." Placing his hand over Jane's little heart, Jonathan said, "Your mama and papa will always be with you, here in your heart. They didn't want to go, but God called them home to be with him. I'll take care of you now." He hugged her close and kissed her sweet little cheek, wet with tears.

"I want my mama now! You go to heaven and get her. You tell God he can't have her. She's my mama, not his!"

Jonathan was at a loss for words. Jane was now crying inconsolably, and Frankford was yelling that he was a liar. He didn't have a clue how to help these children. Elaine was crying again as she tried to explain to the children. He looked over at their governess, who was also softly crying, pleading with her to help, but to no avail.

How could he explain so that the children would understand?

Frankford yelled, "I want to see them now. Where are they? You can't keep me from them. I won't let you."

Frankford ran from the room and Jonathan followed him down the stairs. He couldn't keep up because of his bad knee. Finally, he made it down the stairs and found Frankford in the dining room staring at his parents, screaming at the top of his voice, "Wake up, Mama! Papa, wake up!" Frankford had tears rolling down his face.

Kathryn pulled him into her arms and cradled him against her breasts. "Darling, your mama and your papa need you to be a brave soldier. They're in heaven watching you and loving you just as much as if they were here with you now. I know it's hard for you to understand, but just know they didn't want to leave you, but God needed them, and they had to go. We all love you, and we'll take care of you, I promise. Don't blame your Uncle Jonathan. He didn't want them to go either. Look, he's crying too. Shush, my darling, we'll be right here with you."

Frankford put his sturdy little arms around her neck, buried his face in her breasts and sobbed. Kathryn held him until he cried himself to sleep.

Jonathan looked at Kathryn with anguish in his eyes. "Oh Kathryn, what am I going to do? I don't know anything about raising children. I didn't know what to say to them. Little Jane was up there pleading with me to go to heaven and get her mother. Please help me!"

"I'll help you anyway I can, all you have to do is ask. Why don't you stay here with Roderick and Allison? I'll take

Frankford back to the nursery. Don't worry, children are resilient. They'll make it through this and so will you." Then she left the room.

Jonathan refused to leave Roderick and Allison again until the vicar showed up with the caskets. Hatton and Roderick's valet placed Roderick and Allison in their caskets. They held the funeral the next day, and all the neighbors and tenant farmers came to show their respect. Kathryn worked with the cook to prepare for the wake. Jonathan didn't know what he would have done without Kathryn. Once everyone left, she organized everything for the trip the next day.

Jonathan sent word to Lady Milsom letting her know what had happened to her niece and Roderick. He hated to do it by mail, but she needed to know right away. They were taking Roderick and Allison back to St. John's Wood for entombment next to Jonathan and Roderick's father. He felt numb right now because he had pushed his feelings down deep inside so he could be strong for Elaine and the children, but he was dreading the entombment because he knew it would be the final goodbye.

Chapter 10
- Early September 1823 -

The trip back to St. John's Wood was miserable the next day. It rained the entire time, and the children were fractious. Who could blame them? It took them twice as long to get there as usual. Kathryn was a godsend. He couldn't have done it without her. They arrived too late to take Kathryn to her mother's, and he didn't want to anyway.

Goodman took charge, and soon the children were in the nursery with their nurse and fast asleep. Elaine went straight to her room. Goodman put Kathryn in the blue room, and Jonathan asked her to come to his study so they could talk, once she was settled in.

When Kathryn arrived, Jonathan stood up and asked her to take a seat on the couch, then sat down beside her. "Kathryn, how can I ever thank you for all that you have done over the last two days? I don't think I could have handled any of this without you. I want to ask you something, but I need you to listen to everything before you respond. Can you do that for me?"

"Of course, Jonathan. I'm here for you and I'll listen. What is it that you need me to talk to me about?"

Jonathan gazed into Kathryn's eyes. He could barely breathe, he was so anxious about what he was getting ready to do. "We get along extremely well, and I know that we've become very close friends. It's clear that you already love the children, and Elaine idolizes you. I need your help in raising Frankford and Jane. Elaine will need you to help her when she has her come out in a few years."

"Of course, I'll be happy to help. I've grown to love the children and Elaine."

Reaching for Kathryn's hand, Jonathan's voice shook as he continued. "I know that you don't want to get married, but I would ask you to seriously consider marrying me. I promise it will be in name only, unless you change your mind about that. We would just be living together as friends who are married for the sake of the children. You know I never planned on marrying, but I can't do this alone, and I can't think of anyone that I would rather spend the rest of my life with than you. I have grown to care deeply for you, and I respect you tremendously. Please, will you do me the great honor of being my wife?"

Kathryn had a shocked look on her face. "Jonathan, I don't know what to say. I never planned on marrying, and you know how I feel about my desire to be a professional artist. As I said, I do love the children, and I care about Elaine. I also care deeply for you. I need some time to think about this."

Jonathan took her hand in his and stroked it. "Please, say yes. I promise I'll be totally supportive in your desire to be an artist. I'll help you find a studio in London where you can meet with your patrons. I'll even make sure that everyone in the ton knows how good you are. You'll have so many commissions you won't know how to handle them all. You'll have all the freedom you want. All I ask in return is for you to help me raise these children, and help Elaine with her come out."

"Jonathan, I've been determined for years to never marry. I'm not sure I could do it."

"I understand that, but people marry for many reasons. I think that friendship is probably the best reason. I know you're afraid of being intimate, and I promise that I understand that. I'll never bother you that way unless you decide that is what you want. Please, marry me."

Kathryn released his hand and stood up, and then she turned to him. "I still need time to think about it. I need at least two weeks to consider this. I'm going to return to my mother's house tomorrow after the entombment, and I don't want to see you for two weeks. After that, you may call on me, and I'll give you my answer."

Jonathan stood up and sighed. "I understand. I need to go back to Bristol to meet with Roderick's solicitor and get his affairs in order, but when I return I'll call on you for your answer. I know this is a lot to ask, but could you keep the children for me while I'm gone? They have become so attached to you that I'm afraid they'll be devastated if they lose you now."

Kathryn twisted her hands in agitation, clearly distressed by this talk of marriage. "Jonathan, I don't think that would be a good idea. If I decide not to marry you, they'll be hurt even more after having two weeks to become even more attached to me, and me to them. I need to be alone to ponder this decision, and I won't be able to do that with the children around. I know that you're nervous about taking care of them, but you'll be fine, and you'll have Elaine to help you. Please, I must have these two weeks, or I'll have to tell you no today."

Jonathan realized he couldn't press her any further, or he'd completely ruin any chance of her agreeing to his proposal. "I'm sorry. I wasn't thinking. You're right. I'll take the children with me. I'll muddle through some way. Just remember, I need you desperately and so do the children. I pray that you'll decide to marry me, but I'll give you the time you need. Let me escort you to your room so you can get some sleep. Thank you again for all that you've done."

When they got to her door, she kissed him on the cheek and said good night, then went into her room. Jonathan felt a vise squeeze his heart when she closed her door. He was so afraid she would ultimately say no. All he could do was give her the time she asked for and pray she would say yes. He turned and slowly walked down the hall to his room.

They held the entombment the next morning. Frankford stood there stoically and didn't cry. Jane wouldn't go to anyone else except Kathryn, so she held her during the entire service. Lady Milsom was too distraught to be any help with the children. Her health wasn't good anyway.

Jonathan didn't know what he was going to do with the children once he took Kathryn back to her mother's house that afternoon. Again, Kathryn had arranged for a repast to be served to everyone that came to the entombment. That afternoon, after the children went upstairs with their governess, Miss Mills, he took Kathryn back to her mother. They didn't talk on the ride to Bath.

When they arrived, he helped her out of the carriage. "I'll see you in two weeks. I'll be praying that you'll decide to marry me. All I ask is that you remember it will be in name only, unless you decide differently. I'll set you up with your studio right away, instead of three years from now. There are many advantages to being my wife. I honor and respect you tremendously, and whatever you decide, you'll always be able to count on me to continue to be your friend."

Kathryn solemnly looked into his eyes. "Thank you, Jonathan, for saying that. Your friendship means the world to me, and I would be lost if you decided we couldn't be friends, if I decide I can't marry you. I promise I'll give serious consideration to your proposal."

Jonathan escorted her into the house, and as he was taking his leave, he took her hands and kissed them, then released her and slowly walked out of her house. As Jonathan got back into his carriage, he glanced back and saw Kathryn watching him from the window. He prayed that she would find it in her heart to say yes.

When Jonathan got back to his house, he went looking for Elaine and found her in the music room playing the pianoforte. "Elaine, I'm going to need your help with the children. I know that you're grieving, but I can't do this without you. I've asked Lady Kathryn to marry me, but she needs two weeks before she gives me her answer. Pray that she says yes, because we need her desperately. We'll be leaving at eight o'clock tomorrow morning to return to Roderick's estate. Can you be ready?"

"Oh Jonathan, I hope she says yes! The children love her already, and so do I. I'll say a prayer every day that she says yes. I can be ready to leave in the morning. I'll talk to Miss Mills and let her know so she can have the children ready. How are you doing?" Then Elaine lowered her head, the tears rolled down her cheeks as she continued, "I miss Roderick and Allison desperately, and my heart hurts from the pain of losing them."

Jonathan held Elaine in his arms as she cried. He fought back the tears because he needed to be strong for her. She eventually stopped crying and left to go tell Miss Mills they would be leaving in the morning. As he watched her leave, he was so proud of how she was handling everything. He knew he was putting quite a bit on her young shoulders.

Jonathan spent the afternoon with Whetherby, making sure that all was well with the harvest. "My lord, the harvest went even better than we expected. Let me offer my condolences on the death of your brother. Everyone here was greatly saddened when we heard the news. It's difficult to believe your brother and his wife are gone. You can count on me for anything you need. I want to help."

Jonathan's heart ached at the mention of Roderick and Allison. "Thank you, Whetherby, for handling everything while I was gone to Bristol. I'll be returning to my brother's estate tomorrow, and I expect to be gone for ten days. I'll appreciate your continued support throughout this difficult time. If you need anything, please see my secretary, Stebbins. I'll see you when I return."

After Whetherby left his study, he sat there for a long time. He was feeling the desire to take a drink, but he fought off the temptation. He tried reading, but it wasn't helping. It was even more important that he not give in to the desire for a drink, because he was now responsible for Frankford and Jane. Besides, he wouldn't want to disappoint Kathryn, and he knew she would be if he drank.

As Jonathan continued to think about Kathryn, he felt the tension leave his body. Kathryn had such a calming effect on him. Just thinking of her helped tremendously.

Jonathan clasped his hands together and bowed his head as he began to pray. "Oh Lord, please open Kathryn's heart. Help her deal with her fear. Show her that I will never do anything to hurt her. I know that in your infinite wisdom you will guide her in the right direction. If it be your will that she marry me, I promise I will take care of her and try to heal her wounded spirit with your help. If she says no, I ask that you help me deal with the rejection. Make me strong so I can be here for Roderick's children. Help me deal with the temptation of drink. I can't do it without your loving guidance. In your son's most precious name I pray. Amen."

It had been years since Jonathan had prayed—since before Waterloo. He felt a peace roll over him after he finished praying and knew he would be all right whatever Kathryn decided. He wanted to marry her desperately, even though he knew he wasn't good enough for her. As much as he wanted her, he knew she had to make the decision that was best for her. He went to the music room, and as he began to play he felt the power of the music roll over him, and soon he was lost to the beauty of it.

The trip back to Westland Acres went well, and the children, while sad, behaved very well. He met with Roderick's steward, Bartlow, and the harvest had indeed been very plentiful. "Bartlow, I appreciate you handling everything. I'll need to depend on you in the future. I'll be sending my secretary, Stebbins, here, so if you need anything, all you have to do is ask him, and he'll handle it. I'll be here for the next ten days, and I look forward to working with you. We'll meet every morning at eight o'clock. Is that convenient for you?"

"That will be fine, my lord. Let me speak for everyone here and offer you our condolences. You brother was a fair man, and he treated his tenants well. He will be greatly missed by all of us. You can depend on us to take care of everything for the little master." After their meeting, Bartlow left the room, and Jonathan attempted to go through Roderick's papers, but it was just too painful. He left the study and went to the music room instead.

The next afternoon, he met with Roderick's solicitor and Mr. Brooks read his brother's will. All his affairs were in excellent shape, and he was doing very well on his investments. Roderick named Jonathan guardian to the children, as he had expected. Everything would be held in trust until Frankford reached his majority at one and twenty.

The next ten days went by excruciatingly slow. He wanted to see Kathryn again so badly. He continued to pray daily for God's wisdom, and every night he played the pianoforte to keep his nerves calm.

Over the fortnight, Kathryn spent most of her time alone. Her mother had wanted to talk about her trip and the tragedy of Roderick and Allison, but she refused to tell her mother anything. Marriage was something she had never wanted, but she did want to help Jonathan. She knew he was at a loss when it came to the children, and she had grown quite fond of Frankford and Jane.

Kathryn decided she wouldn't tell her mother that Jonathan had asked her to marry him because she knew her mother would try to talk her into it. This was something she had to decide all on her own. Kathryn just prayed that God would help guide her and help her decide what was best for her.

She knew Jonathan had said it would be a marriage in name only...

And that it would be just for the children...

But...could she really trust him?

Her fear of men was overwhelming, and the thought of putting her complete trust in any man was frightening. Jonathan was the kindest and most gentle man she had ever known, and she did respect him tremendously, but marriage was totally different than trusting him as her friend.

Each day she took long walks with Sarah, and she would sit in Queen's Square and draw for hours. Her mind kept replaying Jonathan's proposal over and over again to the point it felt as if she were going mad. She was torn between wanting to help Jonathan and the children and fear at the very thought of marriage. She wished she had Melody or Helen to talk to. She knew they would give her good advice, but unfortunately, neither one of them were available, and this wasn't something that she felt she could put in a letter.

Kathryn realized that a huge part of her wanted to say yes. She loved the idea of being a mother to Frankford and Jane. She knew she valued Jonathan's friendship tremendously, and the thought of seeing him every day thrilled her because he was the best friend she'd ever had. Kathryn prayed daily for God's guidance, but even after twelve days, she was no closer to making a decision. There were only two more days until Jonathan would return for her answer. She just hoped she would have one for him when the time was up. Looking up at the clock, she realized that it was almost luncheon, so she put down her book, which she hadn't been able to concentrate on anyway, and headed downstairs.

Kathryn's mother was already sitting at the table when she entered. Just as soon as Kathryn sat down, the footman served them. "Kathryn, you seem very distracted ever since you returned from Bristol. I'm sure it was awful for you there. I never asked you—were you able to finish the portrait before the marquess's brother and his wife died?"

Kathryn's eyes filled with tears. "No, I didn't finish it. I do believe I have enough sketches that I'll be able to complete it. When Jonathan comes by the day after tomorrow, I'm going to tell him." Then Kathryn realized that she had let her mother know that she expected Jonathan to come see her, and that she had also called him by his given name in front of her mother.

The duchess looked over at Kathryn with shock in her eyes. "I didn't realize that you used the marquess's given name. You must have grown closer to each other than you led me to believe. I just knew there was an attraction between the two of you."

Interrupting her mother, Kathryn quickly said, "It's not what you think, Mother. Lord Sutherland and I are just friends, nothing more. When he lost his brother, we just slipped into calling each other by our given names. I promise you, it doesn't mean anything other than friendship." Then, changing the subject and hoping to distract her mother, Kathryn asked, "Now, are we still going to that new play this evening?"

"Oh yes, I've heard that it is excellent, and I'm looking forward to seeing it. Lady Milsom and her husband are meeting us there." Glancing up at the clock, the duchess exclaimed, "My goodness, look at the time! I'm due at

Madame Bovary's in fifteen minutes. Kathryn, I'll see you at dinner, and then we'll leave immediately after we eat for the theater." Kathryn's mother stood up and walked from the room.

Thank goodness her mother remembered that appointment. Kathryn hoped that her mother would forget about her slip-up before they saw each other again. She had done so well in keeping her mother unaware of Jonathan's proposal, and she wanted to keep it that way. The last thing Kathryn wanted was her mother finding out about that.

Oh, what was she going to do?

Jonathan would be here for his answer in two days, and she was still not sure what she wanted to do. No, that was not true. If she were honest with herself, she knew she wanted to marry him. That wasn't the issue at all, really.

Oh, if she could just be sure she could trust Jonathan!

He did say the marriage would be in name only.

Once Kathryn returned to her room, she got down on her knees and prayed, *"Dear Lord, I need your guidance and wisdom right now more than ever before. I want to be there for Jonathan, and the children, and Elaine. I know that they need my help. Give me the strength to make the right decision for all of us. I ask this in your son's precious name. Amen."*

Kathryn felt a huge sense of peace wash over her, knowing that she had turned this over to God. She knew in her heart that the right thing was to trust in God to show her the truth.

Chapter 11

- September 1823 -

Finally, it was time to go back to St. John's Wood. Elaine was invaluable in keeping the children entertained on the trip back. The weather cooperated, and the return trip went by quickly. For the next four days, he kept himself busy by riding out with his steward every day. In the evenings, he played his pianoforte long into the night. He prayed constantly that Kathryn would be able to see past her fear and agree to marry him.

The fourteenth day arrived, and it was a beautiful fall day. He hoped it was a good omen, and that Kathryn would say yes. The last two weeks had certainly been the longest fortnight of his life. When he arrived at Kathryn's, the duchess's butler showed him into the drawing room. Kathryn wasn't there, so he went and stood by the window and looked out at the street. His emotions were all in turmoil. He offered up one last prayer while he waited for Kathryn to arrive.

Jonathan heard a noise and turned around...there stood Kathryn. She looked like an angel with all that fiery red hair floating around her face. His heart thundered in his chest and his hands were shaking. She had a soft welcoming look on her face, and he was encouraged.

Oh, please Lord, let her say yes!

He went to her and picked up her hand, bringing it to his lips for a gentle kiss. "Good afternoon. It's so good to see you again. I hope you're feeling well. You certainly look as if you are. You look lovely today, as always. We've all missed you terribly, and you know why I'm here. Have you reached your decision yet, or do you need more time?"

What an idiotic thing to say. He wanted his answer now, not at a later date!

"Good afternoon. I hope your trip went well and the children are doing all right. How are you dealing with everything? You look well rested."

Jonathan tried to conceal his impatience as he answered, "The trip went well, and the children are doing as well as can be expected. They miss their parents dreadfully. I'm dealing with everything, but I miss Roderick terribly. It's hard to imagine that he and Allison are gone. Now, have you reached a decision? Please, will you marry me?"

Kathryn looked at him in her serene, calm way and gave him an encouraging smile. "I've given careful thought to your proposal and all that you offered. I worry that accepting your proposal will be unfair to you. You deserve to have a woman who doesn't have the problems that I have. I truly don't believe I'll ever be able to be your wife in anything but name."

Jonathan interrupted. "I don't want any other woman. If you don't marry me, then I'll never marry. I would rather have you as my wife in name only than to not have you at all. You've become my best friend, and as I said before, I think friendship is the best reason to marry. While I do desire you, that isn't the reason I want you to marry me. I need you in my life, and if friendship is all you can ever give me, I'll be content. Please, say you'll be my wife!"

Kathryn looked directly into his eyes. "As long as you understand that friendship is all that I'm able to give...then yes, I'll marry you."

"Thank God! I promise you'll never regret marrying me. When can we have the ceremony? I don't want to rush you, but I would like to be married as soon as possible. The children are constantly asking about you. They need you. I need you. Please say that it can be soon!"

"We can have the banns read over the next three Sundays, then we can be married the following Saturday. That will give my mother enough time to plan. I want to be married in Bath Abbey where I've been attending church services. My mother didn't get to plan an elaborate affair for either my brother or my sister, and I want her to be able to do this for us. Personally, I would be happier having a small wedding, but I know this will mean so much to her. I hope you understand."

Jonathan was so relieved that she'd said yes that he was willing to go along with whatever she wanted. It was so like Kathryn to put her mother's wants and desires ahead of her own. "Whatever you want is fine with me, as long as you marry me. I'll go talk to the vicar when I leave here and set the date. This will be the longest four weeks of my life, but I'll manage some way. I would like it if you and your mother came for tea tomorrow. I want to show you your new home."

"I'm sure we'll be able to come. I haven't said anything to Mother, but I know that she's going to be thrilled that I'm marrying you. Oh, as a courtesy, you'll need to write to my brother and ask his permission. But don't worry; he'll be overjoyed that I've changed my mind about marriage. Let me go get my mother and we can tell her together. I'll be right back." Kathryn left the room, and Jonathan let out a sigh of relief.

Thank God, she was going to marry him!

He wasn't good enough for her, but he would protect her with his life. He hoped that, after time, she would fall in love with him and change her mind about intimacy, but even if she didn't, he would bear it. He loved her so much that he would do whatever she wanted.

Kathryn wasn't gone long before she returned with her mother. As they entered the drawing room, Jonathan smiled at the duchess. Bowing low over her hand, he said, "Thank you for coming to talk to me. Your Grace, I've grown terribly fond of your daughter over the last two months, and I believe she's fond of me. She and I have something we would like to tell you." He looked over at Kathryn and asked, "Do you want to tell her, or do you want me to tell her?"

Kathryn smiled at her mother. "Mother, Jonathan has asked me to marry him, and I've said yes."

The duchess looked dumbfounded as she looked from Kathryn to Jonathan, and then smiling, she said, "Oh my, congratulations! Kathryn, you've made me very happy." She turned to Jonathan and added, "My lord, you'll make a fine husband for my daughter. Welcome to the family. Now, when do you want to get married? Of course you'll want to have the wedding at St. George's in London next June. Oh, I'm finally going to get to plan a wedding!"

"Mother, we want to get married in four weeks. Bath Abbey is where I want to hold the wedding. You can invite whomever you want, but remember we only have a month to plan everything. Jonathan needs me to help him with the children, so that's why we're marrying so quickly. I'm counting on you to make all the wedding plans, because I know you'll do it beautifully. Can we count on you?"

The duchess looked ready to explode, but then she pulled herself together and said, "Well, Bath Abbey *is* beautiful. Four weeks doesn't give me much time, but I'm so thrilled that you've changed your mind about marriage, I'll do it. We need to get planning immediately."

Relieved that the duchess was being so accommodating, Jonathan said, "Well, I'll leave you to your planning while I go speak to the vicar and secure the date for our wedding. I'll return just as soon as I've made the arrangements." He turned to Kathryn. "You've made me the happiest of men. I'll see you soon, my dear." Then with that said, he bowed to both of them and left the room.

After Jonathan left them to their planning, he went to see the vicar. He was able to secure the date for their wedding, and he sent a message to Kathryn letting her know. He sent a letter to her brother by express immediately. Jonathan would have rather gotten married by special license, but he knew that it meant so much to Kathryn to have this wedding. He was so overjoyed that she'd said yes, he would agree to anything, just to have her as his wife.

When he arrived home, he found Elaine at the stables. "Elaine, I just came back from seeing Kathryn. She's accepted my proposal, and we're getting married in four weeks."

Rushing over to him, Elaine threw herself into his arms. "Oh Jonathan, that's wonderful news. I know you'll be so happy together, and the children are going to be elated. Both of them already love her, and so do I. Where are you getting married?"

Jonathan smiled jubilantly, joy filling his heart. "Kathryn wants to marry at Bath Abbey. I've already talked with the vicar and secured the date, so we'll be getting married in four weeks."

"Oh, I love Bath Abbey. It's so beautiful. Do you think Kathryn will ask me to be in the wedding?"

"I'm sure she'll want you. After all, once she and I are married, you'll be sisters. Kathryn and her mother are coming for tea tomorrow, and she'll probably ask you then. Now, why don't we take a ride? We haven't done that in a while." Jonathan made a mental note to himself to ask Kathryn about Elaine, but he was sure that Kathryn would want her as an attendant.

When Kathryn arrived the next day for tea, he greeted her and her mother and helped them out of their carriage. He watched for Kathryn's expression as she gazed at his home for the first time, hoping Kathryn would love it as much as he did.

He could see delight in her eyes as she said, "Oh Jonathan, your home is beautiful. I'm sure I'll be very happy here. I hope you'll give me a tour of the inside while I'm here today."

"Of course, my dear, whatever you want. All you have to do is ask. Let me escort you and your mother into the house." Jonathan turned to her mother and said, "Welcome to my home, Your Grace. Did you and Kathryn get everything planned for the wedding after I left yesterday?"

As they walked into the drawing room, Her Grace answered, "We have all the important details agreed upon, now we just have to execute our plans. We will be extremely busy over the next four weeks. I would have liked more time to plan, but I know that you're anxious to marry, and I will manage."

After tea, Jonathan took them on a tour of the house. "Feel free to change anything that you would like. My stepmother decorated it shortly before her death fifteen years ago. I did redecorate the music room and the master suite five years ago, but the rest of the house I left alone."

"Jonathan, your home's beautifully decorated. Your music room is delightful, and I look forward to spending time with you there, listening to you play." Kathryn looked over at her mother and commented, "Jonathan is a marvelous pianist. He's as gifted as Mary is. Once we get settled, we'll have you over so you can hear him play." She turned back to Jonathan and added, "Mother loves music, and she'll enjoy hearing you as much as I do."

After they finished the tour, he escorted them to their carriage, and they departed. Kathryn and Jonathan agreed to go and meet with the vicar on Wednesday as Jonathan had arranged. Jonathan watched as the carriage carried Kathryn back to town. She seemed at peace with her decision to marry him, and that relieved his mind. If he thought the last two weeks were long, they would be nothing compared to the next four.

On Wednesday morning, Jonathan picked Kathryn up at nine o'clock so they could meet with the vicar. The meeting went well, and they finalized all the details of the ceremony. They both agreed that they wanted the full mass as part of the service.

After they left the vicar, with Kathryn's maid in attendance, they visited the Pump Room so that Jonathan could drink the water. He had gained relief from drinking it, so now he tried to go there at least a couple of times a week. The water tasted awful, but it did seem to help his knee.

While they were at the Pump Room, Kathryn and Jonathan ran into Lord and Lady Shelton. After shaking hands, Lord Shelton said, "Good morning, Sutherland. It's good to see you again. Are you here for the water? My wife likes to drink it, so we come almost every day." Turning to Lady Kathryn, he added, "It's a pleasure to see you again as well, Lady Kathryn. We're looking forward to you starting our portrait. Are you still able to start in two weeks as you planned?"

Jonathan spoke up. "Shelton, congratulations are in order. Lady Kathryn has agreed to marry me. We'll be married in four weeks. She's going to be very busy..." then realizing that Kathryn would decide if she had time the do the portrait, he quickly added, "but, of course, she'll decide when she can start your portrait."

Lord Shelton clapped Jonathan's shoulder and said, "Congratulations! I'm very happy for both of you. We'll understand if you need to put the portrait off for a while. Just let us know when is convenient for you."

Kathryn, the consummate professional, said, "I would like to go ahead and at least get the preliminary sketches done. Would you be free to come tomorrow morning at nine o'clock? I need to go ahead and get your portrait done because I have to be in Devonshire by the first part of November. While I'm sure I'll be busy, my mother is taking care of most of the wedding plans, so I'll be fine."

Lord and Lady Shelton looked at each other, then nodded. "We'll be happy to be there in the morning. We appreciate your willingness to go ahead and start. We'll make sure that we're available whenever you can fit us in."

"Good, then I'll see you in the morning. I look forward to working with both of you. When you come tomorrow, we'll work out a schedule for the next few weeks."

Jonathan asked, "Shelton, would you stand up with me at my wedding? Since I lost my brother, I would really appreciate it."

A look of shock came over his face as Lord Shelton exclaimed, "Oh, my God! What happened? I'm so sorry about your brother—I didn't know. Please accept our condolences on your loss. I can only imagine how painful this must be. I know how close you were to St. John. Of course, I'll stand up with you. How is his wife handling it?"

Jonathan swallowed the lump in his throat and sighed. "Roderick and Allison both passed together. They had taken out their yacht and were caught in a storm. The yacht capsized and Roderick and Allison drowned. I'm now guardian to their two children. It has indeed been very difficult."

"What a terrible tragedy. If there is anything you need at all, don't hesitate to ask. You know I respected and admired St. John tremendously." Lord Shelton turned to Lady Kathryn and asked, "Are you sure that you can start our portrait? We'll understand if you can't do it."

Kathryn shook her head. "Actually, it will take my mind off everything, so please come tomorrow as arranged."

"Well, as long as you're sure. We'll see you tomorrow at nine o'clock," Lord Shelton said.

As they walked away, Jonathan said, "Are you sure you should be doing this?"

"I want to go ahead and get started. Based on how often Lord and Lady Shelton can come for a sitting, I could possibly get it done before the wedding. Mother is really doing all the planning. All I have to do is go for sittings with Madame Bovary for my wedding gown, and those appointments are in the afternoon. I can't afford to wait, because I need to be in Devonshire by the first part of November. Remember when I told you that nothing will come before my art? Well this is just an example of what I meant."

Jonathan gently took her hand, raised it to his lips, and kissed her fingers. "Whatever you think is best. I just worry that you'll wear yourself out, and then you'll get sick. I understand how important your art is to you, and I shan't stand in your way."

"Well, good. Now, I need to get back home so I can get my studio ready for tomorrow. You're easy. Now I have to deal with my mother. She'll not be nearly as understanding as you are!"

Jonathan dropped Kathryn off at her home and headed back to St. John's Wood. He worried that she was taking on too much, but he knew he couldn't interfere. Kathryn was very stubborn when it came to her art. At this point, he would go along with anything to keep her happy, because he didn't want her to regret her decision to marry him.

He would just have to hope she would be all right. His feelings were growing stronger every time they were together. He hoped as she grew more comfortable with him that she would change her mind about being intimate with him. If he could get her to fall in love with him, then he was sure he could overcome her fears.

After Jonathan dropped her off, Kathryn hurried into the house and up to her studio. She knew that she was taking on quite a bit, but she didn't want to wait to do the Sheltons' portrait. Her mother loved planning events, and Kathryn's wedding would be no different. Kathryn was shocked that she had decided to marry Jonathan, but she trusted him to keep his word about the marriage being in name only.

Kathryn had promised him she would help him with the children, and being married was the only way she could fulfill that promise. Poor Jonathan didn't need to go through this alone. He had loved his brother so much, and she worried that things were happening so fast that he wasn't having the chance to mourn for his brother and Allison. She was determined to help him with his grief. While she could never be his wife completely, she would be a good and loyal companion.

Well, this wasn't getting her ready for her afternoon. She needed to go to her room and freshen up. She had her first fitting with Madame Bovary at two o'clock, and it was noon already.

After luncheon, Kathryn broke the news to her mother. "I ran into Lord and Lady Shelton, and I've moved up their portrait. In fact, they'll be coming every day for a sitting so I can get their portrait done before my wedding."

The duchess grew quite still, and a tense silence filled the room before she furiously said, "Kathryn, how could you do this? You're getting married in less than four weeks. This is most inconsiderate of you. We have far too much to do for you to do a painting at this time. You'll just have to tell them you cannot do their portrait until after the wedding."

Kathryn met her mother's fury without batting an eye. "I will *not* be telling them I can't do their portrait. Nothing…absolutely nothing…comes before my art. Jonathan already knows about this, and he supports my decision. Besides, you love planning events, and I give you full control over any and all decisions in regards to my wedding."

"But Kathryn, we have so much to do, and such a short period of time to get everything planned."

"I'll still have my afternoons free, and you'll just have to schedule things that you need me for in that time frame. I have complete confidence in you, and I know I'll have a magnificent wedding. With you in charge, it will be the most talked about wedding of the year. Now, I need to go upstairs before we leave for Madame Bovary's Salon, so I'll see you in fifteen minutes. By the way, Mother, thank you for doing this for me. I know we don't say this often, but I do love you." With that being said, Kathryn walked out of the room.

Kathryn made it to Madame Bovary's by two, and soon her mother was pouring over the design fashion plates. Kathryn decided on a cream satin with Italian lace overlay on the bodice and skirt of the gown, gold ribbon under the bodice, and seed pearls sown on top of the lace. Her mother was in raptures over the gown. Madame Bovary took her measurements, just to make sure they hadn't changed, and told her she would need her for another fitting on Friday.

After the fitting, Kathryn and her mother went to the printer's shop, picked out the invitations, and ordered them engraved. They took the envelopes with them so they could get them addressed. The duchess was inviting three hundred people to the wedding, which was far more than Kathryn wanted. She tried to get her mother to limit the guests, but she wouldn't hear of it. Their next stop was the greenhouse on George Street. Her mother wanted lilies, even though they weren't in season. The proprietor of the shop assured them that he would find them, along with the white roses her mother had also requested.

Bath Abbey was the perfect place for a wedding. It was an eighteenth century church with graceful fan vaulting and a huge east window that overlooked the courtyard. What was truly amazing was the fact that it was a memorial to, of all people, Beau Nash, who was one of the most flamboyant dandies to frequent Bath in the last century.

After several lengthy discussions, Kathryn and her mother finally agreed to hold the wedding breakfast at the assembly rooms after the ceremony.

The most arduous task was addressing the envelopes, which they immediately went to work on. The duchess had asked several of her friends to help, and by Friday, the invitations were on their way, three weeks before the wedding. Of course, the announcement had already appeared in the London Times and the Bath papers.

Kathryn had so many things to keep her busy that she didn't have the time to dwell on the magnanimous decision she'd made in agreeing to marry Jonathan. She did keep a constant prayer running in her head that God would protect her from harm. As each day passed, her conviction grew stronger, coming to believe…it was all right…to put her trust in Jonathan.

Chapter 12
- September 1823 -

Lord and Lady Shelton were extremely cooperative and came to her studio each morning promptly at nine o'clock. Their three children were very well behaved, and by Saturday the twenty-seventh, the sketches were done, and she was ready to start the painting. She was confident that she would have their portrait finished by the day before the wedding.

The date set for the wedding was the eleventh of October, which would give Kathryn and Jonathan three weeks to rest before they would need to leave for Devonshire. Henry, Melody, and the children would be arriving on the eighth, and Helen, Matthew, and their children were arriving on the ninth. Kathryn was anxious for all of them to meet Jonathan. She thought they would like him exceedingly well. She had received letters from both Melody and Helen, and they were thrilled she had decided to wed and wanted to know all about Jonathan.

Jonathan came to dinner every Sunday after church, and they, along with the duchess, attended the assembly rooms on

Wednesday nights. While she knew Jonathan didn't enjoy going to the assembly rooms, he went to please her. They managed to spend a bit of time together on Sunday afternoons and usually went for a drive. Of course, they didn't get to see each other alone, as it was too cold to use an open carriage, so Sarah had to go along with them.

On the last Sunday that the banns were read, Kathryn and Jonathan decided to take advantage of the unseasonably warm weather and took a walk. Of course, Jonathan couldn't go far because it was too difficult for him with his bad knee, so they walked across Royal Crescent and found a park bench. Sarah discreetly walked away to give them some privacy, while still staying within sight.

After Kathryn and Jonathan sat down, Kathryn asked, "Jonathan, how are the children doing? Are they handling the death of their parents better? I wish I could see them, but things have been so hectic, it just hasn't been possible."

Jonathan straightened out his leg to get more comfortable before answering her. "Jane cries herself to sleep every night and keeps asking me to go to heaven and get her mama. I've tried to explain, but she doesn't understand. It tears my heart apart when she asks me to go get them."

"Oh Jonathan, I'm sure that's very difficult for you. How is Frankford?"

"Frankford has withdrawn from everyone. He doesn't cry at all, which worries me. I hope that once we're married, and you're around him, he'll start opening up again. He's always been such a rambunctious young fellow. It's hard to see him so quiet and withdrawn. He's still doing well with his studies, but he isn't showing interest in any of his other usual pursuits. It doesn't help that the weather has been so dismal. At least today is nice and their governess was going to take them on a picnic."

"How is Elaine? Has she continued to be helpful with the children? I'm so pleased she wanted to be one of my attendants."

Jonathan placed his arm on the back of the bench and his hand brushed Kathryn's shoulder, sending chills down her spine. It surprised her that his slightest touch could cause her to react so strongly. "Elaine's doing as well as can be expected. She has to fight the tears whenever she sees Jane crying, but she's been wonderful with the children. She's very excited about our wedding, and she's thrilled that you asked her to be part of the wedding party. How's the portrait coming along? Are you going to have it finished before the wedding?"

"Lord and Lady Shelton come for their last sitting tomorrow. I'll be through with it by Wednesday, and they can pick the portrait up Thursday morning. I think it's my best work yet. Would you like to see it when we get back to my house?"

"I'm amazed that you've been able to get their portrait done so quickly. I'd love to see it, if you want to show it to me." Then with a downcast look, Jonathan said, "I wish you'd been able to finish my brother's family portrait."

"Oh Jonathan, I'm sorry, I meant to tell you. I plan to finish their portrait. I have some wonderful sketches of them, so I'll definitely be able to complete it. I thought that if you would be all right with it, we could go to Bristol, get the portrait, and bring it back here so I can get it done before I have to leave for Devonshire."

"I'm so pleased you'll be able to finish the portrait. That means the world to me. There won't be enough time to travel to Westland Acres, but Stebbins is there, and I'll have him bring the portrait to you."

"Would you like to come with me when I go to my sister's in November? I'm sure she would be happy to have all of us. Her children would love to play with Frankford and Jane. The Marquess and Marchioness of Ralston also have three boys, and I think they're close to Frankford's age, so the children should be happy there."

"I would love to come with you. I was hoping you would ask me. It would be good for the children, if you're sure we wouldn't be imposing on your sister and her husband." Then changing the subject, he continued, "Oh, by the way, I've already picked out a room you can use as your studio. It has a full wall of windows and gets the morning sun."

"That sounds perfect, Jonathan. I'm sure it's also difficult to go to Westland Acres, because of the memories. I wish there was something I could do to help you deal with your grief. I can remember how difficult it was for me when I lost Nelson. It just takes time to move past the grief." Kathryn's heart went out to Jonathan. She knew he was grieving deeply for Roderick and Allison.

Knowing that talking about Roderick and Allison was causing Jonathan such sadness, she turned the conversation away from them. "Helen and Matthew will be here on Thursday, and I'll make sure they're all right with you and the children coming with me. I'll be very busy and spending each morning at the Ralston's, so you'll need to entertain yourself in the mornings. Matthew likes to hunt. Is that something that you can participate in?"

"I know that you'll be busy in the mornings, but I'm sure I'll find ways to entertain myself, and I love to hunt. I can't walk long distances, but I can stand still with no problem. Since you do quite a bit of that when hunting, I'm sure I would enjoy it."

"Well good, at least I shan't worry about you then." It relieved her mind that Jonathan seemed to understand that this trip wouldn't be a holiday, so she was glad she'd suggested that he come.

Jonathan looked over at Kathryn and grinned. "I also love to ride, and I remember you telling me that Helen and her husband ride the beach whenever the weather permits. Of course, that probably isn't too often in November. In fact, it's starting to get a little cool, so we had better go in. I'm glad we had this chance to talk. I've missed spending time alone with you."

"I've missed it too. And you're right; it is getting a bit cool."

"Well, time to go in. I'm sure your maid is probably freezing standing over there." When they returned to the house, Kathryn took Jonathan up to her studio and showed him the Sheltons' portrait. As he gazed at it, he said, "Kathryn, this is remarkable. It looks finished now. What else do you need to do to it? You've caught Shelton perfectly. They're going to be thrilled with this. Once more people see your work, you'll have so many commissions you'll be able to choose who you want to paint."

"Oh, there's just a few minor touches left, but you aren't able to see them as I can. I'm glad you like it and that you think the Sheltons will like it. I find everyone fascinating—ugly, pretty, old, or young—so I doubt I'll ever want to pick and choose my patrons."

With a look of distaste on his handsome face, Jonathan said, "I can think of some people that you might not want to deal with. Some of the old dragons of society can be very difficult to appease."

"Jonathan, have you forgotten who my mother is? She's the epitome of what an old dragon is, and most of her friends are the same way, so I can't imagine I would have any problems dealing with any of them."

"That's true, I wasn't thinking about your mother. She's actually been very polite and courteous to me, so I don't look at her like that."

"It's because she *likes* you. You're a marquess, and my mother is all about a person's prestige."

"Well, I'll have to make sure that I stay on her good side."

Kathryn looked up at Jonathan. "She has always treated Melody awful, and Melody is one of the nicest people you could ever meet." Then remembering her family with fondness, she added, "Oh, I just know you're going to get along with my family. None of them are high in the step at all."

"I look forward to meeting all your family. I told you I met your brother, but I really didn't get to know him. What's he like?"

"Henry is probably the most down to earth person you could ever meet. Now, if he needs to be, he can be very arrogant and intimidating, but that rarely happens. He detested Helen's husband at one time, but now they're the best of friends and work together frequently in Parliament. I'm warning you, he'll definitely try to get you to take a more active role in the House of Lords. He feels strongly that it's one of the most important responsibilities of a peer of the realm. So be forewarned."

"As I mentioned before, now that my bachelor days are behind me, I want to take a more active role." Then looking down at his watch Jonathan said, "Oh my, look at the time. I've overstayed my welcome. What time do you expect your brother and his wife to arrive on Wednesday?"

As they walked downstairs, Kathryn answered, "I'm not sure when they'll be here, but I expect that they'll make it in time for tea. Why don't you plan to come for tea that day?"

Jonathan took her hand and kissed it as he gazed affectionately into her eyes. "Anything for you, my dear. I'll see you Wednesday at four o'clock." As Jonathan kissed her hand, it sent chills throughout her body. These feelings were growing stronger each time they were together. She was becoming inordinately fond of Jonathan, and if her uncle hadn't abused her, she felt she would have enjoyed intimacy with him.

Oh, why did her uncle have to rape her?

It was so unfair, but then no one said life was fair.

The next few days flew by. She was able to finish the Sheltons' portrait on Tuesday, and they came and picked it up Wednesday morning. Lord and Lady Shelton were extremely pleased with it and promised to recommend her to all their friends. This thrilled Kathryn to no end. Once word spread, she'd have all the commissions she could ever want.

It was a good thing she'd finished the Sheltons' portrait, since Henry and Melody were arriving that afternoon. Kathryn looked forward to seeing them. She hadn't seen them since late May when she graduated from the Art Institute. Little William was almost a year old, and his birthday would be in ten days. She hoped they could have a birthday celebration for him while everyone was together.

That afternoon, Jonathan arrived shortly before four o'clock, but Henry and his family weren't there yet. The duchess held off tea, which was extremely unusual. Once thirty minutes passed, she decided to go ahead and serve. Just as soon as the duchess began to pour, Kathryn heard Henry and Melody arriving.

She jumped up, grabbed Jonathan's hand, and tried to pull him up. "Come on, they're here! Let's go out and meet them." When they went into the entry hall, Kathryn dropped Jonathan's hand and ran into her brother's arms. "Come here, Jonathan, and meet my brother." She was laughing and running from Henry, to Melody, to Mary, and then to the children, and then back to Jonathan. "Jonathan, this is my brother, the Duke of Sanderford. Oh, you said you met him, didn't you? I forgot."

Jonathan bowed. "Hello, Your Grace. We met in Brussels while we were waiting for Bonaparte to make his move."

With a puzzled expression on his face, Henry replied, "I'm sorry, but I remember very little of my time in Brussels before the battle. It's a pleasure to meet you again all the same, Lord Sutherland. Let me introduce you to my wife, Melody." Henry turned to Melody and said, "Darling, this is Lord Sutherland, Kathryn's fiancé."

Bowing low over Melody's hand, Jonathan kissed it. "Pleased to meet you, Your Grace. Kathryn has told me so much about you. She speaks very highly of you."

Smiling pleasantly, Melody replied, "Please, call me Melody. After all, on Saturday, you become my brother. Kathryn wrote me about your brother and his wife. I'm so sorry for your loss. I can't imagine how horrific it must have been to lose both of them at the same time. Thank goodness their sweet children have you to take care of them."

"Thank you for your kind words. It has been very difficult, but I've had Kathryn's support to help me through," Jonathan replied. "If I'm to call you Melody, then please, call me Jonathan."

"All right, Jonathan." Melody turned and said, "Let me introduce you to the Marchioness of Wyndham, my brother-in-law Nelson's widow."

"It's a pleasure to meet you, Lady Wyndham." Again, Jonathan bowed and kissed Mary's hand. "Kathryn tells me that you're an extremely gifted pianist. I play also. I would love to hear you play sometime."

Mary replied, "I would be happy to play for you, but only if you'll return the favor and play for me. And please, call me Mary."

Kathryn looked fondly over at her nieces and nephews. "Jonathan, these are all my wonderful nieces and nephews. This is Mary Elizabeth, Henry and Melody's eldest." The little girl looked up at him, smiled, and then executed a perfect curtsey. "This is Brandon and Magnus, then of course, the baby is William." The two little boys bowed to him like perfect little gentlemen, and he returned their bow. "Here are Mary's children, Roderick and Angela."

When Jonathan heard Roderick's name, Kathryn saw that he tensed up slightly, and she knew it had to be difficult to meet someone that shared his brother's name.

Roderick bowed. "Pleased to make your acquaintance, my lord. This is my sister, Angela." Then the little girl curtsied and Jonathan bowed to her.

Jonathan smiled at all the children. "It's a pleasure to meet all of you. Your aunt Kathryn has told me all about you. I have a niece and nephew, whom you'll meet in a few days. Frankford and Jane are close to your age. I know they'll be overjoyed to meet you."

Kathryn, with her voice full of joy, said, "Everyone, follow me into the drawing room. Mother is in there waiting for all of you to arrive so she can have her tea."

Henry laughingly replied, "Then by all means, let's go into the drawing room. We wouldn't want to keep the duchess waiting for her tea."

Tea was chaotic, but joyous. Happiness bubbled up inside Kathryn when she saw how well everyone seemed to take to Jonathan. He was quite relaxed around her family, so she knew she didn't need to worry that such a crowd would disturb him.

Henry pulled Jonathan aside and said, "I'd like to find a place so we can sit down and talk. Why don't you come with me, and we'll find the library together."

Soon, they found the library and went inside. Henry walked over to the cabinet, poured himself a brandy and started to pour a second one when Jonathan spoke up. "None for me, Your Grace. I only drink wine."

"No problem. Let's sit down and get to know each other better. I must say I'm amazed that Kathryn has agreed to marry you. How did you convince her? Oh, and please call me Sanderford or Henry, none of this 'Your Grace,' please." Henry sat down and took a sip of his brandy.

Jonathan took a seat across from Henry, and then proceeded to explain. "We got to know each other quite well while she was doing my portrait. Then, of course, she was with me in Bristol when my brother and his wife perished in the storm. By that time, I was already in love with your sister, so I asked her to marry me. She didn't say yes immediately, but then I was able to convince her to do it for the sake of the children."

"I'm so sorry you lost your brother and his wife. That has to be tough. You just told me the most important detail—you love Kathryn. I'm still amazed that you were able to talk her into marrying you, but I'm very pleased you were successful. Kathryn has always said that she would never marry."

Jonathan eased his leg out straight, trying to get more comfortable before he answered. "I don't know all the details, nor do I know who, but I know she has been hurt by some man, and it must have been bad. I hope that as we grow more comfortable with each other, she'll eventually tell me more. She did tell me the bastard is dead."

Henry looked menacing as he said, "I can tell you who it was. It was our uncle, my mother's brother. He tried to rape her. Melody and I caught him just in time, but it's made her extremely wary of men. That's why I'm so surprised that she's marrying you."

Jonathan looked Henry in the eye. "I convinced her that I wouldn't expect her to be intimate unless she decides she wants it. I'm hoping she'll fall in love with me and that we can work through her problem, but even if that never happens, I'll always love her."

"What will you do if she doesn't change her mind? Are you prepared to live a chaste life? You're a stronger man than me, if you can do that."

Thinking about how he could explain this to Henry, Jonathan decided to be candid. "When we were first getting to know one another, I thought that nothing would ever come of my attraction to her, since I never planned to marry. My brother was strong and healthy, he already had a son to be my heir, and he and his wife were expecting another child when they died. I have no desire to be with another woman. Kathryn is the only woman I want in my life."

Henry interrupted, "But that still doesn't fully answer my question. How will you handle it if Kathryn never changes her mind? Saying you don't desire to be with any other woman is one thing, knowing you'll be strong enough to be faithful, is another."

Looking Henry straight in the eye, Jonathan put all the conviction into his voice he could muster as he answered him. "Shortly after we met, I went to a brothel. When I left there, I felt as if I had betrayed Kathryn, even though we barely knew one another. At that point, I thought I was merely infatuated with her and that it would run its course, but then when we were together so much at my brother's, I realized I love her. If I can't be with Kathryn, then I would rather live chaste for the rest of my life, because I don't want to be with anyone else."

Henry beamed at him. "Jonathan, welcome to the family. I'll be proud to call you brother. I believe my sister already loves you. There's no way she would say yes, unless her feelings were engaged. She just doesn't realize she's in love with you yet."

"I certainly hope you're right. We had better get back to the drawing room. I'm sure Kathryn is wondering where we are."

When they returned to the drawing room, Kathryn walked over to them and said, "Well, did he pass your test, Henry?"

"He passed with flying colors. I'm happy for you, Puss. Now, where is my pretty wife?" Henry asked.

"Melody took William upstairs to feed him," Kathryn explained. "He started fussing, and she said that he's cutting some teeth. How long are you going to be staying Henry? I hope it's long enough for us to have a birthday celebration for William."

Henry glanced over at his mother. "It all depends on how well Mother treats Melody. I won't have her upsetting Melody in her condition."

"What, you mean Melody is going to have another baby? I'm so pleased for you. I do hope you have another daughter. Our family needs more girls. Mother has been wonderful since I've been here, and she adores Jonathan. I know she loves living here in Bath, and that may have helped to soften her attitude. If she gets too unbearable, you can always come and stay with us. Isn't that right, Jonathan?"

Smiling fondly down at Kathryn, Jonathan replied, "Whatever will make you happy, my dear. Invite anyone you want to our home. I would be happy for them to stay."

"Jonathan, why don't you stay for dinner?" Kathryn asked. "Other than Mother, the rest of us are very informal, and since you can do no wrong in her eyes, she'll not say a thing about the way you're dressed. Please, stay so you can get to know everyone better."

Henry spoke up. "Yes, do stay, Jonathan. I have an extra set of dress clothes and we're close to the same size. I'm sure Melody isn't going to be satisfied until she has her chance to interrogate you. You might as well give up, you're outnumbered."

Jonathan turned to Kathryn and laughed. "I can definitely see that I'm outnumbered. Whatever you want, my dear. I'll be happy to stay."

Everyone went upstairs to get ready for dinner. Abernathy showed Jonathan to a room where he could freshen up and change his clothes. Henry's valet brought Jonathan a spare set of dress clothes for him, and from the looks of them, they would fit.

Thinking back on their conversation, he was glad he had been candid with Henry. He seemed to be a likeable person. In fact, so far, he liked all of Kathryn's family. He looked forward to meeting Helen and her husband the next day.

Kathryn was just glowing with happiness, and Jonathan fell more in love with her each day they spent together. He hoped Henry was right about Kathryn already being in love with him. He just knew that if she were in love with him, she would be able to overcome her fears about intimacy. He would just need to be patient.

As Kathryn was dressing, she thought about Jonathan calling her "my dear," and she decided she liked it. She realized she wanted his affection, even if they never had a higher level of intimacy. She decided she would just enjoy his affection and quit being so suspicious. It would be nice to have companionship.

Marriage wasn't all about physical intimacy. She would try to be a good wife to Jonathan, and she would turn a blind eye to him having a mistress. After all, she couldn't expect him to do without sex just because she didn't want to have any. She knew better than most how driven men were to have sexual congress. She would just have to find a way to let Jonathan know without actually telling him he could have a mistress.

Dinner was a joyous affair. Even the duchess was on her best behavior and treated Melody with the utmost respect. After dinner, the men didn't stay in the dining room, but joined the ladies straightaway. Mary played the pianoforte, and when she was through, she asked Jonathan to play for her, which he said he was happy to do. Everyone agreed they both played beautifully.

At ten o'clock, Jonathan got up to leave, and Kathryn walked him to the door. "Jonathan, when you come tomorrow, go ahead and bring dinner clothes with. I want you to get to know Helen and Matthew just as you have Henry and Melody." Kathryn looked embarrassed as she added, "I wanted to let you know that while I can't be intimate with you, I do want us to be affectionate. So if you would like to kiss me, it would be all right."

"Dearest, nothing would please me more." Then he pulled her into his arms and gave her a brief, yet gentle, kiss on her lips, and then he released her. "I'll see you tomorrow at four o'clock. I look forward to getting to know the rest of your family. Do you think your mother would mind if I brought Elaine and the children with me tomorrow? I hate to leave them out, and I know the children would love being around your nieces and nephews."

"Oh Jonathan, that would be wonderful. Yes, please bring them. What's a few more when there are already so many?" Then she hugged him and kissed him quickly as if she were embarrassed. He hugged her back and then took his leave.

Kathryn went back into the drawing room, and soon everyone went to their rooms for bed. Once Kathryn had changed into her night rail, she sent Sally away. As Kathryn lay there waiting for sleep to take her away, she replayed the evening over in her mind. She was so pleased that her family had responded so well to Jonathan. Of course, she'd been fairly confident that they would all like him. After all, Jonathan was so kind and solicitous of her. It made her feel so safe and cared for.

Jonathan had been so gentle when he had kissed her good night. She realized that it had been her first kiss. Even though she had endured so much pain and humiliation at the hands of her uncle, he had never kissed her. Knowing that Jonathan was the first to kiss her felt special, and she was glad that at least her uncle hadn't taken that away from her. Kathryn reached up and touched her lips as sleep took her away. Her dreams that night were of how safe she felt with Jonathan.

Chapter 13
- October 1823 -

The next morning brought another beautiful fall day. Everyone had breakfast together and then Kathryn, Melody, and Mary took the children across the street to the park. All the children had a wonderful time, and Kathryn enjoyed watching them play. Kathryn turned to Melody. "Henry told Jonathan and me that you're expecting again. When do you expect this baby?"

Smiling, Melody replied, "The doctor says I should have the baby the middle of April. I hope I have another girl this time. Mary Elizabeth has demanded that we give her a sister. She says she already has enough brothers. Henry wants a girl too. Now, tell me all about Jonathan. You didn't tell me he was so attractive in your letter. Are you madly in love with him, or are you like Helen and think you're just marrying for the children?"

"Melody, I truly am marrying him because of his niece and nephew, but I'm very fond of Jonathan. He's a wonderful man, and I wish you could have met his brother and Allison.

You would have liked them. It has been just awful for Jonathan since they died. He and his brother were extremely close. Allison was expecting another child, which only makes it worse." Kathryn got tears in her eyes, and Melody reached over and patted her hand.

"It's all right, darling," Melody said as she gazed sympathetically at Kathryn, "I would say you're due for a good cry. I'm sure it was a terrible ordeal for all of you. My heart goes out to those sweet children. I'm sure they're devastated over the loss of their parents. I'm glad Jonathan is bringing the children with him today. It will be good for them to be around other children. Kathryn, are you sure you're not in love with Jonathan? You seem very close, and I can tell he cares a great deal about you. Don't you want to be in love?"

Kathryn hesitated, but then she said, "No, I don't. After what happened to me...I find the whole idea of intimacy repulsive. The only way I agreed to marry him was if it would be a marriage in name only."

"Darling, I know you had a horrible experience with your uncle, but physical love is actually quite wonderful when two people truly care for one another. When I'm with Henry, it's the most incredible feeling in the world. Sometimes it's so beautiful that it brings tears to my eyes. You already seem quite fond of him."

"I am fond of him, and I told Jonathan last night that it was all right to kiss me, and he did," Kathryn said, and then in embarrassment, she added, "It was quite pleasant, and I even kissed him back briefly, but then I became embarrassed and he left. I've decided that he needs to take a mistress since I can't be intimate with him. At least he'll have a good reason to take a mistress, not like some men of the ton who cheat on their wives for no reason at all."

"Kathryn, I think you need to think about this before you go telling him to take a mistress. What if you end up falling in love with him? Take my word for it. You would definitely not want him to have a mistress then."

Looking disquieted, Kathryn replied, "I'll need to think about this some more. I thought I had the answer with telling him he could have a mistress, but maybe you're right. I might be jealous if I thought he was spending too much time with another woman. I'm glad we talked today. You've definitely given me quite a bit to think about."

"Since you enjoyed his kiss…why don't you do this? When Jonathan kisses you, try kissing him back. You may find out that you'll like it, and if you enjoy his kisses, then you may like his touches also," Melody replied, then with a look of embarrassment, she continued, "I'm not talking about full…ah…intimacy, but just a little affectionate kissing and touching. How does that sound?"

"Well, I guess I could try that. I'm glad we talked today. I'll need to give more thought to this." They spent another thirty minutes letting the children play before taking them back to the nursery so they could get ready for luncheon.

Kathryn thought about Jonathan's kiss last night. It had been pleasant, and it hadn't been threatening. She had actually enjoyed it. If he could just kiss her like that, and nothing more, then she would like it. This touching business sounded frightening. Touching was what her uncle started with, and all of his touches were awful. No, kissing was all right, but no touching.

Jonathan arrived in plenty of time to be there when Helen arrived. He brought Elaine and the children as they had previously discussed. When Frankford and Jane met all the nieces and nephews, they got excited and immediately started playing with them. Elaine was enjoying all the children so she decided to stay with them.

When Jonathan and Kathryn left the nursery, he reached for her hand and raised it to his lips and kissed it. "How are you, today? I thought about what you said last night about affection, and I'm glad that you're receptive to it. I promise that if I ever touch you in any way that makes you uncomfortable, just tell me and I'll stop. I care about you very much, and I shall never hurt you. Would it be all right if I kissed your cheek?"

Kathryn breathlessly replied, "I would like that very much." He gently pulled her into his arms, kissed her pretty, soft cheek and Kathryn giggled. "That tickles."

Jonathan laughed as he gently hugged her close. "I want to hold your soft, delicate hand, nothing more, all right? You have such beautiful hands, by the way. It's one of the first things that I noticed about you."

Kathryn nodded her head and shyly looked down. As he put her hand in his, they walked down the stairs to join the rest of the family.

It felt comforting, holding Jonathan's hand. Kathryn decided that holding hands would be all right. When they reached the entry hall, the door opened, and Helen and her family were arriving. Kathryn dropped Jonathan's hand and ran across the room to hug Helen.

"I'm so glad that you've arrived! Come meet Jonathan. He's right over there. I know you're going to like him." Kathryn pulled her sister over to Jonathan and said, "Jonathan, this is my sister, Helen, Lady Collingswood." Then she turned to Helen and added, "Helen, this is Jonathan, the Marquess of Sutherland."

Jonathan bowed as he kissed Helen's hand. "Hello, Lady Collingswood. I'm pleased to meet you. Kathryn mentions you with fondness, and has told me you're very close. I understand you have a great love of horses. I also enjoy riding quite a bit. While you're in town, you'll have to come out to our home so we can go riding together."

Helen smiled exuberantly. "I do love to ride. It would be my pleasure to go riding with you. Now, none of this formal addressing, please call me Helen, and I'll call you Jonathan. Let me introduce you to my husband." She called over to Matthew. "Matthew, come here and meet Jonathan."

Matthew walked over and shook Jonathan's hand. "I'm pleased to meet you." Then with a grin, he said, "So you're the one who's captured our Kathryn. I'm amazed because she's insisted for as long as I've known her that she would never marry. Congratulations! Kathryn wrote us and told us about the loss of your brother and his wife. Please, accept our condolences. I can only imagine how difficult it would be to lose a brother."

"Thank you. I miss both of them tremendously. Please, call me Jonathan. I look forward to getting to know you," Jonathan replied, and looking fondly at Kathryn, he added, "I'm the most fortunate of men that Kathryn has agreed to marry me."

Helen looked over at her children and said, "Jonathan, meet my children. This is Christina and Catherine, and yes, they are identical. And these two rambunctious boys, who are also identical, are Winston and Nelson. I understand you have a niece and nephew. Are they here with you?"

"We just took them up to the nursery before you arrived. Frankford is six years old, and Jane is Five. We left them with the other children. They're loving every minute of their playtime."

Matthew laughed. "Well, I'm going to get mine up there too. That way they can join the pack. I'll see you at tea." Matthew and Helen gathered the children and went upstairs to the nursery.

As Jonathan watched them leave, he said, "Kathryn, I like your sister Helen and her husband. Let's go into the drawing room and join the others."

Jonathan placed her hand in his, and they went into the drawing room. Kathryn and Jonathan found a seat on the couch and sat down. He continued to hold her hand. Helen returned from the nursery and came over to talk with them. As they were talking, Matthew came over and started talking to Jonathan.

"Why don't we find somewhere so we can talk?" Matthew asked.

Jonathan nodded his head and said, "We can go to the library. I know where it is now, since I went there yesterday when I talked to Henry."

Jonathan led the way to the library, and when they entered, Matthew went to the cabinet and started to pour two brandies. Jonathan spoke up. "Thank you, but none for me."

Matthew looked over at him, raised his eyebrows and asked, "Do you dislike liquor?"

"Actually, I like it too much, so I've decided to stop drinking anything except wine at my meals. I was injured at Waterloo, and from that time on I began using liquor to deaden the pain, but it started causing a few problems for me," Jonathan explained.

Matthew took a seat. "The only time I've ever had a problem with liquor was when I went to my wedding. I was so nervous about marrying Helen that I drank too much. Once we were married, I calmed down and didn't have the need to drink excessively."

"Kathryn tells me you're from Devonshire. I've never been there, but I've heard about the moors. Do you live close to them?"

"We're about six miles from Dartmouth Moors. We live along the coast, and Collingswood Hall sits right next to the sea. Helen mentioned that you'll be coming for a visit with Kathryn the first part of November."

Jonathan shifted in his seat trying to find a comfortable position. "I hope that it's not inconvenient for me to visit at that time, but I would rather not be separated from her so soon after our marriage. Why were you so nervous about marrying Helen?"

"When I met Helen, I was only interested in finding a mother for my daughters. I asked her to marry me two weeks after we met, and then she went to Sanderford Park to get ready for the wedding. Once she left, I realized that we really didn't know each other, and I felt as if I was marrying a stranger and got cold feet. I knew I couldn't back out, so that's why I was so nervous."

"I can imagine that would be quite daunting. You appear to have a good relationship now though."

"Definitely. It didn't take me long to realize what a wise decision I made in marrying Helen. Once we arrived at my estate, we realized we had quite a bit in common, and I have grown to love her deeply. Now, tell me, how did you convince Kathryn to marry you?"

Jonathan explained about how he and Kathryn had met. Jonathan knew it would come out about them marrying in name only, so he decided to go ahead and tell Matthew. "She knew I needed help with the children, and as I said, we had become good friends. She agreed to a marriage in name only. I assured her that I understood she didn't want to be intimate. That's why she said she would marry me."

Matthew looked shocked. "You mean no sex at all? I guess you plan to keep a mistress then. I wouldn't let Sanderford know about this. He would be furious. I had a mistress when I first married Helen. When Sanderford found out about her, he was so enraged that he hit me, and I deserved it."

Jonathan looked him in the eye. "I have no plans to take a mistress. I've fallen in love with Kathryn and have no desire to be with another woman. I'm hoping she'll fall in love with me and change her mind, but even if she doesn't, I'm ruined when it comes to any other woman. All I can think about is Kathryn, and I could never betray her that way."

"I hope for both your sakes that she changes her mind. Has she told you what happened to her when she was sixteen? I'm sure that's why she wants a marriage in name only."

"She's told me a little about it, and Henry told me more and who it was. It's a good thing that bastard's already dead, because I would kill him if he weren't. Well, we had better get back to the others. I'm sure Kathryn is wondering where we went off to." By the time they returned to the drawing room, everyone was leaving for their rooms.

Jonathan escorted Kathryn to her room, gave her a quick kiss, and then squeezed her hand gently. "I'll see at dinner. I think I'll go rest my knee for a while."

By the time Jonathan got to his room, his knee was pulsing furiously with pain. He opened his valise and took out the laudanum that Hatton had packed for him. He found a pitcher of water on a table, poured a glass, and took it. As he gazed about the room, he noticed that someone had laid out his black superfine dress coat with the matching embroidered royal blue waistcoat. Since he had some time before he needed to dress, he sat down in the chair. As he rested his leg on the matching ottoman, he leaned his head back against the cushion and closed his eyes.

Jonathan was very encouraged with Kathryn's response to affection. He was amazed she had kissed him and felt it was promising. If he took it very slowly, he felt that eventually she would trust him enough that she would want to be intimate. Each day he spent with her, he grew to love her more. He thought about his conversation with Matthew, and he knew that he meant every word he had said to Matthew. He would rather have Kathryn in his life than a million other woman, even if they never made love. As he lay there thinking about Kathryn, he fell asleep.

It was seven o'clock when he woke up from his nap, so he had to rush or he would be late for dinner. Someone must have come to his room while he slept because he found steaming hot water available. He quickly washed up, gave himself a hurried shave, and then headed downstairs.

When Jonathan entered the drawing room, his eyes immediately found Kathryn. She looked so beautiful in her blue silk evening gown that he felt his heart skip a beat. Her fiery red hair, pulled back from her beautiful face with curls cascading down her shoulders, showed off her lovely countenance. She looked up, noticed him, and smiled.

Jonathan approached her and took her hand in his. "Darling, you look beautiful tonight. Did you rest after tea? I fell asleep and barely had time to dress and get here in time for dinner. Did you by chance stop by and see the children? I feel badly that I overslept and didn't get to see them. Where's Elaine, do you know?"

"I went to the nursery right before I came down, and the children are fine. Elaine should be down any minute. She's freshening up in my room, and my maid is arranging her hair for her. She wants to look more mature tonight since she's getting to dine with the adults." Looking toward the door, she saw Elaine enter the room. "Ah, here she comes now."

Elaine hurried over to them and said, "I hope I'm not too late. Thank you for letting me use your room Kathryn. I love what Sarah did with my hair."

Jonathan smiled. "Hello, Princess. Did you have an enjoyable afternoon? I feel as if I've neglected you, even though I certainly didn't mean to."

"That's all right, Jonathan. I loved playing with all the children. Mary Elizabeth and Angela are very sweet, and they have taken Jane under their wing. She's happier than I've seen her since Roderick and Allison died. I'm glad you were able to bring us. It's been good for all of us to get away."

"How's Frankford?" Jonathan asked. "Has he made friends with any of the other children? I think one of Melody's sons is close to his age."

Kathryn spoke up. "Brandon's the same age as Frankford. When I was there they were playing pirates, and he looked happier than I've seen him since his parents passed away. I agree with Elaine—I think it's good that they were able to come."

Abernathy came in and announced dinner, so Jonathan escorted Kathryn and Elaine to the dining room. Elaine sat next to Jonathan, and Matthew was on her left side. Matthew kept her amused by telling her stories about his sister Margaret. Jonathan found all of Kathryn's family warm and welcoming, and since he no longer had Roderick to talk to, it was pleasant to have other males to speak with about his thoughts on Kathryn.

Roderick would have been so pleased that he was marrying her. Both Henry and Matthew obviously loved their wives, and Helen and Melody clearly loved their husbands. He hoped that having them to talk to would help Kathryn deal with her fears about intimacy. Jonathan realized he had an uphill battle, trying to help Kathryn overcome her anxiety in regards to intimacy between a husband and wife.

It was a convivial group at dinner that night, which made for a pleasant evening. Jonathan knew Kathryn told him that the duchess treated Melody poorly, but she seemed to be as pleasant toward her as she was with everyone else. Once dinner was over, the duchess led the ladies into the drawing room and left the men to enjoy their port and cigars.

Over their port, Henry asked, "Jonathan, how long were you in the army? I spent almost seven years on active duty and then three years inactive when I had amnesia. That's why I don't remember meeting you. I recovered most of my memory, except for the weeks leading up to the battle, and then the month right after."

"My brother and I joined when Bonaparte escaped from Elba. My father was opposed to us going, but we threatened to enlist as foot soldiers, so he bought my brother and me our commissions. He thought we would be safer as officers. I had no idea how to lead men, but my colonel gave me good guidance."

Henry took a sip of his port, and then he asked, "How did we meet?"

Jonathan took a sip of his port, resisting the temptation to gulp it down, then answered Henry, "We met at all the balls and parties that the ton held in Brussels. When Wellington received the dispatch from the Prince of Orange, he sent most of his officers to Quatre Bras to defend it against Marshall Ney. You and I were among the ones he sent. I lost track of you after that. I received my injury during the final battle. I don't regret going, and if I had it to do over, even knowing that I would be injured, I still would have gone."

With a look of frustration on his face, Henry said, "I wish I could remember the battle, but that whole month is a blank for me. Did you know my friend Hayden as well?"

"Yes, but I didn't know either of you well. I was so young, and I was a little intimidated by you and your fellow officers because you were seasoned, and I was so green."

"I loved being a soldier, but when I married Melody, I knew I didn't want her to have to follow the drum, so I was getting ready to sell my commission when we received the dispatch that Bonaparte had escaped." Henry looked over at

Matthew and said, "I'm sorry Collingswood, this is probably boring for you."

"I actually find this all fascinating," Matthew said. "I wanted to go badly, but my father refused to buy me a commission. I don't have any cousins, and my younger brother was always getting into trouble even as a young boy, so I bowed to my father's wishes. I had my daughters to think about as well."

Jonathan asked, "You must have married very young. Aren't you about the same age as I am? I'm thirty."

"My first marriage was arranged when I was one and twenty. My father thought marriage would have a calming influence on me, but the reverse happened. I hated him for forcing me to marry so young and continued in my wild ways. I was a terrible husband to my first wife." Matthew leaned back in his chair and inhaled his cigar. "I'm an excellent husband now, and I would never do anything to hurt my wife."

"I know I certainly wasn't ready for marriage at that age, so I can understand why you resented being forced to marry." Jonathan inhaled deeply, letting the smoke fill his lungs as he relaxed in his chair. While he now had to watch what he drank, he could still enjoy a good cigar.

Henry stood up. "As interesting as this all is, we need to join the ladies. I'm sure they're wondering what we could be doing for this long."

They found the ladies in the drawing room having tea. Kathryn was talking to Mary, so Jonathan went over to join her. "Hello, ladies. We let the time get away from us while we were enjoying our port. Henry and I were talking about the army and Waterloo."

"That's all right," Kathryn said. "I'm pleased that you had so much to talk about. Mary and I have been talking about the orphanage that we both volunteer at in London. She's a member of the board of trustees now. She's one of only two women on the board."

Jonathan smile over at Mary. "I'm sure you're an asset to that board. It's very generous of you to devote your time to the orphanage. Kathryn told me that you're very involved and have been for quite some time. I admire you for it."

"Thank you, Jonathan," Mary replied. "When I lost my husband, I lost all interest in life and was very melancholy. Melody helped me deal with my grief, and working with the children helped me move past it. I'll never forget my husband, but I know he would want me to be happy. I have been blessed with two wonderful children, and Melody, Helen, and Kathryn are as dear to me as any blood sisters could be."

"I'm glad that they helped you overcome your grief. I'm dealing with that myself since I lost my brother." Glancing over at Kathryn, Jonathan said, "I would be lost without Kathryn. I'm a fortunate man to have her in my life. The grief can be crippling some days, and she helps to ease it for me."

Mary rose. "Well, if you'll excuse me, I'm going up to check on my children. I just want to say that I'm thrilled for both of you, and I hope you'll be as happy in your marriage as I was in mine." She turned to Kathryn and added, "Kathryn, I'll see you in the morning. Have a pleasant evening."

Jonathan turned to Kathryn and asked, "Where's Elaine? Has she gone upstairs? I need to get her and the children. We need to go ahead and leave since we have an hour's drive ahead of us."

"No, she had to step out of the room for a moment. I'm sure she will be back soon. Why don't we go upstairs and get Frankford and Jane? She'll be back here by the time we bring the children down."

"All right." The children had fallen asleep, so Jonathan and Kathryn carried them down to the carriage. Elaine met them on their way down. Once they had the children in the carriage, Jonathan turned to Kathryn, pulled her close, and gave her a gentle kiss on her forehead. "Good night, my dear. I'll see you at the church on Saturday. I'm so grateful you're going to be my wife. Tell your family good night for me." Then he entered the carriage and signaled to the driver.

Chapter 14

- Twenty-four Hours Before the Wedding -

When Kathryn went back into the house, she returned to the drawing room, told everyone that she was retiring and that she would see them in the morning. As Sarah helped her get ready for bed, she thought about Jonathan. He treated her as if she was a fragile piece of glass, and it made her feel very special. He was such a gentle and kind man, she was so grateful she had agreed to marry him. She realized she wanted to be his wife. It was comforting to imagine growing old with him.

Kathryn imagined he would be a sensitive lover, but then she remembered all the pain and humiliation that she went through with her uncle. Kathryn hated her uncle even more than she had before, knowing he'd ruined any chance she had to have a complete loving marriage. If it weren't for him, she realized she would gladly give herself to Jonathan. The tears started rolling down her cheeks at all she had lost because of that depraved man.

Someone knocked on her door, and she asked, "Who is it?"

The voice at the door replied, "Kathryn, it's me, Helen."

"Oh, come in."

When Helen saw her crying, she ran over to her and asked, "Kathryn, what's wrong? Why are you crying? Did Jonathan do anything to hurt you? If he has hurt you, I'll go get Henry, and he'll take care of him for you."

Kathryn shook her head. "No…No…Jonathan is wonderful. That's the problem. He deserves to have a wife that will be his in all ways. Not someone who can never be a true wife to him."

"What do mean a true wife? What haven't you told me? Why can't you be the wife he needs?"

In a halting voice, Kathryn replied, "It's because of our uncle that I can't be his wife in truth. Every time I think about being with a man, I remember what he did to me, and then the thought of being intimate repulses me."

"Oh Kathryn, don't let him ruin this chance at love. I was so pleased when you wrote me and told me about your engagement. I can tell that you both care about each other tremendously."

"Jonathan is the most gentle and kindest man I've ever known. It's not fair to him that I promised to marry him. I can't expect him to live his life without intimacy. I think I need to call off the wedding, but I don't want to. He needs me…to help him with the children, and he says that if I don't marry him, he won't marry anyone else, and then the children won't…have…a mother. Oh Helen, what am I going to do?" By this time she was sobbing, she was so upset.

Helen put her arms around Kathryn. "Honey, does Jonathan know how you feel about…intimacy?"

"Yes...he knows. We're to be married in name only. That's the only way that I would agree to marry him. Oh, it's so unfair to him!"

"It's his decision to make, and if he's willing to marry you in name only, then I think you should let him. I watched him with you today, and it's obvious that he cares deeply for you. You never know, after you're married and you see how kind and gentle he continues to be, you may change your mind. Kathryn, I need to ask you something," Helen hesitated, and then asked, "I know that Melody and Henry stopped Uncle Theodore from raping you, but had he done something to you before that incident?"

It all came spilling out as Kathryn sobbed, "I...I...Yes...he had! He raped me when I...I was twelve years old!"

"Oh my Lord! Does Henry know?"

"No...No...you can't tell him! I've never told anyone, ever. Please promise me you won't tell Henry. I couldn't stand for him to know."

"Shush...it's all right. I won't tell him, I promise. Oh honey, I'm so sorry you had to go through that alone. If that old rogue wasn't already dead, I would go kill him myself for hurting you like that! Did you ever try to tell Mother or Father?"

"You know Mother would never have believed me. She has never acknowledged what he tried to do when Henry and Melody stopped him that time." Kathryn continued to weep as she hung her head in despair.

Biting her lip nervously, Helen said, "Kathryn, you need to tell Jonathan. He needs to know how strongly you feel about intimacy. It's the only fair thing to do. Matthew and I will take you out to his house tomorrow morning." As Kathryn started to interrupt, she said, "No, I won't tell him why you need to go see him. We'll just say you need to ask him something about the wedding."

"I know you're right, but what if he wants to call off the wedding?" she said, as she covered her face with her hands. "Mother will be livid. I really do want to marry him. He's the best friend I've ever had!"

"He's agreed to a marriage in name only so he may still be willing to marry you, but he needs to know everything Kathryn." Helen helped Kathryn get into bed, kissed her on the cheek, and said, "I have a good feeling about Jonathan. I think that he'll still want to marry you, but in case he's thinking you're going to change your mind about intimacy, he needs to know that if you ever do decide to be intimate, it's not going to be any time soon. Has he ever kissed you?"

"Yes, and he was so tender. It was quite pleasant. I told him I wanted his affection...just not the other part." Kathryn leaned back against her pillows and sighed deeply.

Helen smiled reassuringly. "Well, you need to get some sleep. I'm sure everything will work out in the morning. Matthew and I will take you out there early before Mother even knows you're gone. We'll say that Jonathan asked Matthew and I out to go riding, and that won't even be a lie, because he did ask. He just didn't say when. I'll come and wake you at seven o'clock. We'll be at his house by nine o'clock, and then you can tell him everything."

"Thank you, Helen. I feel so much better now that I've finally told someone what Uncle Theodore really did." She yawned and added, "I'll see you in the morning."

Helen patted her on the hand, kissed her cheek, and left.

As Helen made her way to her room, she thought about what Kathryn told her, and she felt rage in a way she'd never felt before. To think about what that licentious, old rogue did to an innocent child sent shivers down her spine.

How could someone be that depraved?

If Uncle Theodore wasn't already dead, she would shoot him herself!

As she entered the room, Matthew looked at her and asked, "What's upset you so much? I can see by your expression, you're furious. Was Kathryn all right? Tell me what's wrong?" Pulling her into his arms, Matthew said, "Whatever it is, we'll deal with it together."

"Oh Matthew, it's Kathryn. You have to promise me you'll never let her know I told you. I promised I wouldn't tell Henry, but she didn't make me promise not to tell you. Promise me." Helen looked up at him with tears in her eyes.

Matthew pulled her into his arms. "Darling, of course I promise. Now what in the world is wrong? What did Kathryn tell you?"

"Remember when I told you that Uncle Theodore almost raped her, but that Henry and Melody stopped him before he could finish? Well, it turns out he'd already raped her numerous times before that night." Helen buried her head into his chest as she sobbed. "She...She was only...twelve, the first time he raped her. Oh Matthew, how could he have done something like that to an innocent child?"

"Darling, I can't answer that for you. There are quite a few sick, lecherous, old rakes in this world, and it's sickening to think that one of them did this to Kathryn. Now I understand why she wants a marriage in name only."

"How do you know about that? I just found out myself tonight. How did you find out?"

Matthew hugged her close. "Jonathan told me this afternoon when we were talking. He says that he's accepted it, and that he loves her anyway. He told me he knows that her uncle hurt her, but I don't think he knows to what extent. I believe he thinks that if Kathryn falls in love with him, she'll change her mind."

"I don't know that she can change her mind. She says that every time she thinks about being intimate with a man she remembers what Uncle Theodore did to her, and then she feels repulsed. Oh, this is so terrible. She doesn't know it yet, but I think she's already in love with him. I told her she should tell him everything that happened to her. He needs to know the full extent of her feelings about intimacy and why she feels that way. Do you think I did the right thing in telling her that?"

"I agree that Jonathan needs to know, but I think he'll still want to marry her. He told me he would rather have Kathryn as his wife than not, even if they never become intimate, because she's ruined him for any other woman. I asked him if he would be taking a mistress, and he told me that he would never betray her like that, even if they never truly become husband and wife. I think he's deeply in love with her."

Helen snuggled against Matthew. "That makes me feel better. I told her we would take her out to see him first thing in the morning. Now, you can't let her know you know why we're going out there. She'd be mortified if she knew I'd told you about any of this."

"What excuse are we going to use? Everyone is bound to ask questions. I'm sure there must be millions of things that she's supposed to be doing tomorrow morning to get ready for the wedding on Saturday."

"We're going to leave at eight o'clock in the morning, before Mother gets up. She never gets up until at least ten in the morning. We could even be back by eleven, and then Mother wouldn't even miss her," Helen said, laying her head on Mathew's broad shoulder. "Just in case she does, I'm going to leave her a note saying that Jonathan asked us to come out and go riding with him, and that Kathryn wanted to come too."

"All right. That just gives your mother something else to be angry at us for. She's actually been decent since we arrived. Do you think she's mellowing in her old age?"

"Don't let her hear you refer to her as old, or she won't like you anymore. Since we need to be up early in the morning, we need to go to sleep." Helen yawned and closed her eyes.

"You mean I can't interest you in a little love play before we go to sleep? Just think how much better you'll sleep if you're all relaxed and satisfied. Come here and let me kiss you, wife!" Matthew gave her a bruising kiss as he hastily unbuttoned her gown. Before Helen could catch her breath, she was naked and writhing as Matthew kissed her hot, deep, and long, setting off an explosion as ecstasy took her away on a hot wave of delight.

After Helen left her room, Kathryn cried herself to sleep. Once she was asleep, her dreams had her tossing and turning as the nightmare started. She dreamed of all the vile things her uncle used to do to her. She woke up gasping for breath from her vivid nightmare. Her body was dripping with sweat, and she was shivering all over. Tears were pouring down her face.

At least she had woken up in her own bed and not wandering the halls as she did as a child.

Kathryn glanced over at the ormolu clock on the mantle, and it was only three o'clock in the morning. The dream was so realistic, that for the first time in years, she craved the oblivion laudanum would give. This frightened her because she never wanted to be addicted to laudanum again. Thank goodness, there wasn't any available. There was a pitcher of water on the dresser, so she got out of bed, went over to it, and poured herself a glass. As she poured the water into the glass, she noticed her hands were trembling.

As she slowly sipped her water, Kathryn's heartbeat slowed down, and she climbed back into bed. She was fearful of falling back to sleep and having another nightmare, so she lay there fighting sleep, but eventually she drifted off. She started dreaming again, but this time she dreamed of Jonathan kissing her with incredible tenderness. In her dream, she told him she wasn't a virgin, that her uncle had raped her when she was twelve years old. He told her he could never marry someone who wasn't a virgin, and she again woke up crying.

Soon she heard the clock striking five, so she got up and got another drink, but this time she didn't get back in bed. She sat in a straight-back chair to keep from falling back to sleep. At seven o'clock, Sarah came in with steaming hot water, so she washed and let Sarah fix her hair, and then got dressed. Sarah brought her breakfast, but she didn't eat anything. She was too nervous about telling Jonathan of her rape. As she waited for Helen, she stared out the window at the dreary day. The day fit her mood perfectly.

When Helen entered her room, she said, "Oh dear, you didn't sleep well, did you? Are you ready to go to Jonathan's?

Matthew's already outside waiting beside the carriage. If you've changed your mind, I will understand why."

"Helen, I have to go see him. It's the only right thing to do. I dreamed I told him about what happened, and that I wasn't a virgin…he said…he could never marry a woman who wasn't a virgin. I'm going to be devastated if he decides he can't marry me. Mother will be furious with me if he calls off the wedding."

Helen hugged her. "Honey, I'm sure that's not going to happen. He's going to understand that it wasn't your fault that Uncle Theodore raped you. If it has you this upset, maybe I was wrong, and you don't need to tell him."

"No, you were right, Jonathan has to be told, and if he can't marry me, then it may be for the best. He deserves to marry someone who can be a true wife to him, not someone like me who has so many problems, and wants a marriage in name only. Let's go get this over with." They went downstairs and joined Matthew in the carriage.

Matthew and Helen kept the conversation lively, but the closer they got to his house the more frightened Kathryn became. Before she was ready, they were pulling up onto the drive that led to the house. As the house came into view, Kathryn felt a crushing weight on her chest, knowing what she had to tell Jonathan.

Goodman came out to greet her. "Good morning, Lady Kathryn. Lord Sutherland is in his study with his steward. Please, let me show you to the drawing room, and I'll let him know that you are here."

Kathryn was too nervous to sit, so she went and stood by the window, looking out at the light drizzle as she waited for Jonathan.

Why was she so upset at the thought of not marrying Jonathan? He'd had to do some serious convincing to get her to even agree.

She knew she would miss him horribly if he wasn't in her life anymore.

As Jonathan came into the room, he said, "Darling, it's wonderful to see you. What a pleasant surprise." He looked over at Helen and Matthew. "Welcome to my home."

Kathryn turned around with soul-wrenching sadness in her eyes. "Jonathan, I need to talk to you about something very important. Is there somewhere we can go so we can speak privately?"

"Of course, my dear. We'll go to the library." He turned to Goodman and said, "Please bring some refreshments for Lord and Lady Collingswood." Jonathan smiled at Helen and Matthew. "Kathryn and I will join you shortly. Please make yourselves at home."

Jonathan placed Kathryn's hand in the crook of his arm, patted her hand, and led her out of the room. When they entered the library he said, "My dear, you look so distraught. What's wrong? I can tell you have something serious you want to discuss. What is it, sweetheart?"

"Oh, this is so difficult. I...need to tell you about something that happened to me. I...I...don't know where to start!" Kathryn began to cry softly.

"Dearest, please don't cry. Let's sit here on the sofa, and you can tell me all about it." Once they sat down, he put his arm around her, pulled her close, and wiped a tear off her cheek.

Kathryn buried her head into his shoulder and sobbed, "I'm...not a...virgin."

"Shush, sweetheart. It's all right...neither am I. Now, just tell me what's troubling you." Smoothing her hair, he kissed her head and rubbed her shoulder.

"When I was a very young child my uncle...he started touching me...I tried to hide from him, but he always managed to find me, and when I was twelve...he...he...raped me!"

"Oh, my poor darling, you were a defenseless child! If you hadn't already told me he was dead, I would be hunting him down and killing him for doing this to you. I already suspected that something like this had happened to you. That's why you're so afraid of intimacy, isn't it?"

"Yes, I know I can't ever be a true wife to you because the very thought of intimacy repulses me. You deserve a woman who can truly be a wife to you. I'll understand if you don't want to marry me." She raised her head and looked at Jonathan. "In fact, I'm releasing you from your obligation to marry me. I'm sure you can find someone else that will help you raise the children. If we marry, then someday you may resent me, and I couldn't bare it if you grew to hate me."

Pulling Kathryn onto his lap, Jonathan said, "Sweetheart, I would never resent you or hate you. I don't want to be released. You're not to blame for what happened to you. Even if you never move beyond your fear of intimacy, I still want to marry you. I told you I never planned to marry. We're doing this for the children, and you'll be a wonderful mother to them. We already agreed we would have a marriage in name only. What happened to you doesn't change the reason we decided to marry."

"It's so unfair to you. You're the kindest man I've ever known. I just want to do what's right for you." Kathryn looked at him through tear-drenched lashes.

He pulled her against him. "I want you to stop worrying about me. I'll be fine. We'll have our friendship, and that means the world to me."

Kathryn interrupted. "But Jonathan, I know that men have certain urges, and I can never fulfill those for you. If you still want to marry me, then I'll marry you, but please feel free to keep a mistress. I know it's the way of the ton. Many husbands keep mistresses, and I promise I'll understand if you need one."

"Darling, I have no need to have a mistress. I would rather spend the rest of my life chaste than not have you in my life. I promise I'll be fine with just your affection. You've been sitting here on my lap for quite some time, and I don't think you found it repulsive." Jonathan gently stroked her shoulders, and Kathryn was shocked to realize she had never felt so safe in her life. "Now, I want you to stop worrying. Go home and get ready for our wedding. You're going to be a beautiful bride—the only bride that I want. Will you do that for me?"

"Oh Jonathan, you're such a wonderful man. I promise I'll be a good wife and a good mother to your niece and nephew. I already love Frankford and Jane very much. Just remember, if you ever do decide you want a mistress, I'll understand." She smiled up at him and snuggled close.

"All right. If I ever do feel that I need one, I'll take care of it, but that isn't going to happen. I'm an adult and have complete control of my urges, so I know I won't need a mistress. Now, let's go join Matthew and Helen." He pulled her close, kissed her tenderly on the cheek, and helped her up.

When they returned to the drawing room, they sat and talked with Matthew and Helen. Shortly after, the three of them left.

On the drive back, Kathryn thought about what Jonathan had said and knew he was going to be a wonderful husband. She still thought it was unfair to him, but at least he knew that if he ever did take a mistress, she would understand why.

Friday afternoon, Stebbins arrived with the unfinished portrait of Roderick and his family. Jonathan had the portrait carried up to the studio he had prepared for Kathryn. Once the footman placed it on the easel, he dismissed him. Jonathan gazed at the portrait and found it hard to swallow. Tears filled his eyes, and he fought to keep them from falling.

Oh God, why did life have to be so unfair?

Roderick and Allison had been so vibrant and in love with each other. Kathryn already had Roderick's face painted, and she had captured his zest for life in his brilliant blue eyes that were so like his own. Jonathan prayed he would be able to raise Frankford and Jane to be the kind of adults that Roderick and Allison would have wanted them to be. He felt that he could, with Kathryn's love and support.

He thought back over the conversation with Kathryn that morning.

Thank God, he'd been able to convince her to go ahead with the wedding.

His heart had stopped for a moment when she told him she released him from what she saw as his obligation to marry her. Her beautiful face had been so expressive, and the sadness in her eyes had torn at his soul.

How could anyone be so licentious with an innocent child?

No wonder Kathryn was repulsed by the thought of making love. The bastard had robbed her of something that should have been her gift to give. Obviously, Kathryn had not told Henry about the rape and abuse, or he would have been dead four years ago.

Jonathan realized he would have the battle of his life trying to help her overcome her fear of intimacy. His desire for Kathryn was intense, but he would have to step very carefully so that he didn't scare her. He had to cling to the hope that as she grew closer to him she would be able to let go of her fear. Whether she did or not, he knew he would love her forever. As he turned away from the portrait, he noticed the time. Jenkins should be arriving shortly, so he left the studio and returned to his study.

No sooner had Jonathan sat down in his chair, than Goodman knocked and told him that Jenkins had arrived. "Good. Please show him in, Goodman."

When Jenkins entered the study, Jonathan said, "Sorry, old friend, my knee is bothering me today or I would get up. I'm pleased you're able to attend my wedding. How was the trip over?"

"The trip wasn't bad for this time of year. When I received your letter about your marriage, I was astonished. The last time we talked, you swore you would never marry. What changed your mind?"

After taking a sip of water, Jonathan told him how he and Kathryn had met. "While Kathryn was painting my portrait, we became very good friends. She's very easy to talk to, and we have quite a bit in common. After she finished my portrait, we traveled to Westland Acres so she could do Roderick's family portrait. She was with me when Roderick and Allison drowned, and she was invaluable when it came to the children. I don't know how I would have made it through, if she hadn't been there. Since I knew I couldn't raise the children on my own, I asked her, and she said yes."

Jenkins raised his eyebrow. "Jonathan, I'm so sorry about Roderick and Allison. I know how close you were to him, and of course I'll miss him myself. We had some good times together, didn't we? It's so hard to imagine they're gone. Sutherland, Lady Kathryn is a confirmed spinster. It's a well-known fact that she never wanted to marry. She's turned down numerous proposals over the last few years. She's extraordinarily beautiful and well liked by everyone, so how did you get her to change her mind about marriage?"

Jonathan grimaced as a pain shot through his knee. He tried to get in a more comfortable position and answered, "She's doing it for the children. She grew quite fond of them while she was at Westland Acres, and she knew they needed a mother. I offered friendship with no strings attached, and I convinced her I wouldn't interfere with her art. That had been her main objection to marriage."

"What do you mean 'no strings attached'?"

Jonathan hesitated, but then he answered, "We've been friends for a long time, so what I'm about to tell you must be kept in strictest confidence. We're going to have a marriage in name only."

"Why in God's name would you agree to that? Well, I guess you'll have to find a new mistress when you get back to town. Maybe this isn't a bad arrangement after all. You get a mother for the children, and you get to continue your life as if you were still single."

Jonathan looked him directly in the eye. "I shan't be taking any more mistresses, nor will I continue to live my life as if I wasn't married. I could never betray Kathryn that way. Jenkins, I've fallen in love with her, and I would rather have her in my life without sex than not at all."

"Well, you're a stronger man than I am. My mother is after me again to get married, so next spring I'll be looking for a wife. But it won't be in name only, I'll tell you that." Jenkins looked at him with pity in his eyes. Jonathan wished he had just kept his mouth shut, but he really did need to talk about this with someone, and he and Jenkins had been friends for years.

"I do not need, nor do I want, your pity! I just hope you can meet someone as kind and generous as Kathryn."

"Sutherland, we've been friends for a long time. I just hope for your sake you don't live to regret this marriage. You're only thirty, and you could live for a long time. I can't see you, of all people, being celibate for the rest of your life."

Jonathan looked at him. "If you had told me two months ago that I would feel like this, I wouldn't have believed it, but my love for Kathryn supersedes all else. I hope that as she gets to know me better, she'll fall in love with me and change her mind about intimacy. It's a risk I'm willing to take. Please, just wish me well. As far as you and marriage go, try to find someone you can love. If you can't find love, at least find someone that you admire and respect."

Jenkins smiled, and then he said, "She's really changed you, Sutherland. All right, I wish you well, and I'll consider your advice about admiration and respect. Maybe I can fall in love. If you can, anybody can."

Jonathan clapped Jenkins on the shoulder and said, "Now, why don't we go out and look at my new colt? He was just born a few days ago." They left the study and made their way out to his stables. They spent the rest of the afternoon joking about the good old days.

Chapter 15
- October 1823 -

Madame Bovary was already at her mother's house with her wedding gown, waiting to do the final fitting so that it would be perfect for her wedding, when Kathryn returned from Jonathan's. Kathryn's mother was furious at her for leaving the house that morning, but when Madame Bovary assured them that she wasn't upset, her mother calmed down. The rest of the afternoon passed quickly. Cousin Harold arrived with his family, along with several other family members. They were all staying at the White Hart Inn across from the assembly rooms.

At tea, Melody came over and asked, "Honey, are you all right? Why did you go see Jonathan this morning? You're not having second thoughts are you?"

"I just feel that my insistence that the marriage be in name only isn't fair to Jonathan, since I know that I'll never be a true wife to him, but he still wants to marry me. I saw Jonathan so I could tell him I wanted him to take a mistress, but he said he didn't need one. I did finally get him to promise that he would take one if later he decided he needed one after all."

"Kathryn, you just need to relax. Jonathan is a wonderful man, and if he wants to marry you, knowing how you feel, then you just need to let him. I have a very good feeling about this. I believe you're going to find that you'll love being married to Jonathan."

"I'm sure you're right. I admire and respect him tremendously, and we do have quite a bit in common. Since I had a restless night, I'm going upstairs to take a short nap before I get ready for dinner. I'll see you then." Kathryn went upstairs and fell asleep as soon as her head hit her pillow. Sally woke her up in time to get ready for dinner.

Dinner was an elaborate affair. The duchess loved to entertain, so she was in her glory. Kathryn enjoyed seeing the rest of the family and was pleased that so many of them had come for the wedding. She had received a note from Susan, Lady Hastings, and she and her husband were coming. Kathryn had become good friends with Susan while they volunteered at the orphanage together.

When Kathryn went up to her room, she was much more relaxed than she had been the night before. Sarah helped her get ready for bed, and then Kathryn sent her away. As she lay there beginning to get drowsy, she remembered how safe she felt when she was with Jonathan. When he held her in his arms, she didn't find it frightening in the least. It must be because she trusted him to keep his word.

She was now at peace over marrying him. She would make sure that he didn't regret their marriage. She would be the best mother possible to Frankford and Jane, and she would take good care of Jonathan's household. As she fell asleep, she had a peaceful smile on her beautiful face.

The wedding was set for eleven o'clock, and Sarah woke her up at eight. She'd slept much better than the night before and felt well rested. Sarah brought her breakfast, and after she had eaten, Sarah had her bath ready. Soon it was time to put on her wedding gown. Helen and Melody came to her room to wait with her until it was time to leave for the Abbey.

Melody gave Kathryn a hug. "Darling, you look radiant. I can see it in your eyes—you're simply glowing with happiness."

"I do feel happy. Thank you for listening to me." Then looking at Helen, she said, "And you too, Helen. I wouldn't have made it through to this day without your love and support."

Smiling, Helen replied, "That's what sisters are for. Now, shall we go downstairs? It's almost eleven o'clock." Arm in arm, the three of them made their way down the stairs.

When Kathryn stepped down from the steps, Henry was waiting for them.

Giving Kathryn a brotherly hug, Henry said, "Sweetheart, you make a beautiful bride. Are you ready to go to the church and get married?"

With her eyes glowing she said, "Yes, I'm ready."

When Kathryn arrived at the church, the abbey was full of all the guests that Kathryn's mother had invited to the wedding. It looked as if all three hundred people had decided to attend. This was a bit overwhelming to Kathryn, but she knew it pleased her mother. She looked around the lovely church. White lilies and roses covered the altar. Purple tulle and white satin bows adorned the end of each pew. Hundreds of beeswax candles were lit, casting a glow over the entire church.

As the music filled the abbey, she placed her trembling white hand in the crook of Henry's arm. He covered it and gave her hand a gentle pat as they started down the aisle. Her knees were shaking, and her hands trembled as she clasped her bouquet. She looked up, and Jonathan was standing in front of the altar in all his wedding finery. He looked amazingly handsome. His piercing blue eyes shone with affection and compassion. Melody, Helen, and Elaine were smiling at her, looking incredibly beautiful in their deep purple gowns.

When Kathryn and Henry reached the altar, the vicar asked, "Who gives this woman in holy matrimony?" Henry looked down at her, his love for her shining in his eyes as he said, "I do." Then he placed her hand in Jonathan's, and they moved forward in front of the vicar, and the mass began.

Jonathan repeated his vows. "I, Jonathan Frankford Courtland, take thee, Kathryn Eleanor, to my wedded wife. To have and to hold from this day forward, for better for worse, for richer for poorer, in sickness and in health, to love and to cherish, till death us do part. According to God's holy ordinance, and there to I plight thee my troth." Jonathan's voice was strong and clear as he smiled into Kathryn's gorgeous violet eyes.

Then it was Kathryn's turn to repeat her vows, and she did so in a quiet, but steady voice. "I, Kathryn Eleanor, take thee Jonathan Frankford Courtland, to my wedded husband. To have and to hold from this day forward, for better for worse, for richer for poorer, in sickness and in health, to love and to cherish, and to obey, till death us do part. According to God's holy ordinance, and there to I plight thee my troth."

As Jonathan slid the ring on her finger, Kathryn felt a sense of peace wash over her, greater than she had ever felt before, and she knew in her heart that she had made the right decision in marrying Jonathan. Meeting Jonathan's gaze, she heard the vicar say, "You may kiss your bride."

Jonathan lifted her tulle veil, then lowered his head, pulled her close, and tenderly kissed her on the lips. Kathryn felt a thrill run through her. There was no fear or apprehension when Kathryn felt Jonathan's lips on hers. He lifted his lips from hers and smiled as he tucked her hand in the crook of his arm. Then they made their way back down the aisle to the vestry where they signed the registry book. They were now husband and wife at last.

Kathryn and Jonathan made their way outside and to the awaiting carriage. Rice and rose petals rained down on them from both sides of the walkway. Once they sat down in the carriage, Jonathan pulled her into his arms and started kissing her—light, feathery kisses on her eyes, cheeks, and lips. As he eased back, he said, "Thank you for becoming my wife. This is the happiest moment of my life. After all the sorrow and pain of losing Roderick and Allison, it's wonderful to feel this much joy again. Please tell me that you're happy, darling?"

Kathryn smiled serenely. "Yes, Jonathan. I'm overjoyed that you're my husband. I'm going to be a good wife to you, and a good mother to Frankford and Jane."

Jonathan cradled her in his arms all the way to the assembly rooms, and she felt very safe and cared for. By the time they entered the rooms, most of their guests had arrived.

They had taken the long route to give the guests time to arrive before they did.

The assembly rooms looked gorgeous. Each white linen-covered table had a candelabrum in the center, with baby's breath and purple ribbons interwoven around the base. Kathryn thought everything looked lovely. It didn't surprise her in the least, since she knew anything her mother planned would be magnificent. They made their way through the well-wishers to the head table, where they took their seats. Jonathan held her hand the entire time, and Kathryn enjoyed the closeness.

Lord Shelton made his toast to their happiness, and then Henry stood up to make his toast. "To my sister, Kathryn, and her new husband, I wish you a life filled with love and happiness. Please remember that I'll always love you, sweetheart, as you and Jonathan go forth into your new life." Tears shimmered in her eyes when she saw the love glowing in Henry's eyes. Then Jonathan's friend, Baron Jenkins, followed with his toast, wishing them many years of joy and happiness.

As Kathryn and Jonathan sat at the head table, she kept looking down at her gorgeous amethyst and diamond ring. It was the most beautiful ring she had ever seen. Jonathan looked into her eyes and said, "Darling, do you like the ring? I picked it out because it reminded me of your beautiful violet eyes."

She gazed into his eyes. "I love it. I've always loved amethysts, and I couldn't ask for a more beautiful ring."

"I promise I'll make you happy. I'll always protect you and keep you safe. You'll never have any reason to regret marrying me. I've reserved the bridal suite at the White Hart

Inn because I want tonight to be special." She stared at him and started to say something, but then Jonathan touched her lips with his finger and continued, "Don't worry, I'll keep my promise. We can still enjoy the luxury of their opulent suite and spend the evening relaxing with each other."

"I know that I can trust you to keep your word. That's one of the things that I most admire about you. I feel very safe when I'm with you, safer than I have ever felt before. I wanted to ask you if you have been able to get the portrait from Westland Acres."

He stroked her hand. "Stebbins arrived yesterday, and he brought it with him. I had it placed on your new easel in your studio. You've caught Roderick's keen love of life in his eyes. I'm so pleased that you'll be able to finish it."

"There's still quite a bit more that I plan to do before it will be complete. I want it to be my best work. This will be the last portrait of them, and it will stand as a lasting memorial for their children. I'm also going to paint a miniature for each of the children so that they won't forget them," Kathryn explained, while feeling Jonathan's hand gently stroking hers.

"Can you paint one for me?"

"Of course, I'll be happy to." As Kathryn gazed around the room she said, "I think we need to mingle with our guests."

They walked hand in hand around the room talking to their guests. Kathryn introduced Jonathan to Cousin Harold, his family, and all the other family members. They came upon Susan and her husband, Lord Hastings, and stopped to talk.

Susan smiled as she gave Kathryn a hug. "Kathryn, you're a beautiful bride. Thank you for asking me to your wedding. I was so pleased when I received your invitation."

"I'm happy you were able to come. This is my husband, the Marquess of Sutherland." She turned to Jonathan and said, "Jonathan, this is Viscount and Viscountess Hastings. Remember I told you that I volunteer with her at the orphanage in London?"

Jonathan bowed. "It's a pleasure to meet you. Kathryn has mentioned you several times."

Susan curtsied. "I've looked forward to meeting you ever since I received your invitation. You must be a very special person, because Kathryn has always vowed to never marry." Then she turned to Kathryn, "I wish both of you much happiness. I'm so pleased you have found Lord Sutherland to share your life with."

"Thank you, Susan. I'm already deliriously happy. I know you had to travel a significant distance to be here. Have you fully recovered from your recent blessed event? I was thrilled for you, when I heard you had a girl."

"Yes, I'm feeling marvelous, and I have the most precious daughter, Laura. My boys are a little put out that I've given them a sister, but they're already starting to warm up to her. Are you still going to pursue your art, now that you have married?"

Kathryn nodded. "I certainly am. In fact, that's how Jonathan and I met. He commissioned me to do his formal portrait. I also did his brother's family before they died. I still have some final touches to do on their portrait, but fortunately it was near completion when they died."

Susan turned to Jonathan. "My lord, I was so sorry to hear of your loss. We met your brother and his wife several times when they were in London for the season. It's such a tragedy to lose both of them at the same time. I understand that they had children. I'm sure they're having a difficult time dealing with their parents' death."

"Yes, it has been difficult, but knowing that Kathryn is going to be by my side as I raise them helps tremendously. The children are already quite fond of her." Jonathan gazed over at Kathryn and smiled. "Isn't that right Kathryn?"

"Yes, and I'm quite fond of them." Then, recalling Mary's news, Kathryn said, "Susan, I understand that congratulations are in order. Mary told me that you have joined her on the board of trustees at St. Mark's Orphanage. I'm sure you'll do a wonderful job."

"Thank you, Kathryn. I'm looking forward to helping the children. Since you're still going to paint, we would like to have you do miniatures of each of our children, and a family portrait as well. When do you think you could do this for us?"

Kathryn glanced over at Jonathan and explained, "Lord and Lady Hastings live in Kent, which isn't too terribly far from Sanderford Park. I would like to accept this commission. We could go there when we leave my brother's after the holidays. Would that be agreeable to you?"

"I would be fine with that. Whatever makes you happy. I agreed that I would never inhibit your art. Kent is lovely country, so I would love to go. Remember, we'll have the children with us," Jonathan reminded her.

Kathryn smiled at Jonathan and then looked over at Susan. "As long as we can bring the children and that time frame works for you, I would be happy to do it."

"That would be wonderful. My boys would enjoy it tremendously. Anything that will keep them from their studies thrills them. We'll look forward to your arrival."

"I'll write you when I have an exact date of when we'll be able to come. It should be around the tenth of the month, but I'll know more once the holidays are here. We've enjoyed talking with you, but we need to move on to other guests. We'll see you in January."

At this point, Kathryn and Jonathan continued to move around the room talking with some of their other guests. Soon it was time to cut the wedding cake. While gazing at the enormous three-tier cake, which had intricately made white sugar roses and lilies decorating it, Kathryn also noticed a filigree pattern that resembled lace adorning it. The cake was so beautiful that it seemed a shame to cut it.

Jonathan picked up the cake knife, she placed her hand on his, and they cut the first piece together. Jonathan's eyes shone brightly as she nibbled her portion of cake. A bit of icing was on her chin and Jonathan wiped it off and then licked the icing off his finger, while gazing into her eyes.

Kathryn felt flutters in the pit of her belly.

In a split second it was replaced by fear.

Oh, why did her uncle have to ruin her!

If he had just left her alone...

She just knew...she would have been able to respond to Jonathan.

Shortly after eating the beautiful cake, it was time for Kathryn and Jonathan to leave. On the way to the White Hart Inn, they stopped by Kathryn's to pick up her valise that Sarah had packed for the night. The rest of her clothing and belongings had already been taken over to St. John's Wood, and Sarah was already there as well. When Kathryn and Jonathan arrived at the door of the bridal suite, Jonathan picked her up and carried her into the room.

With surprise sharpening her tone a bit, Kathryn exclaimed, "Jonathan, put me down! You're going to hurt your knee. You've been on it for hours, and I'm sure it's bothering you."

Jonathan laughed. "I'm fine. You're as light as a feather, and I guess I'm a romantic at heart. When I was young, I always dreamed of carrying my bride over the threshold. Humor me a bit, all right?"

"Well, now that we're inside, please put me down. I want to look at this beautiful suite." Kathryn gazed around the room, noticing the light fruitwood furniture with blue brocade cushions on the couch, and the table set for two. Long-stemmed white roses were lying on the table next to a bottle of champagne that was chilling on ice.

Kathryn thought it was so sweet of Jonathan to plan all this for her. She was getting a bit nervous because she couldn't understand why he'd gone to this much trouble when they wouldn't be consummating their marriage. "I'm confused Jonathan." Then she noticed there was only one door in the room. She went over, opened it, and found that it was a bedroom. "Jonathan, there's only one bedroom. Where are you supposed to sleep?"

Looking Kathryn in the eye, Jonathan replied, "We're going to sleep together in that bed. Just because we aren't going to make love doesn't mean we can't sleep together. I promise...I just want to sleep with you—nothing else. I think that you enjoyed it when I held you earlier in the carriage, now didn't you?"

"I did enjoy it, but when I'm in bed, I wear my night rail. That's quite different from you holding me in my day clothes. I don't want to do this. I've never slept with anyone before. I'll be too nervous to sleep." This was starting to alarm her. The very thought of sleeping with him frightened her. "No, I definitely don't want to do this."

Jonathan stepped over to Kathryn, then pulling her into his arms, gently said, "I want you to do this for me. Just for tonight, I want you to try it. If you don't sleep well, then we won't do it again. You know darling, marriage is not just about making love. I want us to be close to each other physically, without making love. Will you do it for me, please?"

Kathryn looked at him with trepidation in her eyes, but then in a trembling voice, she said, "I guess…we can try it, but I'm sure that I won't be able to sleep, and then I'll be tired all day tomorrow."

Releasing Kathryn, Jonathan casually said, "Why don't you go into the bedroom and change into your night rail? I'm going to change out here. Then we'll have dinner."

Kathryn looked at Jonathan with embarrassment in her eyes. "I'll need you to unbutton my gown and l-loosen my corset." Jonathan gently turned her around and quickly did it for her. Kathryn could feel his fingers brushing against her as they released each button, and it sent sensations running through her body.

Jonathan kissed the nape of her neck. "All done. Just let me know if you need any more help."

Kathryn walked to the door, opened it, and entered the bedroom to change. While she changed into her night rail, which was thick white muslin and buttoned up to her neck, she realized that a small part of her was excited about sleeping with Jonathan. She had enjoyed it when he held her in the carriage, and she did want them to be close.

If it would make Jonathan happy, then it would be worth it. Kathryn had promised to obey him, so she guessed this was the first example of it. She sat down at the dressing table and took down her hair. Once it was loose, she brushed it until it shone, and then braided it so it wouldn't tangle while she slept. Standing up, she took a deep breath and walked to the door, opened it, and entered the sitting room.

Jonathan was already sitting at the table, pouring them each a glass of champagne, when Kathryn entered the room. "Sweetheart, come here. I've poured you some champagne. I've already ordered our food, so it should be here shortly."

As Kathryn took her seat, she surreptitiously looked over at Jonathan and noticed he was wearing a dark blue, silk dressing gown over his nightshirt. His nightshirt opened at the neck and there was some hair peeking out. She wondered if he had hair all over his broad chest. Kathryn also noticed his powerful arms, and as he moved them, she could see his muscles straining against the fabric of his dressing gown. When she realized what she was doing, she blushed and looked down.

"Are you all right? You seem a little flushed. Is it too warm in here for you? I built up the fire while you got undressed. I must have been overzealous. Maybe I should open a window for a moment."

Jonathan started to get up, but before he could stand up, Kathryn hurriedly said, "No, I'm comfortable. I'm just not used to seeing a man in his nightclothes. The fire actually feels wonderful."

Kathryn picked up her glass and took a sip of champagne, trying to calm her nerves. She wished the food would hurry up and arrive—she was starting to feel very uncomfortable.

There was a knock on the door, and she breathed a sigh of relief as Jonathan got up to open it.

The servant brought the food in and placed it on the cart, then departed. The food smelled delicious, and Kathryn realized she was famished. Jonathan took the cover off and served her. As she ate and sipped her champagne, she again glanced casually over at Jonathan. He was eating with gusto and was obviously comfortable being in his nightclothes in front of her, so she tried to relax and enjoy her meal. Jonathan kept topping off her glass, and soon she felt slightly tipsy, but it was helping her relax. By the time Jonathan served the lemon custard for dessert, which was a favorite of hers, she felt much more comfortable.

Once they were finished eating, Jonathan said, "I hope you don't mind, but I need to put some ointment on my knee. I usually put it on twice a day, and I missed this afternoon, so my knee is feeling a bit stiff."

Looking sympathetic, Kathryn said, "I'm sorry that your knee's hurting you. By all means, please go ahead and put the ointment on it. I'm just going to sit here and drink the rest of my champagne." Jonathan went to his bag and got the ointment, took a seat on the sofa, raised his nightshirt to above his knee, and began applying the ointment. He was so matter of fact about it that she wasn't uncomfortable.

Kathryn noticed the scars, and his knee looked red and swollen. "Jonathan, do you need to put ice on your knee? I understand that ice can help the swelling. Does your knee become swollen every day?"

"It's worse today than usual because I missed my afternoon treatment," Jonathan explained. While he continued to rub ointment on his knee, he continued, "Normally, Hatton rubs the ointment on and then wraps my knee with cold compresses, which keeps the swelling down. I know that it's not a pretty sight, but I'm just grateful I didn't lose my leg."

"Thank goodness you were able to keep it. Do you take anything to help the pain?"

"I usually take a dose of laudanum, which does help the pain. I fought against taking the laudanum for years, but what I was doing was using excessive liquor instead, and it didn't work nearly as well as the laudanum does. So now, I take a dose of laudanum in the afternoon, then another dose at night before I go to bed. I sleep much better now than I used to."

While Kathryn watched Jonathan, she continued to sip her champagne. "I know you need the laudanum for the pain, but be very careful that you don't use too much. It's very easy to get addicted to it. Of course, when I was taking it, I took large doses numerous times a day trying to forget the pain of what my uncle did to me. Even though Henry and Melody stopped him that time, it brought up all the memories of the times before when there wasn't anybody there to stop him."

Pulling his nightshirt back over his knees, Jonathan said, "I saw several men getting addicted to it while I was recovering in hospital. That's why I fought against taking any, but as long as I only take it in small doses, the doctor has assured me that I shouldn't become addicted. Will it bother you, seeing me take it?"

"I'd rather not see you take the laudanum, and I certainly don't want to know where you keep it. I had a nightmare the other night and woke up wishing I had some to take, and it frightened me. I don't ever want to go through being addicted again. It was horribly painful to get off the laudanum. I know you need it, so please take it when you need to, but I would rather not be around."

Walking over to the table, Jonathan smiled. "I took my dose while you were getting changed. I'll make sure you don't see it, or me taking any, all right? Well, I'm really quite tired tonight, so why don't we retire to our bed?" Kathryn looked over at him with apprehension in her lovely eyes. "I promise all we're going to do is sleep. I would love to hold you in my arms, but if that's too much for you, I'll understand."

Jonathan pulled her by the hand and they entered the bedroom. He led her around to the right side of the bed, pulled the covers back, picked her up, and laid her down. Then he smiled and pulled the covers up, tucked them under her chin, and playfully touched her nose. He walked around to the other side, slipped out of his dressing gown, lifted the covers, then slid into bed. Kathryn was lying there, stiff as a statute, as he eased over and gathered her in his arms.

Gently stroking Kathryn's shoulder, Jonathan murmured, "It's all right. Nothing is going to happen. Just try to relax and enjoy being close to each other. Now, doesn't this feel nicer than sleeping in a cold bed, alone?" As he continued to softly stroke her shoulder, he hummed to himself. Slowly, Kathryn felt herself begin to relax. She thought that it did feel nice to be with him instead of a cold bed. Jonathan was very warm, and as she lay there, she drifted off to sleep.

Chapter 16
- October 12, 1823 -

Jonathan woke up just as dawn was beginning to break. Kathryn was cuddled up close to him. There was just enough light to see her beautiful face as he looked down at her. Last night had taken every ounce of control he had in him to keep from frightening her. Lying next to her, but not making love, had been torture, but he knew that the only way she was ever going to accept him was if they were physically close. He wanted her to be so used to him that she didn't think twice about him touching her. The last thing he wanted was for Kathryn to feel his arousal, so he continued to mentally beat it down as he lay there holding her in his arms.

Kathryn reminded him of a pet he had as a child. He found the dog beaten and bruised, and he had nursed him back to health. At first, the dog would growl when he came near, but once the dog knew he wasn't going to hurt him, he quit tensing up and growling every time he soothed his pain. Eventually, Max followed him all around everywhere, and they were the best of friends for many years. He hadn't thought of Max in years. He'd been a faithful friend and companion throughout his adolescent years.

Kathryn was emotionally scarred by the trauma she'd experienced with her uncle. It made her wary of physical contact, just like Max had been, so he would have to gently guide her into physical touching. His brilliance at thinking of getting this bridal suite and convincing Kathryn to sleep with him, amazed even him. He was actually proud of her for allowing him to lay in bed with her last night. He knew she was scared to death, yet she still let him hold her, and she fell asleep when she thought she wouldn't be able to.

This was definitely a good start on eventually being able to make love to her. He knew it could take months, maybe even as long as a year, before she would be able to respond sexually to him, but he hoped it wouldn't take *that* long. He just needed to keep taking these small steps daily, and soon she would move beyond her fear. She obviously trusted him, or she would never have gotten into bed with him, let alone let him hold her. Yes, this was definitely a good start.

Looking over at the window, Jonathan watched the sky lighten further. He felt such a huge sense of rightness over his marriage to Kathryn. She was going to be a wonderful mother to Frankford and Jane, and hopefully, once he got her to move beyond her fear of intimacy, she would have her own children to shower her love on. Frankford and Jane already loved her, and she loved them. Yes, God had certainly blessed him when he put Kathryn in his life. Saying a brief prayer of thanks as he smiled contentedly, he slowly closed his eyes and drifted back to sleep.

Kathryn woke up and realized she was still in Jonathan's arms. She'd slept the entire night without any problems. She'd been sure she wouldn't be able to sleep, but she was wrong, and she felt more refreshed than usual. It felt comfortable and safe lying next to him with his arm around her. Her hand was lying on his chest, and she could feel the soothing beat of his heart. Again, she wondered if hair covered his entire chest. Another button on his nightshirt had slipped open, and she could see more hair than last night. She felt tempted to slip another button open and peek at his chest.

Jonathan was sleeping so soundly that surely he wouldn't feel it, if she was very careful. She slowly slid the button out of its hole and gently pushed open his nightshirt and saw silky-looking, black hair scattered across his chest. She wanted to touch the hair and see if it felt as silky to the touch as it looked, but she knew she could never do that. If he woke up, she would be so embarrassed, and he might think it permission to touch her breasts. She looked up and found herself staring into Jonathan's blue eyes.

He smiled. "Good morning, my beauty. Did you sleep well? I know I did. I can't remember when I've awakened feeling so refreshed. Are you hungry? I'm starving. I think I'll get up and go order us some breakfast. Is there anything in particular that you want?"

Jonathan pulled back the covers. His nightshirt had pulled up during the night, and she saw his muscular thighs. She knew she should look away, but the hair that lightly dusted his legs mesmerized her. As he stood up, his nightshirt fell back down, covering his thighs.

Picking up his dressing gown, Jonathan put it on, turned around, and said, "Well, are you going to stay in bed all morning, or are you going to get up and help me find us our breakfast? You know, your braid came undone during the night, and your glorious hair is falling down around your shoulders. Will you sit up so I can see all that amazing hair?"

Looking embarrassed, but wanting to please him, she sat up, and her hair fell down to her waist. "Ah, what an incredible sight. I wish you could wear your hair down all the time. It truly is beautiful. I've imagined what it would look like down, and it surpasses my greatest expectations. Well, I'll leave you to your morning ablutions. Will you need any help with your buttons?"

Shyly looking down, Kathryn replied, "I'm not sure what Sarah packed for me, but I'm sure that I'll be able to manage. I'll see you in a bit."

Kathryn watched as Jonathan limped out of their room. Once he closed the door, she jumped out of bed, went behind the screen, and used the chamber pot. She found a pitcher of water on the washstand and poured the water into the basin. It was freezing cold, but she wasn't going to tell him that. She quickly washed, brushed her teeth, and went to see what Sarah had packed for her. Thank goodness, the dress buttoned up the front, and she didn't need a corset with it.

Once she was dressed, she walked to the door, opened it, and entered the sitting room, then stopped and stared. Jonathan's back was to her...his bare back. He had incredibly broad shoulders, and his back narrowed into a slim waist, then trim hips. She couldn't tear her eyes away. Jonathan must have heard her, because he turned around and smiled. He had soap on his face and it was obvious that he was shaving. She felt her mouth drop open as she gazed at his spectacular chest with that black silky-looking hair scattered across it.

"Oops, caught me with my shirt off," Jonathan laughed. "You're a fast dresser. I see you didn't need my help with your buttons. There's hot tea and coffee on the table. Help yourself while I finish up here."

Jonathan turned back to the mirror and continued shaving. Helen was fascinated as she watched him scrape the hair off his handsome face. Once he was finished, he donned his shirt. She almost hated for him to cover up that magnificent chest.

Oh my goodness, why was she thinking this way?

Jonathan sat down across from her, poured a cup of coffee, and started drinking. She poured herself some tea, added cream and sugar, and then took a sip. There was a knock on the door, and Jonathan called, "Come in."

A servant entered carrying a tray laden with serving dishes. Jonathan must have ordered everything on the menu, because there was certainly quite a bit to choose from. The servant sat the tray down on the cart and left the room. "I ordered a bit of everything, since I'm starving. I didn't know what to order for you, so hopefully there's something here you'll like." He lifted off the cover. "Hum, kippers, sausage, bacon, and ham. What's your preference my lady?"

"I'll take a piece of the sausage and a slice of bacon. Are there any eggs?"

Jonathan took off another cover. "Of course we've got eggs. We've got them coddled and we also have some made into omelets. Which would you prefer?"

"I'll take an omelet, please. I would also like one of those delicious looking muffins. That should take care of me."

Kathryn watched as Jonathan piled his plate high with a bit of everything. Once they finished eating their breakfast, he said, "I've ordered the carriage to be brought around in thirty minutes. Can you be ready to leave by then?"

"I can be ready in fifteen. All I need to do is pack my valise. Is there anything that I can do for you?" Picking up the rest of her muffin, which was slathered with fresh creamery butter, Kathryn smiled over at Jonathan.

"I can think of something. Why don't you come over here and give me my good morning kiss? I'm feeling deprived." Hesitantly, Kathryn sat down her muffin, came around the table, and gave him a peck on the cheek. Evidently, that wasn't what he meant, because he grabbed her by the waist, pulled her down on his good knee, and gave her a very thorough kiss.

Jonathan teased her lips, licking and nipping at her mouth, and when she gasped, he slipped his tongue in, deepening the kiss. At first she was startled, but then she remembered what Melody told her, so she relaxed and concentrated on enjoying the kiss. She felt her heart begin to beat faster, and her breathing became shallow as he continued to kiss her. This kiss was so much more than any of his other kisses, but she found it quite titillating.

Kathryn heard him groan as he lifted his lips from hers. "You have the sweetest tasting mouth. I could kiss you all day, but this isn't going to get us out of here. Go on now and do your packing. I'll let you know when to come downstairs, my sweet."

The hour's drive to St. John's Wood passed quickly. When Kathryn and Jonathan approached the house, Goodman had all the servants lined up to greet their new mistress. Kathryn tried to make a point of repeating each of their names back to them as they were introduced to her, because that always helped her remember everyone's name better. The housekeeper, Mrs. Rollins, offered to show her to her rooms, but Jonathan said he would do that.

Kathryn and Jonathan went upstairs, and he led her to her new rooms. When he opened the door and they entered, she looked around at the beautifully appointed sitting room. The soft shades of peach with accents of sea foam green used to decorate the room made it feel warm and inviting. The furniture looked comfortable, with plenty of cushions on the chairs, and she could just imagine curling up for a good long read. She thought about what it would be like to spend a quiet evening with Jonathan, reading to each other in this lovely room.

The French doors opened out onto a balcony, which overlooked the gardens, and she could see a lake in the distance. The gardens appeared well maintained, and she felt sure that the gardens would be lovely next spring.

Jonathan came up behind her and stroked her shoulders. "My mother loved to garden. I've attempted to maintain them as a memorial to her." Turning her around, he pointed. "Over there is the door to your room, and mine is on the opposite wall. We each have a private dressing room and bathing room attached. I hope you'll be happy here. Please feel free to change anything you would like."

"The sitting room is delightful. May I see my bedroom?"

"Of course, my dear. Follow me." As they entered the bedroom, she noticed that the color scheme matched the sitting room. The counterpane on the bed was a deeper shade of peach with delicate ivory lace trim, and there was a mound of comfortable pillows that she could just see herself luxuriating amongst.

"Jonathan, these rooms are lovely. I'm sure that I'll be very happy here. I don't need to change a thing. Is that the door to my dressing room?"

"Yes, and your bathing room is attached. I had these rooms modernized five years ago when I did my rooms, so there's running water in the bathing room. No need for anyone to carry water upstairs."

"Thank goodness. I have to admit that I've been somewhat spoiled since Sanderford Park has also been modernized. Sarah will appreciate this, and it looks as if she has already put away my things," Kathryn stated as she walked over to the chest and peered inside.

Jonathan walked over to her and took her hand. "Come with me. I'll show you my room."

Jonathan's room was enormous. The bed was huge with a deep green velvet counterpane on it. There were two comfortable-looking wing back chairs with matching ottomans in front of the fireplace. A book was lying on the table between the chairs with a pair of spectacles on top of it, as if someone had just laid the book down.

"Jonathan, do you wear spectacles? I've never seen you with them on. I want to see them on you."

Jonathan reached around her, picked up the glasses and put them on. "Yes, I wear spectacles, but I only need them to read. That's why you've never seen me with them on. What do you think of my room?"

Kathryn walked over to the chairs. Running her hand over the back of one, she said, "It looks quite comfortable, and very masculine. The moss green walls are very serene and restful, I imagine. Thank you for showing me our rooms. They're quite lovely. I'm sure we'll spend many quiet evenings in the sitting room. We'll be able to read to each other this coming winter."

Jonathan pulled her into his arms and kissed her. Kathryn responded, allowing him to deepen the kiss. Kathryn felt a tingling sensation run throughout her body as he pulled her close. When their bodies touched chest to thigh, she felt something hard probe her belly. Realizing it was his manhood, she pushed him away. "Jonathan, I like your kiss, but I get uncomfortable when you pull me too close. Please don't pull me so tightly against you. I could feel your…ah…arousal, and it made me uncomfortable." She sat down in one of the chairs and looked up at him.

Jonathan sat down in the other chair, leaned forward, and took her hand. "I'm sorry, darling. I'll be more careful in the future. I don't want you to be uncomfortable, but just because you arouse me doesn't mean I'll act on it. You're a very beautiful woman, and it's my body's way of responding to your beauty. I promise you I'm quite harmless. I think you'll enjoy having me hold you close, if you realize that you have nothing to fear. Now enough about that. Let me show you your studio. I hope it pleases you. Let's go take a look at it, all right?"

The studio was perfect. Jonathan had furnished it with plenty of art supplies and canvases. The unfinished portrait sat on the easel, and she was dying to get to work on it. She thought it was going to be her best work so far. She wanted it to be perfect for the children and Jonathan, since she knew how much it would mean to them.

After luncheon, she went upstairs to visit the children in the schoolroom. Frankford and Jane were happy to see her and were soon showing her their work. Their governess, Miss

Mills, told Kathryn that both of the children were good students and well behaved. Frankford still seemed a little withdrawn, but Jane was cheerful as she asked, "Lady Kathryn, would you come back later after I finish my schoolwork and have tea with me?"

Smiling down at Jane, Kathryn replied, "I'd be happy to, and please call me Aunt Kathryn. After all, you're now my niece. I'll return at three." Then giving Jane a quick hug, she left the schoolroom.

Kathryn went back to her new studio and spent the next couple of hours working on the portrait. She thought about what had happened in Jonathan's room. She realized she hadn't been afraid, but only nervous, even though she'd felt his arousal. She knew he wouldn't do anything to her she didn't want. She did enjoy having him hold her, and she loved his kisses. They made her feel all warm and tingly.

Kathryn wondered if what she was feeling could be desire, and the very thought shocked her, because she has been sure she would never be able to feel it. She decided that the next time Jonathan held her she wouldn't pull back, even if she did feel him getting aroused. Jonathan had been so logical when he explained why he'd become aroused. She had no reason to be scared of Jonathan. She knew he would never do anything to hurt her. She decided that she just needed to relax and enjoy Jonathan's friendship and affection.

At three o'clock, she went to the nursery, and Jane had everything ready for their tea. They sat at the little table and chairs with two of her dolls, and pretended to drink tea. Kathryn enjoyed it because she'd done this many times with Mary Elizabeth and Angela. After she finished having tea with Jane, Frankford asked her to read him a story, which thrilled her. She spent a pleasant hour with the children, and then went downstairs to have tea with Jonathan and Elaine.

When Kathryn entered the drawing room, Elaine was already there, so she went to the sofa and sat down beside her. "How are you today? I wanted to thank you for being one of my attendants yesterday at the wedding. I have something for you. I hope you like it." Kathryn pulled a beautifully wrapped gift from her pocket and handed it to Elaine.

When Elaine opened it, she picked up the bracelet. "Oh, thank you, Kathryn. This is so pretty. I've always wanted a charm bracelet. You really didn't have to get me anything, but I do love it."

"It's a tradition to give everyone that's in the bridal party a gift as a thank you for being in the wedding. You looked very lovely yesterday, and purple is a good color on you with your golden blonde hair and green eyes. Have you used Madame Bovary's Boutique before?"

"Yes. When Allison came for her last visit, shortly before they died, she convinced Jonathan to allow Madame Bovary to make me a few dresses. They turned out beautifully, and the riding habit fits me better than any I've ever owned. I love riding. Do you ride Kathryn?" Elaine asked, as she sat with her back straight, not touching the back of the chair. Kathryn was impressed with Elaine's manners and comportment. Her governess had done a very good job, and Elaine was a charming young lady.

"I do ride occasionally, so hopefully we can ride together sometime."

"Good. I look forward to it. I'd like to go back to Madame Bovary's because I need some new things for this coming winter. Everything I had last year no longer fits since I've grown two inches, and my chest is much bigger. Do you think I could get some more gowns from Madame Bovary?"

"I'll talk to your brother, but I'm sure he'll agree. Your figure is more mature than the average fifteen-year-old, and I'm sure Madame Bovary can design gowns to fit you, and yet still keep you looking young and innocent. If he's all right with it, we can go tomorrow."

Jonathan came into the room and asked, "Where do you plan on going tomorrow? Is it somewhere I would like to go?"

Kathryn looked up when she saw Jonathan and smiled. "No, it's not. Elaine just told me she needs some new clothes for the winter, and if it's all right with you, I thought I would take her to Madame Bovary to get her new wardrobe. She has the best designs in Bath. Didn't Elaine look nice yesterday at the wedding? Madame Bovary made that gown."

'I have no problems with her using Madame Bovary. Just make sure she still looks like a fifteen-year-old. It's three years before she has her come out, and she's still a child in many ways, even if she doesn't look it." Jonathan took a seat, accepted a cup of tea from Kathryn, and took a sip.

A shadow fell over Kathryn's lovely face as she said, "I couldn't agree with you more. I'll make sure all her new clothes are appropriate for her age. The last thing I would want to do is encourage any man to think she's older than fifteen and available for dalliance."

Elaine spoke up a bit testily. "You're no fun at all. I'll be sixteen on November twelfth, and I am not a child! I'll be making my come out in two years, not three. I think I'll go up to my room now and read." Elaine huffed out of the room.

Jonathan shook his head as he watched his sister leave. "I don't know what I'm going to do with her. When my friend

Jenkins came to visit, she actually tried to flirt with him. Thank God, he has a younger sister and didn't act on it. At least it's fairly isolated out here, and there aren't any young men around."

"I think it's quite natural for a young girl her age to want to try out her feminine wiles. At least it was safe with Baron Jenkins."

"Please, watch her closely tomorrow when you're in town. I know I'm over-protective, but you and I both know it would be easy for her to get into trouble if we don't watch her carefully. Maybe I ought to go with you after all. I could always go to the Pump Room and drink some of that nasty water while you're at Madame Bovary's."

Kathryn put her plate back on the table. "You're welcome to come, but I promise you I'll watch her very carefully. I know better than most that there are wicked men out there who prey on young girls."

"I'm sorry. I don't want you to think that I don't trust you. That's not it at all. I just know Elaine likes to get into mischief. When I'm in London, I'm always getting notes from her governess. I'm hoping that you'll have a calming effect on her." Jonathan picked up a cake from his plate and bit into it. After he swallowed, he said, "Did you try these cakes? These are one of Cookie's specialties and my favorite."

Kathryn smiled. "I did try them, and they're quite delicious. Elaine's really quite typical for a fifteen-year-old. I don't think you need to worry, especially since there are no young men close by. I think she's quite level-headed and mature for her age. You told me that you left her here with only her governess most of the time. If she got into mischief, it was probably her way of getting your attention."

"I know you're probably right, but I'm just having a hard time realizing she's almost grown."

Lightening the conversation, Kathryn said, "I spent some time with the children this afternoon. Frankford is still withdrawn, but he did ask me to read him a book. Jane is darling. We played teatime with her dolls. I plan to spend time with them every day. I also worked on the portrait earlier this afternoon. I should have it finished by the end of next week. Then I'll start on those miniatures you asked me to do."

"I'm so grateful that you're going to be able to finish Roderick's family portrait. I'm going to hang it in the family gallery when it's finished. Eventually, it will go back to Westland Acres when Frankford reaches his majority."

"I'm just grateful I did so many sketches so I could finish their portrait."

"Thank you for spending time with Frankford and Jane. I'm sure you're going to be able to help Frankford get over his grief. I'm going to teach him how to ride. He's old enough, and I think that if he has a horse to take care of, that will help take his mind off losing his parents."

"I think that is an excellent idea. He's the perfect age to learn."

"If he can ride, he'll be able to go out with me. Since he's my heir, he needs to meet all my tenants so he'll appreciate everything that makes up the marquessate. My father did that for me when I was his age. Well, as much as I enjoy sitting here talking to you, I've got a meeting with Stebbins and Whetherby, so I'll see you tonight at dinner." He leaned over, kissed her on the cheek, and then left the room.

Chapter 17

After his meeting with Stebbins and Whetherby, Jonathan went to his room so Hatton could treat his knee. While he was there he took his afternoon dose of laudanum. He told Hatton he wouldn't need him again until seven o'clock. Once Hatton left the room, he leaned back in his chair and closed his eyes. He wanted a drink, but he resisted the temptation. Now that Kathryn was his wife he had an even stronger reason to stay away from liquor. He wondered how long it would take before the craving for liquor would leave him entirely. The last thing he wanted was for Kathryn to see him drunk.

Jonathan wasn't sure how he was going to keep her from knowing he desired her. It was murder last night, holding her in his arms and not making love to her. He just needed to remember he had to take it slow, but still get her used to physical touching. She was definitely responding to his kisses. When they were kissing earlier, he felt her quiver as he deepened their kiss. He wished he knew whether it would hurt or help his case if he told her he loved her. Sitting there thinking about Kathryn was getting him hard, and since he couldn't do anything about it, he decided to take a cold bath.

At dinner that night, Jonathan began to tell Kathryn some delightful stories about his childhood. "You know that Roderick and I were only a year apart. The summer when we were ten and eleven, while we were swimming in the lake, Roderick decided he was going to climb the tree next to the lake and then jump off the tallest branch. I told him not to do it, but he wouldn't listen to me."

"Henry was quite a daredevil at that same age. I'm surprised he never broke a limb from all his antics."

"Well, Roderick did. The lake isn't that deep by the tree, and sure enough, when he jumped, he ended up landing on his side and snapped his arm. He spent the rest of the summer with his arm in a splint and a sling. Father never reprimanded him. He felt that the pain of a broken arm was enough. Roderick was also unable to swim in the lake the rest of the summer."

Kathryn wiped her mouth with her napkin and remarked, "Henry fell out of a tree by our lake when he was around six years old, but Nelson saved him from drowning and taught him how to swim that summer. Nelson taught all of us how to swim when we got that age. We spent many wonderful afternoons out at our lake each summer."

"Roderick always loved the water. That's why it was so perfect when he inherited Westland Acres. As hard as it is to think about losing him, at least he was doing something he loved when he died. We found the yacht, you know. It washed up on the shore about a week after we found Roderick and Allison. It wasn't even damaged that badly. A huge wave must have flipped it over, and they probably didn't even have time to react. Oh God, I wanted to keep our conversation light tonight, but sometimes I just need to talk about them. I'm sorry." He picked up his wine glass and took a sip as he looked over at Kathryn.

With tears swimming in her gorgeous eyes, she said, "I miss them too. I know I didn't know them for very long, but they were both so friendly, and they went out of their way to make me feel welcomed in their home. Jonathan, I want you to be able to talk to me about anything. That's what friends are for. I've never had many friends because I'm a little shy, and it's hard for me to talk to people I don't know."

"It's all right to be shy. It's one of things I find most attractive about you. You're a very good listener too. If you're finished with your dessert, let's go to the music room. I feel like playing tonight. Would you mind listening to me?"

"Of course, Jonathan. I could listen to you play for hours." Jonathan helped her up, and they made their way to the music room.

After he played for about an hour, he suggested, "I'm a bit tired tonight. Are you ready for bed?"

"I'm tired also, so yes, I'm ready to retire."

When Kathryn and Jonathan entered the sitting room, he said, "I'll give you thirty minutes, and then I'll come to you. She looked nervous, but she nodded her head and went to her room.

When Jonathan got to his room, Hatton helped him treat his knee, then departed. He knew he would have to be very careful tonight if he was going to convince her to let him sleep with her again. He decided he would just go in there, get into bed, and see how she reacted.

He knocked on her door, then walked in. "Hello, darling. Did I give you enough time?" Jonathan casually stretched and yawned. "I'm really tired tonight, how about you? Oh, you never said whether it was all right for me to go into town with you tomorrow. I do want to go to the Pump Room and take the waters. Did you plan to go anywhere else while you're in town?"

While sitting at her dressing table, brushing her hair, Kathryn answered, "I thought that after we finish picking out Elaine's new wardrobe, we would go by my mother's and see the family. I'm fine with you coming along. I'm sure Henry and Matthew would enjoy your company."

Jonathan walked over to the bed and pulled back the covers. "All right, then I'll come along. I'm going to get in bed now. Are you coming, or are you going to sit up a while?"

With apprehension on her pretty face, Kathryn said, "No, I'm coming to bed." Walking to the right side of the bed, Kathryn pulled back the covers and lay down beside him. Jonathan pulled her into his arms, kissed her cheek, and closed his eyes. Kathryn laid there for a few minutes all tensed up, but then he felt her body begin to relax. Soon her breathing grew steady, and he knew she had fallen asleep. That went better than he had expected. He thought she would object when he got into her bed, but she never said a word.

Yes, he just needed to take it slow and easy.

Let her get used to him being in bed with her every night.

It might kill him before she finally gave in, but it would be well worth it. As he enjoyed the feel of her sweet body next to his, he slowly drifted off to sleep.

Kathryn heard someone moaning as she woke up from a sound sleep. She realized it was Jonathan. He was thrashing about, and in the moonlight she could see that his face was slick with sweat. He was in the throes of a nightmare. Kathryn shook his shoulder, but he didn't wake up. He started shouting, "No...No...Leave my leg alone!" She tried again to wake him up, but this time he grabbed her to him and cried out again, but he was still asleep. Kathryn let out a little scream.

Kathryn started rubbing his chest and down his arms. She tried again to wake him up, but he continued to sleep. As she continued to massage his chest, he quieted down and quit thrashing around. His breathing evened out, and he became calm. She knew that the nightmare had passed. She continued lying there with her hand on his chest, gently stroking. She felt him roll toward her and pull her against him. At first Kathryn was scared, but then he began rubbing her back. It felt relaxing, and she slowly fell back to sleep.

The next morning, when Kathryn woke up, she looked over at Jonathan to find he was still asleep. He looked much younger when he was sleeping. In fact, he looked quite a bit younger than when she first met him. The lines around his mouth and eyes were less pronounced, and he didn't look as tired either. It was as if she was seeing him through different eyes.

Had she changed, or had he?

Jonathan's arm was around her waist, and when she tried to lift it away, he pulled her against him. Now they were lying face to face on their sides. He started stroking her back, and then he opened his eyes. "Good morning. Did you sleep all right? You look very pretty this morning with your face all aglow. I like waking up with you beside me. I just realized that you're the first woman I've ever slept with."

Kathryn looked startled. "How can I be the first woman you've ever slept with? You told me you weren't a virgin, so I'm sure you've slept with quite a few women."

Jonathan grinned. "Oh, I'm definitely not a virgin, and you're right, I've *bedded* quite a few women, but I never slept with any of them. To be blunt, once we were through having sex, I always left and went home to my own bed. I promise...you're the first woman I've ever slept with."

"Why didn't you want to stay with them all night?" Kathryn asked, finding this conversation fascinating.

"After we finished having sex, I always felt restless. You know what I also just realized? I've never made love to a woman. All I've ever done is have sex with them. I realize now that there's a big difference. Oh, I called it making love, but love never entered into it. It was always for sexual gratification. We haven't had sex, but I do make love to you."

"Now you're really confusing me. How have we made love?"

"Kathryn, there are many ways to make love. When I hold you in my arms and kiss you, it feels different than when I was with other women, and I think it's because I care so much about you." He kissed her and said, "Do you know why it feels different?"

"No, I still don't understand why you say we've made love." Still looking puzzled, she waited for him to explain what he meant.

"I'll try to explain. I've fallen...in love with you. When I kiss you, I make love to your mouth, and when I rub your back, I make love to your back. I never expected to fall in love, but you had me from the first moment that I laid eyes on you. Do you know why I don't want a mistress?"

Kathryn hesitated, but then said, "No."

As Kathryn looked up at him, Jonathan answered her. "I'm ashamed to tell you this, but I think it will help you understand. A week or so after we met, I went to a brothel. I picked out a woman with bright red hair and long legs. She resembled you. While she was pleasuring me, I imagined that it was you. After I left there, I felt incredibly guilty. As if I'd betrayed you. I went back to the brothel one more time, and this time I picked out someone who looked nothing like you, but it didn't matter. All I could think about was you. I again felt that same level of guilt when we finished having sex."

All this was fascinating to Kathryn. Lying there in his arms felt so pleasant as he stroked her back and arms. She felt no fear. Even though he was speaking of sex, she wasn't uncomfortable. She actually found it flattering, and part of her was thrilled that he loved her.

Jonathan stroked her back gently and kissed her cheek as he continued to explain. "So you see you've ruined me for all other women. If I can't have you, I don't want anyone else. I would rather live the rest of my life chaste with you than have to live without you. I hope and pray that someday, you'll grow to love me as much as I love you, and when you do, I think you'll change your mind about intimacy. But even if that never happens, I would still rather be with you."

"Jonathan, I don't know what to say. I've never thought about falling in love because I knew how I felt about intimacy. I don't know what to think about you loving me. I know that I care about you, but I don't think I'm in love with you."

"That's all right, darling. I didn't expect you to say you love me, but I can't help but hope that you *will* one day."

"I can't promise you that I'll ever be able to make love to you, but I will say this, you're the only man that I will ever want to kiss me, and I do enjoy your kisses tremendously. I like it when you hold me in your arms, but I'm just not ready for anything else, and I don't know that I'll ever be. I'm sorry that I've ruined you for other women." Then she looked up at him and added, "Well, actually, I'm not sorry. I don't want you to be with another woman. I guess I'm very selfish."

Smiling down at her, Jonathan said, "No, my darling, you're not selfish. I'm actually encouraged that you don't want me to be with other women. I hated it when I thought you wanted that. I want you to promise me that you won't worry about any of this. Let's just enjoy being with each other, and we'll just let nature take its course. Well, enough about this for now. I need to get up, go back to my room, and get my day started. What time do you want to leave for Bath?"

Kathryn watched as Jonathan got out of bed. "I would like to be at Madame Bovary's by eleven o'clock. Would that be acceptable to you?"

"Yes, just meet me out front at ten o'clock, and we'll leave then. Now kiss me and send me on my way."

And...that's exactly what she did.

Elaine chattered the entire time during the drive into Bath, so it was easy to see she was excited about getting a new wardrobe. When Kathryn and Elaine arrived at Madame Bovary's, Jonathan left them there and went on to the Pump Room. Madame Bovary had a myriad of fashion plates for Elaine to choose from, specifically designed for young adolescent girls. Elaine had fun selecting the styles that would work best for her, and she was very receptive to all of Kathryn's suggestions.

Madame Bovary had a wealth of fabric swatches to choose from. Elaine picked out an adorable pale pink silk for a dinner gown with deep pink rose buds embroidered all over the bodice, and trails of them down the front of the gown. She picked out several day dresses, a new traveling dress, and another riding habit in deep blue, which complimented her complexion.

Jonathan returned for them at one o'clock, and they went to lunch at the White Hart Inn. After they finished a tasty meal of pork pasties, cheese, and crusty brown bread, they went to the duchess's house.

Abernathy told Kathryn that the gentlemen were in the study and the ladies were in the drawing room. Jonathan decided to go join Henry and Matthew. As Kathryn entered the drawing room she said, "Good afternoon, Mother. I hope you're feeling well?"

"I am feeling very well. How are you today? Are you enjoying your new home? I know Jonathan set up a room for you to use as your studio. Did it meet with your expectations?" her mother asked.

"Everything is wonderful. I'm going to enjoy living in my new home. The studio is perfect." Kathryn turned to Helen and Melody and asked, "Would you like to go for a walk with me? The weather is surprisingly mild."

Melody and Helen responded in unison, "We would love to go!"

Kathryn asked Elaine, "Which would you rather do? Go on a walk with us or spend time with the children?"

Elaine answered, "I'd rather spend time with the children."

Kathryn, Helen, and Melody went with Elaine to the schoolroom, and the children were overjoyed to see Elaine. Mary Elizabeth and Angela immediately wanted her to join them for tea, and the boys wanted her to read to them. They left Elaine with the children and went outside for their walk.

Once the ladies were in the park, Kathryn turned to Helen and Melody. "I have something of a dilemma, and I need your advice. Jonathan told me that he's in love with me this morning. I'm not sure that I want him to be in love with me. It makes me feel a higher level of guilt over marrying him, since I can't see myself returning his regard. I can tell by the way he talks that he thinks that I'll eventually change my mind about intimacy, but I don't see that happening. What should I do? I care deeply for him, but this is all a little frightening for me."

Helen spoke up. "Kathryn, I think it's wonderful that Jonathan's in love with you. I know how you feel about intimacy, but I think that over time, as you grow to trust Jonathan, you'll change your mind and want to ah...be with him. Let me ask you something. I assume he's kissed you several times. Do you enjoy his kisses?"

"Yes, he's kissed me quite a few times over the last couple of days, and I have enjoyed them. He's also insisted that we share a bed each night. At first, I didn't want to, but he convinced me that it would help us grow closer to each other. I didn't think that I would be able to relax enough to fall asleep, but I've actually slept quite peacefully. He makes it all seem so natural that I find it hard to object." Kathryn sat down on the park bench, leaving room for Melody and Helen to join her.

They sat down and then Melody shared her thoughts on the matter. "I think that it's very smart of Jonathan to insist on sharing a bed, and it's a promising sign that you've been able to sleep so soundly. It shows that you already trust him. I believe that trust is essential in a loving relationship. I think Jonathan's behavior warrants your trust in him."

Kathryn looked around at the fall leaves on the ground as she replied, "I do trust him. While he obviously desires me, he hasn't acted on that desire. When he kisses me, I can feel him keeping tight control of his passion. I find myself wanting to respond to him, and it surprises me, but I think I've actually felt desire from his kisses. I get a warm, tingly sensation when he kisses me, and I find it extremely pleasant."

Helen nodded. "That's definitely desire you're feeling. That's very promising Kathryn. Has he touched you?"

"Well, he has rubbed my back and stroked my arms, and I felt the same sensations as I did when he kissed me. I find myself wondering what it would feel like…if he touched me more intimately. I'm sorry. I probably shouldn't be talking about all this, but I'm so confused. I really want your help." Kathryn blushed as she told them this.

Melody excitedly replied, "Sweetheart, we love you, and yes, it's a bit uncomfortable to talk about these things, but if it will help you, it's worth a little discomfort. Kathryn I think all of this is very promising. I have a few suggestions for you. This is what you need to do. The next time he kisses you and touches you, make sure you respond by letting him know you're enjoying his touch. Moan or sigh deeply, and he'll know that you're responsive."

Kathryn thought about this for a moment, and then said, "I think that I can do that. I've already wanted to, but I've suppressed it because I didn't want him to try other things, but now I think I'm ready to experience more. Thank you so much for your advice. It's embarrassing to talk about all this, but I really do want your advice. I'm glad you're staying for a few more days so I'll be able to continue to talk with you."

Helen hugged Kathryn. "All I'll add is…you may already be falling in love with Jonathan. Knowing you the way I do, you wouldn't be responding to his kisses and touches unless you were emotionally attached to him."

"You may be right, but I'm so afraid. Oh, this all so confusing!"

"Don't be afraid of love as I was. I denied my feelings for Matthew for months, and even after I realized that I did love him, I still waited several more months before I told him. Life's too short to spend months pondering over this. None of us knows how long we have on this earth. Just look at what happened to Jonathan's brother and his wife."

The ladies returned to the house and joined everyone for tea. As Kathryn traveled back to St. John's Wood, she thought about her conversation with Helen and Melody and decided she would try to do as they suggested. She trusted Jonathan enough to know that if she became uncomfortable he would stop if she asked him to.

Elaine talked the entire way home about all her new gowns and how she couldn't wait to wear them. Kathryn was glad she had gotten Jonathan's approval for Elaine to have her gowns made by Madame Bovary, and she felt he would be pleased with the result. Jonathan laughed and teased Elaine about her gowns, and the trip passed quickly.

Chapter 18
- May 1823 -

When Kathryn arrived back at the house, she went to the schoolroom to visit with Frankford and Jane. She spent an hour reading to them and then went to her room to get ready for dinner. While she was at Madame Bovary's, she had picked up a new dinner gown she had ordered.

Once she was dressed and Sarah finished arranging her hair, she looked in her cheval mirror. As she smoothed down the bodice of the gown, she noticed how the décolletage showed her breasts to advantage. The deep gold silk felt marvelous against her skin and, it complemented her natural creamy complexion. She knew she looked her best tonight, and hoped Jonathan would think she looked attractive.

When she descended the stairs, Jonathan was waiting for her. His eyes glowed with appreciation. "Darling, you look incredibly lovely tonight. Is that a new gown?"

As he escorted her into the dining room she replied, "I picked it up today while I was at Madame Bovary's with

Elaine. I ordered it two weeks ago. I'm pleased you like it. Jonathan, I think you'll be pleasantly surprised when you see the dresses that Elaine ordered. They're perfect for her, and they don't make her look too mature. It was a challenge to pick out gowns that were appropriate, but Madame Bovary had quite a few designs that worked perfectly for her."

Jonathan helped Kathryn take her seat, and then he sat down adjacent to her. "I appreciate you helping Elaine. I realize she's growing up, but I don't want her looking too mature. I know that there are unscrupulous men out there who would love to get their hands on her. I just want to protect her."

Kathryn picked up her napkin and spread it on her lap. "I love that you're so protective of her. I wish my parents had been more aware of what was happening to me when I was a young girl. They were always gone, and Nelson and Henry were quite a few years older than Helen and I, so they were away at school most of the time. I was too ashamed to tell anyone what was happening, but I think that a more involved parent would have realized that something was wrong."

Once the footmen had served the quail and left the room, Jonathan replied, "I agree with you. That's why I watch over Elaine so closely. I know she's very impetuous and could be easily led astray. I'm relieved that you're going to be there with me when she has her come out. I was counting on Allison to bring her out, but I know you'll do a marvelous job. You're even more aware of the dangers that accomplished rakes can be to an innocent young girl than she would have been. Now that we're finished with our dinner, do you want to go upstairs to our sitting room and read, or go to the music room?"

"Why don't we go to the music room? I enjoy hearing you play. I find it quite soothing. I just wish I had taken my music lessons more seriously now that I'm older, but I was so wrapped up in my art that I found them a bother. Of course, I do enjoy singing, and I have a passable soprano voice."

"I didn't realize you could sing. I'll play some pieces that you know, and you can sing for me. I would enjoy that tremendously." Jonathan had quite a few pieces of music she knew. After spending some time in the music room, they went upstairs together.

When they entered their sitting room, Jonathan told Kathryn he would join her shortly. Kathryn went to her bedchamber, and Sarah helped her get ready for bed. She had Sarah leave her hair loose instead of in her usual braid. She knew Jonathan loved her hair and would enjoy seeing it down again. She also chose to wear a matching silk night rail and robe instead of her heavy cotton gowns.

Kathryn decided she would get into bed and wait for Jonathan to join her. Soon she heard him knock and enter her room. She held her breath for a moment as he came into view. He must have taken a quick bath, because his hair was still damp, and she could smell sandalwood soap, which was very enticing. He had on his dark blue silk banyan, and he didn't have a nightshirt on under it. When he noticed her hair loose, his eyes darkened with desire, and it caused those marvelous sensations to run through her body.

Jonathan came over to the bed, pulled back the covers, and climbed in beside her. "Your hair is even lovelier than I remembered. Would you mind if I touch it?"

Kathryn hesitantly smiled. "Certainly you can. I left it loose tonight because I thought you would like it better that way.

You've mentioned several times that you find my hair attractive."

Jonathan ran his fingers through her hair and watched it fall onto Kathryn's breasts. His breathing was shallow and his hands trembled. She could tell he was trying to control his desire. A few nights ago that realization would have scared her, but she actually found it tantalizing tonight. As he reached for her, she went willingly into his arms. Kathryn saw the surprise on his face as she laid her head on his chest.

When he leaned down to kiss her, she kissed him back, and he deepened his kiss. While he nibbled at her bottom lip, she sighed in enjoyment, and he slid his tongue into her mouth. Again, she parted her lips to allow him further access. She placed her hand on his chest, felt his heart beating rapidly. Kathryn felt her heartbeat accelerate too.

Jonathan continued to kiss Kathryn, and she felt her belly knot with anticipation. She groaned just as Melody and Helen had told her to do, and Jonathan gently placed his hand on her breast. As he rubbed her nipple through her silk gown, it grew taut. Kathryn was surprised, but she liked the feelings that were surging through her body.

He trailed kisses down her neck, then lowered his head and slowly took her nipple into his mouth through her silk night rail. Kathryn felt a jolt of electricity shoot through her lower body, and she moaned softly. His hand reached down and pulled up her night rail. When he touched her bare skin, she felt his hand trembling as he ran it up her leg toward the apex between her pretty thighs.

Kathryn was trembling with excitement as he parted her thighs and touched a spot she wasn't even aware was there. The most incredible sensations burned through her body. She felt as if a coil was being tightened inside her body as he stroked the tip of his finger over her cleft. Then she felt his finger begin to slide inside her, and she stiffened.

He immediately pulled his hand away and pulled her gown back down. "I'm sorry. All you have to do is tell me to stop, and I will. I don't want to scare you, but my dear, you don't know how much it means to me that you have trusted me enough to allow me to touch you."

Kathryn timidly looked at him and murmured, "I was enjoying the way it was feeling until you did that last thing. Can we just do everything else except that last bit?"

Jonathan gazed into her eyes. "We can do whatever you're comfortable with. I sensed you were enjoying my touches until the last. Kathryn, you have such a beautiful body, and I desire you desperately. This is the beginning stages of making love. I'm glad you found it enjoyable. Can I kiss you again?"

"Please."

Jonathan tenderly kissed her. While raining kisses all over her beautiful face, he gently kneaded her breasts. Soon her breathing quickened and her heartbeat escalated. She was moaning from the incredible things she was feeling. He kissed her with more passion, and she followed his lead. He continued to fondle her breasts with gentle touches. The feeling was mesmerizing as she felt a rush of desire deep inside her body. She knew she was close to something very special.

They lay there for quite some time as he softly stroked her breasts, arms, and back, then slowly, he raised his head and smiled at her as he pulled her close. "I think that's enough for tonight. We'll just lie together until we fall asleep."

Kathryn smiled and closed her eyes. As they lay together, she felt so safe. She was overjoyed that she'd taken Helen and Melody's advice. She had enjoyed everything they did except for that one thing. Then she had grown a little fearful that what he had planned to do would hurt her, so she had stiffened up. But he had immediately pulled back, so she knew she could trust him to stop when she wanted him to. Kathryn was so grateful that she had listened to his plea when he asked her to marry him, for the children's sake. With a beatific smile on her face, she slowly drifted off to sleep.

Jonathan lay there for a long time just holding her in his arms. It had been the hardest thing he'd ever done, when he pulled back, but he knew it was the right thing to do. He'd kept a tight rein on his passions. He knew that his patience would bring much greater rewards later. He was amazed that she had responded so passionately. He knew he was taking a big risk, pushing a little further than she was comfortable with, but he knew that if he didn't take some risks, they would never reach his ultimate goal of making love to complete fulfillment for both of them. Just as soon as he felt her tense up, he knew it was time to pull back.

When she asked him if they could continue, it just about brought him to his knees, but he stayed in control and continued to tenderly stroke and pet her until she again was feeling the beginning sensations of desire. As he continued to lie there with her in his arms, hard as stone and filled with so much passion that it was painful, he still knew he had done the right thing. Eventually his body calmed down and he fell asleep.

When Jonathan woke up the next morning with her body pressed up against him, spoon fashion, it felt sublime. Her sweet little bottom was nestled against his loins, his arm was around her waist, and he was in paradise. He didn't want to waken her because he just wanted to enjoy feeling her so close against him.

He knew that when she woke up and felt his cock stiff against her derriere, she would pull away. The progress he'd made last night was truly astonishing, much more than he would have ever dreamed in so short a time. This was just their third night together, and he had expected it would take weeks, or even months, before he would actually be able to touch her beautiful body, and yet it had happened last night.

Jonathan felt her wiggle and then stiffen and knew she was waking up. "Good morning, my love. Do you feel as marvelous as I do? I just love waking up with you in my arms. Why don't you turn around so I can give you your good morning kiss?"

She turned toward him and shyly said, "Good morning to you. I'm glad you slept well. I know that I certainly did." She pulled his head down to hers and gently kissed his lips. As she kissed him, she parted her sweet lips and invited him in. While he kissed her deeply, she tentatively probed his mouth with her tongue.

It was the most erotic experience of his life when he felt her untutored attempts to return his passion. As she kissed him, he gently stroked her luscious breasts. She rubbed up against him, so he slipped his hand into the neckline of her night rail and took her nipple between his thumb and forefinger and gently squeezed. Her nipple pebbled up as hard as a small stone.

"I want to see your breasts." Though she blushed, she nodded her head, so he slowly unbuttoned her gown down to her waist. Pushing her gown apart, he gazed at her luscious breasts. She had the prettiest nipples with small dusky pink areolas. Lowering his head, he sucked her puckered nipple into his mouth. He gently massaged her other nipple as he suckled. She moaned with pleasure as she tried to get closer to his hand.

Jonathan reached down, pulled up her gown to her pretty red curls, and touched her sweet little bud of desire. He flicked it with the tip of his finger and felt her tremble in his arms. He wanted to bring her to satisfaction for the first time, so he continued to rub her little nubbin until he heard her gasp and whimper as waves of ecstasy rolled over her. He looked up at her, and she had the most incredibly beautiful smile on her gorgeous flushed face.

She opened her lovely violet eyes, filled with wonder, and said, "What did you do to me? That was the most amazing feeling I've ever experienced."

Pulling her close, Jonathan said, "My dear, God designed your body to feel pleasure, and what you felt was the sexual fulfillment of desire. It pleased me greatly to be able to bring you your first experience of pleasure. With what happened to you when you were a child, I wasn't sure you would be able to relax enough to feel pleasure. Thank you for trusting me, and I promise you have nothing to fear from me."

"Surprising enough, I wasn't scared. I trust you Jonathan."

"Any time I do something that makes you uncomfortable, all you have to do is tell me, and I'll stop. Now, as much as I love lying here with you, I need to get my day started." He rolled out of bed and stood up, leaned over and kissed her on the nose, then smiled as he turned and walked out of the room.

When Jonathan entered his room he was in severe pain from the stiffest erection he could ever remember having. He knew he would have to find his own release, so he took care of business and breathed a sigh of relief.

Oh God, how in hell was he going to do this every night…until she finally allowed him inside her gorgeous body?

Jonathan was determined to find the strength somewhere, because when she did finally let him in, it would all be worthwhile. He just knew that if she fell in love with him, her passions would overrule her fears. The expression of wonder on her pretty face when she reached her fulfillment made him feel his love for her in the very depths of his soul. Her pretty cheeks, all flushed with passion, were fulfillment for him. That was the first time he had ever pleasured a woman without any thought of his own sexual gratification.

Yes, it would all be worthwhile.

All he needed to do was be patient a little while longer.

Once Jonathan left the room, Kathryn continued to lie in bed. She felt so deliciously satisfied. She never imagined that there would be such pleasure found in anything to do with sex. Just thinking about what had happened made her feel a tingly sensation in the place between her legs. She was so grateful to Helen and Melody for suggesting that she let nature take its course.

Jonathan was such a thoughtful and considerate man. She had sensed that he held his passions in check so he wouldn't scare her. She wondered if she would ever be brave enough to give him pleasure by touching him intimately. She knew he had desired her because she felt his arousal against her bottom when she woke up this morning. She decided that she would try to touch him tonight. She would block out the images of her uncle from her mind.

That morning, Kathryn felt energized as she got up and rang for Sarah. Once she finished her morning ablutions, she went downstairs, had breakfast, and then went to meet with the housekeeper, Mrs. Rollins. They planned the day's menu and discussed a problem with one of the maids. "Milady, Nancy, the chambermaid, is in a delicate condition, and I think she should be dismissed. It will set a bad example for the rest of your staff if she continues to work here."

Kathryn looked at the housekeeper and wondered what would be the best way to handle this situation. "Mrs. Rollins, I want to speak to Nancy. Please go get her and bring her here."

Mrs. Rollins brought Nancy to her office, and Kathryn smiled pleasantly at her. It was obvious she was terrified. It showed in the poor girl's deep brown eyes. "Nancy, Mrs. Rollins tells me you're with child. How far along are you, and who's the man responsible for your condition?"

Nancy started to cry. "Please d-don't fire me, milady. I h-have no place t' go. Me parents 'ill k-kick me out when they find out about th' b-babe."

"Shush, no one is going to kick you out," Kathryn said. "Now continue with your story."

"I tried t' stop th' men," Nancy stammered, "but t-they forced 'emselves on me. It was th' young genl'men t-that comes here from Bath. I don't knows their names. They was out riding an' asked me for d-direction, an' when I stopped t' tell 'em...t-they got off their horses and pulled me int' th' bushes. I'm a g-good girl, milady. I was... a v-virgin. I thought

I'd die from th' pain. It hurt real bad, milady. One after th' other did it t' me. Th' others held me down."

Nancy sobbed out her story, and Kathryn was appalled that young men would do something like this. "Nancy, you're not going to lose your position. Could you identify the men if you saw them again? I'm going to get Lord Sutherland, and I want you to tell him what the men looked like, all right?"

"Oh p-please, milady," Nancy cried. "They told me t-that they'd kill me if I ever told anybody about this. Please don't make me tell. They was mean and I...I knows they meant ever' word."

Kathryn went over to Nancy and put her arm around her. "We shan't let anyone hurt you, but these men need to be punished so that they can't do this to another young girl. Nancy, how old are you?"

Nancy continued to sob as she spoke in a trembling voice. "I'm fourteen, milady, and always been a g-good girl. Them young genl'men don't live around here. I never seen 'em afore. Only reason I knows they was from Bath is one o' 'em mentioned it."

Kathryn patted her on the shoulder. "Shush, everything is going to be all right. Stay here with Mrs. Rollins while I go get Lord Sutherland."

Kathryn left the room, went to Jonathan's study, and knocked on the door. When she heard him tell her to come in, she entered and cried, "Jonathan, the most dreadful thing has happened, and I don't know how to handle it. One of the maids has been r-raped by several young men from Bath, and she's now with child." Kathryn had tears rolling down her cheeks as she told Jonathan what had happened. "She says that her parents will kick her out when they find out about the child. Jonathan, she's only f-fourteen. These men need to be punished for what they've done! What can we do?"

Jonathan went to Kathryn, pulled him into his arms. "I'm so sorry you've had to deal with something like this. Can the maid identify the men who did this to her?"

She dropped her head on his shoulder. "I don't think she can. She said they threatened to kill her if she ever told anyone about what happened. Mrs. Rollins wanted to dismiss her, but we can't do that to her."

"Which maid is it? Most of them are daughters of my tenants. I'll talk to her parents and make sure they don't throw her out. Let's go find out, all right?"

Kathryn nodded, and they went to the housekeeper's office together. When they entered, poor Nancy was sobbing uncontrollably.

Jonathan spoke to Nancy in his deep, soothing voice. "Nancy, I'll talk to your parents, and they won't throw you out. You aren't going to lose your position. Lady Sutherland told me what happened. Those young men can't hurt you, because I won't let them. Now please, tell me who they are."

"Milord, I can't tells ye, cuz I don't knows who they was. They was just some young genl'men from Bath. That's all I knows. They talked real fancy like. They was gentry, they was."

Turning to the housekeeper, Jonathan said, "Mrs. Rollins, see that Nancy is taken care of. I'm going to go see her parents and tell them what has happened." He turned to Kathryn and added, "Kathryn, please come with me."

Once they were out of the housekeeper's office, Jonathan said, "Her parents are very strict Wesleyans, so they aren't going to take this well. I just hope I can convince them to let her continue to live with them. I don't want you to worry about this. If they do refuse to allow her to come home, I'll figure out something. Why don't you go upstairs to your studio? When I get back, I'll come and let you know what's going to happen."

Kathryn went to her studio, but she had a hard time concentrating. She went back downstairs to Mrs. Rollins's office and found her alone. "Where's Nancy?"

Mrs. Rollins replied, "I sent her to clean the music room. I thought that keeping her busy would help the poor little thing. I never dreamed that something like this could happen. Those young men need to be found and punished. If they did this to Nancy, they could do it to someone else."

"I agree with you, but since she can't identify them, it's going to be difficult. It sounds as if they were young gentlemen, and it would be impossible to punish them, even if we could find out who they are. Lord Sutherland told me that her parents are strict Wesleyans and won't take this well at all. I hope he can convince them to let her continue to live with them," Kathryn said, as she sat down in the chair.

Mrs. Rollins pushed her spectacles up on her nose and sighed. "I'll keep her busy today, and hopefully Lord Sutherland will figure out what needs to be done."

Kathryn went upstairs and spent some time with the children, but she was too distracted to enjoy it. Since Kathryn always found walking helped calm her down, she went to her room, put on her walking shoes, and went for a walk to pass the time until Jonathan returned.

When Jonathan returned from speaking with Nancy's parents, he found Kathryn in their sitting room. "I talked to Nancy's parents, and they were furious when I told them

Nancy was with child, and immediately said they would throw her out. I let them know how displeased I would be if they did that, and they backed down. I just wish there was some way to punish these young men, but since it sounds as if they're gentry, it would be difficult. Who would take the word of a servant over these young men?"

"Thank goodness you were able to convince her parents. The last thing Nancy needs now is to be ostracized by the very people she needs the most support from."

"How are you handling all this? I'm sure it's brought up painful memories for you."

Kathryn bowed her head and sighed. "It *has* been difficult. Of course, what happened to Nancy is much worse than what happened to me. I can't imagine being raped so many times and by several different men. Oh, how can men do things like this to an innocent young girl?"

Jonathan put his arm around her and pulled her close. "Darling, I can't tell you why some men behave like animals. Sweetheart, you *were* raped repeatedly. Your abuse was ten times worse, because you had to live in fear every time your uncle came for a visit. At least with Nancy it won't ever happen again." Trying to lighten Kathryn's mood, he asked, "Now, did you work on Roderick's portrait today?"

Kathryn shook her head. "I was too distraught to concentrate, so I went for a walk instead. I also went and visited the children. Poor Nancy, my heart goes out to her. Now she's going to have to face being a mother at far too young of an age."

"I wish I could stay and continue to talk to you about this, but I have a meeting with Whetherby." He gently pulled her into his arms and kissed her forehead. "Why don't you go rest until dinner?"

"I think I'll do that. This has been quite distressing," Kathryn said. Jonathan gently kissed her, and she gave him a trembling smile and watched him leave the room.

Chapter 19
- October 1823 -

Kathryn woke up from her nap feeling much better. She still felt terrible about what Nancy would be facing, but at least she wouldn't have to face it alone. Kathryn would make sure that Nancy's child was well taken care of. After all, she had her money from her commissions to help women like Nancy. In fact, there must be a need for a safe haven for other young girls who found themselves in similar situations. Maybe she could sponsor a home in London to help these young women. Kathryn decided that she would talk to Jonathan about it at dinner.

While eating dinner that night, Kathryn broached the subject, explaining to Jonathan what she wanted to do. "Since I don't need the money that I earn from my commissions, I can fund it myself, that way you shan't need to worry that I'll come to you for help."

"Kathryn, I think it's a wonderful idea, but I would like to help. I agree that there must be many other young girls that find themselves in situations just like Nancy's. When we go to

London in the spring, I'll help you find a location for the home."

"Oh, thank you, Jonathan. I'm sure that I can get Melody and Helen to participate in my endeavor. After all, all of us who have volunteered at St. Mark's Orphanage have seen children without a parent to take care of them. With a home like this, there will now be a way for young girls to keep their babies instead of leaving them at the orphanage."

"Whatever you want to do, my love. Now, since we're through with our dinner, why don't we go to the library, and we can read some more of that new novel by Jane Austin."

Later that night, after Jonathan and Kathryn retired to bed, Jonathan held Kathryn and gently rubbed her shoulders. "Darling, you're very tense aren't you? I think you need a massage to relieve some of that tension. Roll over on your belly. If I'm going to do this right, you'll need to take off your night rail. While you do that, I'm going to my room and get some massaging oil. I'll be right back."

While Jonathan left the room, Kathryn thought about this idea of a massage. She wasn't sure she wanted one, especially without her night rail on. Of course, she did like it when he rubbed her shoulders, so maybe it would be all right. She removed her night rail, laid down on her stomach, and pulled up the sheet.

Jonathan came back into the room carrying a small bottle, which he held over the flame of a candle. "I'm warming the oil so it will feel more soothing. It will only take a moment. I hope you don't mind the scent of mint, because this oil has spearmint in it. I'm going to just lower this sheet a bit." He touched the bottle. "Perfect."

Jonathan sat on the side of the bed, poured some of the oil in his palm, and rubbed his hands together. Then he started rubbing her shoulders and arms. The oil had a pleasant, spicy scent that filled the room as he kneaded it into her skin. He used a little pressure as he rubbed her shoulders. Then he poured some more oil into his palms and applied it to her back. She had to admit, it felt very soothing, and she could feel her muscles begin to relax.

As Jonathan kept stroking her back, he worked his way down to her derriere. He pulled the sheet down and started stroking her bottom and upper thighs. She wanted to reach down and pull the sheet back up, but she resisted the temptation. Kathryn felt a throbbing between her legs, and she felt moisture pooling there. Kathryn couldn't imagine what was causing that.

Again, he poured more oil into his palms and massaged it into her body. His hands worked down to her calves. It felt so good, that she couldn't help but moan from the pleasure of it all. Then he started massaging her feet, going toe by toe, and it felt sublime.

"Roll onto your back and I'll massage your front." She looked warily at him, but then she complied. He started at her feet and worked his way up her legs. It really did feel marvelous, and her muscles felt as if they were wet noodles. Then he poured some oil in her navel and slid his hands over her belly, kneading gently.

Jonathan slowly rubbed his hands up to her breasts and massaged more oil on her skin. He never touched her nipples, but they grew taut anyway. Her breathing was becoming shallow, and her heart was beating rapidly. He was now lying on the bed. Jonathan leaned over and kissed her as his hands continued to massage her breasts. His hands were trembling as he finally took her nipple and gently rolled it between his forefinger and thumb.

Kathryn began kissing him back. She parted her lips, so he slid in his tongue. He ran his hand down over her belly and into her curls at the apex of her thighs. She felt his finger touch her core, and she sighed from the intense pleasure. He circled her little nubbin, moving ever closer to the entrance of her body.

Slowly, Jonathan slipped his finger inside her, and she willed herself to stay relaxed. He began to stroke his finger in and out while his thumb rubbed her special spot. Heat poured through her, startling in its intensity. She gasped as sensations surged throughout her entire body. She felt as if she was flying, and then she landed on a soft cloud. As she came back down to earth, he slowly withdrew his hand. He gently kissed her nose. "Do you feel relaxed now?"

Kathryn gazed at him. "If I were any more relaxed, you would have to scrape me off this bed. I think I like massages. Would you like me to give you one?"

"I tell you what…you can give me one next time. I believe that it's time for us to go to sleep. I love you, Kathryn." He lay down beside her, pulled the covers up over them, and wrapped her in his arms. Kathryn was so sleepy that she closed her eyes and fell fast asleep without even remembering she was totally nude.

Kathryn and Jonathan, along with Elaine and the children, went into town on Friday to visit with Kathryn's brother and sister and their families because they were all leaving to go back home on Saturday. When they arrived, Kathryn took

Frankford and Jane to the schoolroom so they could play, and Elaine decided to stay with them. Jonathan went to the study to spend time with Henry and Matthew.

When Kathryn got back downstairs, she found her mother with Helen and her sisters-in-law in the drawing room. As she entered the room, she took a seat. "Hello, Mother. You look well. Have you enjoyed having your family here this week? I'm sure you'll miss everyone when they leave. Do you have any plans for next week?"

"We've had a pleasant visit. Lady Milsom and I are going to London next week. Her son is getting married in three weeks to the Duke of Monmouth's youngest daughter, Lady Ellen. The wedding should be marvelous. I need to do some shopping, so I'm looking forward to the trip."

"I hope you have an enjoyable time." Kathryn turned to Helen and asked, "Are you sure you're all right with me bringing Frankford and Jane with me when we come in two weeks?"

"Of course. We look forward to it. Christina and Catherine are thrilled that Jane is coming for a visit, and Winston and Nelson are enthralled with Frankford. When can we expect you?"

"We're planning to leave on Saturday, the first of November. Since we'll have the children with us, we should get to your house the following Tuesday. We're planning on three days of traveling. Is that how long it takes you?"

"If the weather is good, then you can easily do it in three days. It took us three days to get here, and none of the days was too arduous. Let's go up to the schoolroom and see how the children are doing." Helen turned to Melody and asked, "Do you want to come with us?"

"Certainly, Helen. William's due for a feeding anyway," Melody replied.

Once Kathryn, Helen, and Melody were out of the drawing room, Helen said, "Now, let's go to your old room so we can talk. We want to know how everything is going with Jonathan. Can you believe Mother? She's been pleasant this entire visit. She must finally be mellowing in her old age." They all laughed, looked at each other, and smiled.

They went upstairs to Kathryn's old room and took a seat, and then Melody remarked, "I have to say, I'm quite surprised with your mother's attitude. She's been so pleasant to me. It's as if she were a different person. Henry hasn't had to say anything to her the entire time we've been here. She even had us bring the children to her yesterday afternoon, and while she was a bit stiff, she actually had a conversation with Mary Elizabeth and Brandon. I was so shocked you could have blown me over with a feather. Now, enough about that. Tell us what's been happening. Are you and Jonathan getting closer?"

Kathryn blushed. "Yes, we're getting to know each other much better. I want to thank both of you for your advice. I'm much more relaxed around him. Jonathan's so kind and considerate, and I'm thrilled that I married him."

Helen rolled her eyes. "That's not what we want to know. We want to know if you've made love yet. Has he been able to break through your barrier?"

Kathryn looked down in embarrassment. "He says that we are making love, but just not completely. We sleep together every night and I've...allowed him certain...ah...liberties with my person. He's told me he loves me, and that he's content with whatever I'm comfortable with. Something happened that was truly amazing. He's given me immense pleasure, but I haven't returned that pleasure. He told me he gets satisfaction from watching me, but I know he would rather me do something for him, but I don't know what to do." Kathryn's face turned bright red as she told them this.

"I know you find this difficult to talk about, Kathryn, but we just want to help you. I'm pleased you've allowed him to bring you pleasure. As far as giving him pleasure in return, all you have to do is…ah touch his…ah manhood. I promise he'll love that," Melody answered, blushing profusely from embarrassment.

Kathryn couldn't look at them as she replied, "I've thought about that, but I haven't gotten my nerve up yet. Oh, this is all so embarrassing. I appreciate your advice, and I do want to do what's right for Jonathan, but I get scared that he'll be so overcome with desire that he'll do something I can't handle."

"Kathryn, how do you feel about Jonathan? Do you think you're falling in love with him?" Helen asked.

"I know my feelings have grown much stronger for Jonathan, but I'm not sure that I know how love feels. How did you know you were in love with Matthew?" Kathryn asked. "I know you were determined to never fall in love, but then you did."

"Love wasn't something that I planned on. I fought it determinedly, but it sneaked in when I least expected it," Helen replied, as she smiled at Kathryn. "For me, love is never wanting to be away from him, and when we are apart, thinking about him constantly. I not only love Matthew, I respect him tremendously, and we've become very good friends."

"Jonathan and I are good friends. In fact, he's the best friend that I've ever had. I do think about him all the time, and I respect him. Oh, how do I ask this? Does…ah…making love hurt?"

Embarrassed, Melody giggled. "No, making love doesn't hurt as long as the man does what he's supposed to do. Your body has to be prepared to receive your husband. Lots of kissing helps to do that, and touching you intimately does also. Just let yourself relax. I promise it doesn't hurt. I know what happened to you was horrible, but it had nothing to do with making love. What your uncle tried to do was about power and manipulation."

"I appreciate your help and advice," Kathryn confided. "You've given me more to ponder, and I'm sure that I'll know when I'm ready for more intimacy. This was difficult to talk about, but if it helps me get over my fear, it's worth it. Now, can we go have William's birthday party?"

Arm in arm they walked to the nursery. The children were having a delightful time. Helen and Kathryn read them a story while Melody fed William. Once William had eaten, Melody sat him down at the table in front of his birthday cake, and before she could stop him, he dug his hand into the cake and smeared icing all over his face. All the children shrilled with laughter.

Once they had all eaten the cake, Melody helped William open up his presents. It was so cute to watch him try to tear the paper off and see his expression when he saw what was inside. They spent a pleasant hour with the children, then returned to the drawing room for tea.

The men joined them and soon everyone was enjoying their tea and biscuits. Since they were staying for dinner, Jonathan and Kathryn went up to her old room to rest. As they entered her room, Jonathan pulled Kathryn into his arms, kissed her, and said, "I've been wanting to do that for the last hour. Why don't you lie down and take a nap? I'm going to just slip off my pantaloons and put some ointment on my knee."

Bolstering her courage, Kathryn took a deep breath. "Why don't you lie on the bed, and I'll massage the ointment into your knee? Where do you keep it?"

Looking surprised, but pleased, Jonathan said, "I'll get it for you." He went to his valise and pulled the ointment out, then handed it to her as he slipped out of his pantaloons. He went over to the bed and laid down. Kathryn walked over to the bed, sat down beside him, and spread the ointment over his knee. She worked it into his skin. Her hands trembled slightly as she stroked and kneaded his knee.

"Let me know if I hurt you. I've never done a massage before, and I don't know how much pressure to use. When I see your scars, I'm truly amazed that you didn't lose your leg. I would think that it's terribly painful to bend your knee," Kathryn said, as she continued to massage the ointment into his skin.

"It is quite painful, that's why I have to walk with such a limp. Does it bother you that you're married to a cripple?"

While Kathryn continued to message his knee, she said, "I don't think of you as a cripple, and no one who knows you would. I think it's remarkable that you get around as well as you do. I just wish that it didn't cause you so much pain. Do you need to take a dose of laudanum?"

"I was going to wait until you fell asleep. You said it would bother you to see me take it. I'll be all right for a while longer. My knee feels much better since you rubbed the ointment on it. Why don't you slip off your gown? I'll loosen your corset and you can take a nap." He sat up and turned her around so he could unbutton her gown.

Kathryn stood still as he helped her loosen her gown. "I know you need the laudanum. I'll be all right if you take your dose. I'll just turn away from you while you take it."

"As long as you're all right with it." Once she was through massaging his knee, she removed her gown and laid down with her back to him while he took his laudanum. When he rejoined her on the bed, he pulled her close and whispered, "Pleasant dreams."

After their nap, they dressed and went down to dinner. It was splendid as usual. The duchess had a wonderful chef, so the food was always superb, and everyone was in good spirits. When it came time to leave, Kathryn hugged Melody and Henry and said, "Thank you for coming to my wedding. Jonathan and I look forward to seeing you at Christmas. Have a safe trip back." Then turning to Helen and Matthew, she added, "I'll see you in November!"

After more hugs and a kisses, Kathryn entered the carriage, and as it pulled away, she waved to them as the carriage turned the corner and headed back to St. John's Wood.

The children slept the entire way home. When they got home, Jonathan and Kathryn carried them up to the nursery and tucked them into bed. By the time they got to their rooms, Kathryn could barely keep her eyes open. Jonathan told her he would be back, and he went to his room. Sarah was waiting for her, and she soon had Kathryn ready for bed. Sarah left, and Kathryn went ahead and got into bed. As she started to drift off to sleep, she heard Jonathan come into the room. He walked over to the bed, pulled back the covers, got in, and pulled her close. He kissed her cheek as she closed her eyes and fell fast asleep.

Chapter 20
- Early November 1823 -

During the next two weeks, Kathryn spent her time working on Roderick's portrait in the morning, and playing with Frankford and Jane in the afternoon. Her nights were filled with sensual delights. She still hadn't worked up the courage to touch her husband. Each time she started to, her mind would fill with images of what her uncle had forced her to do.

Her feelings were growing stronger each day they spent together, but she still didn't know if she was in love with him. In the evenings after dinner, they would spend time together in the music room, or in their sitting room reading to each other. Kathryn was very content with her life, and knew that Jonathan felt the same way.

Kathryn, Jonathan, and the children were leaving the next day to go to Helen and Matthew's house. The children were excited about seeing their friends again, and they constantly asked when they were leaving. Elaine wasn't going because she needed to concentrate on her studies, since she'd neglected them ever since Kathryn and Jonathan's marriage.

That evening when Jonathan came to Kathryn, she was determined to give him some of the pleasure he'd so generously given to her. Before he got into the bed, he removed his robe, but he left his smalls on. He slid into bed and pulled Kathryn into his arms. She gladly snuggled close, raised her head, and met his kiss. Returning his kiss with enthusiasm, she opened her mouth to allow him access, and then slid her tongue into his mouth, twining it with his. She breathlessly kissed him back, her mouth pliant and hungry, luxuriating in his taste.

Desire blossomed deep in her belly as she melted into his embrace. His fingers slid down over the soft orb of her breast, turning her nipple into a tight little bud. His lips followed the path that his hand had taken as he gently suckled her breast. Then nibbling his way down to her navel, he swirled his tongue around it as if he were drinking sweet nectar. His hand found her core as he began to gently flick his fingertip across her little pearl. The muscles tensed in her belly from the desire she felt as his mouth followed where his hand had gone.

Jonathan lay between her slender thighs as he kissed the soft flesh of her inner thigh. Kathryn was shocked as he licked his way up her thigh to her mound and silky curls. He caressed the moist, pink folds with his mouth and hand. At first she started to tense up, but then she relaxed as wonderful sensations filled her body. As he licked her tight bud, her escalating cries filled the air. His tongue circled the sensitive flesh around the entrance to her tight portal. The pressure kept building until she shattered into a million little pieces.

As Kathryn gently floated down from the clouds, Jonathan kissed his way back up her body and rolled to the side as he kissed her delectable lips. She tasted her essence on his lips as she reached for his chest and rubbed his taut male nipples. She heard him gasp and knew that he enjoyed the touch. She slowly trailed kisses down his shoulder and chest, nuzzling her nose through the silky hair on his chest until she licked his nipple, mirroring what he had done to her. She laid her hand on his chest as she suckled, and felt his heart pounding at an astounding pace.

Jonathan rubbed Kathryn's back and pulled her close as she continued to suck his flat male nipples into her mouth. Then his throaty cries of passion filled the room. His hand covered his shaft as he jerked from the explosion of his loins. Kathryn watched in amazement as Jonathan slumped back against the pillows. She was stunned by what had just happened and gloried in the expression of sheer bliss on Jonathan's face.

As Jonathan sighed, he said, "Kathryn, my love. I've wanted you to touch me for so long. You've brought me great joy. Thank you, my darling."

Kathryn blushed. "You've sent me to heights I never imagined, and I hope that, in some small way, I've given you pleasure that you so richly deserve."

Jonathan pulled her close, kissed her tenderly. "Pleasure beyond my wildest dreams."

As she watched his handsome face, his blue eyes slowly closed. His breathing grew steady and deep as he fell asleep. Kathryn lay there in shock at what had happened. She knew she had given him immense pleasure and that he had experienced his release. She never expected that just fondling his chest as he had done hers could cause this to happen. She was immeasurably pleased with herself.

As Kathryn watched him sleep, it dawned on her that she...was in love with Jonathan. Her heart swelled with emotion, and she felt tears of joy roll down her cheeks. Part of her wanted to wake him up so she could tell him that she loved him, but then fear raised its ugly head, and images of her uncle kept her silent.

Oh Lord, please help me overcome these fears so that I can be a true wife to Jonathan.

While she continued to ponder the events of the night, she slowly drifted off to sleep.

When Jonathan woke up the next morning, Kathryn was still sleeping beside him. The love he felt for her swelled his heart to bursting. He couldn't believe that Kathryn had touched and fondled him last night. It amazed him that he had experienced such a powerful release from so little, but then it had been so unexpected. When she had allowed him to give the most intimate of kisses last night, his desire had risen to fever pitch. He could still taste her essence on his lips. They had crossed a line of intimacy that he had expected would take months to reach. He just needed to continue to have patience, and eventually she would overcome all her fears and give herself to him completely.

Jonathan slipped from the bed, leaving Kathryn to her dreams, and went back to his room. Hatton was already there to help him get ready for their trip. Soon he was clean and shaved, so he headed downstairs to breakfast. He told Goodman to send Sarah up to help Kathryn get ready. When he entered the breakfast room, he went to the sideboard and filled his plate high with kippers, sausages, coddled eggs, and thick slices of toast slathered in butter, and took his seat at the table. As he ate his breakfast, he perused the morning paper, more relaxed than he had been in years.

Elaine entered the room, filled her plate, and sat down next to him. "I still think you should let me come with you and Kathryn. You're bringing Frankford and Jane, and they've been avoiding their studies as well. It's not fair that you're making me stay behind! I want to come too. I promise I'll behave, and I'll even help with the children. Please...let me come!"

Jonathan sighed as he laid down his fork. "We've been through this several times. This is not a holiday. Kathryn's going to her sister's to work. As you know, she's painting a portrait for the Marquess and Marchioness of Ralston. Frankford and Jane are coming because Kathryn doesn't want them left alone so soon after the death of their parents, and Helen's daughters want to play with Jane. I know you're good with the children, but there shan't be anyone your age to keep you entertained. Miss Tilton feels you have fallen behind in your studies and you need to catch up."

"You're taking the children's governess with you, so why can't we take Miss Tilton too?" Elaine pleaded. "If she comes, I'll still be able to do my studies. I'm going to be so lonely here without you. I miss Roderick and Allison too. I shouldn't be left alone either."

Tears rolled down her pretty pink cheeks, and Jonathan felt guilty. Obviously, the thought of being alone was quite distressing for her. Maybe it wasn't fair to leave her behind. Helen and Matthew would be fine with her coming. Jonathan just didn't want her to think that she was getting her way all the time. Then again, if they left her feeling so resentful, she might get into mischief.

"All right, you can come," Jonathan relented. "But Miss Tilton comes with us, and you'll do extra studying every day. This will *not* be a holiday. Now, if you're coming, I need to let Kathryn know, and tell Miss Tilton that she'll need to pack for both of you. Hurry and finish your breakfast and get changed into your travel clothes. We're leaving in an hour."

As Jonathan left the breakfast room, Kathryn arrived downstairs. "Against my better judgment, I've allowed Elaine to talk me into letting her come with us. I'm going upstairs now to tell Miss Tilton so she can get them ready. Elaine is finishing her breakfast, but then she needs to hurry upstairs and get ready for the trip."

"Jonathan, I really do think it's for the best. She misses Roderick and Allison dreadfully, and she would have been so lonely here without any of us. Helen and Matthew will be delighted to have her. She's very good with all the children, so she'll help keep them entertained. I'll hurry and eat my breakfast, then help her get ready to leave. Sarah has everything well in hand, so I didn't have anything to do until we leave. See you out front in an hour." Kathryn smiled back at him as she entered the breakfast room.

There was quite an entourage ready for the trip when Jonathan finally got everything organized. Jonathan and Kathryn would ride in the main carriage, while the governesses, children, and Elaine rode in the second, and then Hatton, Sarah, and Elaine's maid, Kitty, were in the third carriage. He knew it was probably going to take four days to get there instead of the three they had originally planned. At least the weather was clear, if a bit cold. By the time the coaches were loaded, they were thirty minutes late leaving. Once all Kathryn's art supplies and canvas were loaded into the third coach with the servants, they were off.

The coaches traveled for four hours before they made the first stop to have a light repast at a coaching inn that Matthew had recommended. Jonathan had the entire trip planned out based on information shared with him by Matthew.

By the time everyone had seen to their basic needs and had something to eat, they had lost another thirty minutes of valuable time. Jonathan tried not to let it bother him, but he didn't like the way the sky was looking. The clouds were dark, and he could already feel dampness in the air. And of course, his knee was killing him.

Once they were back on the road. Jonathan relaxed a bit, and he and Kathryn took turns reading some of Shakespeare's sonnets to each other. Kathryn was pleasant to travel with and made few demands.

About an hour after they left the coaching inn, the rain started, and it was torrential. It made travel exceedingly slow. The coaches were slipping and sliding in the mud. It became so bad that they had to make an unplanned stop, hoping the weather would break and they could continue on their way. It began getting dark, and the weather showed no signs of improving, so Jonathan made the decision to stop for the night. It could have been worse—at least the inn was clean, and the rooms were spacious.

The governesses settled the children and Elaine for the night, and after Kathryn and Jonathan told them goodnight, Kathryn and Jonathan had dinner in the private parlor. The food was plain country fare, but well prepared, and soon they finished the meal with their appetites appeased. Over dessert,

Jonathan said, "Thank goodness. It looks like the rain is finally stopping. It's slowed us down quite a bit. At this rate, we'll not get to Matthew and Helen's until Wednesday. If the weather is fair tomorrow, we may be able to make up some of the time."

Covering her mouth, Kathryn yawned. "I'm sure you'll be able to make it up tomorrow. Well, I'm quite tired, so I'm off to bed. Are you ready to come up?"

"I'll be up in a moment. I'm just going to relax here in this chair before I turn in. See you in a bit, my dear." Kathryn smiled at him, then turned and left the room.

Jonathan's knee was bothering him terribly because of all the rain, so he took his laudanum with a glass of port, but before he realized it, he'd drunk an entire bottle and was feeling the effects. He was feeling so pleasantly mellow that he called for another bottle. Eventually he passed out and never made it up to bed.

When Hatton found Jonathan the next morning, he shook his head. His head was pounding, but he refused Hatton's offer to fix him his old remedy. He was quite nauseated at his stomach, and, figuratively speaking, kicked himself for his own stupidity.

When Kathryn came down for breakfast, she looked concerned. "What happened last night? You never came up to bed. I was worried when I woke up this morning."

Hanging his head, Jonathan answered her with embarrassment in his voice. Kathryn deserved better than this. "Kathryn, I'm not feeling very well this morning, but I'll be all right soon. I'm going up to our room to change. Go ahead and have breakfast without me. Can you handle getting everyone organized so we can leave in an hour?"

"I'm sorry you aren't feeling well. I'll take care of everything. I hope you get to feeling better soon. Are you sure you're up to traveling today?"

"I'll be fine, once I have a wash and a shave. Don't worry about me. Thank you for handling everything this morning. I'll see you outside in an hour." He turned and slowly made his way upstairs.

God, why did he allow himself to slip like that?

It had been so long since he last drank himself into a stupor!

Once they were back on the road, Kathryn asked, "What really happened last night? You look as if you haven't slept in a week, and your eyes are all bloodshot."

Jonathan felt terrible remorse and knew he needed to tell her the truth. It was the only fair thing to do. "I behaved very stupidly last night. After you went up to bed, my knee was bothering me terribly, so I took a dose of laudanum with a glass of port. The next thing I knew, Hatton was waking me up this morning. I overindulged on port, so I have a sore head this morning. I thought I could handle a few glasses of port, but obviously, I couldn't. I'm sorry. I shan't let it happen again."

"You should have told me your knee was bothering you so badly. I would have been happy to massage it for you. Next time, instead of drinking too much, let me help you. You need to get some sleep. Come over here and lay your head on my shoulder and rest. I'm sure that with some sleep, you'll feel better soon."

Jonathan looked at her with gratitude in his eyes. Moving over beside her, he put his head on her shoulders and closed his eyes, then fell asleep. His last thought before sleep took him away was that he'd married a saint. Jonathan slept for three hours, and when he woke up, he felt much better. He was so ashamed of his behavior. Obviously, port was too strong for him to drink, and he knew he would have to leave it alone, along with the whiskey and brandy.

Travel was easier that day, and they were able to make up some of the time they'd lost the day before. By the time they stopped for the night, everyone was famished. The governesses took their charges upstairs and had trays sent to their rooms.

Kathryn and Jonathan dined and then retired together to their room. He played maid for her, and she rubbed his knee and wrapped cold compresses around it while he lay on the bed. There was a screen in the room so Kathryn went behind it to undress. When she joined him in bed, Jonathan pulled her into his arms, kissed her, and then felt sleep begin to take him away. He was exhausted from the day's travel, but so grateful to have such an understanding wife. Before sleep completely took him away, he sent up a silent prayer thanking God for bringing her into his life.

When Kathryn woke up the next morning, Jonathan had already gotten up and left the room. There was a knock on the door, and Kathryn let Sarah in the room. While dressing, she thought about Jonathan's problem. He'd been so embarrassed over his slip. Her heart just went out to him when she saw his distress. She could understand how it happened, what with the amount of pain he had to be experiencing.

Traveling had to be incredibly difficult for Jonathan, because he had to sit for such long periods of time. He was too much of a gentleman to stretch out in the carriage to take some of the strain off his knee. Today, she would convince him to recline on his seat, which should help. After dismissing Sarah, she headed down to breakfast.

When she entered the dining parlor, Jonathan was already eating his breakfast, so she filled her plate from the sideboard and sat down across from him. "Did you sleep better last night? I must say you look much better than yesterday. How much further do we have to travel? Are we halfway yet?"

"We're more than halfway, and if we make as good a time today as we did yesterday, we should be there by early Wednesday afternoon, well before dark. I slept very well last night, how about you?"

Kathryn took a sip of her tea, then sat it down. "I felt very well rested when I woke this morning. I stopped by and spoke with Miss Mills, and the children are doing fine. She told me that Elaine has helped to keep them entertained. I'm pleased you allowed her to come with us."

"I'm sure Elaine's been very helpful with the children. I guess it's better that we brought her. I just hope she continues to behave when we get to your sister's house. I'm going outside to make sure everything's ready for our departure. I'll see you in fifteen minutes." Kathryn finished her breakfast and went upstairs to see if Elaine was ready.

The weather held out, and they arrived at Helen's house at two o'clock on Wednesday. As they pulled up to the house, Kathryn caught her first view of the ocean, and the magnificence of it took her breath away. She could understand why Helen loved it here so much. As they were getting out of the carriages, Helen and Matthew hurried out to greet them.

Helen hugged Kathryn and kissed her cheek. "I'm so pleased that you've finally arrived. Did you run into bad weather? It took us longer to get back last week because we had terrible rain part of the way. Did the children travel without mishap? Oh, and I talked to Cassandra, and she's excited about you coming to do their portrait. We're supposed to go there tomorrow for tea. That way you can discuss when you want to have them sit for you."

As they walked to the house, Kathryn said, "We had bad weather the first day, but the rest of the trip the weather was clear. The children did well. We brought Elaine with us. I hope that's all right. I look forward to meeting Lady Ralston and her husband tomorrow. I'm anxious to get started."

Once they entered the house, Helen introduced her to the butler. "This is Wells, and he'll get you anything that you need. Let me show you to your rooms. I'm glad you brought Elaine with you. She'll help entertain the children. My children adore her."

Helen showed them to a suite of rooms, which were lovely. As Kathryn looked around her room, she admired the lovely royal blue counterpane on the bed, which matched the upholstered furniture. Sarah arrived and soon had all her belongings put away. There was a dressing room that separated their bedrooms, which was very spacious. She went and knocked on Jonathan's door, then entered his room.

Jonathan had taken off his shirt and his pantaloons, and he was standing in just his smalls. "Oh, excuse me. I didn't realize you were changing."

"That's all right, sweetheart. I'm always happy to see you. Come here and give me a kiss. I feel as if it's been a week since we've really kissed."

Kathryn tentatively approached him and he pulled her to him. He gave her a slow, hungry kiss that curled her toes. She ran her hand across his chest, burying her fingers in the silky hair. She loved to run her fingers through his chest hair.

Jonathan must have liked it too, since his smalls tented up from his erection. She found it to be titillating, rather than frightening, as she felt it probing her belly. It amazed her that she had come such a long way. Two weeks ago, she would never have believed that she would find Jonathan's erection arousing.

"Sorry, my dear, but you cause this reaction all the time. I'm usually able to hide it from you. I hope it doesn't frighten you. I was just getting ready to put some ointment on my knee when you walked in."

"Since you explained what causes it, I'm no longer frightened when it happens. I'm actually…flattered." Then realizing what she had said, she looked down, saying hurriedly, "Why don't you sit in that chair, and I'll take care of your knee? I'm sure it has to be stiff from traveling the last few days."

Jonathan sat down next to a table where the jar of ointment was sitting. Kathryn picked it up, then rubbed the ointment on his knee and massaged it into his skin, as she knelt down before him. Looking down at his knee, she didn't see the look of desire burning in Jonathan's eyes, but she couldn't help noticing the material of his smalls stretched tightly across his thick shaft. It was so fascinating, that she wanted to reach up and touch it, but she was too shy to do it, especially since it was daylight. Once she finished tending his knee, Jonathan pulled her up and sat her down on his good knee, and then kissed her deeply as she opened her mouth for him.

Jonathan reached behind her, and unbuttoned her gown. Before she knew it, he had it pulled down, along with her chemise, and was feasting on her breasts. Pleasure broke over her, sending ripples of fire up her spine. Her breasts grew heavy, and her nipples taut, as he licked one with his tongue while he gently flicked his thumb over the other.

Kathryn ran her hand over his smooth muscular stomach, and she felt his shaft swell even further under her derriere.

Jonathan groaned. "We have to stop, or I'll never be able to get myself back under control in time for tea. You have no idea what you do to me."

Kathryn smiled coyly. "I'll leave you so you can get dressed. Jonathan, I'm thrilled that you react like that to me. I love how it makes me feel when you touch me. I'm not ready to fully make love with you, but please, just give me a little more time. I'm hopeful that I can conquer my fears, where before I would never have imagined that I would be this comfortable with what we do." She stood up, leaned down, and kissed him passionately, then left the room.

After tea, Jonathan went off with Matthew to see his stables. While they were looking at the prime horseflesh that Matthew owned, Matthew asked, "So, how's it been going with Kathryn? Have you worn down her resistance, or are you still taking a lot of cold baths?"

Jonathan grinned, showing how immensely pleased he was over the situation with Kathryn. "Things are progressing faster than I expected. While we haven't made love yet, she has allowed me quite a few liberties. I feel that she should be able to overcome her fears in the near future. I just know if she would fall in love with me, her passions would burn hot enough to defeat the fears she has. We had a situation with one of the housemaids, and I thought that it would stir up bad memories and set us back for weeks, but she handled it much better than I expected."

"What kind of situation did you have?"

"One of the chambermaids ended up with child, and it turns out she was brutally raped by several young men from Bath. She was unable to give any type of description, other than that they were gentry. I expected Kathryn to fall apart over it and withdraw back into her shell, but she handled the entire episode with a calm demeanor."

Mathew looked at him with a shocked look on his face. "That's awful. You couldn't get any information? I guess it wouldn't have mattered anyway, if they were gentry. Who would take the word of a chambermaid over a member of the gentry?"

"That's why I didn't push the issue. I went and talked to the girl's parents, and at first, they wanted to kick her out, because they're very strict Wesleyans. Then I told them that I would support Nancy and her child, so they relented and said they would keep her. So tell me about some of these racing horses. Do you ever take them to Doncaster and race them?"

As they walked out of the stables, Matthew turned to him and said, "Sanderford owns Doncaster Stables, and he's let me breed some of my mares with his Arabian stallion. I expect to have some births any day now. I've raced Jezebel and won. That was a nice purse. The odds were ten to one. If I can have a few more runs like that, I would become a much wealthier man."

"I didn't realize Sanderford owned Doncaster Stables. That's one of the best breeding farms in England. I'll have to talk to him about breeding some of my mares. Matthew,

Kathryn mentioned that Henry used to detest you, but now you're the best of friends. What changed?"

Matthew looked embarrassed. "I think I told you about my mistress. Well, Henry blamed me for causing Helen so much grief, and I deserved it. Cecilia made Helen's life miserable the first year of our marriage."

"Kathryn told me about it. At least you were able to move beyond it. I'm sure that it was hard on Helen."

Looking tormented, Matthew replied, "It was my own stupid fault. I should have broken it off with Cecilia before I ever went to London to look for a wife, but unfortunately, I didn't. That's something I'll regret all my life. I'm truly blessed to have her as my wife. Eventually, Sanderford forgave me when he realized how much I love Helen."

"Well, I'm glad he was able to forgive you, and that you're now good friends. I really like Sanderford, but I'll make sure I don't ever get on his bad side. We had better get back to the house. Kathryn will be wondering what we could be talking about for so long."

Chapter 21
- Mid November 1823 -

Once the men went outside to the stables, Kathryn and Helen went up to see the children. They spent a pleasant hour in the nursery before going to her sitting room to talk. As soon as Kathryn sat down, Helen asked, "How have things been going for you this past fortnight? Jonathan seems relaxed and happy, and so do you. Have you let him make love to you yet?"

Kathryn smiled affectionately over at her. "I'm immensely happy. Jonathan's a wonderful husband. I've fallen in love with him. We still haven't made love, but I'm feeling much more comfortable with the idea of intimacy."

Helen smiled triumphantly. "Oh Kathryn, that's wonderful. I'm so pleased that you've fallen in love with him. I just knew the two of you would have a wonderful relationship. I liked Jonathan from the very beginning, and I knew you wouldn't have married him if you hadn't loved him. I promise you won't regret making love. When you love someone, it's the most amazing experience of your life. I have some news to share with you. I'm going to have another baby. I'm two months along, so the baby is due in late June. I just became sure this week."

"Helen, how do you know when you're with child? I've always wondered how a woman knows before she starts showing."

"Well, if you have regular monthly courses, it's fairly easy to tell, because they stop when you're with child," Helen explained. "I just missed my second one in a row, so that's how I know that I'm about two months along. I love my sons, but I do hope that I have a daughter this time."

"I hope you do too. I'd love to have a baby. Thank you for telling me this, because I'm hopeful about overcoming my fears. It's just that if Jonathan were to lie on top of me, it would bring back horrible images of what my uncle did to me. As long as he stays on his back, I find it much less threatening."

"Kathryn, there's many positions that can be used for making love. The man doesn't always have to be on top." Helen looked embarrassed, but then she continued speaking. "In fact, oh...this is so embarrassing, but if it will help you...I ah...enjoy it quite a bit being on top. It gives me a sense of power, and I love it!"

Kathryn's cheeks flushed. "Helen...oh my...I can't even imagine. I'm glad we talked. I do find it embarrassing to talk about it all, but if it will help me overcome my fears, then it will be well worth a little embarrassment. Well, I need to go to my room and get ready for dinner. Are you sure you're all right with Elaine taking her meals with us?"

"Oh, of course. When I first got married, Margaret, Matthew's sister, was only sixteen, and she always ate with us. I think that by the time they're fifteen they should eat with the family."

"Oh good, I know she's thrilled about it." Kathryn was relieved, because she knew how much Elaine was looking forward to being included. "She's almost sixteen anyway. Her birthday is on the twelfth. I'm hoping that once Jonathan sees her behaving, he'll start letting her eat with us at home. He's actually quite old-fashioned about some things."

Helen grinned. "Well, sixteen is an important birthday, so we'll have to give her a small party."

"Thank you, Helen. I know Elaine would enjoy that. Well, if I'm going to be ready in time for dinner, I need to go back to my room. See you at dinner." Then, with a wave of her hand, Kathryn left and went to her room.

Elaine was on her best behavior that night, and dinner was a jovial affair. After dinner, the ladies left the gentlemen to their port and cigars. Kathryn worried about that since she knew Jonathan had problems with drinking, but she just had to have faith that he would be able to handle it. She followed Helen and Elaine to the drawing room.

Once the ladies left the room and the port was brought to the table, Matthew started to pour two glasses, but Jonathan spoke up. "Ah, none for me, Matthew."

"Jonathan, what do you drink?" Matthew asked. "You don't drink brandy, and now you don't drink port. I noticed you at dinner, and you barely touched the wine, and what you did drink, you watered down."

"I...don't seem to be able to handle spirits very well," Jonathan explained, feeling embarrassed about having to admit his problem. "I do still drink watered wine, but only with my meals. I was still allowing myself port, but on the trip here, I overindulged on it, so I've decided that I shouldn't drink it either."

"Why do you think you drink too much? Everyone overindulges at times."

"It all started because of my injury," Jonathan admitted. "I was in so much pain, and I drank to get some relief. Right before my brother died, I had started drinking whiskey every night, and I was barely eating any food. We went to the assembly rooms in Bath, and to make a long story short, I got drunk and made something of a spectacle of myself. At first, I thought that if I would just left the whiskey alone, I'd be all right, but then I overindulged on brandy, and now port. So I don't want to take a chance that I'll get drunk again."

Matthew had the footman take away the port, and requested coffee instead. Once the footman returned with the coffee, they just enjoyed their cigars, along with the coffee. "For the rest of your stay, we'll just have cigars and coffee, no port. I can take it or leave it, so I'll just leave it while you're here. I think you're a strong man to recognize that you have a problem and then do something about it. I think that my younger brother has a drinking problem, so I respect anyone who can leave it alone."

Jonathan felt a huge sense of relief that Matthew didn't seem to judge him for having a drinking problem. "How old is you brother? Is he out of school?"

"Gregory's one and twenty, and he's in the navy. He was sent down from school when he was eighteen. I haven't seen him in two years, but he writes occasionally and seems to like the navy. Before I bought him his commission, he was drinking and carousing around with his friends all the time.

The worst part was the gambling. He even had to fight a duel because of it. Before my boys were born, I worried about what would happen if I died without an heir. I was ecstatic when Helen had the twins and greatly relieved, to say the least."

Hearing Matthew talk about his brother made Jonathan think about how he'd lived his life before he met Kathryn, and he felt so grateful for the changes he'd made in his life. He still knew he wasn't good enough for her, but he was determined to never live that way again, so Kathryn could be proud of her husband.

"Your brother is still quite young, and you never know — he may have changed. Two years can make a big difference at that age. Well, I'm sure that the ladies are wondering what we're doing. Shall we join them?"

After Jonathan and Matthew joined the ladies, they went to the music room, and Jonathan played while Elaine sang. Everyone had a pleasant evening, and Helen assured Jonathan that he played as well as Mary. At ten o'clock, everyone retired to their beds. Jonathan was proud of Elaine. She'd handled herself very well tonight. It was hard for him, but he had to accept that Elaine was on the cusp of womanhood. Thank God he would have Kathryn there to help when she made her come out in two years.

When Jonathan arrived in Kathryn's room, she glanced over at him, giving him what she hoped was a seductive look. "I think that I'm ready to take another step closer to making love. You have to promise me that you'll just lie on your back and let me explore. When you lean over me, I get images of my uncle, and that's what frightens me. Will that be all right with you?"

"Sweetheart, whatever you want. I'm yours. I'll just lie down beside you and put my arm around your shoulders. Is that acceptable to you?"

"Yes, it's just if you lean over me too much that I get scared. I do like it when you hold me in your arms." Jonathan let her take the lead. She leaned over him and started kissing him passionately, and he responded. He rubbed her back and stroked her shoulders. Kathryn started kissing down his chest and she took his flat nipple into her mouth and began to suckle while she gently rolled the other one between her thumb and forefinger. She ran her hand down his smooth stomach and toyed with the waistband of his smalls.

His breathing became shallow, and he made a slight groan as Kathryn pulled the tab loose. Once they were untied, she pushed them down a little bit. Her hands were shaking, but she was determined to touch him. She reached inside his smalls and gingerly touched the tip, but when she felt something wet, she pulled back.

"That's my seed you felt. I promise it won't hurt you. If you really want me to enjoy this, let me show you how I would like you to touch me." Jonathan took her hand, guided it down to his shaft, and showed her how to stroke him through his smalls.

She fondled and touched for a long time, and then he gently moved her hand away. "If you keep doing that, I'll explode, and I don't want to frighten you. When a man gets too excited, he releases his seed, which comes out of the tip of his shaft, and right now I'm very close to that happening."

"Don't you want that to happen? Would it make you feel pleasure as you have made me feel pleasure, if you release your seed? I want to give you the same pleasure that you have given me."

"Sweetheart, if you're sure about this, then just keep rubbing me through my smalls." Kathryn tentatively smiled up at him and started rubbing him again. She squeezed his shaft, and she felt it swell and grow even harder as she continued to touch him. It was actually quite exciting to watch Jonathan's face as she fondled him. She found herself becoming aroused. She ran her hand up and down his shaft. She started moving her hand faster as she squeezed his member. Suddenly he gasped, letting out a deep, keening sound, and then fell back against the pillows with the most contented smile on his face that she'd ever seen.

"Did you feel pleasure, Jonathan?" she huskily asked.

"Oh, yes," he replied, "Now let me return the favor. Roll onto your side facing me so I can touch your luscious breasts."

Kathryn lay there waiting in anticipation as he began to stroke her breasts. He kissed her deeply and soon their tongues were dueling. Kathryn's breath grew shallow, and her heartbeat accelerated as his hands traveled down her body to the apex of her thighs. He slipped his hand between her slender thighs and touched her special spot, ever stroking faster and faster. Then he sent her spinning dizzyingly over the edge into ecstasy. They lay there in each other's arms as her breathing returned to normal.

"Thank you, darling, for the gift of your trust. I love you, and I just want you to be happy. You've brought so much joy into my life, and you have made me a better man. When I first met you, I was just going through the motions. I wasn't really living, and now I feel like a new man. I hope that someday soon you'll trust me enough to throw off all your fears and truly be my wife, but you take as long as you need. I'll be waiting right here when you're ready, my love."

He gently kissed her forehead, and then they fell asleep.

The next day, Kathryn and Helen arrived at the Marquess and Marchioness of Ralston's estate at four o'clock for tea. The butler showed them into the drawing room, where Lady Ralston was waiting for them. As they entered the room, she said, "Helen, it's so good to see you. This must be your sister, Lady Kathryn."

Helen hugged Cassandra. "Yes, Cassandra, this is my sister, Lady Sutherland. She recently married the Marquess of Sutherland. She arrived yesterday."

Cassandra beamed as she handed a cup of tea to Kathryn. "Lady Sutherland, welcome to my home. I've looked forward to meeting you. Congratulations on your marriage."

Kathryn took a sip of her tea, and then she said, "Thank you. It's a pleasure to meet you, Lady Ralston. Helen has told me what good friends you've become. I appreciate the opportunity to do your family portrait."

"Please, call me Cassandra. I'm sure that we'll become good friends. I'm so pleased that you're able to do our portrait. We've talked of having it done for a while now, but we wanted the children to be a little older. Brian is now six years old, John is five, and Lucian is four. I hope you're used to rambunctious little boys, because mine certainly are."

Kathryn nodded as she smiled over at Cassandra. "Oh yes, I have quite a few nieces and nephews. I've painted all of them several times. I recently did a family portrait for the Earl and Countess of Shelton, and they had three children. Then I did a family portrait for my husband's brother and his wife before they died. My husband is guardian to their two children, so I'm very used to children and love to paint them."

"I was so sorry to hear about your husband's brother and wife. I'm sure that was just dreadful. Helen told me about it. Please accept my condolences on your loss. From what Helen told me, you were there when it happened. I'm sure that you were able to help Lord Sutherland a great deal. Now you're married to him. Did you fall in love with him when you helped him get over his loss?"

"It was very difficult, and I'm just glad that I could be there for my husband. Of course, we weren't married when they died. I met my husband when I painted his portrait, and we became good friends. Then when his brother and his wife passed away, we grew closer. He asked me to marry him and help him raise the children. We fell in love after we married. I never expected to marry, but I'm very happy, and he's very supportive of my art."

"Well, I'm happy for you as well. I'm glad you enjoy children, because, as I said, mine are definitely a handful. Now, when can you start our portrait?"

"I'm ready to start right away. I'll need to do preliminary sketches of each of you, which should take about a week, depending on how many times a week we can meet," Kathryn explained. "I like to observe the children at play while I sketch them. This keeps them from having to sit too long. I'll want to do sketches of you and your husband separately, and then I'll need to do a sketch of all of you in the setting we choose for the portrait."

"We're more than willing to accommodate as many sittings as you need. My sons and I can be available every day, but my husband won't be available until next week. He had to go to one of our other estates and won't return until late Sunday."

"That will work out fine. I'll do the sketches of you and your sons this week, and I'll sketch your husband next week. I should be able to start painting by the following week. Did you have a room in your house that you would like for the background?"

Cassandra looked thoughtful, obviously thinking about Kathryn's question. "Hum, I do like our morning room. Would that work?"

"I'd like to see the room, and meet your children today, if possible." Then remembering that she hadn't told her what time was best, she added, "Oh, and I like to do my sketching in the morning, if possible."

Cassandra stood up. "If you'll follow me I'll take you to the morning room, and then take you to meet my children."

When Kathryn saw the morning room, she could understand why Cassandra wanted to use it. The room was delightful, full of sunshine from the large bay window, and decorated in a tranquil shade of blue with beige accents. "Cassandra, this is a lovely room. It will work perfectly for the portrait."

"Oh, good. I do really love this room, and it's where we spend quite a bit of our time," Cassandra explained. "Now, let's go to the nursery so you can meet my boys. Just follow me." Cassandra turned to Helen and said, "I'm sure this is boring for you. I apologize for leaving you out of our conversation."

"Please, don't worry about me. I'm fine. I'm just pleased that you want Kathryn to do your portrait. I promise that you'll not regret it."

As they walked upstairs to the nursery, Cassandra said, "I know that you said mornings are best for you. Would nine o'clock be all right? I do find that my sons are better behaved right after they've had their breakfast."

As they entered the nursery, Kathryn replied, "Yes, nine o'clock will work perfectly." Cassandra's sons were adorable. They had pale blonde hair and big blue eyes, and they resembled their mother quite a bit. Kathryn knew she would enjoy painting them. They spent about thirty minutes visiting before heading back downstairs. Once they were back in the entry hall, Helen and Kathryn left, with the understanding that Kathryn would return the following morning at nine o'clock.

The next few days flew by. Kathryn spent every morning with Cassandra and her sons. The children were very well behaved, and she was able to do several sketches of the boys, and she also had quite a few good sketches of Cassandra. Her afternoons were busy, what with spending time with Helen, and then a couple of hours with the children. Frankford and Jane were having a marvelous time.

Christina and Catherine were such exuberant little girls and always came up with different games to play. Elaine spent her mornings at her studies and joined the children in the afternoon, reading to them and playing with the girls as they played with their dolls. Kathryn thought that Jonathan worried too much about Elaine. Kathryn found her to be very helpful with Frankford and Jane, and they just adored her.

That Sunday, after Mass, Helen and Matthew had an unexpected guest arrive. Matthew's brother, Gregory, came for a visit. Gregory was a lieutenant in the royal navy, and his ship was in Plymouth being repaired, so he had two weeks leave.

Helen warned Kathryn that Gregory was a bit wild and that she would want to keep Elaine away from him. "I don't think he would do anything to her, but just to be on the safe side, I would make sure Elaine is chaperoned at all times. Gregory is a very handsome young man, and he's only one and twenty, so Elaine is bound to find him attractive."

Kathryn looked worried. "Oh dear, and Jonathan has already caught her trying to flirt with one of his friends. I'm sure you're right. I'll be extra careful and keep her away from him as much as possible."

That afternoon at tea, Matthew introduced Gregory to Kathryn, Elaine, and Jonathan. Helen had certainly been right about him being a handsome young man, with his dark blonde hair and blue eyes. She could tell that Elaine thought he was handsome by the way her cheeks flushed as they were introduced. Jonathan looked worried, and she could just imagine what was going through his mind.

Once everyone sat down to drink their tea, Jonathan asked, "How long have you been in the navy? I was in the army for a short time back in 1815."

Gregory grinned broadly. "I joined in the winter of 1821, and I love it. I've always loved the sea, and Matthew taught me to sail when I was quite young. I've traveled to quite a few foreign places, which I've enjoyed tremendously. I particularly enjoy France. Did you fight in the Battle of Waterloo? Is that how you ended up lame?"

With a reserved tone in his voice, Jonathan answered, "Yes, I did fight in that campaign, and I was injured during the final battle. I took a bullet in my knee."

Gregory grimaced. "Ouch, that sounds painful. I'm surprised you didn't lose your leg."

Matthew interrupted. "I think that's enough questions. You need to realize that there are ladies present, and they don't need to hear all this." He looked over at Jonathan and said, "Please, excuse my brother and his impertinent questions."

"Think nothing of it. Well, I do believe we'll go upstairs, since we've finished my tea." Jonathan turned to Kathryn. "Why don't we take Elaine with us and visit the children? I haven't seen them today."

When they left the room, Kathryn could tell that Jonathan wasn't happy. She knew he didn't enjoy talking about the war, and certainly not about his injury. Gregory was definitely impertinent.

When they arrived at the schoolroom, Frankford was entertaining Helen's boys by reading to them, and Jane was playing with Christina and Catherine. Elaine went over to the girls and started talking to them. Kathryn and Jonathan spent thirty minutes with the children, then left and went to their rooms.

There was a completely different atmosphere at dinner that night. It was obvious that Elaine loved the attention Gregory was paying her. Gregory was charming to her, and Kathryn could see that Elaine was smitten with him. Jonathan had a brooding look about him all throughout dinner, and she was glad when it ended. The gentlemen didn't spend very long over their port and cigars. When they entered the room, Helen asked, "Jonathan, I enjoyed it when you played the other night. Would you play for us again tonight?"

"I would be happy to, and Kathryn can sing. You wouldn't mind, would you, my dear?"

"No, not at all."

They entertained everyone until the footman brought in the tea, which Helen served. Matthew turned to Gregory and asked, "Jonathan and I are going quail hunting tomorrow. Would you like to go with us? The weather should be nice enough. We would like for you to join us."

After Gregory took a sip of his tea, he replied, "I'd be happy to join you. I haven't been hunting since I joined the navy almost three years ago. I look forward to it."

At ten o'clock, everyone retired to their rooms. Jonathan joined Kathryn in the bed, but since they were both tired, they kissed and went to sleep. Around midnight, Kathryn had her nightmare. She dreamt that her uncle had come back and that he was chasing her down a long hall. She kept running faster and faster, but he was gaining on her, and just as he reached for her, she woke up with a gasp. She looked around, dazed, and realized she wasn't in bed. She was in the library. She'd been sleepwalking, which she hadn't done in years.

Kathryn was relieved that no one had stumbled across her. As a child, her parents had punished her for sleepwalking, so she had always felt as if she were doing something wrong whenever she did it. She went upstairs to her room and quietly slipped back into bed. Thankfully, Jonathan didn't wake up. She lay there for quite some time, worried about what had just happened. She was afraid to sleep, and she fought it for as long as she could, but eventually she nodded off.

The next morning, when Kathryn woke up, Jonathan had already left to go hunting. She lay in bed trying to figure out why the sleepwalking was back. She felt so happy and content in her new life with Jonathan. She couldn't imagine why it would start again. Kathryn glanced over at the clock and realized she would be late for her appointment with the Ralston's if she didn't hurry. To make up time, she skipped breakfast and left right away. She barely made it, and since it was the first time she would be meeting Lord Ralston, she was relieved that she arrived on time.

Kathryn enjoyed meeting Lord Ralston, and while she worked on her sketches of him, he told her amusing stories about his early years. Kathryn was able to get several good sketches. "Thank you, Lord Ralston. If it's convenient for you, I'd like to continue tomorrow at the same time. Then, on Wednesday, I'll want to do a sketch in the morning room with all of you. I should be able to start painting next Monday. Is that agreeable with you?"

"It sounds as if that would work, but let's find my wife and make sure that it works for her and the children."

They found Cassandra in the drawing room, and once Kathryn explained everything, Cassandra said, "Oh Kathryn, that's wonderful. I'm impressed that you'll be ready to start painting next week. I'll make sure that the servants know to leave everything alone. We'll forgo using the morning room until you don't need it anymore. How long will it take to complete the portrait, once you start painting?"

"I should have it done by the end of next week, if all goes well. I'll need all of you to sit for me every day next week. Will that work for you?"

Cassandra looked at her husband and he nodded. "That will be fine. I can't wait to see the portrait. I'm sure it will be wonderful."

"I hope that you'll be pleased. Thank you for giving me the opportunity to do your portrait. I'll take my leave now. Lord

Ralston, I'll see you tomorrow at nine o'clock." Cassandra escorted her to the door, hugged her, and then Kathryn left.

Chapter 22
- Mid November 1823 -

Today was Elaine's sixteenth birthday, and she was feeling very downcast. As of yet, no one had wished her a happy birthday. Turning sixteen years of age seemed like an important thing to her. Surely they hadn't simply forgotten. After she finished playing with the children, she put on her walking shoes and went for a walk. Since it was such a nice day for November, she took the path down to the beach. She walked all along the shore, and by the time she was through with her walk, she was feeling a little bit better. Elaine loved the ocean, and a sense of peace came over her whenever she spent time on the beach. She remembered all the fun times she had had this past summer with Roderick and Allison.

Oh, why did they have to die?

Why was life so unfair?

Poor Allison had been with child, so there were three lives lost that terrible day. She missed them terribly. As she walked along the shore and thought more of Roderick and Allison, tears began to roll down her cheeks.

Elaine was happy that Jonathan had married Kathryn, but he was so absorbed with her, that he didn't have much time for her. That's probably why he had forgotten her birthday. Of course, Kathryn was busy painting so that was probably why *she'd* forgotten.

Her cheeks were quite cold from the tears, so she wiped them away with her woolen scarf, turned around, and made her way back up the steep path, which led back to the house. Her heart was aching for Roderick and Allison, and because no one had remembered it was her birthday.

That evening, when Elaine entered the drawing room, everyone was already there. Gregory was standing by the fireplace, and he looked incredibly handsome. Looking over at her, he gave her a charming smile. Elaine felt an odd feeling in the pit of her stomach whenever he looked at her. He walked over to her and said, "Hello, you certainly look lovely this evening. I had a good time with your brother today when we went hunting. What did you do today?"

Before he could continue, Kathryn and Jonathan came over and interrupted. "Happy birthday, Princess! Just think, you're now sixteen."

Everyone else stood up and cried out, "Happy sixteenth birthday!" As they all clapped their hands, Elaine felt a little silly that she'd thought everyone had forgotten her birthday. Kathryn gave her a hug, and so did Helen.

Oh, I'm so glad they remembered after all!

Elaine's heart swelled with joy. Of course, she wished their timing had been better. She'd been enjoying Gregory's attention. She surreptitiously glanced over at him, and he was watching her with an intense look in his eyes. It thrilled her that he seemed to be interested in her. Goodman entered the room and announced dinner, so Jonathan offered her his arm, and everyone went into the dining room.

Dinner was superb. Helen was so sweet to have planned this for her. After everyone finished the main course, Goodman rolled in a cart that held the prettiest birthday cake she'd ever had. There were pink sugar roses with delicate green leaves adorning the cake. He placed the cake in front of her and handed her a silver knife so she could cut the first piece. Everyone sang to her, wishing her many more. The cake was delicious! Lemon with lemon curd filling had always been a favorite of hers.

Yes, this was turning out to be an excellent birthday!

After dinner, Jonathan and Kathryn gave her a beautifully wrapped present. When she opened it up, a gorgeous strand of matched pearls came tumbling out into her hands. "Oh, thank you! These are just beautiful. I've wanted pearls for ages." She gave both of them a hug.

Helen handed her another present, and it was a set of earbobs to match the pearls. Elaine was so overcome she started crying. "I thought you had forgotten it was my birthday. Thank you so much for this wonderful party, Aunt Helen."

"I'm just glad we could do this for you. You've been so helpful with all the children. We wanted to show you that we appreciated it," Helen said.

Elaine thought this was the best birthday she had ever had. After she finished opening up her presents, they went to the music room, and Jonathan played for everyone. At ten o'clock everyone went upstairs to bed.

As Elaine went down the hall, she heard a noise and looked around. Gregory was there in a recessed doorway. He put his finger to his lips, letting her know to be quiet and motioned for her to follow him. Elaine looked down the hall. Everyone had already entered their rooms, so she followed Gregory into a room.

Gregory closed the door. "Happy birthday. I would have gotten you a present, but I didn't know it was your birthday. You know what I would like to give you? A birthday kiss, if you'll let me."

Elaine looked at him and nodded her head. Then he gently touched his lips to hers. He didn't touch her anywhere but her lips, and it felt incredible. She was trembling from the excitement of receiving her first kiss. When he ended the kiss, he said, "You have the softest lips I've ever felt. I've wanted to kiss you from the first moment I saw you. I wish you were older. I find you very pretty."

"I've never been kissed before. Your kiss has made my birthday very special, thank you. I should go to my room now. Ah...I've been taking walks on the beach every afternoon around three o'clock. Maybe...I'll see you one of those afternoons. Good night." Elaine opened the door, looked both ways, and then, with a wave of her hand, she went to her room.

After finishing all her sketches on Friday, Kathryn spread them out before her. She was very pleased with the results. Monday she would be able to get a good start on the portrait since the children were so well behaved. Kathryn loved painting children, and Cassandra's boys were adorable. She felt sure the portrait was going to turn out well.

Kathryn decided to take the day off on Saturday because Helen wanted her to come with her to the village to do some shopping. Since Kathryn felt Elaine deserved a treat for being so helpful with the children, she decided to ask Elaine if she wanted to come with them.

Finding Elaine in the music room, Kathryn asked, "Would you like to go to the village this morning? Helen told me there were some delightful shops for us to explore."

Elaine gave Kathryn a hug. "Oh Kathryn, I would love to come!"

Bigbury-on-Sea was a delightful seaside village. As Kathryn watched all the activity on the dock, she decided that she wanted to paint the scene, so she turned to Helen and asked, "Can we go down to the docks sometime? I'd like to bring my sketch pad and do some sketches of all the workers."

Helen looked at her. "I don't think that would be a good idea, Kathryn. Those men live very rough lives, and they can be quite crude at times. On one of my first visits here, I strolled along the boardwalk, and they made some very rude comments. Matthew told me to stay away, so I have."

"Oh, I never thought about that. I guess I'll have to do it from memory then. Look, there's a bookshop. Can we go in?" Kathryn asked. "I want to see if they have a new Minerva Press novel."

"Of course, I would enjoy a new novel myself. I'll see if they have any books for my children as well." The bookshop did indeed have what they were looking for, and after they made their purchases, they moved on to the millinery shop where Kathryn found a lovely chip straw bonnet with lavender ribbons. Elaine picked out a bonnet with bright yellow ribbons that tied on the side. By the time they got back to the carriage, their arms were laden with their many purchases.

Once Elaine settled back in her seat, she looked over at Helen and said, "Thank you, Aunt Helen, for allowing me to come with you today. I enjoyed myself tremendously. Bigbury-on-Sea is a delightful place. In fact, I've quite fallen in love with this entire area. I loved spending time on the beach in Bristol, and being here has brought back some fond memories of my brother and his wife. It's nice to remember the good times for a change."

Kathryn was pleased to see Elaine so animated and hear her talking about Roderick and Allison without tearing up. Elaine was right—it did feel good to remember the good times for a change. Losing them had been dreadful for both Jonathan and Elaine, and of course, the children too.

Smiling, Kathryn said, "Elaine, I'm glad you're able to remember all the wonderful times you had with them. Even though I only knew Roderick and Allison for a short time, I had grown quite fond of them. They were such vibrant people. Now, why don't you try on your new bonnet? It's quite fetching on you."

Since it was a pleasant day, Kathryn went to the nursery and got Frankford and Jane and took them for a walk on the beach. Even though it was cold, the sun was shining brightly, so the children were able to run and play in the sand. Kathryn enjoyed watching them play. It was good to see Frankford so happy. He had been so withdrawn since Roderick and Allison had passed away. This was a good idea, bringing them on this trip. Jane had even stopped asking them to go to heaven and get her mama. Both children were beginning to move past their grief. Kathryn enjoyed watching the children play tag and was glad she had interrupted their studies.

When Elaine got back to the house after her visit to town, she decided to go out to the stables. Lord Collingswood had quite a few beautiful horses, and she wanted to ride one of them. While she was at the stables, she encountered Gregory, and he asked, "Were you planning on going for a ride? My brother has several gentle mares to choose from, and I'm sure he wouldn't mind you riding one of them. I'd be happy to take you riding this afternoon."

"Oh, I'd love to go riding, but I'd want a more spirited horse. I've been riding since I was six years old, and I'm a very accomplished horsewoman." Elaine coyly smiled at Gregory as she asked, "Would you take me riding on the beach? I've always found the ocean fascinating, and I'm sure I would love riding along the shore with the wind in my hair. My brother Roderick used to take me out on his yacht before he died, and I found it exhilarating."

"I'm sorry about your brother and his wife. I'm sure that you miss them terribly. I understand that you were visiting them when it happened. Please accept my condolences." Then lightening the mood, Gregory gave her a charming smile. "Now, we can definitely go riding on the beach. Why don't you go get changed while I have two horses saddled for us? We'll meet back here in fifteen minutes."

Elaine was thrilled that Gregory wanted to go riding with her. She again felt that odd sensation in the pit of her belly. Delighted by this turn of events, she replied, "I'll be back in ten. Thank you, I appreciate you taking me riding."

Elaine felt a rush of anticipation course through her veins. She'd been trying to talk to Gregory ever since he had kissed her the night of her birthday. He was an extremely handsome young man with his dark blonde hair with gold streaks running through it. His piercing blue eyes seemed to see down into her soul.

When she got to her room, she quickly pulled out her new riding habit. It was a good thing that it buttoned up the front, because she didn't want to have to get her maid, Kitty, to help her. She didn't want anyone knowing that she was going riding with Gregory. She knew that neither Jonathan nor Kathryn would approve. They treated her as if she were still in leading strings—especially Jonathan! She loved Kathryn, but since Jonathan had married her, he had practically ignored her most of the time, and she was getting tired of it. This was her chance to have some fun.

By the time she returned to the stables, Gregory was waiting for her with the horses, and he helped her mount. When he lifted her up by her waist, she felt that flutter in the pit of her stomach again. It was an odd feeling, but very exciting. She was disappointed when he let her go once she was in the saddle. Soon they were on the beach, and Gregory said, "Since this is your first time riding on the beach, we'll start out at a walk until you get used to how it feels on the sand. Once you're comfortable, we'll give them a good run. My sister went to a school in Bath. Do you go to school there?"

"No, my brother doesn't think I need to go to finishing school. I'm hoping that Kathryn will help me talk him into letting me go. Mrs. Manning's School for Young Ladies is supposed to be one of the best finishing schools in England, and it's not as if I would have to travel far away."

As they slowly meandered along the shore, Gregory said, "That's the name of the school my sister Margaret went to, and she seemed to love it. Of course, she only went for two years because she got married at sixteen. She married one of my best friends from school. At the time, I was very angry at Peter for compromising my sister, but they've been married for three years and seem to be happy. Let's pick up the pace since you've had a chance to get used to the sand. Tell you what—I'll race you to that post down there."

Elaine laughed. "Get ready to eat some sand!"

And off she went.

The wind was blowing so hard that the cold stung her cheeks. Nonetheless, it felt marvelous. She was racing toward the post, and they were neck and neck. At the last moment, he inched ahead and won the race. Considering that Gregory was used to riding on the beach, she felt she'd done an excellent job keeping up with him.

As the wind ruffled Gregory's hair, he said, "You really *are* an exceedingly good rider. You almost beat me, and I've been racing on this beach my entire life. What did you think of your first ride along the shore?"

"Oh, this has been the most amazing experience of my life! I must look a fright now that the wind has blown my hat off, and I've lost most of my pins. Thank you for bringing me riding," Elaine glanced over at Gregory and added, "I've been a little bored during my stay here. Kathryn is always over at Lord and Lady Ralston's estate, and Jonathan goes off with your brother. I love my niece and nephew, but I needed a break from them. How did you end up in the navy? Was it something you always planned to do? You seem quite young to be a lieutenant."

Looking slightly embarrassed, Gregory said, "I hated school, and I joined the navy shortly before my nineteenth birthday. I hate to tell you this, but I was sent down from Cambridge for some misdeeds with some of my...ah...friends.

Matthew was furious, and he gave me the choice of either the army or the navy, and since I have always loved the water, I chose the navy. I'm glad I did."

Gregory reined his horse in. "Since I'm the second son, I needed to find a career where I could make money, and some of the prizes are very lucrative. I've gotten to see some of the world, and I love it. I've already been promoted once, and I plan to be a captain soon. I want my own ship. By the way, you look beautiful with your golden hair all around your face. I think you're quite pretty. Of course, you already know that. I hope you didn't think I was too bold the other night when I kissed you?"

"No, I didn't think you were too bold. I enjoyed your kiss. It helped to make my birthday special. I'm glad you like the navy. If I were a man and needed to find a career, I would choose the navy too."

"Well, I'm certainly glad you aren't a man. You are far too lovely, and it would be a shame if this world weren't graced by your beautiful countenance. We'd better get back before someone comes looking for us. I enjoyed our ride tremendously. We'll have to do it again before I leave next week."

Elaine and Gregory headed back to the house. When they entered the stables, since no one was there, Gregory touched her cheek, then lowered his head and gave her a gentle kiss. "I wish you weren't so young. I'll have to come look you up in a couple of years. Well, you'd better run along before your brother catches you with me. He would have a fit if he knew I'd kissed you. I'll see you at tea."

As Elaine and Gregory left the stables, they ran into Jonathan. Elaine could tell by his expression that he was furious. "Who told you that you could go riding, young lady? You need to go to your room and change your clothes and straighten up your hair. It's almost time for tea. We'll talk more about this later."

As Elaine went into the house in a huff, she heard Jonathan say, "I want you to leave my sister alone. She's only sixteen years old, and she shouldn't have gone riding with you. You should have at least taken a groom with you." She stopped so she could hear Gregory's response.

"You're right, we should have taken a groom. I promise nothing happened. We just went for a ride on the beach. I'll not spend time with her again. Now, if you'll excuse me, I need to go change for tea." Elaine felt a searing pain in her heart as she heard what he said. Her brother had to ruin everything for her. Now Gregory was going to stay away from her. Feeling despondent, she hung her head and hurried up to her room.

Jonathan watched as Gregory walked away. He was very concerned about Gregory taking his sister riding. Elaine knew she shouldn't have gone, and she certainly didn't ask permission. Jonathan was sure that Kathryn would never have given her approval for her to go riding with Gregory. Helen had warned Kathryn that Gregory was a wild young man, and of course, Matthew had told him some alarming things about his brother.

The last thing Jonathan would ever want was for Elaine to end up like Matthew's sister and have to get married at such a young age. Jonathan knew that Elaine was easily influenced and could be quite impetuous on her own, without someone encouraging her. He would need to watch his sister very closely. If he'd had any idea that Matthew's younger brother was going to be here, he would never have let Elaine come here with them.

Jonathan went up to his room, and Hatton was there, waiting to help him. He gave him his dose of laudanum and then rubbed ointment on his knee. He didn't have time for the cold compresses, and he knew he would regret it later.

Jonathan had enjoyed spending time with Matthew. They had ridden his estate, and he was impressed with how well-run it was. In fact, he liked Matthew quite a bit and was glad that he was his brother-in-law. In fact, he liked both his brothers-in-law.

Henry had talked to Jonathan about some bills he was working on in Parliament and had asked him if he would join the committee. Now that he was married, he wanted to take a more active role in Parliament, so he told Henry that he would. Jonathan glanced over at the clock and realized that he needed to get downstairs now, or he would be late for tea.

When Jonathan saw Kathryn coming out of her room, he joined her and they headed downstairs. As they descended the stairs, he said, "Hello, darling. Did you enjoy your trip to the village? I had an enjoyable day with Matthew. At least I did until I found Elaine with Gregory. She went riding with him on the beach, and she didn't take a groom. She didn't ask me if she could go. Did she ask you?"

Kathryn gasped. "No, she certainly did not. I would never have given her my permission. How long were they together without a chaperone? You know Helen warned us that he wasn't to be trusted. I hope nothing happened. Surely he wouldn't try anything with her. She's barely sixteen."

"He promised he would leave her alone, but I just don't trust him. He shouldn't have invited her to go riding with him in the first place. We need to watch her closely so they don't have a chance to be alone again." Jonathan glanced around the drawing room and noticed Elaine was across the room talking to Gregory. He immediately walked over to them. "Elaine, we need to talk. Come with me."

Jonathan took her upstairs to their sitting room. "Elaine, please sit down. We need to talk about what happened this afternoon." Then he looked directly at her and asked, "Why did you go riding with Gregory? You didn't ask permission from either Kathryn, or me. I'm sure you realized that we would have told you no. You promised me that if I let you come with us you would behave. I'm very disappointed in you."

Her face growing flushed with anger, Elaine jumped up. "I'm so tired of you treating me as if I was still in leading strings. I'm sixteen now. The reason that I didn't ask permission was because I knew you wouldn't give it. I wanted to go riding on the beach, and since Gregory asked, I accepted. Nothing happened. He was a perfect gentleman the entire time. You're making this to be much worse than it is."

"Now, young lady, you need to calm down. I'll not tolerate you speaking to me in this manner."

Elaine put her hands on her hips and gave Jonathan a withering look. "I've spent most of my time here with Frankford and Jane. I love them, but I needed some time away from them. Is that really so bad? You spend every day with Matthew, and Kathryn is always over at Lord and Lady Ralston's working on their portrait. It's as if I don't exist. You know, I'm grieving for Roderick and Allison too, but neither one of you have asked if I'm all right. Please understand that I'm bored. I just wanted to have a little fun."

Jonathan stood there feeling horrible as he realized they had been ignoring her. "You're right. I have ignored you. I guess I can understand that you wanted to have some fun, but Gregory isn't a safe person for you to spend time with. Helen and Matthew told us that he's a very wild young man, and he's always getting in trouble. I'm just trying to protect you. I want your promise that you'll not go anywhere with him again.

Calming down, Elaine sat back down. "I promise I shan't go anywhere with him again." Looking coyly over at Jonathan, she added, "I would like to talk to you about something else. I'd like to go to finishing school. I want to meet other girls and have some friends. I'm really getting too old for a governess. Please let me go to school."

"I didn't realize that you wanted to go to school. I don't have a problem with sending you. I'll look into it when we get back home. Now, we'll only be here for another week, and then we'll be going home. If you want to go riding, let me know, and I'll take you, all right?"

"Oh Jonathan, thank you so much. I promise. I'll do whatever you want. You won't regret sending me to school. I'll stay away from Gregory, but I hope you'll take me riding this coming week. You know how I love to ride. Can we go on Monday?"

"If the weather permits, I'll take you. Now, why don't you go to your room and rest before dinner?" Jonathan watched as Elaine left the room and felt badly that they'd been ignoring her. He was so enamored with Kathryn that he hadn't been giving Elaine the attention he used to.

After Elaine left, Kathryn came in. "I just saw Elaine leaving this room, and she looked elated. What is she so happy about? Did you talk to her about Gregory?"

"Yes, and I feel awful. She accused us of ignoring her, and she's right. I've forgotten that she lost Roderick and Allison too, and misses them as much as I do. She's promised not to spend any more time with Gregory, and I've promised that I'll take her riding on Monday. She also said that I treat her as if she's still a child. As she pointed out to me, she did just turn sixteen. It turns out that she wants to go to school. I never thought about it, to be honest with you. I told her I would look into sending her when we get back home. Did you go to school?"

Kathryn sank down on the sofa. "Oh Jonathan, I feel terrible. I've been so busy, what with the portrait and all. I just didn't consider how Elaine must be feeling. To answer your question about school, no, I didn't go, but I wanted to. I think that it's a good idea to send her. There's a very good school in Bath. My old governess teaches there. If you send her there, she'll still be close enough that she can come home on weekends. I think it's an excellent idea. They'll get her ready for her come out much better than I could."

"Well, I'll definitely look into it when we get home. Since we're speaking of home, when do you think we could go back? From what you told me, you should be finished with the portrait by the end of the following week. Can we leave then?"

"If all goes well this week, I should be finished by Friday or Saturday. We can go home the following Monday. As much as I've enjoyed doing this portrait, I'll be glad when I'm finished. I need a break. I've done four portraits in a row, with very little time in between. I look forward to the quiet of St. John's Wood. Well, I'm going to my room now. I'll see you later at dinner." She stood up and went over to him, gave him a quick kiss, and left the sitting room.

Chapter 23
- Mid November 1823 -

That evening, when Jonathan retired to his room, his knee was aching terribly. Hatton rubbed ointment on it and wrapped it as usual. He took his dose of laudanum, but it didn't seem to help very much. He felt a strong temptation to drink, but he fought it. He didn't want to go to Kathryn with liquor on his breath. Besides, if he took the first drink, he wouldn't be able to stop, and he would end up drunk. Hatton retired for the night, and Jonathan sat there for a while with the cold compresses on his knee, and finally the pain eased up a bit.

Jonathan was making progress with Kathryn. She hadn't told him she loved him, but he knew she had strong feelings for him, and he believed that if he could ever break through her shell, she would be a passionate woman.

Well, enough woolgathering, it was time to go join his lovely bride!

When Jonathan entered her room, Kathryn was sitting at her dressing table brushing her fiery red hair. He walked over.

"Let me do that. I've always wanted to brush your lovely hair." He took the brush from her hands and began to run it through her hair. It felt like the finest silk. As he continued brushing, he felt himself becoming aroused. He could tell she was enjoying it as well by the blissful expression on her beautiful face. He laid the brush down and ran his fingers through her hair, watching as it fell down her back.

Their eyes met in the mirror, and Jonathan leaned down, brushed her hair to the side, exposed the nap of her neck, and kissed it. He began to slowly stroke her shoulders, and he heard her breath quicken. Pulling her up into his arms, he turned her around, and then kissed her deeply. When she parted her lips, he slid his tongue into the sweet cavity of her mouth. She tasted sweeter than cherries, and her luscious scent overwhelmed his senses.

Nibbling his way across her cheek to her earlobe, he gently sucked it into his mouth, and Kathryn gasped as his tongue licked her ear. Jonathan placed his hand on her breast and felt it swell as he rolled her nipple through her night rail.

"Darling, take off your night rail so I can see your gorgeous body. Have I told you what a delectable body you have?" She looked up at him, reached for her gown, and slowly pulled it up her body and over her head, letting it drop to the floor.

Jonathan felt his heart accelerate as she uncovered her delectable body. Her pert nipples were hard as pebbles, and he leaned down and captured one in his mouth, teasing it gently with his teeth and lips. Kathryn pushed his robe off his chest and began to run her delicate long fingers through his chest hair, which always drove him wild. She had no idea how that excited him.

"I love it when you do that." Jonathan shrugged off his robe and it fell to the floor. Her eyes widened when she saw that he was completely naked. He'd always left his smalls on, but not tonight. He took her hand and pulled her over to the bed, and she sat down on the edge.

"Lie back."

Kathryn lay back as he parted her lovely thighs, leaned over, and licked her core. His tongue caressed the moist pink folds exposed to him. As he gently sucked her bud of desire, he took his finger and circled her tight passage. Jonathan slowly, and gently, slid his middle finger inside her. He felt her muscles tighten. "Just relax. I'm not going to hurt you."

Jonathan slid his finger in to his first joint and then stopped to give her a chance to accept him. When he felt her opening up for him, he pushed his finger the rest of the way in, then slowly drew it out, and then slid it back in. She gasped, but didn't tighten up, so he continued. He breathed deeply of her clean, womanly scent, and he felt his cock grow hard as a rock. He leaned his head back down and licked her core as he stroked her with his finger.

Kathryn's breathing grew shallow, and she was writhing under his head and hand. When he knew she was close to her release he stroked faster and sucked on her pretty little pearl, then he heard her whimper, and she let out a breathless scream as she fell over the edge into bliss. Jonathan looked up into her sweet face all aglow from her passion. She'd never looked more beautiful.

He pulled her up so she could look into his eyes, then he kissed her, took his shaft and rubbed it across her glistening wet nether lips, but he felt her stiffen up. "It's all right, I'm not going to hurt you. Trust me, I'm going to just put the tip in. If it hurts, I'll stop. I promise." Jonathan pushed the tip of his shaft in. It felt like heaven.

Kathryn's pretty face tightened up, and she cried, "No…No…I…can't do this. Please don't make me!"

He pulled out and gathered her in his arms. "Shush, it's all right. I promised I would stop, didn't I? You're my sweet, brave girl for trying. I love you, sweetheart." He gently rocked her until she stopped crying and trembling. It just about tore his heart in two, to see her like this.

Oh God, he hoped that bastard was burning in hell!

Even that was too good for him.

"I'm sorry, Jonathan, but it brought back the memories of him lying on top of me, forcing his manhood inside me. Oh God, I wish these memories would leave me!"

Jonathan continued to tenderly stroke her back. "It's all right, we'll get through this together. I love you enough that even if it never happens, I'll still love you forever. I hope that someday you can return my love, because then I'll have my deepest desire fulfilled."

"Jonathan, I do…I've…fallen in love you. I really do want to be your wife in every sense of the word. Please continue to be patient with me. I'm not going to let that weasel ruin what I know will be beautiful." She reached down and wrapped her hand around his shaft as she said, "Teach me how to pleasure you."

Jonathan looked into her sincere little face, tenderly smiled at her, and nodded. "Squeeze my shaft." He guided her hand up and down his cock. As he drew close to his release, he groaned, and then kissed her ravenously as he shot his seed over her belly. He held her tightly as his breathing returned to normal, and his heartbeat slowed down. Jonathan went over to the basin, wet a cloth, then brought it back to the bed, and gently cleaned her belly.

"My sweet, wonderful girl. Thank you." He picked her up in his arms, and pulling back the covers, he laid her down, then slid into bed beside her and gathered her into his arms. He tenderly kissed her temple. "Go to sleep, my love." He lay there and tried not to let this disappoint him. Kathryn had told him she loved him.

Those were the sweetest words, yet bittersweet, because even though she loved him, she couldn't give herself to him. Jonathan felt rage building in him against the bastard who did this to her.

Oh God, how were they going to make it through this?

He knew he had pushed her a little too far tonight, but God, he wanted her so badly.

He wasn't sure he could keep this up much longer. Maybe it would be better if he left her alone for a while. Eventually, he dropped off to sleep, holding his beloved wife in his arms.

Kathryn woke up to the sounds of moaning and crying. She felt Jonathan's chest under her head, and his heart was thundering in his chest. He was clammy and shaking all over, and then he shouted, "Never…leave my leg alone! Help me, Roderick! Don't let them cut my leg off," Kathryn gently stroked his chest, and then he grabbed her to him. The sudden movement surprised Kathryn, causing her to scream, and he woke up. He looked at her with terror in his eyes. "Oh God, did I hurt you? I'm so sorry. I didn't know what I was doing."

Kathryn gently smiled. "It's all right. You can't help your dreams. You didn't hurt me, it just scared me a little when you grabbed me, but I'm fine. I know what it's like to have nightmares. I had one last week. I'll go months and not have a nightmare, and then all of a sudden, they'll start up again. The one last week was quite disturbing, because I found myself in the library when I woke up. I haven't done any sleepwalking in several years. One thing that I've learned is that I can't control them. All I can do is live through them. I know they can't hurt me."

"I know you're right, and that I can't control them. I used to drink myself into oblivion, but I know that isn't an option for me anymore. What I just realized was having you beside me made it less horrific when I woke up. The next time you have a nightmare, wake me up— especially if you've been sleepwalking. I can just imagine how frightening that would be. I want you to be able to depend on me to help you through it. Don't try to deal with it on your own, all right? I wonder what could have caused your nightmare again. I'm going to get up and get myself some water. Do you want any?"

"I'm not sure what triggered that dream or the sleepwalking, but I promise that if it happens again, I'll wake you up. Thank you for offering me the water, but I'm fine. You'll come back to bed, won't you?"

"Yes, right after I drink some water." Jonathan came back to bed after he drank his water, and they lay there in each other's arms until they fell back to sleep.

The next morning when Kathryn woke up, Jonathan was already gone. She lay there thinking back over what had happened last night. Rage rose up in her when she thought of what her uncle had done to her.

Why couldn't she let it go?

She desperately loved Jonathan and wanted to let him make love to her fully, but every time he tried to take their love to completion, she would get the terrible images in her mind of what her uncle had done to her, and she felt as if she were suffocating. Feeling so helpless, she started crying. As the tears coursed down her cheeks, she prayed, *"Lord, help me with this. I know you don't want me to be tormented. You have sent a wonderful man in my life, and I deserve to have a full, loving relationship with him. Help me overcome my fears so I can be a true wife to Jonathan. Lord, I place this in your hands. In your son's precious name I pray."*

When she finished her prayer, she felt much better and rose from her bed more determined than ever to overcome her fears.

Kathryn stayed on schedule and finished the portrait on Friday. Lord and Lady Ralston were thrilled with it. They told her they would be recommending her to all their friends. Kathryn was pleased with the way it turned out, but her best work so far, in her opinion, was the portrait of Roderick and Allison. When she got to Helen's, she went looking for Jonathan so she could tell him that she was finished with the portrait. She found him at the stables with Matthew.

As Kathryn approached him, Jonathan turned to her with a bright smile on his handsome face and asked, "How did it go this morning? Were you able to finish their portrait?"

She smiled. "Yes, I finished it. Lord and Lady Ralston loved the portrait, and they said they would be recommending me to all their friends. What have you been doing this morning?"

"Matthew and I just returned from a ride on the beach. I must say, even though I don't like to be out on the sea, it's very pleasant to ride along the shore. I'll miss it when we leave on Monday. What do you have planned for this afternoon?"

"Since it's such a nice day, I thought that I would take the children for a walk after luncheon."

"Well, I hope you have an enjoyable afternoon. I would love to come with you, but you know that I can't walk long distances. Well, I need to rub down this horse and give him some oats, so I'll see you at luncheon." Kathryn gave him a smile as she turned around and went back to the house.

After luncheon, Kathryn took Elaine, Frankford, and Jane for a walk in the woods behind the house. They had a pleasant walk, and the children got to run off some of their excess energy. As they walked along, she said to Elaine, "I want you to know that I appreciate all you do for the children. You have really helped to keep them entertained. I know that you've been bored, but just think—when we get back home, Jonathan is going to enroll you in Mrs. Manning's School for Young Ladies. Are you excited?"

"Oh yes, I'm looking forward to it very much. I can't wait for the holidays to be over with so I can start. Do you know why I decided that I wanted to go to school? It's because of the conversation I had with Gregory. He told me about his sister, Margaret, and how much she enjoyed school. You know, he was very nice and polite to me, and a perfect gentleman. I know that you don't like him, but I don't think you've given yourself a chance to know him."

"I can understand how you might find it flattering for a young man to pay you attention, but Helen told me things that make me very leery of him. Besides, you're entirely too young to be developing a tendre for him."

"I know I'm young. I'm *not* going to fall in *love* with him. I just wanted to be his friend. Helen and Matthew haven't seen him in almost three years, and even I know there's a big difference between eighteen and twenty-one. He's been here for almost two weeks, and I haven't seen any wild behavior."

Elaine had a very valid point. "You're right, there is a big difference in three years at that age, and I haven't seen any wild behavior either. I don't object to you being friends; just don't go anywhere alone with him. He did promise your brother that he would leave you alone. Enough about this, you have so much to look forward to. I just know you're going to love finishing school."

"I agree. I'm sure that some of the other girls will be making their come outs when I do, so I'll have friends when I go to London in two years for mine."

"I would have liked to have gone to school, but my parents refused to send me. At least I did get to go to the Art Institute, thanks to Henry and Melody. Well, it's time to gather the children and head back to the house. The sky is darkening, and it looks like we're going to have a storm. Let's hurry." They made it back to the house just as the rain started. Kathryn hoped that Jonathan didn't get caught out in it since he had gone over to one of Matthew's tenant farms that afternoon.

Once Kathryn left the children in the schoolroom, she went to her room to freshen up for tea. At four o'clock, she joined Helen in the drawing room, but the men weren't there. "Have Jonathan and Matthew returned yet? I certainly hope so, because this is a very bad storm."

"No, they haven't come back yet. I imagine that they'll probably stay at the Miller's place until this storm passes. That's what Matthew usually does. Did you finish the portrait this morning?"

"Well, I won't worry since you're sure they aren't out in this weather. I did finish, and as much as I love to paint, I'm ready to take a short break. My next commission is for Susan and her husband. I'm supposed to do their portrait after the holidays. Since they live in Kent, which isn't too terribly far from Sanderford Park, it just makes sense to go there after we leave the park. Are you sure you and Matthew won't come? It won't seem the same without you."

"I know I'm going to hate not going, but I've been so sick from this child, I can't even think about taking such a long trip. I'm thrilled about the baby, but the timing could have been better. Kathryn, how is everything with Jonathan? You've been so busy that we haven't had a chance to talk." Helen reached over and took a biscuit from the plate on the table.

"Helen, I can't seem to overcome my fear. Jonathan is very understanding, but I know this is so hard on him. I want to make love, but whenever we try to…you know…I get images of what my uncle did to me. I don't know what I'm going to do."

As Kathryn sat there crying, Helen put her arm around her. "Honey, I'm so sorry, but I hate that you're letting that horrible man have power over your life. It's bad enough that he did those things to you, now he's ruining your chance at happiness as well. Please, try to put it behind you so you can have a full marriage."

With determination in her voice she said, "I know you're right. I never looked at it that way! I am giving him power, and I don't want to do that anymore. I'm glad we talked. That's the most helpful thing you've said to me. I refuse to let that awful man ruin my life any longer. I love Jonathan, and I want to make love with him. I know he would never hurt me."

Helen patted her hand. "Good for you. I know you can do this. I'm going upstairs to dress for dinner. I'm sure Matthew and Jonathan will be home soon. See you in a bit."

After Elaine left Kathryn and the children, she wandered down to the music room. She went through some of the sheet music, but didn't find anything to interest her. She sat there and just picked at the keyboard. She was pleased Jonathan had agreed to allow her to go to school. She knew that she would enjoy it.

She heard footsteps and looked up. Gregory was standing there, just inside the door. He pulled the door closed and walked over to her. "Did your brother give you a hard time about going riding with me?"

"A little bit, but I told him that he'd been ignoring me, which made him feel guilty. I brought up going to school, and he's agreed to send me after the holidays. He also made me promise not to see you alone. I don't understand why he doesn't want me to see you." She looked up at him and smiled as she added, "I think you're nice. You treat me like a grown up. Jonathan is so old-fashioned, and he treats me like a child."

"You're definitely not a child. I wish you were a couple of years older. I'd really like to get to know you better. Your brother has a good reason for mistrusting me. I've been wild my entire life. The navy has given purpose to my life, and I'm finally growing up. I'm going to succeed, and I'll have my own ship in a few years. Then I'll prove to my brother that I'm not the wastrel he's always thought me to be. If I give you my address, will you write to me? I know you're leaving on Monday. Can I have…another kiss? This will be the last time we'll have a chance to see each other alone."

"I'd like for you to kiss me. I'll write you. I'll be having my come out in a couple of years. Maybe I'll see you again then. I'll be eighteen in two years, so maybe we can get to know each other better then."

Gregory pulled her into his arms and gently kissed her. When she responded, he deepened the kiss and pulled her closer. Elaine felt a tingly sensation run through her body as he brushed his tongue across her lips. She gasped, and he slid his tongue into her mouth.

Elaine tentatively put her tongue in his mouth, and he groaned, then broke their kiss. "We have to stop. I could go on kissing you, because it feels so good, but it wouldn't be right. I promised your brother I'd leave you alone. In two years, I'll come looking for you. I hope you'll write, and I'll write back. I'm going to leave you now. I don't want you to get into any more trouble because of me." He hugged her close, playfully kissed the tip of her nose, then let her go, and walked out of the room.

Elaine watched him leave and wished desperately that she was two years older now.

Chapter 24
- Late November 1823 -

After Kathryn took the children back to the schoolroom, she decided she would take a short nap so she wouldn't be tired tonight. She was going to make love with her husband if it was the last thing she did. Kathryn knew Helen was right, and she wasn't going to let her uncle have power over her any longer.

When Kathryn got up from her nap, she rang for Sarah and had her prepare her a bath. Kathryn had picked up some lavender-scented soap and bathing salts when she had been in town the other day. After she washed her hair, she leaned back in the tub and thought about Jonathan.

She would seduce him tonight, not that Jonathan would need much inducement, but being bold would help her get the courage she needed to finally make love with him. When the water began to cool, she stood up, and Sarah poured fresh water over her to rinse the soap away. Then Kathryn wrapped herself in a big, fluffy white towel.

Going to her dressing room, she picked out a rich purple dinner gown that she hadn't worn before. Sarah fixed her hair in a flattering arrangement, and once Kathryn was dressed, she looked over her reflection in the cheval mirror and knew she looked her best. The gown accentuated her generous bosom, and the silk fabric draped her tall slender body to perfection.

Oh yes, Jonathan wouldn't be able to keep his eyes off her this evening.

With a bright smile on her face, Kathryn headed down to dinner.

When Kathryn arrived downstairs, Jonathan wasn't in the drawing room, and she noticed that the storm hadn't abated. Disappointment flooded her face as she walked over and sat beside Helen on the sofa. "Are Jonathan and Matthew still not back yet? Surely they will arrive soon. I hate to think of him being out in this weather when he's already been fighting off a slight cold for the last couple of days."

"I doubt they'll return until this storm is over. As I said earlier, Matthew will have made arrangements to stay out at the Miller's place. They'll have an uncomfortable night. I hadn't noticed that he had a cold. This weather won't be good for him to be out in, but I'm sure he'll be fine. Of course, it's only eight o'clock, and the storm could still blow over in time for them to return tonight. You certainly look spectacular tonight. You must have big plans for Jonathan. I know he'll be pleased."

"I must admit I'm nervous, but also excited. I'm going to seduce my husband tonight when he returns. I refuse to believe that this awful storm won't end. I just wish it would hurry and get over with before I lose my nerve." Just as she said this, Elaine walked in and joined them, and then shortly after that, so did Gregory.

Kathryn tried to relax as she watched Gregory and Elaine talk. After her conversation with Elaine, she realized that she had probably been biased against him, based on what Helen had said about him. She had to admit, he had behaved like a perfect gentleman, other than those few impertinent comments he'd made when he first arrived. Elaine had made a very good point when she pointed out that three years did make a big difference at that age.

The dinner was superb, but Kathryn was getting so concerned about the storm that she could barely eat a thing. After dinner, they went to the drawing room, and Gregory joined them right away, suggesting that they all play some cards. Kathryn tried to concentrate, but she was just too nervous about Jonathan being out in the storm. She played dismally, and she and Helen ended up losing quite badly to Elaine and Gregory.

At ten o'clock, she excused herself and went to her room, after she made sure Elaine went to hers. She knew Jonathan was counting on her to watch out for Elaine and make sure she didn't have any opportunity to be alone with Gregory. He had been polite, and very respectful, while they played cards, so he must have listened to Jonathan's request to leave Elaine alone.

Being restless while she waited for Jonathan to return, she quickly undressed and dismissed Sarah. Not wanting to give up entirely that the storm would end and Jonathan would return soon, she dressed in her most alluring night rail. Pacing the sitting room, she planned in her mind what she would do when Jonathan finally returned. She just hoped he wouldn't be too tired.

At midnight, Jonathan had still not returned, and the storm continued to rage outside, so she finally accepted that he wouldn't be back until morning. Kathryn hung her head in disappointment and went to her empty bed. She just prayed Helen was right, and Jonathan was safe. After tossing and turning, she eventually nodded off to sleep.

The next morning, Matthew and Jonathan were finally able to make it home at eight o'clock. Refusing any breakfast, Jonathan went up to his room and ordered a hot bath because he felt chilled to the bone. It had been a miserable night. He and Matthew had slept in the Miller's barn, and it had been freezing. As he soaked in the tub, he began to cough, and his throat felt scratchy. By the time he got out of the tub, he knew he was sick. He certainly hoped this wasn't something catching. He would hate to give it to Kathryn, or anyone else for that matter.

Turning to Hatton, Jonathan haltingly said, "Hatton, I need to lie down and take a short nap." Clearing his throat so his voice wasn't so scratchy, he added, "Please return in time for me to dress for luncheon. I'm sure I'll feel better after I sleep for a few hours."

When Hatton came to waken Jonathan for luncheon, he was sleeping so soundly that he was hard to wake up. When Hatton finally got him awake, he was so ill that Hatton barely got the chamber pot to the bed in time for Jonathan to cast up his accounts. He fell back against his pillow and croaked, "Please…I need…some water." Hatton brought him the water, but he was so weak, he could barely drink it.

God, he felt awful!

Jonathan could barely swallow, his throat felt so swollen, and he felt sure he had a fever. Once he finished the water, he tried to say, "I'm...too ill...can't go downstairs...tell my wife..." then he passed out.

Hatton rushed downstairs to get Lady Kathryn and tell her about Jonathan's condition. He found her in the dining room. "My lady, Lord Sutherland is very ill. I think you need to send for the doctor. He has a fever, and he's passed out."

Kathryn looked startled. "Hatton, what's wrong with him?"

Hatton, with worry in his voice, said, "I think he has a putrid throat because he was having a hard time talking. I need to get back to him, but please send for the doctor."

With a worried look on her face, she said, "I'm coming with you. I'll ask Wells to send for the doctor right away."

Seeing Wells in the hall, she said, "Wells, my husband is extremely ill. Will you please send for a doctor immediately?"

"Of course, my lady. I'll send him up straightaway when he arrives," Wells replied. "Please, let me know if you need anything else."

Kathryn rushed upstairs to Jonathan's side. When she went over to his bed, he looked terrible. He had dark circles under his eyes, and his face was flushed. He was struggling to breathe as he coughed. At least he was awake again.

"Kathryn...you...shouldn't...be in here," Jonathan croaked, "I don't want you...to catch this."

He tried to sit up, but then he started coughing violently and sank back against his pillows. Kathryn felt his forehead. "Jonathan, you're burning up with fever. Hatton, get me some cloths and cold water."

Jonathan was grateful for her help, but very concerned that she would get sick, so he tried again to send her away, but she refused to go. He was just too weak to argue, so he let her bathe his face. Her gentle touch was quite soothing.

The doctor arrived, examined Jonathan, and said, "My lady, he has lung fever. Make sure he takes this medicine every four hours. It should help his cough. You need to bathe him in cold water to try to bring his fever down. Oh, and get him to drink plenty of liquids so he doesn't become dehydrated. I'll return tomorrow morning to check on him."

As Kathryn escorted the doctor from the room, she said, "Thank you, Doctor, for coming so quickly. I'll make sure that he takes this medicine."

Jonathan felt so frustrated because everyone was talking about him, but not to him. And even though he tried to talk, nothing came out. He had completely lost his voice. Finally, he gave up, leaned back against his pillows, and closed his eyes.

Jonathan's fever was raging. Kathryn and Hatton bathed him with cool water and gave him the medicine, but it didn't seem to help. Kathryn refused to leave his side. She sent Hatton to bed, and he told her he would return in four hours to relieve her. Kathryn sat vigil through the night, continuing to bathe Jonathan in cool water. His temperature kept rising. One minute he would be burning up trying to toss his covers off, and then the next, he would be shivering. This went on all through the night.

Hatton came in at eight o'clock to relieve her. She left his side just long enough to freshen up, and then she was back again. Helen tried to get her to take a break, but she still refused to leave Jonathan's side.

Dr. Moore came at eleven o'clock and examined Jonathan. "Just keep bathing him with cool water. Has he kept the medicine down?"

"No, every time I give it to him he throws it back up. He's keeping a little water down, but that's all. I'm so worried about him. How long do you think he'll be like this?"

Dr. Moore answered, "There's no way to tell. However, the longer his fever stays high, the greater the chance he may not make it. At this point, it is in God's hands. Keep trying to get him to take the medicine. It is vital that he take it. I'll return tomorrow morning."

Once the doctor left, Kathryn sent Hatton to get more towels, and she laid her head down on her arms and wept. Helen came into the room and placed her hand on Kathryn's shoulder. "Oh Kathryn, you have to rest. You're going to make yourself sick if you don't get some sleep."

Kathryn looked up with tears rolling down her cheeks. "I can't. Don't you…understand? Just when I'm finally feeling brave enough to let him make love to me, this happens. I don't…want to lose him. He's so ill, and his fever keeps climbing. I don't know what to do!"

Helen hugged her. "You're not going to lose him. We'll keep bathing him in cool water. In fact, I'll have a tub filled with cold water, and you can bathe him there. Maybe if he's immersed in cold water, it will help to bring down his fever."

Once they had the tub filled with cold water, Hatton managed to get him in it. Jonathan was shivering, but she kept pouring cold water over him until the water turned tepid. Hatton put Jonathan back in bed. They finally got him to take some of the medicine, and it stayed down. He did seem a little cooler after the cold water bath, but after a couple of hours, his temperature was climbing again.

For two days, they continued to give him the cold water baths, and his temperature would go down, but then it would start to rise again. Jonathan was delirious and kept shouting for them to leave his leg alone. He called for Roderick over and over again. It was tearing Kathryn's heart apart to hear him. She knew he was trapped in his nightmare, and she couldn't help him.

On the third day of Jonathan's illness, after the doctor finished his examination, he shook his head. "I'm afraid that if his fever doesn't break soon, he'll die. I'm surprised he's lasted this long. I think the cold water baths may be the only thing that's keeping him alive. Keep giving them to him, and get the medicine down him. I'll return in the morning."

Hatton left Kathryn as the clock struck three to go to his bed. Kathryn wouldn't leave Jonathan's side. After Hatton left, she crawled up on the bed beside Jonathan, and whispered, "Please come back to me. I don't want to lose you. Oh, my darling, if you'll just get better, you can make love to me any time you want. Just please come back to me!" Kathryn was so tired she couldn't stay awake any longer, and she fell asleep.

When Kathryn woke, just as dawn was breaking, she looked over at Jonathan and noticed he was breathing easier. She felt his head and it was cool. His fever had finally broken. Her heart filled with love and hope, since she knew he was going to be all right now. She lay beside him, watching him sleep peacefully as she allowed herself to slip back into a more restful slumber.

Kathryn felt a hand on her back as she came awake. She looked up into Jonathan's brilliant blue eyes as he asked, "Why are you lying here in your clothes?"

"Oh, my love, you've come back to me! You've been so ill. I was afraid you wouldn't make it. Thank God your fever broke in the night."

"Sweetheart, I would never leave you. How long have I been ill?"

"Six days," Kathryn told him. "You had lung fever, and yesterday the doctor told me you might not make it. All I could think about was that I might never be able to make love to you, just when I'd decided that nothing was going to keep me from it. I've been so scared."

Jonathan huskily said, "Darling, just give me a couple of days to get my strength back, and you can show me how determined you are. Nothing could make me happier. Do you think I could have something to eat? I'm starving."

"Oh yes, let me ring for something right way." Jonathan ate some chicken broth and then fell asleep. Hatton came in to relieve her. "He woke up, and he's even eaten some chicken broth. He's going to be all right."

"That's wonderful, my lady," Hatton said with relief in his voice. "Why don't you let me sit with him while you get some sleep? He'll probably sleep most of the day."

Since Kathryn was exhausted, she agreed. "I'll sleep for a few hours, but when he wakes, send for me immediately."

Kathryn slept solidly for six hours, and when she woke up, she hurried through her ablutions and returned to Jonathan's side. He was just waking up and immediately wanted food. The doctor had been in to see him and had told Hatton he could eat soft foods. If he tolerated the soft foods, then he could try something more solid. Jonathan ate an entire bowl of porridge, then fell asleep again.

Each day Jonathan grew stronger, and on the third day, he dressed and spent the day downstairs. Kathryn read to him in the morning, and in the afternoon, he played the pianoforte for her. Jonathan joined the family for dinner and appeared completely recovered. Kathryn wondered if he would be ready to make love soon. She hoped he was, because now that she'd made up her mind, she wanted to do it before she lost her nerve.

After entering their sitting room, Jonathan turned to Kathryn. "I'll join you in thirty minutes." Then he walked into his room. Kathryn watched the door close, and her belly was all aflutter with anticipation. She went to her room where Sarah had her bath ready. She filled it with her lavender bathing salts and used her lavender-scented soap. She didn't linger, because she wanted to be ready and waiting when Jonathan came to her.

At dinner, Kathryn noticed that Jonathan had had a gleam in his eyes, so she knew he was healthy enough to make love. She felt as if she would die of excitement. Her heart was thundering, and her pulse was jumping. She dressed in the apricot night rail that Helen had given her to wear tonight. It was so sheer, it was almost transparent. The sides were open with little bows tied strategically to keep it on. Sarah had left her hair loose, and it cascaded around her shoulders and down her back. She nervously stood by the bed while she waited for him to arrive. As the door opened, she realized she was trembling, but she was determined to make love tonight.

When Jonathan gazed at her, he had a ferocious expression in his eyes that caused a fierce rush of pleasure to run through her veins. He boldly met Kathryn's gaze. "Your beauty leaves me breathless." His face was intent and flushed with desire as he slowly moved across the room. When he was standing next to her, he asked, "Are you sure you're ready for this? Because if you're not, tell me now before I lose control of my senses. Please, tell me you're ready."

She smiled at him. "I want to become your wife in all ways. Please make love to me."

Jonathan picked her up and laid her on the bed, then untied his robe and dropped it on the floor. Kathryn's eye grew large when she saw how aroused he was. He climbed into bed beside her. "As lovely as you look in this gown, I think we can take it off, don't you?"

He pulled the bows, and the gown fell open. Staring at her luscious breasts with hunger in his eyes, he slowly pulled the gown completely off and tossed it to the floor. Jonathan ran his hands across her breasts, and her nipples tightened with desire. Leaning over, he took one of the little dusky pink buds in his mouth, using tongue and teeth to arouse her further. He lifted his head and kissed her hot, deep, and long as his hand traveled down her belly toward her fiery red curls.

Kathryn's heart was pounding and her pulse was fluttering as his hand gently parted her thighs. "Open for me, my love." She relaxed her muscles, and her thighs fell apart. As he deepened his kiss, his fingers parted the slick pink folds that covered her sex, then he brushed the tip of his finger across her core, and she quivered with wild delight. Jonathan kissed his way down her body until he lay between her thighs. He breathed deeply to capture the luscious, titillating scent of her arousal, and then he lightly licked her feminine core. A sudden rush of heat ran through Kathryn's body.

As Jonathan circled her love bud with his tongue, he slipped a finger inside her sweet passage and began to stroke in and out, faster and faster, as his tongue licked her secret spot. She felt a tightening deep in her belly, and then she burst into flames of passion as she went soaring higher than she'd ever soared before. A satisfied growl emerged from deep in his throat as he drank of her body's juices.

Jonathan kissed his way back up her body and then rolled to his back. "Straddle my hips with your pretty thighs. When you're ready, guide my shaft inside. You have complete control."

Kathryn's eyes opened wide, but she nodded her head as she moved into position. Trembling, she hesitated a moment before rubbing her love juices on his shaft. Slowly, she lowered herself over him until he was deeply buried inside her body. She looked at him in astonishment. "It doesn't hurt! It feels amazing."

"That's just the beginning." As he lifted her by her waist, he lowered her as he thrust upward inside her incredibly tight channel. He groaned and trembled as he moved faster and wilder, showing a loss of his control. Her muscles began to contract as need built higher and higher. She went over the edge into bliss, vaguely aware of his groaning release as his warm seed filled her for the first time.

Slowly and softly, she returned to reality as she lay on top of him. Once his breathing returned to normal, he said, "That was the most earth-shattering experience of my life."

"It was beyond my wildest expectations. I never knew it could be so overpoweringly exquisite." As she lay there, she listened to the steady beat of his heart, and it gave her a sense of fulfillment she never expected. "Jonathan, I never expected to fall in love like this. When you lay there close to death, I knew my life would never be complete again if I lost you."

Jonathan pulled her close. "Darling, I'll never leave you. You…are my heart. It only beats for you. Thank you for allowing me to share your life. Before I met you, I was aimlessly making my way through life, but now I have purpose. I have been completely turned around by your love." Snuggling together, they slowly let sleep take them away. Neither one of them had to worry about any nightmares that night.

The next morning when Kathryn woke up, she looked over at Jonathan, and her heart swelled to bursting. All her fears were gone. They had come so far! Jonathan was the most patient and understanding man in the world. As she continued to gaze at him, she couldn't get over the change in him. When she had first met him, he had looked so sad and weary. The lines around his mouth and eyes had been much deeper than they were now. While she wished she hadn't had to go through the horrific experience with her uncle, she realized that it had made her a much stronger person.

Jonathan opened his eyes and met her gaze. "Good morning. Did I dream last night, or was it real?"

Kathryn gently smiled at him. "It was real, and it was the most amazing experience of my life. I never imagined it could be like that. Thank you for being so patient with me, my love. Last night you said you'd been turned around by love. Well, darling, you've given me a life that I never thought would be possible for me. Because of you, I have a husband who loves me and two beautiful children. Hopefully, with time, we'll have more. Jonathan, I want to have your baby. I can think of no greater joy than holding your child in my arms."

Jonathan pulled her close. "Well...let's get to work on that." And they did...just that.

Epilogue

Kathryn and Jonathan, along with Elaine and the children, left Helen and Matthew's house two days after Jonathan's recovery from his illness. Just to make sure Jonathan didn't overtax himself, they set a leisurely pace. Despite their slower travel, they were able to make it back to St. John's Wood in four days. When Kathryn saw the manor house, tears welled up in her eyes. She was so overjoyed to be home.

Once they had the children settled in the nursery, they were able to go to their rooms and spend a quiet evening, just the two of them. Jonathan ordered dinner served in their sitting room, and after eating, they made love until dawn. Now that Kathryn had let go of her fears, she was anxious to try it all, and Jonathan was more than happy to show her. They spent their first week back in bed more than out, and Kathryn gloried in every minute of it.

Jonathan went to Mrs. Manning's School for Young Ladies and registered Elaine for the winter term. Elaine told them she was ecstatic and couldn't wait for the term to start. Kathryn was so pleased that Jonathan was allowing Elaine this opportunity. She just knew it was the right thing for her.

They left for Sanderford Park on the fifteenth of December. They had another pleasant trip and were able to make it in four days. When they arrived at the park, Henry and Melody came out to greet them. Melody took one look at Kathryn's face and said, "All is well. I can see it shining in your eyes. I'm so happy for you, Kathryn. Henry and I have both been praying you would find true happiness and peace in your marriage, and you have, haven't you?"

Kathryn smiled at both of them. "Beyond my wildest dreams. Thank you, Melody for all your help. I don't know if I would have been brave enough without you and Helen giving me such good advice. Now, when does the rest of the family arrive?"

Henry announced, "Mother arrived yesterday, and Lady Helton is due tomorrow. The rest of the family will be here on the twenty-second. Helen and Matthew will be the only ones not coming this year. Let's get you in out of this cold. I do believe that I feel snow in the air." Henry turned to Jonathan and clapped him on the back. "Follow me, Jonathan. We'll go to my study and talk while the ladies catch up."

Melody showed Kathryn to their rooms. Sarah was already there getting everything unpacked and put away. Smiling, Melody said, "Once you're settled in and had a chance to freshen up, come to my sitting room so we can talk. I want to hear everything. See you in about thirty minutes."

Jonathan and Henry went to his study, and once the door was closed, Henry asked, "How did you do it? I felt that you would never be able to break through her fears. I'm so relieved I was wrong."

Smiling over at Henry, Jonathan took his seat. "It all comes down to patience and abiding love. Your sister is the best thing that ever happened to me. Before I met Kathryn, I was going through the motions of life, but not really living. My life has been completely turned around by her love."

"I'm happy for you, but I'm happier for my sister. Jonathan, she's glowing. I'm so grateful Kathryn met you," Henry said. "I've worried about her for years, but I know she's in good hands now."

Jonathan hesitated, wondering if he should tell Henry about what happened to Kathryn.

"Henry, please don't let her know I've told you this, but I feel that you deserve to know. Your uncle raped Kathryn when she was twelve years old, and it happened repeatedly until you stopped him when she was sixteen. If the bastard weren't already dead, I'd be hunting him down like a dog."

Henry looked tormented. "Oh God, no! Why didn't she come to me and tell me? How could that depraved rogue do that to an innocent child? I should have realized there was something more to her fear of that old bastard. Melody and I talked to Kathryn numerous times, but she never said a thing. I wish I'd killed that bastard when I had the chance."

Jonathan looked at Henry. "Kathryn was ashamed to tell you. The only reason she told me was that she didn't think it would be fair to marry me without me knowing the full extent of her fears. Remember the morning before our wedding when Helen and Matthew brought her out to my estate? That's when she told me."

"Thank you for being so patient with her. Your love has finally healed her from all the horrible things that bastard did to her. I'm proud…to call you Brother." Henry walked around his desk and pulled Jonathan to his chest. "My sister is truly blessed to have you in her life."

Jonathan was overcome with emotion. He couldn't believe how different his life was now. He returned Henry's hug and said, "Thank you, Henry, but I'm the one that's truly blessed. I'm the luckiest man in the world to have her in my life. And the feeling is mutual. I'm honored…to call you Brother." Then lightening the mood, he asked, "How long have you owned Doncaster Stables? Matthew told me that you have an Arabian stallion. I would relish the opportunity to breed some of my mares with him."

"I have one of his colts here. Why don't we go out and take a look at him? Follow me my friend!"

When Kathryn entered the rooms Melody had given her, she looked around and smiled. It felt so strange to be here again. Melody had put her and Jonathan in the rooms she and Henry had used before he became the duke. Kathryn glanced around and spied the French doors that led out to the balcony.

Lost in memories, she could remember as a young girl sitting out there with Melody, admiring all the gorgeous roses that first spring so many years ago. Melody was so dear to her, and she thanked God every day for bringing her into all of their lives. Henry and Melody had a wonderful relationship, and so did Helen and Matthew. Now, Kathryn could say the same about her relationship with Jonathan.

Enough reminiscing, it's time to go talk to Melody.

When Kathryn knocked on the door, she heard Melody's sweet voice say, "Come in." Kathryn entered the room, and Melody greeted her with a smile. "Please, come take a seat and tell me everything. Obviously, you've overcome your fears. Your face is just glowing. Kathryn. I'm so happy for you."

As Kathryn sat down, she said, "Jonathan and I are wondrously happy. He's the most incredible man. I'm so blessed to be married to him. When he became so ill, I was petrified that I would lose him. I knew that if he made it through, I would show him how much he meant to me. Melody, you were so right about making love. It's truly an amazing experience, and now I can't imagine why I allowed my fears to keep me locked away for so long. Helen told me I was giving power to my uncle, and she was right. Once I realized that, I was able to let go of my fears... Well, enough about this, how are you feeling? You're glowing, so your pregnancy must be going well."

"Oh yes," Melody said. "I'm just a chubby little ball of happiness. I can't believe I'll soon give birth to my fifth child. It seems like yesterday, when I first came here and met all of you. I do wish Helen and Matthew could have come, but I understand her not wanting to travel now that she's expecting again. Oh goodness, look at the time. We'll be late for tea, and you know how upset that makes your mother. She's been pleasant so far, so I want to keep her that way!"

Kathryn and Jonathan enjoyed spending time with all the family, and they even had a lovely white Christmas. The biggest surprise of all was when her mother hugged Melody on Christmas day before everyone, and told her she was a wonderful wife for her son and that she made an excellent duchess. Henry and Melody were so pleased. The duchess spent time every day with her grandchildren. Kathryn just wished Helen could have been here to see the change in their mother.

The children enjoyed playing with all their cousins, and when it came time to leave they cried, but Jonathan and Kathryn assured them they would see their cousins again in the spring. They left Sanderford Park on the seventh of January to travel to Kent so Kathryn could do Susan's family portrait. She enjoyed spending time with Susan and her children. Since the family was able to sit for her every day, she was able to complete their portrait in ten days, and then they headed home.

When they arrived home from their travels, Kathryn helped Elaine pack. Elaine was very excited about going, and Kathryn was happy for her. She was starting the term a bit late because of their trip to Susan's, but Mrs. Manning assured them that Elaine could catch up with the other pupils. Once Elaine was settled in school, they were able to relax.

Kathryn enjoyed managing Jonathan's household. She spent her mornings meeting with Mrs. Rollins and Cookie, and her afternoons she spent with Frankford and Jane. Both of the children were doing much better. While they still missed their parents, they were moving past their grief. Jonathan had given Frankford a pony, and was teaching him to ride and take care of him. Kathryn loved to watch Jonathan with Frankford. He was so patient and loving with him. Kathryn knew that when they had children of their own, he would be a wonderful father.

Her evenings she spent with Jonathan, either listening to him play the pianoforte or reading by the fire in their sitting room. The nights were glorious, filled with passion and tenderness. It still surprised Kathryn that making love was so fulfilling. She had never imagined that it would be such an earth-shattering experience. Jonathan had truly helped her overcome all her fears.

Spring came quickly that year, and soon it was time to leave for London. True to his promise, Jonathan had been in touch with his solicitor, and he had located several properties for her to look at for her studio as well as the safe haven for young girls. Frankford and Jane were coming with them, but Elaine was staying in school.

They had a pleasant trip and arrived in London on the fifteenth of March. The house in Bloomsbury was lovely and so beautifully decorated that she was happy with it just as it was, even though Jonathan had said she was welcome to change whatever she liked. Kathryn was anxious to go look at the properties that Jonathan's solicitor had located, so they went there the day after they arrived in town.

Kathryn fell in love with a house on Curzon Street. It had a room on the top floor that ran the length of the house, and one wall was filled with floor to ceiling windows that received the morning sun. She turned to Jonathan with tears of joy in her eyes. "Oh Jonathan, this is just perfect. I couldn't ask for a more beautiful location for my studio. Now I just have to find the clients."

"Darling, you'll have so many that you shan't know how to handle them all. Once we give the party displaying all your work, everyone will want you to do their portrait. When they see some of your landscapes, they'll want one of those too. I do hope you'll still make sure you have time for me and the children."

"Always. As much as I love my art, you and the children are now first in my life." She rose up on her tiptoes and gently kissed his lips. He pulled her close, and soon they were lost in true love's embrace.

The day after Kathryn found her studio, Henry sent word that Melody had given birth to a little girl. Kathryn and Jonathan rushed down to Sanderford Park so they could admire the new baby. Henry and Melody were so pleased with their new daughter, and Mary Elizabeth was parading around the house telling everyone that, at last, she had her very own sister. Melody and Henry named the baby Miriam after Melody's beloved aunt, and of course, Lady Helton was pleased. This child would look just like Melody when she grew up, which thrilled Henry. He told them that he had pictured having a daughter as beautiful as his darling Melody ever since he had married her.

When they returned to London, Jonathan took Kathryn to all the properties that his solicitor had located as possible sites for the Safe Haven for Young Girls. They found a lovely old manor house on the outskirts of London that they thought would work perfectly.

Kathryn met with a great many vicars, telling them about her plans, and within a month, the Safe Haven was up and running. Jonathan had found a woman to run the operation, and the vicars had already sent several young girls to live at the Safe Haven.

One evening in late May, as they were lying in bed after they had finished making love, Kathryn lazily gazed up at

Jonathan. "Remember what I told you would give me my greatest joy? Well, it's finally happened. Darling, we're going to have a baby!"

Jonathan looked at her with tears in his eyes as he said, "Are you sure? When will the baby be born? Are you feeling all right? Oh, my love, you have made me the happiest of men."

"Yes, I'm sure. The baby should make its appearance in late November. I'm feeling marvelous. I've had just a tiny bit of morning sickness, but just as soon as I eat breakfast, I feel much better."

"Let me show you how happy you've made me." Jonathan gathered her into his arms and passionately kissed her. Feeling love sweep her away, Kathryn returned his kiss just as passionately. That night he took her to heights beyond what she had ever experienced before. As she felt exploding waves of blissful sensations fling her over the precipice and into oblivion, Jonathan made one final thrust as he cried out, "My darling…my love…now and forever!"

The End

Made in the USA
Charleston, SC
19 August 2013